THE BAPTIST

A Native American Odyssey

PAUL PG

BRIGHTON PUBLISHING LLC
435 N. HARRIS DRIVE
MESA, ARIZONA 85203

THE BAPTIST
A Native American Odyssey

PAUL PG

BRIGHTON PUBLISHING LLC
435 N. HARRIS DRIVE
MESA, ARIZONA 85203
BRIGHTONPUBLISHING.COM

COPYRIGHT © 2013

ISBN 13: 978-1-62183-183-9
ISBN 10: 1-621-83183-3

PRINTED IN THE UNITED STATES OF AMERICA

First Edition

COVER DESIGN: TOM RODRIGUEZ

ALL RIGHTS RESERVED. THIS IS A WORK OF FICTION. ALL THE CHARACTERS IN THIS BOOK ARE FICTITIOUS AND THE CREATION OF THE AUTHOR'S IMAGINATION. ANY RESEMBLANCE TO PERSONS LIVING OR DEAD IS PURELY COINCIDENTAL. NO PART OF THIS PUBLICATION MAY BE REPRODUCED OR TRANSMITTED IN ANY FORM OR BY ANY MEANS, ELECTRONIC OR MECHANICAL, INCLUDING PHOTOCOPY, RECORDING, OR ANY INFORMATION STORAGE RETRIEVAL SYSTEM, WITHOUT PERMISSION IN WRITING FROM THE COPYRIGHT OWNER.

DEDICATION

This book is dedicated to the Native American people of North America and their struggle for dignity and survival. This book is dedicated to all those that support the cause of Native American rights and sovereignty, people such as David Geffen, whose commitment to the Native American cause has been an inspiration. This book is dedicated to the struggle to free Leonard Peltier, the Native American activist, unlawfully locked away in a federal prison for life without parole. Leonard Peltier has not and will not receive a fair trial. Mr. President, do what is fair and right to the native people of this land; bring justice to Leonard Peltier. Grant him clemency! Let him go free! Peltier does not deserve to rot in prison! His continued incarceration is an affront to the principle of fairness and the aspirations of the original people of this land.

Paul PG

Acknowledgements

In the life of a writer, there are people you rely on whose support and encouragement are vital to the success of the project. I am deeply grateful to the unwavering and unconditional love and support my wife Ancy and my children Anil and Bibin have given me over the years while I was engrossed in researching and writing the book. I hope that the finished product proves worthy of their sacrifice.

Don McGuire, Acquisitions Editor at Brighton Publishing and the entire staff, including the graphic designers and the editors, who have been instrumental in giving the book its structure and shape. I will remain deeply grateful to Don for the numerous hours we have spent discussing various aspects of the story and the publishing process. Above all, there was the confident backing for the book.

Finally, a word of gratitude to the reader for your interest in the book.

PROLOGUE

The Catechism of the Catholic Church states clearly that homosexuality is morally depraved and intrinsically disordered. Under no circumstances can it be approved. This is the doctrine of the church. As Catholics we must adhere to the teachings of the church. There's no ambiguity."

"The members of the ICA object to the parish support of gays."

"Father Tosco gave permission to a declared gay group the use of the parish center. It's wrong and we strongly condemn it."

"The Pastoral Council approved it."

"It doesn't matter. It must be rescinded."

"Father Tosco owes the parish an apology."

"It's unfair to accuse Father Tosco. The Pastoral Council reviewed the request and approved it. Father Tosco supported our recommendation. That's all."

"The group requested permission to meet and pray. Father Tosco forwarded the request to the council."

"The council shouldn't have done it."

"As far as the council was concerned, this was a request from a group of Catholics. Their sexual orientation was a non-issue."

"Sexual orientation is an issue. That's why the church has a clear and strict policy on homosexuality."

"This is not a political debate. This is a religious issue. As Catholics we are bound to conform to the teachings of the church."

"We won't allow our parish to be a refuge for homosexual groups."

"If they had approached the Pastor as an unidentified group of Catholics and wanted a place to meet and pray, it would be different. That wasn't the case. They identified themselves as a gay group."

"They profess a way of life that's contrary to church teachings. They have no place in our parish community and we won't allow it."

"Why do we have to take such extreme positions? By allowing them to meet and pray, we are not condoning homosexuality."

"They are Catholics, like you and me. The only difference is they are gay."

"We are not theologians. We're Catholics. We don't interpret church doctrine. We obey them. It's that simple."

"The Parish shouldn't support any group that defines itself around sexual practices, especially those the church considers as depraved."

"The parish has an active support group for divorced Catholics. The church does not sanction divorce as a rule. Should we ban this group?"

"We are not here to debate dogma. The Parish support of a homosexual group is a contradiction of church doctrine and we won't allow it."

"The Pastor must rescind this action. We want it taken care of at the parish level. If not, we will take it up with the bishop."

"Father Tosco, you have not spoken?"

"I'm shocked. I didn't see a contradiction of church teachings in allowing them to meet and pray at the parish center. I saw an opportunity to engage a group of Catholics."

"Would you approve a request from a group of self-declared prostitutes, if there were such a group?"

"If a group of Catholics came to me seeking permission to meet and pray, I would give it favorable consideration. It's not permission to practice or an approval of their lifestyle. We have programs for recovering alcoholics. We have support services for returning Catholics. We allow various ethnic groups to meet and pray and worship together. They all enrich parish life and the faith experience."

"Father Tosco, the ICA is an ethnic group. You are not comparing the ICA to a group of homosexuals, are you?"

"Please, please. Let's not make this into anything more than what it is. This is a specific issue. I have stated repeatedly, I believe in sharing responsibility in the management of the parish with the Pastoral Council.

I discussed the matter with the council and with their approval, issued the permission."

"Father Tosco, do not lay the blame on the council for your actions. You are using the council as a cover. It was your idea. Don't drag them into this."

"The Pastoral Council has an important role to play in the parish community. I give a lot of decision-making authority to the council. I stand by their recommendation in this case. Yes! I know what you are going to say that as Pastor, the decisions are ultimately my responsibility. I take full responsibility."

"We should give credit to Father Tosco for empowering the council and making the council responsible for parish activities. Many pastors pay lip service to community involvement. Father Tosco practices it."

"That's well and good. However, it's the Pastor's obligation to ensure the parish community obeys the rules of the church."

"Let's not blow this out of proportion. I personally have no objection to allowing the group to meet and pray here. The council had no problems either and thus the decision was made."

"The council is only an advisory body."

"The final decision is the pastor's. I understand and as I said, I take full responsibility. You have expressed your feelings. I respect that. If there is significant objection from the parish community, and the council wants to rescind it, I will go along with your wishes."

"Are you asking us to conduct a referendum to prove the majority opinion of the parishioners?"

"I want it to be a council decision. It's a matter of principle for me to give the council as much authority as I can in making decisions that affect the Parish community. If the council wants to rescind, I will rescind."

"You are leaving it up to the council. You want them to take the heat."

"Of course not. Pastors come and go. The community stays together. It's your parish; it's your community; it's your council. If there is any blame I'll take it. I'll take the responsibility of rescinding the permit if that's what the council wants. However, I want it to be a council decision.

But more importantly, I want to see the community stay together."

"Let's hear from the council then."

"We will include this on the agenda for our next monthly meeting. You are welcome to join and express your opinions. The council meetings are open to all parishioners."

"We have made our position very clear. There's no need for us to come to another meeting to repeat the same arguments."

"We won't accept anything less than a rescission."

"We have the mechanism to resolve conflicts. What's important, as Father Tosco said, is for the parish community to be one and worship together."

BOOK OF PETER

"The Reverend Scanlon, before being appointed the first bishop of Salt Lake City, traveled extensively through the lands that would eventually become part of our diocese. The legend is, he and his companions managed to get lost among the numerous canyons and hills that make up the landscape of southern Utah. After wandering around for several days, they were desperate with no food or water. To add to their woes, Rev. Scanlon fell seriously ill. Fortunately, they were discovered by a small band of Paiutes who took them to their village, nursed Rev. Scanlon back to health, and cared for them until they could resume their travels."

"Is this true or just another story?"

"It is in his diaries and must be true. He was very grateful for what the natives had done. When he became bishop, he went back to the native village and signed a covenant with the tribe promising to open and operate a mission for them."

"Why a mission?"

"He had two reasons for doing this: he wanted to show his gratitude and wanted to help improve their situation by offering religion, education and healthcare. Eventually he hoped he would be able to convert them and other native tribes around and thus expand the ministry. That is the history of the Paiute native mission."

"Whatever happened to the mission?"

"It's still there!"

"I never heard of it."

"There is a reason why! The mission has been inactive for over sixty, maybe seventy years."

"Why worry about it then? Why is it on the agenda?"

"When I was appointed VG, I was given three tasks by the bishop; fiscal responsibility, improved interaction with local parishes and renovation of the Cathedral of the Magdalene."

"It's not possible to be fiscally conservative until we finish the renovation of the cathedral."

"We are in a tough predicament. We've tried very hard to keep the renovation within budget but to no avail. It's extremely frustrating."

"What has the renovation got to do with the Paiute mission?"

"It came up while I was reviewing the various ministries. I wanted to see where we could cut back and save some money. I came across a few projects like the Paiute mission that are inactive."

"If the mission is inactive, it's not costing us money, is it?"

"The mission is not costing us any money, although in a way, it does affect the budget."

"I don't understand!"

"Year after year, the Finance Committee earmarks funds for all existing projects, various ministries and items like the Paiute mission. At the end of the fiscal year unused allocations are retired back into the general fund. It's normal accounting practice. These are the kind of irregularities I am trying to get rid of."

"Its impact can't be that bad."

"True! But it does create a phantom account we really don't need. The mission is inactive but not non-existent. The bishop is unwilling, like his predecessors, to shut it down. It's like a sacred relic that nobody venerates but can't be thrown away. If there is a strong push from the Diocesan Council, I can make a case with the bishop to eliminate the Paiute mission."

"We are in full support of your recommendation! Will that do?"

"Yes! That's a good start."

"You said the bishop is unwilling to shut the mission down. As long as he is of that mindset, what would be the purpose of our recommendation?"

"We can try. Here's the dilemma—the covenant signed by bishop Scanlon with the native tribe remains. The bishop won't unilaterally dissolve it. He'll agree if the Paiute tribe agrees to dissolve the covenant. This lets me start a discussion with him."

"Why not send someone out there to meet with the natives and get a signed dissolution? Will that satisfy the bishop?"

"The natives won't care! I would be surprised if the tribe knows about this covenant. Not after all these years!"

"It should be easy enough. Anyone could go and get a signed dissolution."

"It may be easy but then again, it could prove to be not so easy. Here's the scoop. We have no record of any involvement with the mission for a very long time. I have not and I don't know of anyone who has visited the mission. All we have is some old records and diary notes."

"It means the natives have no use for it. They would not object to closing it. They won't care whether we close or not close the mission."

"Probably not! Here's what's really strange. It's odd how it all ended. The last priest assigned to the mission never came back; we never heard from him again."

"Something happened to him?"

"No! He just quit. He left a note at the mission and took off. It was three months before someone realized they hadn't seen him or heard from him and decided to go check, only to discover the letter."

"That is a strange story."

"According to his letter, he never met the natives. He couldn't find them."

"Why was he sent there if there were no natives?"

"I guess nobody knew. My guess is that the mission was already in decline and we didn't have someone there on a continuous basis."

"This is really weird."

"Where does that leave us now, if we want to shut it down?"

"We need somebody to go out there, find the tribe, discuss with them the futility of keeping the mission open, and then convince them to sign the dissolution of the covenant."

"There may be no one left in the tribe for us to meet with. Many native tribes have become extinct or just dispersed."

"That could be true. But we need to make the attempt. We can't merely rely on a note left by a priest over sixty years ago. If the tribe exists, then we will get a signed dissolution. If the tribe is not to be found, I can recommend to the bishop that the mission be closed."

"We'll have to reactivate the mission to close it. Crazy!"

"Who can we send? It would have to be a priest, I would imagine, especially if we have to reopen the mission first."

"Yes!"

"But who would want to go?"

"It would be no more than a temporary assignment."

"How about Father Tosco?"

"Why Father Tosco?"

"He has run into problems at St. Bonaventure's, as we know. He may want to take a little break."

"We can't reassign him, even temporarily, because there are problems."

"He may want to get out of there. You know how it is when the parishioners take up arms against the pastor."

"He should have been a little more careful."

"I hear it's getting worse and approaching a flash point. The local press got wind of the story and published a scathing editorial excoriating the church's attitude toward gays. Father Tosco is accused of leaking the story to the press although I don't believe he did."

"That does not sound good."

"The parish is deeply divided over the issue. The ICA is on the far extreme right. If there are any moderates left, no one dares challenge the ICA."

"I don't think Father Tosco can resolve the issue or reconcile the factions."

"He's getting it from every side. It's a mess."

"The ICA has made him into a radical liberal, a threat to the church."

"The rest of the parish is blaming him for stirring up the mess."

"He may be ready for a change of scenery."

"I'm sure he sees the writing on the wall. He can't continue as pastor."

"We need to tread carefully. We can't move him because there is a powerful lobby working against him."

"Neither can we turn a blind eye to the sentiments of the parishioners."

"You have to be sensitive to the dilemma facing priests. The diocese can't change pastors because of pressure from powerful groups; it will undermine the role of pastors. It'll take away the credibility of priests."

"I think the situation has deteriorated to a point of no return. No matter what Father Tosco does at this point, it won't be well received. Too bad."

"We can't let it drag on any longer; it will only make matters worse."

"Maybe it's a good idea to approach Father Tosco with the Paiute mission proposal. He may be looking for a face-saving escape."

"He, who has not sinned, let him throw the first stone! With those words, Jesus silenced the self-righteous hypocrites who had gathered to stone the adulteress woman to death. Jesus had the humanity to forgive a sinful woman. He didn't condone her behavior. He didn't take her aside and chastise her. He sent her away with a warning to sin no more.

It was a lesson to the crowds who came prepared to enjoy a gruesome spectacle. They would have stoned the woman to death in the name of religious fervor. The very same people who probably were participants in her adultery had no moral compunctions in condemning the woman. The words of Jesus still ring true, with as blunt a message. 'Judge not and you shall not be judged!' We are quick to condemn and punish our neighbor while we refuse to look at our sinfulness. Sure, what they had planned was in accordance with the Jewish Law. Jesus didn't challenge the law. But he wanted those who would take law into their own hands take a look at themselves and prove they were beyond reproach.

In another instance Jesus mocks those who 'would behold the mote in their brother's eye but consider not the beam in their own.' Time and time again he taught us to be tolerant of others and their mistakes because we ourselves are not perfect. We have frailties; we have weaknesses; we commit sins. Let's not be quick to judge others. Let us show tolerance toward our fellow humans.

We live in a diverse society. We live among people whose customs and practices we may find objectionable. There are neighbors around us who embrace ways of life that we find morally reprehensible. While most neighbors among us live in accordance with God's commandments, we find some whose conduct conflicts with our beliefs and the teachings of the church. In those times, remember the words of Jesus and his message of tolerance. Tolerance is not an acknowledgement of what is wrong as right. It is a willingness to accept that we are imperfect too.

Brothers and Sisters: God has given us two commandments: 'Love God and love your neighbor.' All other commandments are derived from these two. The first one is the easy one. It's easy to love God who you can't see and feel and who is perfect. It's much more difficult to love your neighbor who you see and feel each day and who has many imperfections. Welcome with open arms all of God's children irrespective of who they are. Do not pick up the stone to punish your neighbor or one day we too will have to face the rebuke from Jesus."

"This is an extract from the Sunday bulletin. Given the circumstances, that was pretty heavy."

"I don't think the message was lost on his detractors."

"He decided he was going to say what he had to say."

"I guess he's no longer concerned if people love him or hate him."

"Those are words of a man who wants to get it off his chest, come what may."

"Father Tosco has got himself into a no-win situation."

"The Parish Council rescinded the permission given to the gay group. They're upset but understand the reality."

"That's the end of that, I guess."

"Not really. Things didn't resolve the way we would've hoped. Having tasted victory, the ICA wants to flex its muscle further. They want the pastor removed. Other parish groups who are not fans of the ICA accuse the Pastor of buckling under to the ICA. They accuse him of being weak. They too want him removed. The Pastoral Council is unhappy over the controversy and questions his administrative ability. Several members have resigned."

"His attempts at parish democracy have come crashing down on him."

"Welcome to the new Christian community: Anarchy in diversity."

"I'm sure he'll learn from this. Change does not come easy to the church."

"What do we do now?"

"It would make things easier for everybody, if Father Tosco requests a transfer out of St. Bonaventure's."

"He has. He has requested to be reassigned. That means we don't have to initiate it. We would have had to but now we are doing him a favor. He has also agreed to take on the assignment to close the Paiute mission."

"'What the patient wanted is what the doctor ordered.' So the saying goes."

"What happens when he's done with the mission? It shouldn't take long."

"I want to make sure his exit from St. Bonaventure is graceful and orderly. He must feel he's not being banished and exiled. The mission task alone would not have been substantial. I appointed Father Peter Tosco as Diocesan Director of Ethnic Ministries. The mission is part of the Ministry."

"That's wonderful."

"Who has been in charge of the Ministry so far?"

"I am or should have been. I must confess I have not given it the attention such an important Ministry demands. As a diocese, we need to take stock of the ethnic communities within the diocese, address their needs and help support their growth. It'll all be part of Father Tosco's job now."

Day 1

March 1, 1985

Peter Tosco, priest, Catholic Diocese of Salt Lake City
Title: Director of Ethnic Ministries

Today I am embarking on a new journey, a new job, into the unknown, with unproven skills for the task ahead of me. Within the span of a few months, my life has turned upside down. From the serenity and calm of a quiet parish life, I have been thrown into the middle of a tornado.

I take full responsibility for making the decisions that catapulted me into this situation; but even knowing what would have transpired, I would not have done anything differently. I'm not sure why I decided to keep this diary, but maybe one day in the future, I may need to reflect back and seek some rational explanation for the journey of my life. I hate to admit it; I'm feeling very insecure. Did I take on this assignment to escape from St. Bonaventure's? Did the diocese manufacture this assignment to ease me out of the eye of the storm? Does it matter? I accepted the assignment and the past is past.

Here I am on my way to meet with a native tribe I know nothing about. To set the record straight, I know very little about Native Americans, other than what I've read in novels and history books—and of course, seen in movies. I had very little time to do research on this tribe and the Catholic Church's relationship with them and other tribes within the diocese. I picked up as many books on Native Americans as I could find in the Diocesan library and the local library. I also found a couple of books on Father Junipero Serra, the great California missionary who converted many of the native tribes there. I was also given a medium-sized box of old documents and a folder with a copy of the covenant Bishop Scanlon had signed with the Paiute tribe. The box, I was told, contained copies of his diary notes and scattered records of the mission's activities since it was established. I will have to learn as much as I can, if I can, before I meet with the natives, if I meet with them.

Accompanying me on the journey is Brother Francis Rodriguez, a fine young man in the final phase of his preparation for priesthood. He is of the serious type, not moody or anti-social, just serious. He didn't seem particularly excited or anxious about the trip. There wasn't a whole lot of conversation, but it was not unpleasant.

I was told the natives might have moved away from the mission site. We had to be prepared to search for them. We rented a U-Haul trailer that we attached to my car, and we put together supplies of food and water for a couple of weeks. We brought along two tents and two mountain bikes, just in case. There was a rectory attached to the mission, but after all these years, who knew in what condition it would be in. We were told the mission was in the middle of tough terrain and to expect many difficulties.

There was an old hand-drawn map of the mission in the folder. I hoped it was reliable. I had borrowed a Rand McNally from the chancery, but there was nothing about a village anywhere in the vicinity of the mission location. It showed the main freeways, but gave no further details of a native reservation or a human habitation in the general area.

Francis was driving. In about an hour, we expected to be turning off the freeway and heading South East across open land, toward a line of hills. Once we got to the junction of 17 and Interstate 15, we would take 17 for about half-a-mile, and the turnoff should be toward the right. There should be some markings through the desert showing the road to the mission. It was about a four-hour drive from Salt Lake City, and I had wanted to reach there around mid-afternoon. That would give us time to survey the area in daylight. We started later than I had wanted, due to a last minute meeting called by the VG.

When we arrived at the junction of the freeways it was a little past three. The hand-drawn map was apparently not to scale and a little fuzzy as to where the turn off was. We drove for about two miles on 17, but saw no turn off or any signs of a road. The hills were there, all right.

The mission was situated on the other side of the hills and we had to find a way through. It occurred to us that we were not going to find any signs of a road. What was in the map would have been nothing more than a trail and would have disappeared over time. We decided to take our chances and head straight toward the hills. We had to be careful because of the trailer. It was a good five miles across bumpy terrain to the hills and as we approached, we could see where a natural passage through a depression in the hills had been modified into an access road. We parked and walked over to the top of the pass, not knowing what lay beyond.

It was quite chilly even though it was a clear and bright day. There was a crisp wind blowing at our backs from the west. The view from the top of the pass was remarkable. There was a dry and broad valley stretching for miles from where we stood to a group of much larger hills to the South. Cutting through the heart of the valley, but closer to where we stood, was a large ravine. It ran parallel to the hills we stood on and ended about a quarter of a mile to our right. The ravine was fairly wide where it came to an abrupt end. To the left, the ravine ran like a slithering snake with many-a-curve and curl for as far as we could see. Between the ravine and the hills we stood on, there was a small plateau, barren and flat.

Directly below was the church, a small rectangular building facing the plateau. From the look of things, it was a structure that was not willing or fully ready to succumb to the demands of time and nature. There was a metal cross standing above the roof at the front, facing the ravine. It was distinguishable as a cross but it stood at an angle and appeared close to losing its hold on to the roof of the church.

At the rear of the church and to its left, was the rectory. It was built deep and almost entirely into the hillside. The road sloped gently to the side of the church and there was enough space there between the church and the rectory to park the car and the trailer. Whoever built the church had selected a good spot, protected as it was from the wind and the full impact of the sun.

It required a stretch of the imagination to call it a church unless every building with a roof and a cross above it could be called a church. Four stone pillars in the four corners supported a tin roof that showed its age and the effects of the inhospitable weather. It was no more than 40' x 20' inside. There was a raised, stone platform to the rear of the church which would be the altar, and there was a two-foot high wall on the two sides. The entrance was through the front marked by four steps that ran the width of the building. The floor was filled with sand. There were remnants of weeds where some suicidal seeds had tried to take roots when some past storms brought wetness to the sand.

Beyond the front of the church was an open area about thirty-feet wide and fifty-feet deep, and from there the land sloped down to the plateau below. It was a ghostly appearance, but unlike some abandoned shacks in deserts, the church had stood its ground. It was very quiet and there were no signs of birds or any other creatures. It was a little eerie, but charming at the same time.

We went back and drove the car and the trailer carefully down the slope to the side of the church. We backed in and parked close to the door to the rectory. We looked all around but there was not the slightest movement. There were no huts, no teepees, no tents, no cattle, horses, or any other living thing as far as we could see. If I had dreamt of driving in, meeting with the natives and getting out, those thoughts were quickly extinguished. This would not have a quick ending after all. One look at the desolation before us was enough to convince us both that the Catholic mission had no purpose being here.

We decided to look around the church and the rectory to make sure there were no surprises hiding there, coyotes, rattlers, or anything more sinister. The door to the rectory was made of solid wood and the ravages of time had left indelible marks on it. There was no lock. A wooden bolt held the door in its place. There were no signs of a break-in. The bolt didn't respond favorably to repeated kicks or our combined exhortations. Francis fetched a hammer from the car and after a few good smacks it decided to comply and move with many a groan and disapproval. I directed my flashlight to get some idea what it was like in there. The inside was a haven for the inevitable cobwebs strung from every conceivable protrusion. There was a thick coating of dust on everything. It was not as bad as one would have imagined for a place that had not been inhabited for over half-a-century.

It was cooler inside. It was large enough for one person to live comfortably. There was a small bedroom to the left with the bed and covers undisturbed. Everything was neatly arranged. The small dining room cum office was directly in front. It was lined on the bedroom side with an open shelf full of books. The table was set for two with china and cups that had intricate designs on them. It was spooky. To the right of the entryway was a tiny kitchen with a wood stove with logs, ready to be lighted. There was a neat pile of firewood stacked next to the stove. Pots and pans hung from a ceiling rack warmly embraced by the cobwebs. Beyond the kitchen was an open enclosure with a stone tub that obviously served as a bath and there was a toilet tucked neatly at the very end. The last person here had left the place in perfect condition for the successor to walk in and call it home.

There had to be a source of water, and much as we searched, we couldn't find any hidden fountain or stream. We would have to do some heavy duty dusting and cleaning before we could make the rectory habitable. We were not in any mood for cleaning work today. It could get quite cold during the night but we decided to brave the elements and sleep in tents rather than inside the rectory. There wasn't much of a wind down there, although we could hear it high up on the hills. We found an open fire pit on the rectory side of the church; and as night fell we would have a campfire to keep warm, cook our dinner, and scare off unwelcome visitors.

We set up the tents inside the church enclosure and then took a walk toward the ravine. Our main objective was to find water. There had to be a source or they wouldn't have built a church and a rectory there. There was none, not easily visible anyway. It was puzzling. There had to be water or people wouldn't have lived here. We had brought a fair supply of bottled water, but that was for consumption, not for personal hygiene. Maybe there was water inside the ravine. The shadows of the hills were creeping toward the edge and soon it would be dark.

As we approached we could see to the right where the ravine ended. Nature had done a marvelous job sculpting the end of the ravine into some remarkable shapes. It was not as deep as where we stood but the walls were steep and rugged. Where a little bit of soil had found a foothold, the rock face was covered with desert plants common to the area. The canyon was dark and deep to our left. If we expected to see the shiny reflection of water at the bottom, we were disappointed. It was totally dry as far as we could see.

The little plateau we stood on and the plains on the other side of the ravine were flat and mostly devoid of vegetation. But further, we could see the ghostly silhouettes of desert plants until everything merged and disappeared into a misty haze. We had the mountain bikes and could explore the area tomorrow. It would have been great to have water for a nice bath, but we were now mindful of the need to conserve our water supply until we found a source. We cooked a simple dinner, said our prayers, and then went to bed tightly wrapped inside our sleeping bags. The adventure had begun.

Day II

We woke up early to a bright and clear day. The air was chilly and had a bite to it when the occasional gust of wind found its way to us. The night had been uneventful but very cold. I may have heard the howls of coyotes or maybe wolves in the distance but I wasn't sure. I would not call myself an outdoorsman and Francis was no exception. We said Mass and after a simple breakfast took our bikes and ventured out to explore the surroundings and look for the native village. We would return before the sun got hot. Even during early to mid-spring, the sun can get pretty hot during the day and it didn't make sense, getting sunburned.

We rode along the ridge on our side of the ravine to our left. We had two things on our minds, signs of native life and a source for water. Occasionally we stopped to peer over the edge of the ravine. It was the same story. There was no sign of water. However, it was obvious that there had been water inside the ravine at some time in the past. There was driftwood and other debris on the floor of the ravine that could only have been brought down during floods. Flash floods were not unknown in deserts, and it wouldn't take much rainfall to make a lake out of these canyons. It was apparent that there had not been any sizable rainfall for quite a long time.

Soon we were past the hills that stumbled to a stop in a vast field of disorderly rocks to our left. The ravine wound its way through the desert toward the row of rocky hills to the east. To our left, the uneven terrain extended some distance until it was swallowed up by awesome-looking rock formations. Even as we took in the beauty of the rugged landscape, we were constantly on the lookout for signs of a native village. There were none. We decided that it was futile to try and find a way to the other side of the ravine from where we were. That could wait for another day.

By the time we got back to the church, the sun was directly above us and it was hot. We decided we would clean up the rectory and make it livable. It would certainly be cool inside and safe. We would bring our perishable supplies inside, including the bottled water.

Where are the natives?

Day III

We slept in our tents for a second night. The rectory had to be thoroughly aired out before we could sleep inside. We said Mass, had a small breakfast, and then set out on our bikes but this time we went around to the southern side of the ravine. We went as far as we dared keeping close to the ravine so that we wouldn't get lost. Distances and landmarks can be deceiving in deserts and canyon lands. There was no sign of a native village or human habitation.

We didn't stay out too long, and by noon came back to the coolness of the rectory. We talked about a variety of topics. Francis was well-read and had an inquisitive mind. But conversation between two people can have its limits, especially when the two people are by nature what you would call introspective. There were longer periods of silence than conversation. Yet, it was natural and neither of us found it uncomfortable. It gave me time to read up on the native tribes of the area.

No sign of the natives. Where are they?

Day IV

Thoughts of a quick meeting with the natives, signing the dissolution of the covenant and return had lost all shades of optimism and were replaced by nagging doubts that maybe there were no natives around anymore. How long should we hang around? How long can I keep Francis down here? What else can I do to track down the natives, if they're still around? Should I call it quits and go back?

At dusk we looked all around, the plains and the hills, to see if there was any smoke rising out of teepees, any music, any reflections of metal objects, anything that would betray human presence. At the same time, we tried to make our presence visible, all to no avail.

Speaking of Francis, he seemed to be enjoying this much like a camping trip. He never complained nor made suggestive remarks about the foolhardiness of the trip. He never showed any discontent about the lack of comforts. I couldn't share his level of nonchalance. The worst part was not being able to have a bath. We could unhitch the trailer and drive out south or north until we found a store or a gas station, but I couldn't remember seeing a store or gas station within twenty-to-thirty miles from where we were. Still, the choice was there. All we had to do was to keep driving until we found something. The city of St. George couldn't be that far down to the south.

There had to be water somewhere close. There had to be. We would have to do with an occasional sponge bath until we found a water source. We would forgo shaving. The ugly rubble on both of our faces was starting to make us look different.

After Mass and breakfast, I showed no inclination to set out on another trip. Francis wanted to go and I let him venture out on his own. I took the opportunity to start reading the books I had brought with me. Knowing the history of the Paiute tribe and other Native American tribes in and around Sothern Utah could come in handy when I met with them. Will I get to meet them, though? Am I wasting my time here? There was nothing else to do. I might as well read the books and enhance my knowledge.

The Paiutes of Utah were one of the oldest of Native American tribes. A peaceful nation, they paid the prize for their non-aggression as well as survived because of it. They were nomadic, but stayed within a limited range. They were hunters of small game such as deer and rabbits. Their access to buffalo was limited. They were expert seed and root gatherers and had an intimate knowledge of the cycle of seasons and what the land provided. They were kind and helpful to pioneers, missionaries, settlers and prospectors that flooded through their territories. Their concept of land ownership was simple; it was for everyone, and there was plenty of it. Thus, there was no need to possess and defend it. That probably factored into the lack of structures built with human hands.

The Paiutes suffered greatly under the mismanagement and foolhardy experiments of the US government and the Bureau of Native American Affairs. They suffered terribly under pressure from the Mormon Church, which had established itself in the Salt Lake Basin and started a process of expansion. Systematically, the tribe was victimized by greedy groups of settlers as they passed through. Each and every group severely impacted their way of life and their chances of survival. But they did survive, even through the dissolution of tribal status, relocation, and restoration.

The Paiutes of Utah were divided into five different bands, each recognized as a separate nation by the US government. Each had its own reservation and governmental system. This area where the mission stood was part of the Cedar City reservation. Much of the land was arid desert and desolate canyons, not of sufficient quality to support their nomadic way of life. Many members moved to cities and led a hand-to-mouth existence on meager wages as unskilled laborers. Their land holdings were vast, but too poor to support agriculture. Wherever there was water and could support agriculture, white settlers or organized religious groups had moved in and driven the natives out. Canyon lands that would attract visitors and tourists were made into national parks. The Paiutes, much like natives all over, were left with nothing to provide for their livelihood.

The interaction between the Paiutes and the Diocese of Salt Lake City was the result of the adventures or misadventures of the Rev. Scanlon before he became bishop. Apparently, he had come into contact with a splinter group of Paiutes because subsequent dealings with the natives appear to have been limited to a small band and not with any of the bigger groups. It was possible that many or all of the natives of this group converted to Catholicism at some time. I could think of no other explanation for the ongoing support of the mission by the diocese. As time passed, interest in the group must have lessened as they were reduced to no more than a hundred members toward the end of the records. Attempts at expanding the faith among other native tribes were non-productive.

Francis returned before noon. He had found a trail leading down to the ravine floor and wanted to go back and explore it some more. If there was a trail, it was created in all probability by humans and not by animals. We had yet to see an animal around. He was confident that somewhere within the deep ravine there would be water; there had to be. I promised to go with him the next day.

Day V

The view from the canyon floor was breathtaking. The undulating formations of the walls, carved over centuries by the hand of nature, left us stunned by the bewildering array of colors and shapes. The sides were steep thus lending an ethereal quality to the deep blue of the sky beyond and the occasional shadows created by the passing clouds.

It was also much cooler down here and very still. I was surprised that there were no trees growing within the canyon. The walls were rocky and mostly inhospitable for vegetation. There were some indistinguishable footmarks of animals on the canyon floor, and there were a few birds flying and nesting overhead among the recesses of the rocks. I thought I heard the sounds of rattlers or whatever may have been disturbed by our surprise visit, but I was in no mood to go investigate. When we spoke, the sound of our voices echoed off the canyon walls with a resounding boom, and for some time we were like children shouting at the top of our voices and listening to the reverberating echoes until they faded. There was no sign of water anywhere. But there were plenty of signs that this canyon held water and plenty of it at various times. The signs were recorded visibly on the canyon walls.

Then it struck me—this is the Little Bend River and this is the Little Bend valley. The documents in the folder talked about the mission being built on the banks of a river. If so, the natives must have lived on the plains surrounding the river. But what happened to the river? Why was it dry? When and how did it dry up? It couldn't have been too long ago. Without water, the natives couldn't have survived around here. The river that had supported this community had dried up and deserted them. They must have been forced to move on. It was a recent event; that was for sure.

I shared my insights with Francis on the way back. Little wonder there was no native village here anymore. The realization forced me to rethink my options. My enthusiasm and hopes of catching up with the natives soon, took a dramatic nosedive. Without the river and the water to support them, they could have moved away or even disbanded and merged into neighboring tribal communities.

Day VI

Francis wanted to climb to the top of the hills at our back. I too wanted to see what was at the top and what we could see from there. I was hoping that we would have a wider view of the surroundings and maybe catch a glimpse of human habitation.

The canyon side of the hills was steep making access impossible. But on the other side of the hill, the slope was gradual and fairly easy to negotiate. There was a discernible pathway slinking its way upward. Large rocks and formations along the way provided some periodic protection from the sun. The ground was barren except for the occasional scraggly desert plant with its dark brown stem and sickly looking leaves. It has never ceased to amaze me how vegetation can find sustenance and survive in the harshest of environments.

As we wound our way around to the top, the marks of humans were plentiful, none of them recent, unfortunately. The natives had frequented these hills and there were numerous indentations on the rocks that had a distinct native quality to them. Human hands had rearranged some of the smaller boulders.

The view from the top was spectacular. We could see for miles all around. I looked closely in every direction. There were no signs of a human settlement as far as I could see. But there were plenty of signs at the top to indicate this area had all kinds of significance for the natives. We found an area of great interest at the very top in the shape of a small plateau. It appeared to be a ceremonial ground. The rocks had been moved around to create a fairly large flat and circular area. The earth had been smoothed, and then trampled firm. Even-sized rocks were placed around the enclosure creating an open arena. The clearing could easily hold well over a hundred people. Standing in the middle of the circle, I had an unobstructed view of the heavens and the land around. There was a fire pit at the very center of the circle, with a faint trace of ashes in it. Again, none of the signs pointed to human visits to the site anytime in the recent past. The dry weather and the infrequent rainfall had helped preserve some of the markings.

From what I'd read, I had a little insight into the belief system of the natives and how it affected and permeated into their everyday social life. They believed in the Great Spirit—Wakan Tanka—who had absolute power over every aspect of nature, its existence, and its manifold variations. Of course, this included all living things and humans were no exception. Nature was the manifestation of the power of the Great Spirit and his gift to humans at the same time. Humans sought harmony with nature, taking what they needed but always maintaining a healthy respect for it.

Nature provided for them and sustained them. There was simplicity in their beliefs, and these beliefs dictated their way of life. It was a day-to-day existence based on a deep-rooted belief that nature would not betray them, not in the long run, anyway. Nature may act oddly now and then, but was predictable over time. Nature had to be appeased and revered because nature was the manifestation of the Great Spirit and beyond the scope of human control. When humans erred and exhibited evil tendencies, Wakan Tanka punished them in the form of a natural calamity, fierce winter storms, an extended drought or other misfortunes such as an epidemic.

Humans sadly had a proclivity for behaving badly. They therefore held the Great Spirit with a mixture of fear and respect and made peace offerings on a routine basis. Everything that happened only happened because the Spirit willed it. It was all part of destiny and even if humans failed to understand the mysterious workings of the Great Spirit, it behooved them not to challenge them. If only life were that simple.

This retreat at the top of the hills had to have a religious significance. Here they would be close to the abode of the Great Spirit and commune with him through the ministrations of the shaman, their spiritual guide.

We went back to the church, almost in a reverie, both of us comfortable with our own thoughts. Francis seemed unconcerned by what was happening or what was not happening. I was restless, unsure of what steps I should take. Should I just abandon this quest and return to the city? If I choose to stay, what would be a reasonable period time to remain here? How will the Vicar General and the bishop evaluate my efforts if I return empty handed?

I was determined I was not going to give up that easy and return without accomplishing my task, if at all possible. Should I give myself another week, two weeks, a month? Tomorrow would mark the end of one week since we got here. I decided another two weeks would be the absolute possible maximum. But, I couldn't hold back Francis here. He had many things to do with his preparations for his ordination. He was an excellent companion, but beyond companionship, there was no justification to keep him here. This was my task to accomplish or fail.

Day VII

After Mass and breakfast, Francis was ready to leave on his bike for more exploration. I was staying back having decided it was time to discuss his departure. I would do it as soon as he got back.

I explained to him my decision to stay for two more weeks. I would attempt to contact the natives and get our mission accomplished. There was no reason for him to stay that long. I was in no danger. There were enough supplies to last me for two weeks. I would expect him back on the fourteenth day from today. If in between, I ran into the natives or they found me, I would complete my task and ask them to drop me off at the nearest town or maybe even back to the city.

As expected, Francis was all up in arms over the idea of leaving me alone, and it took a lot of persuading before he could be convinced to depart. He would leave tomorrow. We moved all of the supplies into the rectory. He would take my car and the trailer back. There was no point in paying rent for the trailer and having it sit here for no reason. The mountain bikes would stay. They were mine.

Day VIII

I felt a touch of sadness as I watched Francis drive away. Much as he had tried until the last minute to convince me he should stay, I was equally adamant he should go. This adventure had now to do with me and with me alone. This was my challenge and I didn't want to drag Francis into it. Win or lose, it was best that I went at it alone. I knew I would miss his company, especially if this dragged on longer. I was stubborn. But as the car and trailer drifted over the pass, and all I could see was the dust trail left behind, I sensed feelings of apprehension creep in. Have I allowed my frustrations get the better of me? Is it wise to be around these parts, all by myself? I was no outdoorsman.

These were only fleeting thoughts, quickly and quietly dispelled. If the native tribe existed around these parts, I would find them; it didn't matter how long it took. If I gained nothing else from this expedition, I would go back with a better understanding of native culture.

I didn't feel like doing anything the rest of the day. Francis had been good company and I missed his presence. I decided to move inside the rectory and live and behave like the pastor of the mission, albeit without a flock. I was not afraid of being alone. It was the lack of sound and movement that was bothersome.

Day IX

My first full day alone in this wilderness came and went. It was uneventful. I found an old branch of a tree and tied a white bath towel to one end to form a flag and attached it to the handle of the bike. Thus equipped, I rode around along the ravine until noon, hoping that it would catch someone's eye. If it did, no one bothered to respond. I spent the rest of the day reading, sitting in the shade of the church.

Day X

I was convinced the natives were out there somewhere. I kept whispering to myself that I could sense it. Somehow I had to get their attention. The flag display hadn't worked. But I would keep it going. I would stick to a routine each day. I would ride around the ravine, displaying my white flag until around noon, and then spend the rest of the day, resting, reading or doing nothing. I would take another shorter ride around before dusk. Such a schedule would prevent me from procrastinating whether I should go or stay. The daily routine would give me something concrete to do other than sit and brood.

Then it occurred to me that there was nothing more visible than fire after dark. It was a matter of creating a large enough fire that could be seen for miles around. As I started thinking about it, it appealed to me as my best option to attract attention. But, how would I build a large enough bonfire, short of setting the rectory on fire? The answer came to me fairly quickly. Nature had provided me with highly flammable material in plenty. There were lots and lots of tumbleweeds all around the plains. I could see them take off on their ghostly journeys each day when the wind picked up. Many of them were caught among rocks and crevasses. All I needed was a long rope to which I could attach the globular weeds, and with the help of the bike, drag them to where I wanted.

Invigorated with the new possibility, I ventured out as soon as the shadows of the hills became visible over the valley, armed with my bike, a flag, and a long rope tailing me. I gathered up the little mounds and strung the rope through them. If anyone was watching, it must have been a comical scene, with me riding the bike with a white flag, dragging a parade of dry tumbleweed; another Don Quixote on a wild mission. Again and again I went out hunting for more tumbleweeds, and each time I returned laden with the booty which I stashed away next to the church so they wouldn't roll away again. I was a modern-day cowboy, rounding up the wandering tumbleweed. Just for good measure, I added a few 'whoops', emulating cowboys. I felt exhilarated.

As night approached, I surveyed my day's work and felt proud of what I'd done. It was time to put it to the test. I piled them up into a heap in the middle of the little plateau, about midway to the ravine. Starting with a large base, I tossed the tumbleweeds one top of the other until I had a pyramid about four-to-five feet high. It was more work than I anticipated. They were so dry, my hands and face were smarting from the scrapes of the prickly mass as I tossed them into the pile. I was sweating, itchy, and kicking up a lot of dust in the process.

I waited until it was pitch dark. All it took was some old newspaper scraps and a match. I lit the newspaper, tossed it into the heap, and then ran back as fast as I could toward the church. Like a child watching fireworks, I stood enthralled as the fire caught, the conflagration hissed and crackled into life, and went up in one huge ball of fire. It took a few minutes to get my vision cleared after the dazzling burst of fire and light. I kept my eyes riveted on the distant plains and hills for any signs of human activity such as flashing lights or sounds. If the natives were around, they had to be on the other side of the canyon or among the hills. They couldn't help but see the sudden burst of fire.

There were no rewarding signs. I stood there for a long time, until the last of the embers had died down and darkness enveloped everything. I was disappointed. I went back to bed weary and exhausted from the day's toils.

Day XI

I woke up physically and emotionally drained. I guess this is what happens when you get your hopes up high, and then there is a letdown. I said Mass as usual and walked listlessly around the area where I had lit the bonfire to see if there were any footsteps or signs of visitors. None.

I hadn't had a bath in days. The stubble of hair on my face was starting to lengthen long enough for me to grab a handful. For lack of anything better to do or as a means of self-inflicted penance, I stuck to my routine and went out on the bike collecting more tumbleweeds. As the day came to a close and darkness spread, I set up the bonfire and watched it blaze, and then die away. Again, I scanned the distant hills and surrounding areas for a glimmer of light or life. There was none.

Day XII

Am I wasting my time here? Are there any natives left in these parts? If there are, would they understand that I'm trying to catch their attention? Why go out again and collect tumbleweeds? Is there anything else I can try that I haven't tried already? Lack of a proper bath and eating canned food were affecting not only my energy, but my morale as well.

I convinced myself I couldn't give in to self-doubt and went out once again hunting for tumbleweeds. If I had the means, I would have lit the fire in the ceremonial pit at the top of the hill. There was no way I would have been able to drag the tumbleweed up the hill. There were logs at the bottom of the ravine, but I didn't have the will to attempt hauling them out. They would have burned longer but it would require too much effort. I had to make do with tumbleweeds.

I had to go further out to find them and there were not as many. Yet, it gave me something to do. I made a bonfire with less tumbleweeds. The size of the fire was not important. I didn't bother to hang around looking at the hills. I lit the fire and walked away. I did it because I had to do, and there was nothing else to do. Slowly the futility of my efforts became obvious. I was wasting my time and all that was left for me to do was to wait for the arrival of Francis and leave.

Day XIII

Hunt for more tumbleweeds. I knew I was weaker and growing more and more desperate. It was a hopeless exercise, but again I had no other options. Eight more days and Francis would be back. In the meantime I had to make the effort, hopeless though it was.

Tonight would be the last time I built the bonfire. I had tried to replicate the native smoke or fire signal. It hadn't worked. Enough was enough. My supply of water was getting low and becoming a concern. There was enough canned food. I wasn't eating much anyway. Eight more days and that would be the end of this ordeal. I knew if I wanted I could get on the bike and make my way to the freeway and wave down some passing car or truck. But I was determined I would do it only as a last resort. I wasn't there yet. I would wait it out until Francis showed up.

I spent most of the day reading. I didn't have to force myself to do that. I re-read the documents with growing passion, slowly understanding the misery the poor natives had endured. I wanted to read more, learn more, and understand more.

The native people were not the monsters painted by popular fiction. They were real and ancient people with a unique civilization that had been destroyed and their population decimated by the white settlers. But there was something more shockingly appalling; the terrible treatment of the natives was not just a thing of the past, it continued even today. The most benevolent and humane of all global communities, the United States of America, the champion of human rights, allowed the natives in their own homeland to live in utter misery. It was shameless.

I was weary, dirty, and hungry. I moved around mechanically. As night fell, I cursed and kicked the remainder of the tumbleweed together. Life can serve out some ugly and unexpected adventures. What am I doing in the middle of this desolate wilderness? A catholic priest marooned in the middle of a desert, burning tumbleweed in the hope some native tribe, who may or may not be out there, would see it and come out to investigate? I could have laughed if someone told me about such a story but the problem was I was living that story. I tore up some wrappers from the cans and water bottles to start the fire and lit it.

What happened next was so unexpected and so sudden, I was totally unprepared for it. As the fire roared to life, I turned to walk away. There was the sudden neighing of horses and a wild scrambling of hoofs. Stunned by the noise and the movement I whirled around. I was scared out of my wits. In the sudden confusion, I lost my footing, and fell flat on my face. I lay there dazed, trying to get the dust out of my face, trying to take in large gulps of air, and trying to steady my racing heart, all at once. Finally I half-turned and started to get up only to lose my footing on the soft sand and this time fell on my back. Thus laid out in the most ridiculous manner possible, I looked up to see three men on horseback towering over me. The horses must have panicked momentarily at the sudden burst of fire, but they were under control now. I could see them in the dim light, tossing their heads and prancing around. There was no visible expression on the faces of the riders. In the occasional glimmer of embers lighting up in the wind, I caught the glint of the muzzle of guns that, although not pointed at me, were in my general direction.

"Get up! You are trespassing on a native reservation! What are you doing here?"

It was embarrassing. I must have been such a sorry sight with my unkempt beard and hair, dirty jeans and jacket, and dust covering my face. I struggled to get up, and with some effort managed to stand.

"Who are you?"

"I can explain. Can we go over to the rectory and sit down?"

"Don't move!"

"All right! I am Father Peter Tosco, the new pastor of the mission."

"You are what?"

"The pastor of the mission!"

"Pastor! Mission? What are you talking about?"

"Can we sit down please and talk?"

"All right, but no tricks! Don't try anything funny."

"No I won't. I told you I am a priest of the Catholic Diocese of Salt Lake City. I was sent to take charge of the mission. I have to meet with the Paiute natives. Do you know them?"

"We know nothing about a mission or a Catholic Diocese or any diocese."

"Why do you want to meet with the Paiutes?"

"Where are they?"

"We are Paiute."

"Thank God! My prayers have finally been answered."

"We are not here to answer your prayers."

"I want to meet your chief."

"Chief! What Chief?"

"Go on! What's all this about?"

"The diocese wants to know if you want the mission here."

"What mission? There is no mission!"

"This is the mission."

"This is no mission. Nothing's happened here as long as I can remember."

"Exactly! If there is no need for the mission, the bishop wants to terminate the covenant."

"What covenant? This is crazy."

"You better talk to the council. This doesn't make any sense."

"When and where can I meet them?"

"Head straight out toward the hills. As you get near, you will see the village. You can't miss it."

"You will see a few broken down cars as you get close to the village."

"When can I come?"

"You can come anytime you want to. Evenings are better."

"Wait! I have no way of getting there except my dirt bike. Can they come here to meet me?"

"Did you get here on a dirt bike?"

"My friend dropped me off. He will be back in a week to pick me up."

"This is the craziest thing I have heard in my life. We'll talk to the folks. They can decide if they want to come and meet with you."

"Please! I need to meet someone. Would you ask them to come? And, if it's no trouble, could you ask them to bring some water with them?"

Without a reply, they turned and rode away into the darkness, shaking their heads.

It was not the kind of encounter I'd anticipated but it didn't matter one bit. I had finally made contact. I had broken through. The most difficult part of my job was done. I knew where they were. If nobody showed up tomorrow, I will get on my bike and ride to the village. Nothing will stop me now. Hopefully, they will come.

My task will be quick. The natives have no need for the mission. They will quite willingly sign the dissolution document. Once my task is accomplished, I'll wait out the one week for Francis to come. Yes. That's what I'll do.

Day XIV

I didn't sleep well last night—I didn't sleep at all. My mind was racing. The strategy had worked. Thank God for tumbleweeds. I was in a state of shock. It was all ending soon. The chief or elders or leaders of the tribe would come. From the sound of things, they have no knowledge of the covenant. I would have some explaining to do to make them understand what this is all about. They would have no problem signing the dissolution. Why would they? They had nothing to gain or lose by it. That would be the end of it. I'll go back to the diocese, a winner.

I got up early with renewed energy. I was as dirty as I had never been in my life. I didn't bother to fix something to eat. I wasn't hungry. I sponged myself clean using a little more water than usual. I decided that shaving could be dispensed with. It wouldn't make a difference. The natives who came would have a description of me of which I would never be proud. So be it.

After Mass, I busied myself with various tasks, most of them unnecessary. The dissolution form was ready to be signed. I kept looking toward the area where the river ended. The natives had ridden toward that side and it seemed the only possible route to the hills. As morning gave way to noon and then toward evening, I started to get a little nervous that maybe they wouldn't come. Why would they come? What was in it for them? I convinced myself they would come. They had to.

The shadows had already crept over the edge of the ravine when in the distance I saw a swirl of dust moving in my direction. It made sense. They were driving over rather than coming on horseback. It was faster. I walked down to the lower plateau to welcome my visitors. After much waiting a pick-up truck finally arrived. I was puzzled and disappointed to see there was only one person, the driver—a young guy—in the truck. He could have been one of the guys from yesterday. I wasn't sure.

"Father Tosco; the council wants to meet with you at the village, if that's okay with you."

"Sure. No problem!"

"If you are ready!"

"I am ready."

"Do you need to get anything else?"

"No! I have everything I need."

"Let's go then!"

"Why the change in plans? I thought they were going to come here."

"Most were of the opinion it would be better if you met with the whole village. That way, people can see you and hear what you have to say."

"I would love that. I hope they won't mind. I'm not very presentable."

"That's all right. This way, you can have a nice bath and eat before you return."

"That's even better."

"Sit tight. It's going to be a bumpy ride. There are no roads around here."

"What's your name?"

"Tony."

"Were you one of the guys who came out yesterday?"

"No, my brother was. I came home this morning and heard about it."

"What do you do?"

"I go to school in Provo and I have a part-time job there. I come home on some of the weekends when I'm not working."

"How many people live in the village?"

"Are you asking how many people live in the village now or how many we are as a community?"

"How about both?"

"We are altogether fifty-seven members including men, women and children. There might be thirty-to-thirty five people living in the village at any given time."

"What about the rest?"

"We're in neighboring cities attending school or working."

"I had given up hope of ever meeting your folks."

"They had seen you. Wasn't there another guy with you?"

"Yes, Francis. He went back a week ago."

"What are you doing here?"

"A long story. You want me to tell you now or wait until later?"

"I guess I can wait."

"If your people saw us, how come no one came to check on me?"

"They've been keeping a close eye on you. At first they thought you were campers or a research group that would eventually go away.

It's seldom people wander this far from the freeways, and they usually all go away quickly. We leave them alone. When you kept lighting the fire each evening, someone got the idea maybe you needed help."

"Indeed. Thank God the guys came. I was running out of options. How come your people don't live around here anymore?"

"There's no water here. There's a place among the hills with a spring. We live there."

"How do you get to the freeways from your village?"

"There's a dirt road further south that leads to the freeway. The village is less than two miles from fifteen when you take that road."

"Too bad we didn't know about it. It would have made my job so much easier."

"The folks had no idea you were looking for us."

"I'm surprised you decided to leave us alone."

"There was a time we used to keep a lookout for intruders and chase them away. It really is not worth the trouble. There's nothing of value here."

"The rectory looks in good shape. Nobody seems to have vandalized it."

"It's kind of hidden and you have to know it's there to find it. I haven't been down here in years."

We fell into an easy silence and in about half-an-hour I started seeing signs of human habitation. We drove onto a dirt road that turned left toward the hills. There were occasional broken-down vehicles abandoned along the side. Soon we could see the village nestled in a hollow among the hills. The road stretched on beyond the village and onto the other side where it inclined toward a clump of trees.

There were teepees arranged in a circular fashion leaving a large open area in the middle. The earth was pressed down into a hard and smooth surface. The teepees were of different sizes and with different trims. I could see smoke coming out the top of most of them. The smell of food was in the air, and my stomach growled in response and anticipation.

The flaps of the teepees were open toward the center of the village. At the opposite end of the courtyard, and to the right, was a large tent much like the ones used at outdoor parties, large enough to hold a couple-of-dozen people. There were seven or eight children running around and playing in the yard. We parked about a hundred feet from the entrance to the village among a group of vehicles in various stages of wear and tear. As we approached, the children came running noisily to meet us. When they realized there was a stranger with Tony, they became quiet and cast shy glances at me without making eye contact.

"Go kids, go and play! Come on, run along."

"This place is hidden from the outside world. It's so very quiet. No wonder I couldn't see any signs of you."

"It's pretty quiet here. There is no TV since we have no electricity. Occasionally some guys will turn up their radios, but it's usually the younger ones, and most of them are away at school right now. It gets a little lively during the weekends."

"I wish I were a little more presentable. I must look awful."

"It's okay. I am going to take you to the teepee to the left of the large tent there. That's set aside for visitors. Behind that you will find the bathroom and the toilet. Why don't you get yourself cleaned up and when you are done, just come on over to the large tent. We are meeting there."

"I have never wished for a bath like I do now—never in my life."

"Take your time."

Inside the teepee were colorful woven rugs covering the entire floor, and on one side was a roll of blankets. There was a bath towel with a small bar of soap. I grabbed the soap and the towel and exited on the other side of the teepee to find an odd-shaped enclosure, which had to be the bathroom. There was a large, open, synthetic tank filled with water and a small bucket hanging on its side. There was no shower. The sight of the water was enough to thrill my senses, and greedily I stripped and scooped up the water and poured it over my head and body again and again. The water was pretty cold, but it didn't matter.

I wondered what their water supply was like and decided to be careful how much water I used in case it was limited. It felt so good. My whole body felt ticklish after the cold bath. It would have been nice to shave and get rid of the scrubby beard. There was no comb either and my fingers would have to pat down the hair somehow.

The first thing I noticed as I came back to the teepee was the rich smell of freshly cooked food—and indeed there was a tray set inside with a combination of bread, meat, and stew. The smell was so inviting, it set my stomach growling again. I went for the food like a ravenous hyena with no thought of decorum. It would have been embarrassing if someone were watching. When I was done, the tray was as clean as if it had been licked a hundred times. I didn't know what was in the stew. It didn't matter. It smelled good and tasted even better. I felt a lot more confident as I walked out to the large tent.

They were waiting, the men on the floor in a semi-circle, three deep, and the women to the rear. The children were there, but further back as they tried to push through the women to take a peek at the stranger. As I entered, one of the men gestured to me with a sweeping motion of his hand to proceed to an empty spot on a heap of blankets, a lone seat facing the rest. I was not accustomed to sitting on the floor, so I made myself as comfortable as I could on the blankets. I waited for the leaders to start the conversation.

"Father Tosco, I am Doug Wilson, and I am the president of the council. We are members of the Little Bend band of Paiutes. I understand you are here regarding the mission."

"First, I want to thank you for your hospitality, the food and the bath."

"You are welcome!"

"I am here as a representative of the Diocese of Salt Lake City. The bishop sent me here to discuss the future of the mission with you."

"There is no mission."

"There was and technically there is. Been here for over a century!"

"There is nothing happening there!"

"We know! It's been at least sixty years now since there's been any activity. The last priest who was sent here quit after failing to meet any of your people. From what I understand, you stopped participating in the mission activities."

"And now, you want to reactivate it. Is that correct?"

"No. Well, yes, maybe. It all depends on what you want. We can reopen the mission if it serves a purpose."

"What is that purpose? You want to make us Catholics?"

"We don't try to convert people against their will."

"What is it then you want?"

"It's not what I want that's important, but what you want."

"We. Nothing. Isn't that pretty obvious?"

"Sounds like the mission lost its purpose a long time ago."

"Why should we be talking about a mission if it has no purpose?"

"The mission was started to provide your people with education, healthcare and religion."

"None of which happened."

"It's not happening now for sure and that's why I am here. The diocese feels the same way you do. The mission has no role here anymore. They want to close it."

"There's nothing open to close. It's already closed."

"The diocese wants to close it formally. You see, the mission was opened following a covenant signed by the then bishop and the leaders of your people. The current bishop does not want to close it unilaterally. He wants to dissolve the covenant with your consent, and then close the mission."

"Why this sudden interest in a defunct mission?"

"The diocese is in the process of consolidating its services and reviewing its commitments. Our resources are stretched thin and we want to phase out or eliminate obligations that are obsolete. This mission is listed for closure."

"It's pretty obvious the mission does not serve any purpose at all. It would be up to you to decide what you want to do. For all we care, go ahead and close it. It's not our mission; it's yours. It's your call."

"I brought a copy of the covenant and I also have a dissolution form. The bishop has signed it. Once you sign the form we will formally close the mission and that'll be the end of it. The bishop has made it clear; the mission will only be closed with a mutual dissolution agreement between you and the diocese."

"Father Tosco, no disrespect to you, but we want to make it clear we won't sign any document. We don't trust the white man's documents, even if it's from the Catholic Church or the bishop. It's not that we suspect you of bad intentions or a hidden agenda. We have suffered plenty by signing documents from the white man."

"I understand and I respect your concerns."

"It's of no importance to us whether the covenant is dissolved or not. We don't care if the mission is closed or not. We won't sign any papers."

"That's fair."

"Is there anything else we can do for you?"

"No."

"What should we do with the church and the house? We don't need them. But, as a place of worship we want to show proper respect."

"Don't worry. You are free to do as you please."

"What are your plans?"

"I'll be returning to the diocese in a few days, now that my work is done."

"Are you going to stay longer?"

"My friend will come and pick me up a week from today."

"A week's a long time. Do you want us give you a ride somewhere?"

"That's awfully nice of you. I can manage for a few more days. I may not get such an opportunity again to be by myself to meditate and reflect on things. I promise not to light any more fires."

"That was pretty clever."

"If I get too lonely or bored, can I come over?"

"Sure!"

Day XV

I went to bed wondering what lay ahead. Was I disappointed? I had failed to get the dissolution signed. I would be going back empty handed. What would the bishop and the VG think? I was sure they would decide I had failed. It would make no difference to them the difficulties I endured in meeting with the native people. It would have been nice for my ego if I had been able to get the signature. But, when I woke up, I didn't feel bad at all.

I kind of felt proud and had a new respect for the natives for refusing to sign the meaningless form. Time and time again these people had been swindled and cheated by unscrupulous white folks and their treaties, contracts, and agreements. Good for them to stand up and say no. I found myself thrilled they had upended the neatly laid out plans of the diocese. I was not disappointed. Their defiance was cool.

I was sure the kindness and hospitality they had shown me had something to do with how I now felt about them. These were good people. Fate may not have been very kind to them, but they had managed to retain their dignity and pride.

The village had no electricity, gas, running water, or any of the amenities we consider routine to civilized life. Why? This in the heart of the most advanced country the world has ever seen. Do they not have rights equal to other citizens of this country? Where are all the humanitarian advocates that fight so hard for immigrant rights, minority rights, asylum rights, and numerous other rights? How come they don't care about the plight of the original people of this land?

Where is Amnesty International that does such a magnificent job ferreting out abuses and exposing them fearlessly the world over? Where are all those folks who fight tooth and nail for the rights of native animals but turn a blind eye to what is happening to the native humans? They all pursue worthy causes. If only they would move a finger to protect the rights of the indigenous people of their country.

Many animals and plant species are facing extinction through human encroachment and loss of habitat. The indigenous people are facing a different type of extinction through the termination of their culture and their way of life. The young members of the tribes see very little hope in a future within the confines of their reservation. They are leaving their homes and their traditional way of life to mingle into mainstream society. The natives of the continent are being reduced to a shadow of their proud past and will soon be preserved as frozen images in museums and as caricatures in the white man's folklore.

It would be a tough few days ahead before Francis came. This morning I had second thoughts. Maybe, I should have accepted Doug's offer to drive me back. I could, still. If Doug had signed the dissolution I probably would have taken him up on his offer since I would be going back victorious. Now, I was in no-such hurry. I knew these were special days, the kind that I would not come by for a long time to come. I will enjoy the freedom and solitude as best as I can. My mission was accomplished even though I had failed. I had met the natives. Under the circumstances, that was a victory.

Day XVI

What kind of a life will I be going back to? Will I continue as Director of Ethnic Ministries or be given charge of another parish? It was reasonable to expect I would end up in a parish in some remote corner of the diocese where I couldn't cause any problems. Instinct told me the VG didn't like me personally. Truth be told, the feeling was mutual, although in my case, it was distrust more than dislike. There was something about the man that projected a craving for power and control. In and of itself, it's not a bad thing, I suppose. But, his need had to be fed by submissive followers who didn't challenge him. He was ambitious. He enjoyed and welcomed authority. It would be best for me to stay clear of him or at least not cross paths with him too often, no more than was absolutely necessary.

I had brought some water in a couple of large containers back from the village. I emptied the water into the trough inside the kitchen and gave the containers to Tony to take back. That was the only offer I had accepted from them. I had enough canned food to last me for the few days until Francis came.

I would keep myself to a routine each day. I would say Mass in the morning and then go for a walk along the ravine and return before the sun got too hot. The rest of the day would be spent inside the rectory reading and writing my journal. It was cathartic to be able to write the journal and get my anxieties out of my system.

As evening shadows swept in I went up the hill to the sacred circle at the top. I sat in the middle of the circle facing the sun as it went down. I imagined how the shaman would have sat where I sat, with the people around him, as he performed the rituals and interpreted the meaning of events that affected them. I was a shaman of sorts without the reverence that was accorded to them. Once the sun set and the stars came out, I went back to the rectory. It was a glorious display of the heavenly bodies when seen from the sacred circle, without the slightest whiff of a cloud and unaffected by city lights.

Day XVII

I was almost done reading all the books I had. One fact came as a big surprise, even though it shouldn't have been. Why are Native Americans called Indians? Of course, I had known the answer but never dwelt on it. All my life I had accepted this without questioning it. How strange? It made me feel silly that I hadn't given it much thought until now. It was more a reflection of how little the native people had entered into my thoughts all of my life.

Columbus was on a quest to find an alternative sea route to India and its wealth of spices that fetched more value than gold in Europe. Columbus calculated that he could sail west and arrive in India rather than take the perilous journey around Africa and the treacherous waters around Cape Hope. He reached land and firmly believed he had reached India. So, he called the natives Indians and to this day we enshrine his stupid blunder. What did Columbus discover other than what already existed? Sure, he was a great seafarer and adventurer—but discoverer of America? He may have discovered America as far as Europe was concerned. I could admire him as an adventurer. But to call him the Discoverer of America was ludicrous.

I guess it fit in with the pattern of Euro-Christian imperialism to consider their world as the center of the universe and their beliefs as the true belief. As I thought more about it, I felt somewhat chagrined that Columbus is revered as a hero even today. His treatment of the natives had been criminal, and he should have been held accountable for genocide, not hailed as a hero honored with a national holiday. Ask the Taino how they feel about the reverence given to Columbus. Well, you can't; there's none left, thanks to Columbus and his followers.

Day XVIII

Three more days to go and I would be on my way. I stuck to my routine, enjoying the solitude and the quiet.

The native people of this continent have occupied this land for thousands of years. They received the white settlers with kindness. It made me angry to recall what the white settlers did to them in return. Leaders of the newly arrived immigrants decreed that the natives were less than human and, therefore, like animals, they could be hunted down or slaughtered without fear of sin. Like European colonials who used Christian missionary zeal to disguise the plunder and looting of far-off lands, the newly arrived settlers, too, hatched plots to separate the natives from their lands and starve them out of existence. The Mormons made the natives the lamanites of their scriptures, the lost tribe, and the evil avatars. Every group competed to create sordid myths and in every myth, the natives became the despicable villains. They created fantastic fiction about native people, and then embraced it as fact.

There was no limit to the extent of the maligning. The natives couldn't have dreamed up the Mountain Meadow Massacre. Will we ever know the real truth? Who ordered the LDS militia to attack the California-bound wagon party? Who devised the strategy to disguise the militia as natives so that the blame for the massacre would fall on the natives? Can the Mormon Church wash its hands off the blood of the 120 innocents that perished at Mountain Meadows?

Day XIX

I started putting the rectory back in order. What would become of the church and the rectory? It would be up to the Paiutes to decide that. I couldn't imagine the diocese wanting to pick up the odds and ends left in the rectory. I would leave things as I found them.

Even without a signed dissolution, I didn't see the diocese wanting to do anything further with the mission. The bishop may have a change of heart and decide to close it anyway, with or without a signed dissolution. If he so wanted, he could come up with a lame-duck argument that the mission was de facto dissolved. The natives had been given a chance to formally dissolve the covenant. They chose not to, not because they objected to the closure but because of some fear of signing documents. It would fade into history. Such is life.

Day XX

My last day at the mission. I will miss this place. I am thankful for the experience it gave me. I learned a few things about Native Americans, which I will take back with me. A great race of people. Fate had not been their friend. They deserved better.

Who knows, I may yet have some contact with native people in the future in my role as the Director of Ethnic Ministries. If the VG is serious about the Ministry, I will do a thorough research to identify how many people of native descent were followers of the faith in our diocese. Given the opportunity, I will do something to highlight their presence and try to enrich their Christian experience. But, without accomplishing what I had been sent here for, I could be considered unqualified for the post. Whatever. My life had been enriched by my contact with the native tribe and it'll remain with me forever.

Day XXI

I packed up my belongings. I indulged myself by having a good sponge bath, and ate a 'sumptuous' breakfast finishing off the last of the canned food. I had rationed my supplies to ensure there would be enough to last me until today. I couldn't imagine Francis wanting to eat something once he got here. We could eat on the way back. I kept a couple of bottles of water for our trip back. We would leave soon after Francis arrived. There was no reason to linger here.

Noon came and went. It was now four in the afternoon. I wondered what was keeping Francis. True, we had not set a fixed time and schedule for his arrival. I had figured he would come early and get back to town before dark. There was no sign of Francis. Evening came and darkness fell—and still, no Francis.

I was getting concerned. Did the car break down on the way? Did he get mixed up with the date? It soon became clear it was too late to leave today, even if he arrived. But first, Francis had to show up. I climbed to the sacred circle and kept a lookout toward the Western horizon for signs of the approaching headlights. By nine o'clock I gave up hope of Francis showing up, and made the weary decision to bed down for the night. There would be no dinner, not that I cared too much about it. Sleep was slow in coming and when it finally came, it was of the uneasy kind, leaving me more tired than relaxed.

Day XXII

I waited and waited all morning. I didn't say Mass, as I would have had to unpack and get everything out. There was no more food, but that didn't bother me. Eating out of a can for extended periods will do that to your appetite. The day wore on and I was getting more and more concerned, wondering if something had happened to Francis. There was no way to find out. Morning faded into afternoon and night.

Day XXIII

What do I do now? There was no food and I was down to my last bottle of water. Francis had not come. I had no explanation for his negligence. He knew I was here by myself. How could he miss the pickup date? Did he forget? My heart was sinking as afternoon crept toward evening.

I was getting desperate. Without food and water, what were my choices? I couldn't hang around here any longer. Should I take the bike and ride toward the freeway? It was too late for that today. I would wait for daylight and do just that. I could ride along the same route Francis and I had taken when we first arrived. Once on the freeway, I could flag someone down to take me to the next gas station. I had money in my wallet. I could find my way back to the city. What happened to Francis?

Day XXIV

I have been without food for almost three days now. I could feel it. My strength was draining, but it was the lack of water that was most troublesome. I was puzzled as well as worried for Francis. Much as I tried, it was impossible not to feel betrayed. Where are the people that were responsible for my wellbeing? What are my choices now? I had hardly slept. In turn I was angry, frustrated, sad, concerned, and afraid. Do I have the energy to ride the bike to the freeway?

I knew I had to leave. Staying here longer could be disastrous. It was appalling what they had done to me. It felt like lead in the pit of my stomach, to realize I was alone in this world. Nobody was looking out for me. Nobody had missed me. How come nobody at the diocese is concerned about my whereabouts? I had been gone for three weeks. Doesn't anybody care? If I perish here, no one would even know about it who knows for how long. I was on my own. I started to understand what my last predecessor must have felt sixty-plus years ago. No wonder he decided to take off rather than go back. Times have changed, but not attitudes.

I vacillated and procrastinated longer than I should have. It was a difficult decision to make, which way should I go? I was weak in body and spirit and it made decision-making all the more difficult.

Should I ride toward the freeway or to the village? The distance to the freeway was farther than the village. If I went to the freeway and if something were to happen to me en route, there was not the slightest chance anyone would find me before it was too late. Then, once I got to the freeway, I would have to find someone willing to stop and give me a ride. I had never done it before. Can you imagine someone stopping for me, standing next to a lonely freeway, with a bicycle, looking like a lunatic? The more I thought about it the less appealing it became. It was too much of a risk to try to find my way back to the city that way.

On the other hand I could ride to the village. It was sure to result in a positive outcome. All I had to do was get there. The rest would take care of itself. It should take me no more than a couple of hours at the most. Once there, I could be guaranteed reasonable welcome, shelter, food and water. The more I thought about it, the village became the better choice. The sun was up, but I could tally no longer.

It was after 11:00 a.m. by the time I finally departed. I packed the minimum into a backpack—especially the sacramental items—and set out on the bike to the village. I would come back later to pick up what I'd left behind.

I knew all I had to do was follow the tire marks and they would lead me to the village. They were pretty visible. I wrote and left a note on the door of the rectory for Francis telling him where I was headed, and how to get to the village to pick me up. That is, in case he ever showed up. I was sure something must have happened to him. He didn't seem the type to be irresponsible and abandon me.

It was tough going. The mountain bike moved slowly as I hit the soft earth of the desert. I knew I had to conserve my energy of which I had very little in reserve. I tried to keep my mind on positive thoughts. The problem was such thoughts didn't last very long. I couldn't believe that Francis would abandon me here and the diocese didn't have a back-up plan. Do I matter to any of them?

I had no experience traveling in desert lands. The heat of the sun and the difficulty of the terrain were making progress difficult. I knew I must get into the mindset of a distance runner, put myself on autopilot and keep riding. I had a quarter of a bottle of water left, and I had to fight the temptation to reach for it and swallow it in one gulp. I kept my eyes glued to the tire marks in the soft earth.

The sun was getting hotter by the minute. I dared not stop to rest knowing that I had to keep pushing forward. I had the notion to dump the bike and walk the rest of the way. No, I needed the bike. At least it kept my feet off the soil. I would push on with the bike as far as possible.

Much as I tried to remember the features of the land from the last two trips to and from the village, I couldn't seem to recognize anything familiar. My vision was playing tricks on me. The tire marks kept going on and on. I looked up toward the hills but there was a haze over the land and I couldn't be sure it was the hills I saw in the distance. There were all kinds of undulating dunes that I couldn't remember from my earlier trip. I guess I must have been focused on my conversation with Tony and not paying attention to the landscape while he drove. Why would I? I never expected to return to the village on a bike.

I stopped to take another little sip of the precious water. The backpack felt like it was laden with rocks. I would be better of not having that burden to carry around. I decided to drop it off somewhere where I could come and retrieve it later. I looked around for an identifiable landmark and saw a cluster of rocks about a hundred yards to the right. There was nothing else that was distinguishable around. I rode toward the rocks and was relieved to see there was a depression on the other side providing a little bit of shade. I decided to take a break while I deposited my backpack there.

I pulled off my shirt and tied it around my head like a bandana. The sun felt hot on my exposed skin and it was odd being semi-naked in the sun. I sat in the shade resting for a little bit. Did I make a mistake by riding out in the sun toward the village? Should I have ridden to the freeway instead? Should I have tried to catch the attention of the natives with another bonfire? It was too late for such thoughts now. I knew I had to stay focused and determined to fight through the fatigue, hunger and thirst. I couldn't linger any longer, as I had no idea how long it would take to reach the village. The sooner I got there the better. I pushed the bike up the incline and threaded my way back following the trail I had left behind.

I couldn't believe that I'd been riding through the desert for close to two hours. I should have been at the village by now. I looked for the outline of the hills and they didn't seem to be any closer than from the mission. I could feel a twinge of despair but with a shake of my head, dispelled it quickly. I kept plodding forward in the direction of the hills. I rode when I could and pushed the bike along when the going got tough. I was reluctant to let go of the bike. It gave me something to cling to.

It looked like the sun was not where it should be. I was headed in a general southeasterly direction but from the angle of the sun it looked like I was going southwest. How can that be? I was still following the tire marks left behind by the pickup. The two clearly defined tire marks ran parallel to each other on and on. Looking more closely, I realized that there was something odd about the tire marks.

Why were the tire marks so clearly defined? I was picked up and dropped back which meant a total of four trips over the same route. The tire marks shouldn't be defined. It then occurred to me that Tony might have come to pick me up the first time from a different direction or left by a different route after dropping me back. With a sick feeling, I realized I must have somehow followed the path he took that one time. One trip would leave clear tire marks unlike the others, which would have been disturbed by the multiple trips.

That posed a dilemma. Where exactly was I headed—or to be precise, where did the tire marks I'm following lead to? I didn't have a clue. But, it was clear the tire marks were leading me away from the village. Should I retrace my steps until I catch up with the split where the other tire marks diverged? I was on the road I shouldn't have taken. If I kept going forward, would it eventually intersect the mud road to the village from the freeway that Tony had mentioned? Would it? How far would that be? I had wasted precious energy because of the error and there was no immediate relief. How far have I traveled on the wrong route?

I guess it is not in human nature to retrace and go back willingly. My initial urge was to keep going in the same direction knowing that eventually it would meet with the road to the village. I had to decide and decide quickly. That was not the safe option. The other would lead me to the village for sure. I would backtrack and follow the path that I knew led to the village and not take a chance into the unknown.

It was painful and extremely tedious as I rode and pushed the bike back. I had no idea how far back I would have to go. It couldn't be that far. I was no longer conscious of time. The heat was unbearable. The air was dense with dust and it was thick in my throat and nostrils. I stopped and tore off one arm of the shirt and pulled it over my mouth and nose to keep the dust out. My lips were parched dry as a bone; I took the last sip of the water and wet my lips as best I could.

I ploughed on afraid that I might lose consciousness and collapse. Fear started creeping in. It was unlikely anyone would find me because no one would be looking for me. I would not survive on my own. If I couldn't find the village before nightfall, what should I do? How would I spend the night out in the cold and in my weakened condition? Thoughts of angry coyotes and prowling rattlers conjured up fearsome visions. I had to reach the village. There were no other options.

After what seemed ages, I came to the spot where several tire marks meshed together and I could see where the majority of them took an easterly direction. There were hoof marks as well. It was too late and futile to analyze how and why I had missed the marks. The correct marks slid into a shallow dry creek, a remnant of some past desert flood. I had a vague recollection of going through the creek with the banks on either side about as high as the windows of the pickup.

I was standing on the south side of the creek and looking ahead I could see where it curved to the right a couple-hundred yards away. Riding the bike in the gravel bed of the creek was impossible. I decided to cut straight across and slide into the creek bed at the curve. I thought about abandoning the bike, but decided against it. Half-blinded by the sun, I urged myself to push the bike along.

A combination of factors accounted for my fall. The incline wasn't steep and looked easy enough to negotiate. The soil was not firm and gave way as I positioned the bike to push it ahead of me down to the bed of the creek. As I was holding the bike with both hands, it gave me no chance to recover once I lost my balance. My weakened condition made it impossible to take evasive action and break the fall. I have no recollection of the sequence and nature of what happened. However it happened, it was enough to knock me out.

Who knows how long I lay there. When I came to, I was sprawled out on the creek bed with the bicycle draped over me. There was a heavy pounding in my head. It didn't take me long to realize where I was and what had happened. I extricated myself from under the bike and with some relief found that no bones were broken. It looked like I had taken a decent knock on my head. I could feel the pulsating pain. I must have several cuts and bruises on my face. I could feel and taste blood in my mouth. The blood had dried and mixed with the dust and sand. The bumps and bruises could have resulted from the bike falling with me or it could have been the result of banging my head on some fairly large-sized pebbles on the creek bed.

There was no time to take a full inventory. As long as I could walk, I had to move. There was rising panic my strength would soon give out and I would be stranded for the night. The sun was heading for the horizon and I probably had no more than one hour of sunlight. I had no idea how far away from the village I was. No matter, I had to keep moving. The will to survive remained strong.

All I could do was keep moving. I dared not abandon the bike, although riding it now was impossible. But I needed something to hold on to. I would walk the bike until it became impossible to do so. The pain from the bump on my head was becoming unbearable. As I felt around, it was not difficult to locate it—there was wetness around it. I looked at the redness on my fingers with nonchalance. I seemed devoid of sensation or comprehension although I was looking at my own blood. Was I about to lose consciousness?

It was impossible to say if the hills were getting closer. At one point it did and then it didn't. I kept going in a half daze, no longer aware of the surroundings except vaguely fixated on the tire marks. I didn't stop again to rest. I didn't even seem to have the energy to stop. On I went, dragging myself through the heat and the dust towing the bike along. Dusk was falling fast and soon it would be dark.

All on a sudden, the hills were directly in front of me. And there was the mud road. I made it. It was now a matter of gathering together whatever energy I could muster and getting through that final incline. As a long distance runner finds new strength at the sight of the finish line, I felt a sudden surge of adrenalin. I moved forward with renewed energy, out of sync, and out of balance. I couldn't push the bicycle any further, not up that incline. It was slowing me down. As I passed the first abandoned car on the side of the road, I let go of the bicycle and it rolled back and fell on its side. Almost immediately, I fell. My body would not let me get up. I struggled and slowly raised myself on my hands and knees and straightened my head. That's all it took. The world took a vicious spin and wouldn't stop. I closed my eyes to fight the sudden dizziness and nausea. I fell flat on my stomach and the world went black. But not for long, though.

Somewhere deep in the recesses of my brain, I knew I couldn't succumb to unconsciousness. If I lay there, I may not be discovered until morning or there was the risk of getting run over if someone was driving back to the village in the dark. The instinct for survival was stronger than I imagined. I started to crawl toward the village, on hands and knees, keeping to the side of the road—collapsing, and then moving forward.

The dogs found me before anyone else. Their barks and excited whelping brought people out with their flashlights. I struggled to get up so that I would be visible. I made it to one leg and the other knee before I collapsed and fell forward on my face. I am sure they must have thought that the dogs had confronted a raccoon or a coyote. What they found was someone in tattered clothing, covered in dust, and lying face down in the dirt. I could faintly hear the sounds of the people and the dogs, but I had no strength to move, and no sounds would come out of my mouth. Someone came and turned me over. My eyes were swollen shut. I couldn't see anything, but I could sense the flashlights. I lay there barely alive. All I knew was that I had reached my destination. The rest would be in the hands of fate and the native people.

"Isn't he the priest who was here a few days ago?"

"It's him. Give me a hand. Let's take him inside and get him some water."

"What happened?"

It seemed the whole village was around me now. A couple of the guys lifted and carried me, and then put me down on something soft.

"What's he doing here?"

"How did he get here?"

"Didn't he say that someone was coming to pick him up?"

"He doesn't look very good. Where's Sarah?"

"Look at that bump on his head."

"Is he stupid or what to try and walk to the village?"

"Come on. Stop talking and get me some water."

"We may need to get him to a hospital."

I had made my second inglorious entry into the village in a week.

Day XXV - XXXV

What happened the next few days can only be described as pure agony. I have no clear recollection of anything, whether it was day or night or what day it was. I would gain consciousness for brief intervals and fade back. I can still feel the dread of those brief moments of lucidity. I was thankful for passing out and becoming oblivious of what was happening.

I came to sometime in the middle of the night. It was very quiet and it was dark. There was a candle or a lamp burning inside the teepee casting an eerie glow. I was almost in a trance before I realized, with alarm, that I was sick. My whole body was burning with a fever. My eyes felt like lumps of burning coal, and tears started to flow out of the still swollen lids. Without warning, nausea hit me. I started retching, but nothing was expelled. It seemed that my very entrails were ready to explode through my mouth. Thankfully, I lost consciousness again.

As if in a dream, I heard voices both male and female. There were hands ministering to me, feeding me some liquid. That would set off a fit of coughing and vomiting. I was past caring about what was happening to me or what was being done to me. I was in a state of total helplessness. I kept falling in and out of consciousness.

Day XXXVI

All on a sudden, I was awake and I knew things were different. I could sense it. My mind was clearer and there was an awareness I didn't have for some time. I could hear the sounds coming from outside and could distinguish them. I was inside a teepee at the native village. I was lying on the floor on a bed of blankets. I didn't feel the heat emanating from my body as in the last few days. I just knew I was feeling better.

I was afraid to open my eyes. There was no way to know what time of day it was, although I was sure it was day. The fogginess slowly lifted and I was almost fully awake. Was there anyone else inside this teepee? I didn't want to make any sounds until I was fully aware of my surroundings. How many days have I lain like this? It was a sinking feeling thinking of the trouble I had caused these good people. They didn't have to do this. I had done nothing to deserve their goodwill.

My back felt stiff and sore. I decided to turn over on my side. It really hurt and the effort was almost too much for me. Slowly I opened my eyes, prepared for bright sunlight. Instead it was rather, dark but not dark enough to block out everything inside the teepee. I felt very weak, but my mind was clear. I could recognize where I was and remember what had brought me here. Whatever happened since would remain shrouded in mystery until I had a chance to talk to someone.

I decided to get up and slowly raised myself up on my right elbow. A mistake. Everything went wrong without warning. The world around me started spinning slowly at first, and then with vicious momentum. All I could do was close my eyes and fall back onto the blankets. I must have let out some kind of a cry as my head hit the floor where the bump was still raw. There were hands that held me down. I could hear indelible murmuring sounds. I closed my eyes even more tightly, trying to stop the spinning and the nausea that was building up. And then I started retching uncontrollably, unable to throw up anything, yet unable to stop.

Who knows how long it lasted but I could feel the hands holding my head all the while. The convulsions subsided. A wet, cool towel was applied to my forehead. The headache, a splitting attack, was sudden and brought hot tears to my eyes and with it involuntary groans. I heard someone enter. I dared not open my eyes for fear that the nausea would return.

"What happened?"

"He's coming to, finally. He must have had a bout of nausea. It's a good sign. He'll be okay in a little while. Don't worry. I can manage."

"All right. Call me if you need me."

"Ask Sally to make some more honeyed tea. He'll be thirsty in a little bit."

It was a female who was taking charge. Who was it? I wanted to believe what she said was true, that I would be okay soon. I was smarting from the retching episode. My head was laid back on something soft. I laid there with my eyes closed. I hadn't lost consciousness. I was aware, yes, painfully aware of things happening around me. I could feel the dizziness subside a little. I didn't want to take any chances. I kept my eyes tightly shut. Slowly, I drifted back to sleep.

There was no way to tell how long I'd slept. But when I awoke, the headache was mostly gone, mercifully, along with the nausea and the dizziness. I didn't dare open my eyes, and I didn't want to take the risk of getting up. I was thirsty, and my lips and mouth felt like gravel. As though by inspiration, there were those hands again, gently lifting my head—and a bowl of liquid was at my lips. I took some sips, wetting my lips and mouth. Even in my state, I could smell and taste the lemon and the honey and it felt good going down. I was afraid that the nausea would return, but thankfully nothing happened. I took a few more sips, and then the bowl was removed, and my head was back on the cushions.

This time I didn't go back to sleep. I was aware of movements behind my head. I was relieved that the nausea stayed away. I opened my eyes slowly. It was light outside but the sun was setting. I laid there with my eyes slowly adjusting to the light.

"Would you like some more of the tea?"

"Um," was the best that I could do! I couldn't frame any words. My tongue appeared to cling to the roof of my mouth.

"I'm glad you are feeling better."

I tried to nod my head in assent, and paid the price as a sudden jolt of pain reminded me of the bruise I had on my head.

"That's all right. We'll talk later."

Another groan was all I could muster.

"Don't try to get up. You need to take it easy for a few days. The bump on your head has not fully healed. I have a few chores to take care of. I'll check in on you later and see if you are ready to eat something."

It was a gentle voice. Although spoken in a low tone, almost as a whisper, there was authority in that voice. It was the voice of someone who could take charge, knew what she was doing, and didn't invite dissent. There was a rustling of clothes as she rose and left. I laid there savoring the quiet, but afraid to move.

What a mess I had got myself into. The last thing I wanted to do was force myself on the tribe. I must have put a serious strain on their resources, particularly in terms of time and effort to take care of me and keep watch over me for however long I had been out of commission.

The gnawing feeling was back again, and along with it some serious resentment. Obviously, nobody had showed up from the diocese. I had left a note at the mission so Francis would know where to find me. It wasn't a charitable feeling I had toward Francis and the VG at the moment. They had abandoned me and I could be dead for all they cared. Where do they think I am now? Do they think that I've absconded just like the last priest sent out here? Is that what the VG wants? How will I put my faith and trust in the Diocesan authorities in the future?

"Father Tosco, are you awake? This is Doug."

"Yes. Thank you."

It was more of a squeaky groan than a reply.

"You had me worried for a few days. I wanted to take you to a hospital. But, Sarah said you would be okay here."

"Sarah?"

"My wife. She has been taking care of you. She's a good healer. I trust her word more than doctors'."

"She was right. I am so very grateful."

"Her mother and grandmother were experts in the art of healing and native medicine. Sarah studied under them and is very skilled in the healing traditions."

"I am a believer."

"Do you feel okay to talk? Can you talk?"

"Yeah!"

"So, tell me. You were supposed to have left a few days after you came to visit us. What happened?"

"Nobody showed up and nobody has shown up since, I assume. I left a note at the mission, if you're wondering how anyone would find me here."

"I am sure there must have been some miscommunication."

"Yes!"

"Don't worry about it. We can drive you back once you are released."

"He's not ready to travel and won't be for a few days."

"Sarah, I was not talking about packing him off right away. When he is ready, one of us will drive him back. That's what I was saying."

"I'll tell you when he's ready to travel."

"I do need to get back as soon as possible."

"Doesn't sound like someone is anxiously waiting for you."

The moment the words were out of my mouth, I sensed the foolishness of my statement. But, Doug's unintended barb hurt even though he had not said it with any sarcasm.

"True. Still, I must get back."

"Let's worry about that later. It's not in my or your hands anyway. We must leave it up to the boss."

"That's right. I will fix a small dinner for you, Father Tosco. After that, stay in bed and rest for the night. By morning you should feel okay to get up. We will fix you a nice hot bath and you will feel a whole lot better."

"Whatever you say, Dr. Sarah."

"That sounds better."

"I see you are learning fast, Father Tosco. In our village, when Sarah speaks, others listen and obey."

"Don't mind his words, Father Tosco."

"I won't, but I get the cue."

"Doug, you can stay with him a little bit longer. Don't tire him out with your questions. I'm going to get his dinner."

"I would not have known what to do with you, were it not for Sarah."

"I feel fortunate."

"She is a remarkable woman."

"I must agree. Whatever she did, worked."

"She knows what she's doing."

"She's very confident in what she does."

"Here she comes and I better leave. I'll be back in the morning. Ask for me if you need anything, even at night. Just yell out! I am close by."

"Good night!"

"Doug, please! Can you help him sit up? How's your head feeling Father "Tosco?

"A lot better now."

"I made a gruel with ground grains and nuts. Not very tasty, but healthy. You won't know the difference, anyway, the way your mouth must be feeling. By tomorrow morning you should feel ravenous, I promise."

"I dare not disagree with you."

"Eat as much as you can even if you don't feel like eating."

I forced myself to swallow whatever it was she had made and made it through almost half the bowl. It didn't taste like much, but like she said, I had no sense of taste anyway.

"I have some more of the tea. You need lots of fluids. Honeyed tea is the best. Drink as much as possible while it's still warm and then go back to sleep. I will check in on you before I go to bed."

"Can I say thanks for your efforts, Sarah?"

"No!"

Day XXXVII

I knew I was feeling a whole lot better the moment I woke up. I wondered how I had slept so soundly. Maybe it was the honey in the tea or something else Sarah had added to it. It was still early. The sun had not risen yet. My body felt weak but I could sense I had turned the corner. I lay there, trying to piece together the fragments of my life to make sense of what was happening. Life had taken some unexpected turns, all within the space of one month and a few days. Quo Vadis? Where do I go from here?

It was impossible not to feel bitter about what the diocese had done or not done. I could have perished while trying to make my way to the village. I would have perished for sure if I had not made it to the village. Did they not care where I was or what was happening to me? In a few days, I would be well enough to travel. I had to go back to the diocese. What else is there for me to do? What will happen next? I hadn't accomplished what I came out here to do. Looking back on the whole affair, what was so important about this covenant? It was not of much consequence whether the tribe agreed to dissolve the covenant or not. In truth, I had come out here and nearly lost my life, all for naught.

I wished there was something I could do for the tribe. I felt embarrassed. I had over-extended their generosity and hospitality. They had given freely of the little they had. Yet, there was a genuine spontaneity in their attitude, which was touching. Reverend Scanlon was also a beneficiary of the same care and concern more than a century ago, so much so he felt obligated to do something lasting for them. What could I do?

It was sad to see this noble race of people living in such poverty. In a sense, I had become like them, slowly deteriorating into irrelevance. How could they try and preserve their culture and way of life? The odds were stacked up against them and the challenges appeared insurmountable. How could Doug and the tribal elders convince the younger generation of the importance of preserving their culture, their traditions and customs? Not only this tribe but also every native nation must be facing the same dilemma. What did they have to offer to their future generations? Maintaining the status quo would only lead to a threadbare existence and ultimate extinction. It was sad, but I could see no possible way out and no solution for their survival. Yet, they must survive.

I wished there was something I could do to help this group live with dignity. If only they could have a fighting chance. They didn't have the resources to improve their standard of living or build for the future. I felt a genuine desire to help them but, unfortunately, I was the one in need of help and surviving on their generosity.

The entrance to the teepee was folded back and a woman came in.

It had to be Sarah. I was seeing her for the first time. I may have seen her the first time I was here but couldn't recall her face. During my first visit, the women of the village had sat behind the men and they hadn't spoken. I knew who she was; she had a presence about her that radiated a quiet confidence and poise.

"You are awake, Father Tosco. Hope you are feeling better too."

"Yes, I am; a whole lot better just like you predicted. Thank you so much."

"There is a nice hot bath waiting for you. I am sure you must be dying for one. Take your time with it and when you come back, I'll have a nice breakfast for you and you'll feel almost as good as new."

"It bothers me that you had to go to so much trouble on my account."

"We can deal with that later, Father. Go on and have your bath."

Slowly I raised myself up and stood up under her watchful eye. I got to my feet all right, a little shaky but the expected dizziness didn't materialize. I took a few hesitant steps. Nothing untoward happened. With small steps, I walked in the direction of the bathroom. I could feel her eyes on me but she didn't move to assist. I was okay.

They had filled a tub with steaming water and there was the smell of herbs or flowers they had added to the water. It must have taken them some time to heat the water. I felt uneasy about all the trouble I was causing them but the water was so inviting, I didn't hesitate for long. I lowered myself into the tub and let the heat and the scents take over. I could feel my skin respond with a pleasant sensation. The people of the village were putting out a lot of effort for me. It was touching. I sat there, absorbing the heat of the water. It felt good to be cleansed of the smell of my illness. There was an unruly growth of facial hair, but that could wait. I stayed in the water until it had lost all its warmth. I scrubbed myself with the soap as fiercely as I could and took another dip in the water. I felt whole again.

When I went back to the tepee, I found my clothes all washed and folded, waiting for me. Once I was back in my clothes again, I started to feel like a human being. I was weak and I knew I had lost a lot of weight. But, I was back on my feet and moving around under my own power.

The breakfast consisted of stuff I couldn't easily recognize and I decided not to ask. What mattered was that it tasted good and I could feel hunger again. There was the honeyed tea to which I had started to take a liking. Doug and two other guys showed up as soon as I had finished my breakfast.

"You are back on your feet Father Tosco!"

"I feel bad I had to be such a nuisance."

"Not at all."

"Nothing unusual as far as we are concerned. Sarah was happy to get a chance to exercise her medicinal powers. We hardly ever get sick."

"What are your plans now? Sarah has decreed that you won't be fit to travel for two more days."

"I would like to get back to the diocese. May I take you up on your offer to drive me back?"

"Certainly."

"I will pay for all of your expenses, of course."

"If you want to pay the guys for gas, that's fine. Nothing more!"

"What you have done and what you continue to do can't be repaid in money and I don't want to insult you. But I do have some money on me if only you will allow me to give you some."

"That's all right. Don't worry about it."

"If I can do something, anything, please tell me."

"One of us will take you back. You will need to obtain a release from Sarah first."

"I shall not defy her orders."

"Will you ever come back here?"

"I hope to and soon, if you will allow me."

"You are welcome anytime Father Tosco."

"How would I get in touch with you?"

"There's a native outpost about twenty miles south on 15. We have a mailbox there, if you want to send us any mail."

"You can also leave a phone message for us there, although, a response may not be forthcoming for days."

"I understand."

"We have a Summer Festival starting first weekend in June. It's an occasion for us to get together as a group and re-establish bonds. It's a fun time with story-telling, dances, and feasting."

"It's one way we try to preserve our tribal customs and practices."

"That's nice."

"Why don't you come? It lasts a week. It's nothing fancy or anything. But, it's one get-together that most members of the tribe attend."

"I will certainly be here."

"Should we send somebody to the church to pick up your stuff? Do you need to go back?"

"If it's okay with you. My bags are packed and ready. Also, my backpack is somewhere behind a bunch of rocks on the way here."

Day XXXVIII

I felt good enough to take a walk. I walked slowly toward the clump of trees I had seen on the other side of the village. I stopped on the way to greet the women and children that were around. I invited a couple of the children to join me, but they appeared shy and I didn't push the issue not knowing how the people would react to such overtures.

There was a fair-sized pool right in the middle of the clump of trees. A thick rush of reeds grew around it. I found an old tree trunk and sat on it facing the water. It was not very deep but the water was clear. There was a well-beaten path from the teepees that led to the water's edge. I heard the neigh of horses and looking up saw four or five horses stabled in a secluded area on the side of the hill.

Looking carefully at the water, I could see a few fish swimming around at the bottom. They looked like minnows. It's surprising how life forms find their way even into secluded pools such as these. I'm sure at some point in the past, there must have been storms that brought flood waters and with it, stray fish which became stranded in the pool.

I was stranded here too, in a different sort of way. But unlike the fish, I could find my way back from where I came. That always brought up the question: What would I do when I got back to the diocese? I could always be assigned to a parish. I had the experience and the seniority to be a pastor and I was sure there were parishes that needed one.

I wanted to do something meaningful with my life, something a little more than a pastor-ship, although that's what the majority of priests did. Why had the diocese failed me? Whether it was miscommunication or willful negligence or whatever you wanted to call it, the sum and total of it was I remained stranded and forgotten. How can you be loyal to someone who betrays you or by sheer indifference shows you that you're irrelevant? I decided I would never again allow anyone to treat me as irrelevant. That included the diocese. I would find my mission in life, whatever that was.

I had dinner that night with Doug and Sarah in their teepee. There was a gathering of all the people after dinner.

"Father Tosco plans to go back home the day after tomorrow. He wanted a chance to meet all of us together."

"I am very grateful to you for taking such good care of me. I have never experienced so much kindness in my life. I do not know what I can do to show you my appreciation for what you have done."

"What we did we would do for anyone in your situation!"

"It's different from what you read and what other people would have you believe. I am referring to your hospitality and care. You have opened my eyes."

"We have been the victims of such propaganda ever since the white man set foot on this continent. That is the tragedy of our people."

"It's not right."

"What happened to the covenant that you were talking about the last time you were here? Is that why you were coming back here?"

"No, not at all! That issue is closed. I was stranded at the mission. I ran out of food and water. Nobody came from the diocese to pick me up. I thought I would seek your help. I didn't expect to end up the way I did."

"You were lucky!"

"You could have killed yourself."

"Don't worry about the covenant. I'll tell the bishop that you do not wish to dissolve the covenant. He can take whatever action he wants."

"It's not we don't want to dissolve the covenant. Would it matter one way or another? We have a bad feeling when it comes to signing documents."

"We fear it'll work against us in the future."

"It always has. Why should we sign something that's irrelevant to us?"

"I understand and I have no problem with your decision."

"We have nothing against you personally."

"I know that and believe me I won't take it personally."

"Father Tosco, will you come back here?"

"I will. Doug has invited me for your summer get-together."

"That's great. You'll get to meet all our members. It should be fun too."

"Your hospitality and concern, it's extraordinary. I'm extremely obliged, to Sarah particularly. I didn't deserve this kindness. I shall not forget."

"You make Sarah proud Father Tosco. She got a chance to showcase her healing powers and now we are going to hear about it for ages."

"Wait till you get sick."

"I would like to have a prayer service tomorrow morning. It's a gesture of gratitude to God, the Supreme Being who protects us and guides us. I want to offer prayers for you, the wonderful group of people who chose to welcome me into your midst and cared for me in my time of need."

Day XXXIX

I conducted a modified Mass and prayer service with a little homily. I thanked them again for what they did for me. I tied that into the message of Christ, the message of love for your brethren. I described how the covenant had been established a long time ago, as a result of the tribe's kindness to Bishop Scanlon. I also expressed my desire to do something for the welfare of the tribe, something that would help them maintain their traditions and culture and at the same time allow them to enjoy the benefits of progress. What I could do and what they would have me do, we could decide together. Later that morning, I took a walk up the hill with Doug.

"I have been thinking Doug. What I went through here had to be for a reason. More and more I am starting to believe I was brought here for a purpose. What happened couldn't have been just coincidence."

"What do you mean? I don't understand."

"It's incredible that no one has come from the diocese to pick me up. It's even more incredible that no one at the diocese has missed my absence and tried to find out what happened to me. It's almost a month-and-a-half since I've been gone."

"It does sound strange."

"Why did I decide to come back here? I could have tried to reach the freeway instead. Was it destiny?"

"As far as I am concerned, these things happen; that's that. You never can figure it out, can you?"

"I guess not; except, I feel strongly the Lord had a plan all along."

"What kind of plan?"

"The Bible is full of stories of people the Lord chose for a purpose. There's the story of St. Paul who started out hating Jesus and persecuting his followers. The Lord knocked him down from the horse, blinded him, then opened his eyes to the truth and he became the most dedicated of disciples. It was not about St. Paul. Jesus had a plan for his followers and Paul was chosen as a tool to implement his plan. God may have a plan for you and he may be using me as his tool."

"Sometimes I feel even god has deserted us. What plans can God have for us, now that we are almost destroyed? If there's a plan, it will be to wipe us out entirely."

"I understand why you feel that way. But we must not lose hope. We must do our part and let God fashion his grand design, as he sees fit."

"You have things of your own to worry about, without having to be concerned about us. What will you do when you get back?"

"No idea. I'll find out soon. How about you? What are you looking for?"

"All we want is to maintain our culture and traditions. It may be an impossible dream. We are like the buffalo, squeezed out of habitat, hunted into near extinction, a relic of the past with no place in the future. Natives and their way of life are destined for history's scrapheap."

"A way of life has many facets. Like all races, you have evolved, you have adapted, and you have changed. But there are principles on which are built the foundations of the tribe. Behavior can change with time while the binding bonds that make up the fundamental core must remain strong."

"We have evolved a lot for sure. From being nomadic, we settled down and became attached to one local area. The changes you see are external. We are the same people at heart and we have the same yearning. We are and we want to remain a free-spirited people. Driving cars and wearing jeans don't make us different."

"Exactly!"

"I worry about how we can hold the community together. Our numbers have steadily declined. Our biggest problem is survival."

"I can see that."

"Parents with school-age children move out to where the schools are. They find jobs and become part of a new community. Young people move to where they can find jobs. Eventually, many marry into the general population and fade away. There's nothing we can offer to draw them back or hold them together. It's a slow but certain slide into extinction."

"What if you could offer them reasonable comforts and opportunity for growth? Would they then want to stay connected?"

"Certainly! There's not one Paiute who's not proud of his or her heritage. We are a proud people. But, pride alone won't do."

"I agree!"

"We are very passionate about our culture and way of life. In our heart of hearts we know we'll do everything possible to preserve it. However, we know we can't stem the tides of change. The end is inevitable.

"It's not a whole lot different from what's happening to other communities such as farmers nationwide. The children see the futility of grinding it out on the farm. You are at the mercy of the weather conditions and when you have a crop, the economics dictate what you can make of it. They want to move on and pursue a different life that is predictable and sustainable. Yet, there are those who keep trying to make it succeed because it's their way of life.

"Our problem is more fundamental. Our culture is under assault. Can our children take pride in our heritage when it's an object of scorn? Do we see it as a burden that chokes out our ability toward progress? Many are starting to feel that way."

"Maybe there's a happy compromise. Maybe what's realistic is a future where the youth seek education and jobs elsewhere but return periodically to the tribal communes to live as themselves for a brief period."

"Look at us! This village has no material comforts to offer them. We have no running water, no telephone, and no electricity. There's no TV. We are far away from urban areas. The children have nothing to keep them occupied."

"Do you think if you had some of these so called comforts, the youngsters would come more often and spend more time here?"

"I believe so. When they see that the village can provide some of the basic comforts, they'll find it attractive to come more often. They may not settle down here for good but they would maintain the contact. Then, as they get ready to retire, there is a home waiting for them here."

"You are right!"

"To do that, we need resources; we need money; we need influence; we need clout and we have none of these."

"I have heard that native tribes receive federal assistance."

"That's a myth. Most tribes receive nothing. Many nations have reservations but like what you see out here, it's nothing but wasteland. We receive absolutely nothing. What's more, we are not even recognized as a native nation."

"Why is that?"

"A long story. It resulted from the stupidity of the Bureau of Native American Affairs."

"You are Paiute, right?"

"Correct. Paiutes are a large group divided into Northern Paiutes and Southern Paiutes, and they are spread out all the way from Arizona to California, Nevada, Washington, Colorado, and Utah. We are part of the Southern Paiute usually referred to as the Paiutes of Utah. It's officially made up of five different groups, Kanosh, Koosharem, Indian Peaks, Shivwits, and Cedar City. We are part of the Cedar City band."

"But you said you were not recognized?"

"The Paiutes of Utah were terminated as a nation in 1954 and regained recognition in 1980. During this period of reorganization and recognition, the first four bands, Kanosh, Koosharem, Indian Peaks, and

Shivwits were recognized without dispute. Then they came upon a bunch of smaller Paiute bands, some as small as two-to-three members. Rather than investigate the individuality of these smaller bands, the Bureau grouped them together as the Cedar City Band, for no reason other than they lived within a geographical area around Cedar City."

"You were made part of the Cedar City Band?"

"Exactly! The unfortunate part is, we were not consulted and we didn't know this was happening until it was completed."

"I am sorry if I sound ignorant. How does it affect you whether you are recognized as a separate band or you are part of the Cedar City Band?"

"We are a separate band and have refused to join the Cedar City band. We won't give up our heritage. We are the Paiutes of Little Bend. We can't cease to be who we are to suit someone else's convenience. If we give in, we are done."

"Are other tribes facing the same predicament?"

"As I said, the Cedar City Band is made up of almost forty tribes, of different sizes. The smaller bands welcomed the opportunity to become part of a recognized band and thus get some protection. We are mid-size as a tribe. We want to remain independent. The Cedar City Council won't let us break away."

"Why? Why would they want to hold on to a group like you hostage, if you don't want to be a part of them?"

"There are land holdings at stake. There are grants at stake. The size of the reservation and the amount of the grants are based on the specific number of members within the band. If people leave and get recognized as separate bands, lands for the new band have to be carved out of the existing reservation. Federal grants will be divided proportionately."

"Do you foresee a solution?"

"No! We have disputed our inclusion into the Cedar City Band ever since we became aware of it. The Bureau won't deal with us. As far as they are concerned, it's a done deal and we are part of a recognized Band. We are not represented on the Cedar City Council and they won't entertain any move on our part to secede for obvious reasons."

"What are your demands?"

"We want to be recognized as a separate Paiute Band, Paiutes of Little Bend. With that in place, we want the Little Bend Valley reserved for us."

"What's that to do with not accepting benefits, which are rightfully yours?"

"If we accept or share in the grants received by the Cedar City Band, it will weaken our demands, in our own minds and the minds of others."

"How? Why?"

"It will be equivalent to acknowledging their authority and resigning our identity. No! We won't do that."

Day XL

It was Tony who drove me back to the city. He was on his way back to Provo. I was apprehensive how I was going to be received and how I was going to confront the VG. I was his responsibility. I thought about making a phone call from one of the gas stations on the way to announce my return, but decided against it. Having endured so much neglect, it would make more sense to walk in unannounced and see his reaction.

I went directly to the VG's office. His secretary told me he was at a meeting with the Police Commissioner downtown and was not expected back until 7:00 that evening. I left a brief note for him, and then called my friend, Fr. Pollock. He was the Pastor at St. Ann's, in the city. He was an older priest and someone whom I looked up to as my mentor and confidante, kind of like a confessor. Luckily, he was home and yes, he had a room available and he'd be happy for me to stay for as long as I wanted.

I picked up my car from the chancery parking lot and drove out to St. Ann's Parish. That night over dinner, I described to Fr. Pollock my visit to the mission. I had to tell someone. It was humiliating to learn that my name had not been mentioned anywhere by anyone as missing or having gone to the mission. He was surprised I had been gone for forty days. Apparently, no one had noticed my absence. In truth, my existence or lack thereof was of little concern to no one.

I was curious to find out why Francis had not returned to pick me up. I called the Seminary and asked to speak to Francis. I was told that he had been sent to a parish in Mexico for the final phase of his training and to learn Spanish. He had left the day after his return from the mission. That explained why he had not come to pick me up. Why, then, did he not delegate the task to someone else?

"Father Tosco. Good to see you back. How did it go?"

"Depends on how you look at it."

"I heard you were having a tough time catching up with the native tribe."

"It took some time, but eventually, I did."

"And? Did they sign the dissolution form?"

"No. They won't. Not that they care about the mission or want it there. They just won't sign any documents."

"That's silly!"

"I tried to reassure them no harm would come from signing the dissolution. I'm sure they understand. But, as a matter of principle, they won't sign the document. They don't trust white man's documents."

"Oh well. Maybe, they'll change their minds later on. What does it matter? It has little relevance, really. The bishop insisted on it. We tried."

"I would like to offer an alternative."

"What?"

"These are good people. They are spiritual even though they are not Christians. We could bring them back to the church, with a little effort."

"Different from what has been tried in the past."

"I believe not a whole lot of effort was put into maintaining the mission."

"What difference would any new effort make?"

"I'm not sure. I was there for almost a month. I lived with them for some time. There's potential there. Before we decide to close it down, I want to give it another shot."

"You lose me, Father Tosco."

"I want to reopen the mission. I am confident we can make a change."

"What are you talking about? I don't want you to take this too seriously. The covenant was signed a long time ago, in a different era and for a specific reason. We are under no obligation to honor an obsolete covenant. I'm not going to waste any more time on it."

"Why don't we give it one more chance?"

"Why would we want to expend time and personnel on something that serves no purpose for anyone?"

"I want to give it a try. Give me six months. I made contact with the Paiute tribe. I know their ways and have come to understand their needs. I know I can do something. If after six months, I can't make a difference, then I will close it down and return."

"Dissolving the covenant was but a formality. What you want to do is different. Why?"

"If we succeed we can make a difference in the lives of these people."

"Father Tosco, I can see you are serious about this. Why would you want to invest your time and energy on such a project? Is it worth the sacrifice?"

"Monsignor, I have spent a lot of time thinking about this. These people need all the help they can get to survive. With your permission, I want to go back to try and help them. That was the original goal of Bishop Scanlon when he signed the covenant. I want to try and fulfill it."

"I can only shake my head in disbelief. Are you that serious about this?"

"There's something about these people that has touched me deeply. Their genuineness, their sincerity, and their desire to survive are heart-warming. We can help them or at least say we tried."

"Let's say I'm in agreement and the bishop gives his blessing. What then?"

"I want some financial support."

"That could be a problem. You know we are struggling for funds. The bishop wants to complete the cathedral by the end of the year."

"Monsignor, I am not asking for much. Two-thousand dollars a month for six months plus my stipend."

"What can you do with twelve-thousand dollars?"

"Not a whole lot, I know. But I have a plan."

"What kind of plan?"

"I am not sure I can explain it now. I haven't worked out the details."

"That does not sound very encouraging. We can ill afford to throw twelve-thousand dollars away and we need every priest we have available."

"The money and the time won't be wasted, I promise you."

"If I didn't know you well, I would say this is crazy!"

"Maybe I'm crazy! What do we have to lose? I promise every penny will be used wisely; every penny will be put to good use; every penny will be accounted for! Monsignor, I ask for your permission to give it a try."

"Yes, of course. I will give you permission. I'm going to have a tough time explaining this to the bishop. All right, I'll support you, although unwillingly."

"Thank you, Monsignor! You won't regret it."

"My problem will be convincing the chancellor and the bishop that the resources are being spent on a worthy cause."

"I don't want to cause you any trouble, Monsignor. Let's forget about the money, if that's the problem. I will use my personal savings. Give me permission to go back to the mission for six months. That's all I ask."

"Father Tosco, don't misunderstand. You took me by surprise, that's all. I will make sure the money is made available as you requested. I can see you are very passionate about this and I won't stand in the way."

"I am grateful."

"Be careful. If something isn't going right, please quit and return right away. I know nothing about the mission and the native people. There's no electricity and no phone. You'll be all by yourself. Your safety is a concern."

"Don't worry. I'll be all right."

"Is there anything else? When do you plan to leave?"

"Tomorrow, if it's okay with you."

"That soon? Well, keep me posted."

What was I getting into? Did I have a plan? No, not really. Maybe, I was still smarting that nobody had missed me for almost two months. I had nearly died and the diocese, my so-called family, was oblivious to it. What was it that induced me into making a sudden decision to request permission to go back to the mission? I had surprised myself. Maybe, it was not a sudden decision after all. Or was it? Or, did I have an idea at the back of my mind all along. I just had not recognized it.

I was annoyed that the monsignor had not even bothered to ask what I had been doing at the mission for forty days. Even though I had shaved and made myself presentable, the marks of my illness would have been visible if he chose to look at me closely. The bishop had not enquired about me and I hadn't seen him. I think, in the end, it was this lack of concern for my well-being that sparked the quick decision to go back to the mission, to get away from here as soon as possible, to get away from it all. Having blurted it out, I didn't feel any regrets, whatsoever. His final show of concern for my safety was so hypocritical, I could almost have laughed. In the end, I was glad I had made the request to go back to the mission.

I wanted to do something for the natives. That part was true. I had been thinking all along how and what I could do for the tribe. I had some loose ideas, nothing I could clearly articulate. It was not as much out of gratitude for what they had done, but from a conviction that I should do something. Not many people are given the opportunity to live with them and get to know them as well as I had. In turn it gave me a chance to do something meaningful with my own life which in the last few months seemed to have gone adrift in a strange river, destination unknown.

Now that I had the permission to go, I had to make plans for my departure. At least in my mind, I would be at the mission for the long haul and had to make certain I was sufficiently equipped and supplied. There was no turning back now. I must leave before the VG had second thoughts, not about my departure but about the possible loss of $12,000. I was sure he would be reluctant to discuss this with too many people, as he would be hard pressed to explain why he committed so much money on a crazy project. I must get out of here quickly. I knew I would have plenty of time to meditate and think things through before devising a strategy once I was back at the mission. I had no misgivings; I knew I would be happier there than here.

Everyone has dreams of doing one thing or another. In most cases, the dreams remain what they are, just dreams. And the majority of the time, when you try to put the dreams to the test of reality, they fail miserably. In my case, reality was driving the dream. My reality was that I wanted to get away from the prying eyes of the diocese, at least for some time while I tried to figure out if I could assist the native tribe. For that reality to take shape, I had to have a dream. The problem was the dream had very little reality attached to it.

One month-and-a-half ago, I had not spent one minute of my life worrying about the plight of Native Americans. I had very little knowledge of America's native people, and what little I knew was a muddled montage of stories, history, and movies. So much had happened since then. I had met and lived among authentic native people in a native enclave. I had experienced their struggles as they fought to survive against unbelievable odds. They had welcomed me and cared for me, as few people would have. In just a short while, the tribe had become the center and focus of my thoughts, and their future had become a big part of my dream.

What if the tribe had turned stone cold on me and showed me none of the warmth and concern they had during my illness? Would they now see me as a pest? What exactly did I have to offer them that would benefit them? What exactly could I hope to accomplish with such little funding? I was a man on a mission, to a mission, without a plan and seeking answers where there were too many questions. But I couldn't look back now. So what if the plan failed? If I failed or if I failed to succeed, I could always return to the diocese and become a pastor somewhere.

I would have my car. I wouldn't be grounded. I wouldn't be dependent on the natives as before. I had enough supplies and the ability to replenish them as needed. Once back at the mission, I decided I would stay at the rectory. Loneliness would be a factor. Water would be another. But, within one hour I could be at the village—and if all worked out reasonably well, I would have company, food, and enough water. I would take as many books as I could to keep me company.

If the decision to return to the mission was taken rather hastily, the departure was even quicker. The lack of a clear and studied plan was replaced by a stubborn determination to push ahead. The success of the whole enterprise was contingent on the premise that the tribe would extend the same level of welcome as I had experienced before.

During the long drive to the village, I rehearsed time and time again how I would present my return to open a mission I had come earlier to close. The original mission was opened to provide religion, education, and healthcare to the native tribe. What exactly would I do for them? I had no medical skills to provide healthcare. Ironically, they were pretty well set in that regard and I was the beneficiary of Sarah's healing skills. They had no need for a school there. I could provide them spiritual guidance. Is that what they needed, though? It was disquieting to break down things that way. There were no answers. I tried to sweep these uncomfortable thoughts out of my mind. Let me get there, set up camp, and then allow things to take shape and let it happen.

I arrived at the village just before noon and wasn't too surprised to find that Doug and the other guys were gone on some errands. Sarah was there, and she and the other women showed real surprise at my return. I got no indication whether they were happy or annoyed. The natives are not usually in the habit of wearing their emotions on their sleeves.

"Father Tosco, you kept your word. I didn't think it would be so soon."

"I knew I had to come back and this time I am back for a long time."

"What do you plan to do?"

"I am not sure. I am going to reopen the mission, for sure."

"What will you do there?"

"I wish I knew. But whatever I do, it'll be with you and for you."

"That's nice to hear."

"When are the guys going to be back?"

"They usually get back before dusk. Do you want to wait for them?"

"No thanks. I am going to drive over to the rectory. Would you ask them to come over when they have the time? Doesn't have to be today; tomorrow morning or evening would be fine."

"Are you sure? Once they get back, you can all drive over there together."

"I think I'll go now and get situated. I can unpack and put things away."

"All right. How is your health? How do you feel?"

"I feel good. Don't have much of an appetite. Other than that, I feel okay."

"Be careful. You are still weak. No outdoor activities for a couple of "weeks.

"Yes, Doctor Sarah."

Driving through the desert, I could see a long trail of dust behind me. This time I didn't lose my way. It was as well that Doug and his friends were out when I arrived. If they came to visit me, it would signal that they accepted my return. If they failed to show up, that would be bad news. If they came and appeared hostile, that would spell doom to my enterprise. Their initial response would mean a lot to my future here.

Nothing at the mission seemed to have changed since I left, not that there was any reason to expect anything different. I parked the car at the front of the rectory and put things away. I had come prepared for a long stay. I had several plastic containers in which I could bring water from the village as needed. I knew I would be a frequent visitor at the village. I would live at the rectory but would spend as much time as possible at the village.

Doug, Freddie, and Mike drove up early the next morning. They looked and sounded matter-of-fact.

"Welcome back Father Tosco. Glad to see you."

"Thank you. Come on over, we can sit inside the church. Are you guys in a hurry to return to the village?"

"Hurry? No, we're never in a hurry."

"I brought you some cigars. I don't know if they are good or just okay. I saw most of you smoked cigars when I was here last time."

"One of our bad habits. These are not bad."

"Offering tobacco is an important custom among native people."

"Good. I guess I did something auspicious."

"Do you mind if we light up?"

"Go ahead. It'll be the last time you get to smoke inside the mission."

"Thanks!"

"When you said you would return, we didn't take you seriously. Why did you decide to come back?"

"I don't know. It all started when you refused to sign the dissolution papers. It got me thinking. Maybe, the mission has a purpose. I talked to my superiors and got the permission to return and reopen the mission."

"You are here; we are over there; how are you going to make it work?"

"I will have services here every Sunday and I am hoping you will come."

"What about the rest of the time?"

"Give me a few days. I am not ready to discuss any plans yet. I haven't finalized them. Whatever they are, you will be part of the decisions."

"You must have some ideas."

"For starters, how about defining the native way of life we talked about? Let's try and figure it out."

"We talk about our way of life in a nostalgic way. But we don't have a clue what it should be in the present context."

"Let's then try to figure out what it should be and then work toward making it real. It must be something good, right?"

"Good, yes. Practical? Maybe not."

"Sometimes we wonder what it's we are trying to preserve and for whom. The younger generation seems to want to get away as fast as they can."

"Because they see no future here for them individually or as a nation."

"Exactly. We have nothing to offer them."

"You told me that if you offer them basic comforts, electricity, television, some form of entertainment, and something to feel proud about, they'd come more often."

"I am sure they would."

"They seem to love it for a few days when they are here."

"We are here all the time. We have nowhere to go. We want those who leave to return more often and stay longer. That would make us feel like a people, a community."

"Why don't you have electricity? Why don't you have telephones?"

"Money, Father Tosco, money! It needs a lot of money to bring these things to the village. We don't have money."

"Let's talk about how to raise money to bring electricity and telephone to the village."

"It's not enough to get them; we will need to pay for them. We can't afford these things. It will add to our expenses and we are in a financial bind as it is."

"Again, money is the solution. Money is the problem and the solution. But my question is this: Let's say you have these amenities at the village. What makes you believe your members will want to come back frequently?"

"Everyone makes it a point to come for the summer and fall festivals. There's a lot of excitement and enthusiasm for a week. But then they are in a hurry to go back."

"They come because there's stuff happening. There are dances, hunting trips, storytelling and traditional cooking. We dress up in native attire. In short, we transform ourselves into who we are, true Native Americans, for the weeklong festivals."

"There are events for the elders; the women are busy doing things, the youngsters roam around freely and the children can play all day without too many rules."

"For weeks ahead we plan the festival and make sure everything and everybody is okay and having a good time."

"If I understand you correctly, you want to create the same atmosphere year round, like what you have during the festivals. You feel that can make your folks connected to the home base more firmly."

"That would change life completely for the community."

"Right now, to be honest, we live and wait for the two annual festivals. That's what keeps us together."

"It shows they want to belong. It shows they are proud of who they are. It shows they take pride in their tribal heritage."

"That alone is not enough to hold them here longer. They want more."

"You can't have fun and festivities all the time."

"There are issues with schooling for children, jobs and even professional careers that force some of our members to stay away."

"What are your long-term goals? Having fun can't be the only goal."

"We want to provide them a tribal village, where they can come when they can, to relax, to reunite and relive who they are."

"We want a tribal center where we can preserve our culture."

"We want the tribal village to be our primary home to which all members come as often as they can."

"They would return here when they retire to be among family and friends."

"We want a place where our elderly receive care and protection surrounded by their own people, practicing their customs."

"Last time when I was here, you talked about recognition as a separate and independent nation. Is that not a goal?"

"Yes! We won't feel secure without recognition and reservation."

"How about we try to do something about it first?"

"There's not much hope of success."

"Nobody will listen to us."

"We are too small. We have no money."

"Father Tosco, our problems are many and can't be solved easily. Why would you be concerned with our problems?"

"I don't know if I can express my feelings in a way you'll understand. During the few days I spent here with you I experienced briefly what the native way of life is. True, I was seeing it from the outside. But, I became convinced that preserving the native identity, the culture and the way of life is important not only for you but also for posterity. Look at all the efforts undertaken to protect and preserve plant and animal life. Why? It enriches our experience on this planet. It's important to protect an ancient race of people and their culture. The United States boasts of its multicultural ethnic diversity as one of its greatest assets. The native citizens of the land must be at the forefront of this highly touted diversity. They must not be forgotten."

"We appreciate your concern. Not many people share your sentiments."

"We ourselves don't feel confident we can save our identity for much longer. We argue a lot if it's worth the effort to try and preserve it."

"The odds may be against you. But, you must keep trying. If you stop trying, you are accepting defeat."

"It is hopelessness rather than defeat."

"Hopelessness born out of helplessness."

"It doesn't take much to rekindle hope. Think about it. If you don't try, you won't know if you can succeed. If you try and it fails, try something else or keep trying until you can try no more."

"We don't know what more we can do."

"I don't either, and I don't know what you have done so far. But, what's the harm in trying again. I don't have much in resources but what I have, I intend to use toward the success of the mission. This is your mission and it can succeed only if you succeed."

"Father Tosco, we're open to ideas and suggestions. What'll you have us do?"

"For starters, we must have a strong spiritual foundation. It's our faith in God, the Supreme Spirit that gives us the strength to fight for our rights. We must put our trust in him and go to him during our periods of despair and sorrow. I would ask you to attend the Sunday services. This is not about converting to Christianity. It's about faith in God. It's like a child's trust in a parent. From God we draw comfort, strength, and hope."

"We will attend Sunday services."

"I wish to come over to the village when I can and meet with you to plan and discuss things. We must set concrete goals."

"You are welcome to the village any time."

"As individuals and as a group, I want you to think of things you want to get done and how they'll help you reach your goals. In the meantime, I am going to give you feedback from an outsider's point of view."

"Father Tosco, if we don't sound too enthusiastic, it's not for lack of desire for change. We find it difficult to get our hopes up high."

"We are like fighters who have been knocked down so often that we no longer have the heart to rise and fight again."

"You won't fall and you won't fail."

It was a long time before I fell asleep that night. There was an excitement building up inside me. Ideas started swimming around in my mind, most of them too fantastic to deserve a second thought. The tribe must get recognized as an independent nation. That would open up a few doors. How could I help them in that regard? I had no political know-how and didn't know any politician personally. I knew nothing about the Bureau of Native American Affairs.

I woke up early still feeling the excitement within me and as I drove out to the village, some of the ideas started taking shape. It was obvious I had to start by doing something about their material well-being. They should have access to some simple comforts of life. That meant money.

"Good morning Father Tosco."

"Good morning Doug. Hope everyone is well."

"Yes, thank you. The folks know you are coming and everyone who is free will join us in a few minutes."

"Can we meet around the pool? It looks cooler out there."

"Sure. Would you like to have something to eat and drink?"

"No. I am fine.

"Sarah, would you let everyone know we're meeting at the pool?"

Doug and I chatted while we walked to the pool and until others showed up. They took their seats on tree trunks, rocks and on the ground.

"I want to thank you for allowing me to come back. I came back because I feel strongly I must do something to help this community. The humanity you showed me when I was ill meant a lot to me."

"You don't have to feel obligated to do something because we took care of you when you were ill. We would have done that for anyone."

"I'm not doing anything out of a sense of obligation. I'm here because I'm convinced it's important to protect and preserve this tribe's history and heritage."

"What do you plan to do?"

"I met with some of you yesterday and I have been thinking ever since, thinking about how you can bring the entire community together and improve your financial situation."

"How? That's not going to happen, unless we win the lottery."

"Do I have specific plans? No. Do I have ideas? Yes. I'm sure you have ideas too. I want all of us to put our heads together and pool ideas that can bring about change."

"It would be nice if we could get electricity."

"We can have fans, refrigerators, and washing machines."

"Do you know how much it would cost to bring electricity to the village?"

"I'm not sure, but it probably would be prohibitive. The village is almost three miles from the freeway."

"Can the Bureau of Native American Affairs provide the funding? Can the State of Utah pitch in and help?"

"The State of Utah is under no obligation to provide electricity to a native reservation. The Bureau is a sham. They won't do anything."

"The Bureau will tell us to go through the Cedar City Council, as we are part of that band."

"How about approaching the utility directly?"

"No utility company would want to invest a ton of money to bring electricity to the village for the sake of a few people. It would not be economically feasible."

"What have you done so far? Have you applied for electricity?"

"No."

"Have you met with the Bureau? Have you discussed it with Cedar City Council?"

"No!"

"We are going to change that. We can't assume it won't work, not unless and until we have tried. Let's meet with people at the Rocky Mountain Power Utility. Let's see what they have to say."

"That's true! What do we have to lose?"

"Do not put restraints on your hopes and dreams. Let them fly!"

"If we had telephones we could call them and get an appointment."

"That should be on our agenda too. We should find out how to get a telephone connection here."

"I can't imagine the telephone company pulling several miles of line to bring a single telephone connection for us."

"Let's stop by the telephone company and find out how we would go about getting a connection."

"How long will all this take?"

"Let's find out. Since none of us are very knowledgeable, we have to ask and get the answers."

"It may take years to get it done."

"It could all be a waste of time.'"

"There are many obstacles we'll have to face. Failure is always a possibility. If we focus on failure, it'll stop us from action. We must overcome the fear of failure. We must focus on action. Yes, Sarah."

"We know how hard we all work to try and make both ends meet. It's been tough for all of us. We all agree we must change our ways if we are to survive. We don't know how. Father Tosco is suggesting we try. If we fail, what have we lost? Nothing. If we succeed, it will mean so much for us."

"Sarah speaks with wisdom. It's true. We have nothing to lose."

"We must make things happen. It can only happen by trying."

"What we must avoid doing is…doing nothing."

"They may have funds for social welfare programs. We may fit the criteria."

"We can go meet with the power and phone companies."

"On the same trip, we should try to meet with the governor, the senators and the congressmen and find out what they can do."

"I am sure our demands will sound crazy to them."

"It is no crazier than sitting around and wishing for the return of the native way of life, and doing nothing about it."

"Let's do it. There is nothing to lose by trying."

"Let's stop talking and do something. When do we start?"

"I will be here at 8:00 tomorrow morning. I'm driving.

Self-doubt extracts a terrible emotional price. It was a crazy idea. Nobody would have believed we would do this except we were doing it. What if we end up not meeting anyone? What if the people we meet laugh at the ideas? What if it takes years to get it done? How long will the tribe stick with it, if there were no quick results? Am I doing the tribe a disservice by giving them false hope? What if it fails? Will they end up worse off than before?

I had spent much of the night in prayer. I tried to convince myself that a lot of people throughout history had accomplished great things but had very little going for them at the start. There was one problem. They all had greatness and I had none. I had little or nothing to show as past accomplishments. But, it was too late now. I had made a commitment to the tribe and there was no backing out.

Doug, Freddie, and John were waiting for me as I arrived. The project was on. The whole village came out to see us off. Nothing was said but in their eyes, I saw expectation and a flicker of hope. I saw Sarah watching us with an amused look in her eyes. Or was it a challenge? She was some woman. Yesterday, with one stroke, one statement, she had changed the momentum from talk to action. It was done with ease. We took to the road.

"It'll take us four hours to get there. That leaves us about four hours to do something today. We need to plan what we are going to do so we don't waste any time."

"Let's meet with the utilities reps today. And if time permits, the state representatives too".

"We will get the addresses from the phone book when we stop for gas?"

"Are these people going to take us seriously?"

"Probably not."

"Do we take ourselves seriously?"

"We must!"

"If nothing happens, if nothing changes; we go back to life as usual."

"No, we can't. We won't accept defeat and return empty-handed. There's no going back to life as usual."

"All these years, we have talked and wished for change, but didn't do a thing. Now, finally, we are doing something. That's change."

"Did you watch the women this morning when we left? They came out to send us on our way. It was like they were sending us off to a battle or a buffalo hunt, like in the old days."

"They are looking for change. They expect us to bring about the change."

"We must! We will! We won't fail. Change is here."

"If we return empty handed, it could make matters worse."

"It won't! This is not a one-shot deal. This is only a start."

"Father Tosco, see the freeway entrance? We take 15 North."

"Okay!"

"Once the tourist season starts, there'll be a lot more traffic on these freeways. It's still pretty quiet. Wait for another month."

"Getting back to what we were talking about. Sounds like you have concerns about the cost once you get electricity and telephone."

"Yes. We don't have a fixed income. The majority of our income comes from working members and the Social Security of retired folks."

"I may have a solution."

"What?"

"I came back to re-activate the mission. The diocese knows the mission has no income. I have funding to run the mission. I can use it as I see fit."

"What has that to do with the cost of electricity and phones?"

"I can pay for the cost of bringing electricity and phones to the mission, as long as it's within reason. I have funds to pay for the monthly cost. If the mission is successful, the support will continue."

"What makes a successful mission?"

"Participation by the people for whom it was built, the Paiute Nation."

"What do we have to do?"

"Attend services and be part of the mission activities. What you are doing now would qualify as a mission activity."

"Who makes the decision whether we are participating or not?"

"Me!"

"The mission and the village are at two different locations. Getting electricity to the mission won't make much difference to the village."

"You're assuming that the mission must remain where it is today. It was built there because you lived close by. You moved. The mission can move too. The mission is not just a structure. The mission is a living thing. It should be where the people are and where it's needed."

"Are saying that you plan to move the mission to the village?"

"The large tent could serve as the church. Do I have your permission?"

"Sure, by all means. That would make it easy for us to attend services."

"Father Tosco, we don't want you to go to so much trouble for us."

"Why not? That's why I came back. I want to make the mission successful. There can be no mission without you."

"We are not Catholics. Will that create a conflict?"

"There were no Catholics among you when the mission was established."

"Do you expect us to become Catholics?"

"Let me make myself very clear. I didn't come back here to force you to convert and become Catholics. It's something you must want and request. Conversion is a calling from God."

Determination and desperation can be strange bedfellows. They can force you to take on foolhardy enterprises. I had decided to ride into town like an old western sheriff and challenge the local bad guy. Here, I had planned to walk into the office of the utility company and meet with the person in charge of approving new services and get it done, now. Of course, I knew that a large corporation doesn't operate that way. You need an appointment, and you need to know who you want to meet and you need a clear proposal. We had none.

I knew I would not in all probability be able to meet with anyone of the rank and stature that could give us the answers. But, I hoped we would be able to get an appointment if not today, then maybe for another time. Time was of the essence. If I wanted to win over this group of native people, I needed action, and I had to show results, not just ideas. Yes, we were doing something and there would be results. I was hoping it would be a positive.

"How can I help you?"

"We want to meet with someone who can give us some information."

"What kind of information?"

"These gentlemen are members of the Paiute tribe and they want to find out how then can get electricity to their village."

"Do you have an appointment?"

"No. We don't know whom we should be meeting with."

"I don't know whom you should be meeting with."

"How about the office manager?"

"She's in a meeting. Please hold. Yes. What were you saying?"

"Do you have someone in charge of Community Affairs?"

"Sir, please hold. Sir! I do not have the time to answer all your questions. I have to handle the front desk and answer the phones."

"I understand. Can you call a supervisor—any supervisor?"

"I don't know who is available. I have to explain to them what you want before I can get someone to talk to you."

"How about someone in customer service?"

"Why don't you have a seat? Let me see what I can do."

"Thanks!"

"She is none too happy."

"It's understandable. We have no appointment and we don't know whom to meet."

"What if we don't meet anyone today?"

"We will meet someone today. Will that person be able to provide us any useful information? I am not sure."

"How long should we wait?"

"We have no appointment. We'll wait as long as we have to."

"Sir, I can't get hold of any supervisors. They are in a meeting. I will be happy to take a message and have someone call you."

"We'll have to wait. There are no phones on their reservation."

"What do you mean, wait?"

"We'll wait until the manager or supervisor is done with the meeting."

"They may have other meetings. I don't know what their schedules are."

"We'll take our chances."

"All right!"

"Gentlemen, what can I do for you?"

"That was quick. Can we sit down somewhere and talk?"

"Unfortunately, we don't have any conference rooms available."

"These are members of the Paiute Tribe. They live on a reservation. We are here to find out how we can get electricity to their village."

"I have no idea."

"Can you find out?"

"Sir, it's not my department."

"What, helping us?"

"That's not funny."

"We're not trying to be funny. We drove almost four hours to come here to get some information. We don't have time to be funny."

"Sir, you can't walk into an office like this without an appointment and expect to get things done."

"That is why we are asking for your help. Can you find out who can provide us with this information?"

"This is crazy."

"Madam, these folks do not have electricity. They do not have a phone to call for information or make an appointment. I'm sure you can help people like that too."

"Sir, my job is to manage an office. I don't deal with these types of requests. That's up to customer service."

"Would you get hold of a supervisor in Customer Service?"

"I don't have time to call all the supervisors to find out who is available."

"Can you ask one of your staff to make the calls?"

"They have things to do."

"I am sure. But, we are not leaving until we meet with someone."

"Don't threaten me. I will call security if I have to!"

"You consider this a threat? How about if we sat and blocked the front entrance? Would that get someone down here quickly? How would you explain creating a scene for refusing to help us?"

"Oh my god! What a day! Have a seat."

"That's two unhappy people."

"There'll be more."

It should have been pretty evident that the Office Manager was not going to be of much help. At least, we got the name of the Manager of Community Outreach, a Mr. Anderson. I left him a note that we would be back the same time a week from today.

We were a little better prepared when we walked into the telephone utility's office. We asked for the Manager for Community Outreach. Of course, he wasn't available. We left him a note asking for an appointment the same day a week from today. We had time. We decided we would pay a visit to the congressman's office.

The Federal Building was only blocks away. William Conway was a first time congressman in his early forties and he represented the third district, which included the Little Bend valley. Mr. Conway was in Washington as congress was in session. We met with his Secretary for Social Services. How could the Paiutes get electricity and telephones?

How would the tribe go about seeking official recognition? A very sympathetic and concerned individual, she said that she would have to do some research about the tribe. She understood the plight of the tribe and would do all she could to help. What kind of help? She would have to get in touch with the Bureau of Native American Affairs and get a status report on the tribe. She would certainly find out what, if any, assistance was available through the bureau. That was the best way to go.

Was there any benefit in approaching the state? Utah has its own department for native affairs. We could try if we wanted to but she didn't think it would be of much help. No harm in trying. There was little the state could do toward recognition of a native nation.

Could she put in a call to the utility department to find out what the chances were of getting electricity to the village? She said she would, although she wasn't very hopeful. Did she know if there were federal programs to support alternative energy production? No! Yes, she would meet with us a week from today at 11:00 a.m. We helped ourselves to some coffee and cookies and took leave. She was good at her job, and was smooth and savvy. On the way out, I picked up some literature on the congressman.

We knew it would be late by the time we got back to the village. We had dinner at a small restaurant and then got back on the road. Everyone had an opinion on the events of the day, but they were mostly negative. I wasn't surprised. They were a small group. Why would anyone take any interest in their welfare? I felt a twinge of sadness for them. Once a proud people, they had roamed over this vast land, as masters of their destiny, living their way of life, until, they were run over by the vast hordes of greedy settlers. Now, they were destitute, a shadow of their former selves, shorn of their pride, trying to survive in a new and alien world that despised them. But they had nowhere to go. They belong here.

I was determined to help them. I had my self-doubts. But, I wouldn't back down. For some inexplicable reason, my path had crossed theirs, and they had shown more than ordinary humanity in the way they cared for me. They were good people with wonderful values that had withstood the passage of time.

As the group fell silent, having vented most of their frustrations, I reminded them that this was our first foray into the unknown. Each time we did something, we would learn something. As we learn more, we become skilled at doing the right things more often. But now, we had no choice but to meander through dark alleys and hit some dead ends.

"We will find the light at the end of the tunnel. How long will it take? As long as it takes to succeed! That is not a cliché. We must go after small successes. We will build on them and get to our final goal: recognition as an independent nation. It's important not to look at things only in absolute terms of success and failure. Nothing is a failure as long as we gain something from it."

We got back to the village well after dark. There wasn't much to discuss. I was going back to the rectory. As I drove back, my mind was working overtime, trying to figure out what I could or should do differently next time. Getting electricity would take time. I must do something for them that worked in the short run. They needed a source of income, dependable and sustainable.

There was something that was ticking at the back of my mind during the trip back from the city. Now, as I drove back alone, it came back to me like a wake-up call. They, like many of the native tribes, were pretty good sculptors of wood and the women were excellent weavers of blankets and baskets. I had seen some of the artifacts they had made. Doug had mentioned that they took their products to the outpost further south, and sold them. It helped supplement their income. During the tourist season, I am sure these outposts did a thriving business in native crafts. The products were of good quality and original but didn't fetch the tribe much money. Won't they be better off if they open and operate their own outpost? They had the people to run the store, and if they ran it on the reservation, they would be exempt from taxes and other formalities.

As I had passed the intersection of the two freeways, it had sparked an idea. The intersection would be an ideal spot for a native outpost with maximum visibility and exposure. There was one problem; it was too far from the village.

I made a quick decision and went back to the village around noon the next day, although I hadn't planned to be there before Sunday. I asked Doug to join me and drove to the native outpost where they sold their stuff. On the way, I asked him about their products and how much they got paid for them. I knew it represented a sizeable part of their income.

Freddie was the master sculptor. Others helped collect the materials and grind and polish the products. Almost all of the women were skilled in weaving baskets, knitting the blankets, and making jewelry and other trinkets. They worked in an unhurried and relaxed manner, working when they had the time and the inclination. Once every month they took the merchandise to the outpost. On average, the wares fetched about $300-$400 a month. During the winter months, they didn't sell anything but kept making things so that they had enough stock to sell when the tourist season started in mid spring.

We walked around inside the store. It wasn't very large but was stocked with what tourists usually look for. Native wares were sold in a separate part of the store. Even at this early part of the season, there were a few customers looking at the stuff. I was interested in the prices and the variety of items they sold. They weren't cheap. Doug pointed out to me some of the items they had sold to the outpost last year. We spent maybe half-an-hour in the store before heading back.

"Doug. Have you ever considered selling these products yourself?"

"No! Why?"

We met in the open space late that evening after dinner. I had stayed back and accepted Sarah's invitation to eat with them. Some of the women and most of the men joined the assembly.

"As you all know, a few of us drove to the city yesterday to find out how we can bring electricity to the village. I'm sure you heard what happened, which wasn't much. We'll be going back next week to see what more we can do. As we were driving, an idea came to my mind. I know you make quite a lot of native wares, sculptures, blankets, baskets, native jewelry, and other items, and sell them to the outpost. You make really good stuff. Today, Doug and I drove out to the outpost. I was astonished at the mark-up. Compared to what they pay you, they sell the items at four times the cost. I am wondering why you can't open your own store and sell the products to the public yourself."

"We have no experience running a store. We know nothing about selling things."

"Are you willing to do it?"

"It's pretty easy the way we have been doing so far. We sell to the outpost, get paid in full, and come home. We don't have to wait to get paid. It's very simple and convenient."

"We run no risk. They do. If it does not sell it's their problem."

"You know they pay you a lot less than what they sell it for."

"Of course."

"If we start our own store and it fails, the outpost won't buy from us anymore. Then, we are in trouble. We need the money."

"They will buy from us anytime. They make a lot from the stuff."

"There's nothing wrong with them making money. That's how businesses work. But you could be making more money if you sell it yourself."

"The way we are doing now, we don't have to worry about storing the stuff, pricing, returns and complaints. We don't need a store."

"You don't need much space. All you need is a tent, really. It doesn't have to be big; just big enough to display stuff you want to sell."

"We have never done anything like it before."

"You have a perfect spot for the store at the junction of the two freeways."

"That's true. It's a far better location than the outpost. It has visibility."

"The junction is too far away from the village."

"Without a store where would we keep the stuff at night?"

"We need a large amount of merchandise to open a store."

"There has to be some money to invest, money which we don't have."

"There's no water or electricity there."

"Listen. Here's what I am thinking. What you make and sell is aimed at tourists and tourist season covers April through November at the most. A large tent like this one here is all you need to display merchandise. One or two people can run the store. I guarantee success."

"What guarantee?"

"I will guarantee that you make double what you get when you sell to the outpost. If not I will make up the difference."

"How can you do that?"

"Because I am confident it'll work. Let me explain. You are paid $500 a month for your products by the outpost. I guarantee up to $1000 each month. If you sell for less than $1000, I'll make up the shortfall."

"We can't let you do that. We won't let you take the risk."

"That's the attitude I am trying to change. You know you can sell more than $500 a month. That's what the outpost is paying you. They mark up the price at least four times what they pay you. You mark up two times and there's your $1000. It's pretty simple. There's no risk at all."

"Father Tosco, you make it sound simple. It's not. We can't accept your offer."

"Why not? You make good and original items, the kind of stuff tourists are looking for. They are non-perishable and durable. You have the personnel and the time to operate the store. What you make from sales is almost entirely profit."

"The outpost is well established for many years. They have the experience and they have the customers."

"It's a tourist driven business. Tourists are not loyal or repeat customers. They will stop and buy where it's convenient."

"Father Tosco, we need to think about this. It's a great idea and I am certain it can succeed. However, the risk is yours only. That's not fair."

"Fine. I want you to think about it. Let me explain my plan in full. I will give you an advance of $3000 now for three months. Let's say we open the store in the last week of May, on Memorial Day, the official start of the tourist calendar. You'll need some of the money to prepare and build the store. At the end of August, we will do the accounting. I will continue the guarantee of $1000 per month for three more months which takes us to November, the end of the tourist season. At that time, you will calculate what you made and repay me the $6000. I'm confident you will make much more than $6000. I see no risk at all for my money."

"I think what Father Tosco is proposing makes a lot of sense. But it only makes sense if we are willing take some risks."

There was Sarah again. She had that uncanny ability to say the right thing at the right time. You could see a shift in their attitude immediately.

"My only fear is you will run out of things to sell."

"We hesitate to act because we are afraid of failure. We could never attempt what Father Tosco is proposing because we didn't have the inspiration and the capital. Father Tosco is giving us both. Now, the challenge is ours; do we or do we not."

"What would we do about the merchandise at the end of each day?"

"We can bring it back to the village each night."

"We can't leave the tent there overnight."

"Taking down the tent and putting it up every day is not very practical."

"We need something stronger than a tent to withstand strong winds. We will need to have a regular store with walls and a roof."

"If we had a trailer, we could have a couple of us live there. The stuff can stay there too. That will save us time and effort to transport things each day."

"First, we need to decide if we want to do it. If we decide to do it, we can find ways to do it properly."

"Why would we not want to do this? There is some risk but there'll always be some risk regardless of what we decide to do. The only way to avoid risk is by doing nothing and let things be as they are."

"We have lived our lives with no plans for the future. We merely exist and live day to day. We must change that. We can't let this chance pass by!"

"Father Tosco is asking us to take advantage of our strengths. We will be making the things we sell. We are good at making things. There is a demand for them. How can it fail?"

"We don't need a lot of money for start-up costs. There's hardly any investment. It's mostly labor. We have plenty of that available."

"Yes, there's great potential to make good money. But timing is important. The tourist season is almost here. If we want to do it, we must do it now."

"I don't think it's possible to do it this year. We don't have enough time."

"It doesn't require a lot of time to get it going. We can do it overnight if we want to do it."

"If we want to do it, do it now, this year. If we postpone, we'll never do it."

"We can do it now. We are not talking about building a big store. We only need a simple display center. People traveling on the freeways can't possibly miss seeing us because of the location."

"We have enough in stock that we made over the winter months. That'll be enough to get started."

The entire village was present for the Mass, including small children. I could sense excitement and anticipation during the service and as we met afterwards. The women seemed a little more animated than usual.

"Father Tosco, there's strong support for the store. We think it's a great idea. If not for you, we would not even have considered it."

"There's no time to waste. We must open as soon as possible."

"We want to look into getting a trailer to store the merchandise and for a couple of us living there."

"We can build a store, something more than a makeshift tent."

"We want to do it."

"Good. Let's go over what we need to do. We need to have two of you go around and look at pricing at the outpost and similar stores, if any."

"Can you Eddie and Joyce do that?"

"Sure!"

"We need a couple of tents, a large one for the store and one or more for people to live in. A used trailer or RV would be great."

"Brian and Stella, can you drive to Provo and look for tents? See if you can pick up some magazines for used trailers or RVs."

"We'll do that!"

"The location must be marked out. We must plan where we're going to set up shop. We'll need a parking area and a work area."

"We will visit the spot tomorrow and draw up a plan.'"

"Here's the advance."

The Summer Festival was already scheduled for the week following Memorial Day. There was a lot of discussion whether to open the store before or after the festival. They had always held the Summer Festival in and around the village. Some of the elders voiced concern that opening the store before the Summer Festival would be a distraction. They needed a lot of time to plan and organize the events. Others countered that the store was more important than the festivities. Eventually, the store outweighed the festival in importance. They were not sacrificing the festival in favor of the store. They were going to have both. The store would open for business on Saturday of the Memorial Day weekend.

More animated arguments followed whether the festivities should be held near where the store would be built. They'd always had them close to the village, and it had advantages. It was secluded from public view and water was readily available. Some of the women pointed out that if the festivities were held near the store, the visual attraction could be a big boost for the store. That clinched it. The festival would be held near the store.

Once the decisions were made, there was a quickening of pace and the tribe displayed the kind of energy I hadn't seen before. If I had concerns about their lack of initiative, they proved me wrong. I came to the conclusion that what was missing in their lives was a sense of direction. Once they got rolling, they were a pleasure to watch.

They decided that the actual work on the store wouldn't begin until the very last moment. They would clear and get the location ready, but wouldn't put up the tent until the night before opening day. The store would go up overnight.

Not a lot of work was needed to prep the spot. It was fairly flat. The area was cleared off brush and boulders. A boundary line was created with rocks and boulders that were plentiful. They marked out the location for the teepees for folks to stay during the festival. The festivities would take place between the store and the teepees. It would be visible from the freeways. The space would look like a large arena, flattened and trampled firm, and covered by a large tent with the teepees in a semi-circle around this covered arena. Portable toilets would be rented and water would be trucked in each day in two large containers such as used by construction crews.

Brian and Stella had found someone who wanted to get rid of an old trailer. It was free, but they'd have to haul it away. They had checked it out and determined it would serve their purpose. They were given the green light to find a moving company and get it over as soon as possible. If it could be hauled, then, it was strong enough for their purpose.

The trailer would be placed behind the store. All who were not involved with site preparation were busy creating as many items as possible for sale. They had the winter stock, but the more they had the better it would be. They wanted to make sure it was not a skimpy-looking store when it opened.

My greatest joy was watching Freddie, the master sculptor. I watched in fascination as chunks of wood came to life in many forms. He had only a few good tools and the material wasn't great. It didn't seem to matter at all. Freddie was truly an artist. The inspiration and the skills were there. He was a quiet individual who never complained—he let his work speak for him. His approach was simple. Rather than search for the right kind of material for the idea he had, he used the material at hand to generate ideas. Given the right combination of time, tools, and proper material, I was sure he'd create high-quality sculptures. He was that good. Here of course, the goal was to create decent artwork quickly and with minimum materials. Others chipped in with sanding, polishing and painting the work. Buffalo heads, horses, native chiefs in headgear, wolves, native women in traditional attire, and all kinds of birds, including eagles and owls, took shape under their skillful hands.

Doug and I went back to the city as scheduled, to keep our appointment with the utility companies and the congressman's office. The manager at the electricity utility was very helpful and promised to do all he could to get us connections to the trailer from the power supply at the freeway junction. He was very interested in the idea of putting up a solar farm at the reservation if it was cost-effective. A project study would be ordered. The telephone utility promised to send someone out to the location to evaluate the situation.

We met with the congressman's secretary, and she was as polished as before. She had talked to the Bureau of Native American Affairs. Unfortunately, there was nothing that could be done because they were not an independent tribe. Our best option was to approach the Cedar City Council and submit a proposal. There was an annoying quickness in the way we were received and dismissed. The tribe didn't represent a valuable asset to the Congressman, obviously.

Privately, I made plans to move the mission and myself close to the store. The idea first came to me as I watched the preparations to put up the large tent that would be the centerpiece of the festival. The arena with the tent cover would serve as the church until something firmer could be built. The church would be visible from the freeways.

Members started arriving all through the week prior to the festival. They remained at the village through Thursday. On Friday, they packed up and departed to the new location. There was a lot of work to be completed there. For two weeks now, most men worked on location from early morning till late in the evening. Newcomers joined the work parties without hesitation. There was a lot of excitement.

The trailer arrived on Wednesday before opening day. It had seen better times, for sure. It received a thorough cleaning and after some deft paintwork, looked as good as new. It had a small bedroom, a matching kitchen, and a toilet. It would serve their purpose.

The atmosphere at the village and the store was nothing short of chaotic. By their count, forty-nine members out of the total fifty-seven were present although it felt like and sounded like an army had moved in. It was noisy, crowded and crazy, with children running around all over, dogs chasing each other while darting in and out among the children, and everybody talking at the same time.

The last several days had been intense, with long hours of work at the site, followed by endless meetings in the evenings, of elders and mostly men. The women cooked and cooked and cooked some more. I was in the thick of it all, and everyone seemed comfortable with my presence.

It was a little after noon on Friday; we were all assembled at the new site. It was impossible not to be amazed at the transformation that had taken place in a couple of weeks. The trailer was parked facing the fork of the two freeways. The tent for the store was pitched directly in front of the trailer so that it looked like a very large awning attached to the trailer. There were spaces marked out for parking further to the front. There was access from both freeways.

The festival arena looked welcoming with the large multi-colored tent covering the entire open area and the teepees erected neatly around. Tonight and for the week following, they would sleep here. People could be seen traveling along the freeways, slowing down to take a look, I'm sure, wondering what was going on. It must have had the appearance of a small traveling circus or a carnival.

There was still more work to be completed. The display items would be set up at night. There were no events planned for today. It was a time for fun and laughter. Teepees were allocated. Duties had to be assigned. People had to be fed. There was an area further back of the large tent assigned for cooking, and soon smoke was billowing around carrying all types of aromas.

A general gathering of everyone over twelve was called around 7:00 in the evening. I was invited and took a seat among the council of elders. There was much excited talk of traditions, why it was important to preserve them, and how they must continue these traditions. They talked mostly in English but, on occasion, would argue in their native dialect. It was apparent everyone knew about the store, but there had to be a formal announcement and approval. That came when Doug, clearly the leader, not only in his bearing, but also by virtue of the headgear he had on. He first asked for the peace pipe. It was lit and passed around the council of elders. I took a symbolic puff and passed it on.

The assembly grew silent and solemn. Doug began to speak. He spoke with quiet dignity and poise. I couldn't understand what he said as he decided to talk in their native dialect. He was not going to make an exception because I was present. There was general agreement and assent as evidenced by the prolonged nodding of heads. Once the animated gestures quieted down, Doug continued in English. At sunrise on Saturday, which was the following day, there would be a formal blessing of the site and the store. A shaman had been invited from the Kaibab Paiute tribe to officiate. I was surprised when Doug turned to me and asked me to conduct a service at the open arena immediately following the tribal blessing. I was more than happy to oblige.

I returned early, well before sunrise, after having retired to the rectory the previous evening. I hadn't slept at all. The excitement I felt was so overwhelming that I couldn't find sleep. My dreams were taking shape. My sudden and foolhardy enterprise was becoming a reality. The native people had been reluctant at first, but they'd caught on fast and now they were into it, with heart and soul. There would be trials and missteps in the future, but for now, it was all fun and happiness. What would the first day be like? Would there be customers visiting the store? Would they buy anything?

Everyone was decked out in native attire. The men with painted faces and suntanned bodies, walked around with stern expressions. Women had their finery on and children had little floral garlands around the necks. I looked oddly out of place with my jeans, shirt, and collar. We moved to an open space beyond the perimeter of the teepees and sat in a semicircle facing east. The shaman was already there, with a fire pit and various offerings in front of him. Everyone grew silent.

As the eastern horizon displayed the first signs of light, the shaman began chanting, making offerings that were tossed into the fire pit. The sweet smell of herbs was carried around by a gentle breeze. Occasionally, the people joined in the chants, sometimes swaying sideways and back and forth. Then at a given sign from the shaman, the warriors stood up resplendent in traditional attire, holding painted shields and feathered spears. Someone began to beat a drum, and the men stomped around keeping rhythm with the drumbeat, their odd movements punctuated with acrobatic leaps. It looked like some sort of a war dance. Occasionally for no apparent reason the dancers would let loose an earsplitting scream. The women kept chanting throughout. The dance lasted for about ten minutes, and then they all sat down. The shaman completed the ceremony by making offerings.

We then moved inside the large tent to celebrate Mass. I was a shaman of a different kind. I wanted to make sure that the service would be as similar as possible in spirit to the service we had just witnessed. I took the opportunity to convey a message of hope, faith, and determination.

"Jesus was preaching to a large group of people who had been following him around. As the day wore on, he realized they hadn't eaten. Despite their hunger they had stayed on to listen to him. He asked his followers to go around and collect whatever food people had with them. They found someone who had five loaves of bread and another two fish. There were over five-thousand people present. Jesus worked a miracle and fed the whole community.

Religion and spirituality are all important to the moral structure of our lives. The mission is here, I am here, to bring you the good news of Christ. But as Christ was conscious of the physical needs of the followers, this mission is here also to assist in the material well-being of the Paiute people for whom the mission was created and exists.

The mission is proud to be a part of your present and hopes to remain a part of your future. May God bless your enterprise and bring success and comfort to you, your families and your future generations."

Once Mass was over, we moved to the front of the store. It looked totally different from the previous evening. Displays were set up with the baskets and blankets hanging from the ceiling, and the sculptures standing on piles of rock or blocks of wood. Each item had its own price tag. Other handicrafts were arranged at various parts of the pavilion. There was more than adequate space for people to walk around. It was all set up for quick and easy removal at the end of the day, and to set up again in the morning. There was a small table and a chair at the front entrance for the cashier. They had festooned the outer parameters with flags. It looked rugged but pleasing. There was a large sign hung between two poles that read: Paiute Native Crafts.

The shaman completed the blessing of the store and the trailer. They were in business. There was another dance by the warriors. Some vehicles traveling along the freeways honked as they passed by. Soon, a car pulled in and the occupants came out to watch the proceedings. As soon as the dance was over, they left without a word. I'm sure they saw it as a religious ceremony and didn't want to disturb us.

Then, there was food. I knew food always played a big part in their festivities. The ceremonies over, it was time for the inauguration of the Summer Festival. There were lots of activities to come. The action moved to the covered arena. A couple stayed back at the store. Yes, we could call it that now.

The Summer Festival was a weeklong affair. I was the only non-native present. The festival was a combination of a family reunion, a long picnic, and a never-ending Thanksgiving celebration.

There were councils and war dances. There were traditional dances. It looked like they would erupt into a dance without any warning. There was a lot of color, native attire, and bare bodies. I could understand the longing of these people to preserve their identity and their pride. Watching them indulge themselves and relive the lifestyle of their forefathers and emulate how they had lived for countless centuries before, it was impossible not to share their nostalgia.

All through, I could see that they remained very much focused on the store. This was the future, and festivities couldn't make them forget tomorrow. Most of the women, residents, and visitors alike stayed busy with their hands, making things while relaxing. Freddie was often absent from the fun and frolic. I knew he was hard at work somewhere.

There was considerable interest from travelers along the freeway. There were dances, mock battles, and chanting and singing. Several of the young warriors in full regalia rode around on horseback, kicking up dust. Some of them moved further out to show off their equestrian skills or just to enjoy themselves. There were competitions of all sorts.

Occasionally, cars pulled in, but they were more interested in watching the dances than in buying anything. Some did end up buying a few small items. As the days progressed, off and on, cars pulled up, mostly out of curiosity to find out what was happening. There was no mistaking this was a native store. It was colorful and original.

The women were busy cooking and cooking. Doug too was seen riding around on horseback in his feathered cape and headgear. He was beaming proud and made no attempt to conceal it.

Soon the festival was winding to a close. There was one big final feast Saturday evening. Sunday morning came, and as the day wore on, families were seen getting ready to pack up and leave. You could hear people expressing disappointment it was ending but making demonstrative commitments to return to see how the store was doing.

Monday morning came. Most of the visitors had left. All the teepees were taken down. The large tent remained. By evening everything was put away and everyone had returned back to the village, all except a couple that stayed back at the trailer. They had decided they would take turns to remain and run the store, one week at a time. In the morning, four or five of them would go to the store and remain until closing time. For now, closing time would be as soon as it started getting dark.

Freddie had decided he would build a shed next to the store and work there during the day. As we had expected, customers hung around to watch him work. He ignored the attention, if he sensed their presence at all. The more time customers spent at the store, the more they would buy. Soon, women came to weave baskets, make jewelry, and knit blankets, or do whatever else they did in full view of the customers. The tribe was catching on.

I had made new plans of my own. Now that the store was in place and seeing first-hand the advantages of the location, I decided to move and live there. I would invest some money and find a suitable trailer for me to live in. Similarly, I planned to purchase a new or used tent as large as the one they had used to cover the arena. It was a good location for the church. Doug and I were driving out to the store together when I broached this to him.

"Doug, I am thinking of moving the mission close to the store."

"Why?"

"As the store grows, there will be a lot more activity around here. I want to expand the mission and open the services to the general public."

"That's fine."

"It may be tough to call it a church in a conventional way. I got the idea from the arena and the tent you put up for the Festival. That should work well for the time being. But, I need some help in putting up the church."

"Father Tosco, all you have to do is ask."

"I'm thinking of naming it St. John the Baptist Catholic Mission. Do you have any objections to the name and moving the mission here?"

"No! That sounds good! When do you plan to make the move?"

"Not sure yet."

"Is there any help you want from me?"

"Not yet. I've asked Freddie to build me a small altar and a sign we can put next to the freeway with the name of the church and the time of Sunday service."

"I am sure he'll do it for you."

"I want to put up a large cross but with a native twist. I want a totem pole with Biblical themes carved on it and a cross at the top. Would that be offensive in any way?"

"Not at all."

"I have one more favor to ask of you—will you come with me to meet the bishop and the Vicar General to discuss what we are doing here?"

As I'd expected, the bishop was out of town or unavailable. It was

95

difficult to gage if the VG was pleased or annoyed or didn't care at all with the update I gave him. Maybe it was a mixture of all of these. He was pleased that I wasn't asking for more money. He was annoyed that the mission would remain open. He didn't care what I was doing. He had no opinion about the mission being moved next to the store and was unconcerned about the name of the church. He was gracious and polite to Doug. Doug played his part and invited him and his Excellency the Bishop to visit the mission.

We didn't stay too long. I needed to pick up some supplies for the church and then we left. We stopped by the utility companies. They were working on it. We could expect to have the electricity connection to the store in about a month; the phone connection would take longer.

I was pleased to see a couple of unfamiliar cars parked in front of the store as we drove back. The women were busy dusting and straightening the items. It was hot. There were three customers, walking around looking at various items, checking prices. They picked up a few small items and left. The total sale for the day was a little under $50. Freddie was in his shed.

"I should have the altar ready for you in a couple of weeks."

"Take your time. Don't let it take you away from the needs of the store."

"This is my break, working on the altar."

"Father Tosco wants to commission you for another job."

"It's a bigger job. I want to make a tall cross we can plant next to the Freeway. But, I want the cross on a totem pole."

"I have never made a totem pole. I will give it my best shot. You tell me what themes you want on the pole. The cross should be easy to make."

"Will do."

"Father Tosco, we need to make some decisions, quickly. We need a real store. We can't survive with this tent."

"I agree."

"It's not practical taking down all the merchandise and re-displaying them each day. But, if we leave it out there at night, it might get vandalized. Dust is a problem too."

"I agree."

"If the store becomes a success, we'll move the village close to the store."

"What about water supplies?"

"We got a good deal on the two containers we rented for the festival. One other thing, most people who stop by are looking to buy water, coffee, beer, or cigarettes, and use rest rooms, of course. The location is ideal for a convenience store. Once people stop here for these 'essentials' they are sure to buy other items that catch their fancy."

"It's a good spot for a real store. The more conveniences you can provide the more the people who will stop by and linger longer."

"Electricity will allow us to expand services."

It took three weeks for Freddie to finish the altar and make a sign with the name of the church and the time of the service. It was going to take him some more time to come up with the totem cross. I didn't want to pressure him as he had a lot of work to do. Sales had picked up a little. Tourist traffic was on the increase. Weekends were getting busier.

I ended up spending more money than I intended on the trailer and the tent for the church. The trailer was going to be my home and I needed basic comforts. It came with a small generator, propane tanks, and a small kitchen with a refrigerator. It would be delivered any day now.

The day after the trailer arrived, I arranged a work party to put the tent up. The church sign was posted close to the freeway, next to the store sign. The church was dedicated and the first Sunday services were held on June 12th. Afterwards, I invited the whole village over and hosted a nice barbecue lunch for them, complete with beer and wine. Two families who had stopped by the store joined the services and I invited them to stay for lunch. When they left, they insisted on donating something and dropped off $20 per family.

Services would be at the new church from now on and I would be living in my own trailer. This meant they would have to come over for Sunday services. Someone proposed that since the entire village was there on Sundays, why not have a barbecue lunch after services. It sounded like a good idea and it was eagerly agreed on. Why not?

The weather was getting hot and I was concerned how people would deal with the heat during the service. We got some welcome news.

We would get electricity connected in a matter of days. Both trailers would be hooked up. I could turn on the AC and survive inside the trailer.

I didn't have to worry about food. Whoever stayed at the trailer cooked for me too. There were five or six members who came to the store each day to help out or just hang around.

The arrival of electricity was a big event for all of us. It was particularly satisfying as we now had a positive outcome for our efforts. There is no better motivator than success. Doug came every day and Sarah came with him when she could. Doug was showing signs of being a little more assertive. I could sense he was proud of what they'd accomplished.

We met and talked often and whoever else was free would join in. It was remarkable how much Doug relied on her for support. It was intriguing how they could communicate with a look or a facial expression. For someone with little knowledge or experience in family dynamics, it was a revelation to witness the intricacies and intangibles of married life.

The store continued to improve in sales day by day. We all knew by the end of the first month that the store had beat out my guarantee. It was heartwarming to witness their excitement and growing sense of purpose. Each weekend there were more and more members coming back to visit.

The totem cross was almost ready and I had selected the spot where it would be planted. We made a little hill with rocks of various sizes and the totem cross was planted on top creating my little Calvary. It stood almost fifteen feet high and was visible for some distance. At the foot of the cross was a sign: St. John the Baptist Catholic mission; Mass and Services at 10:00 a.m. on Sundays. The church was ready, and the pavilion would provide protection against the sun for about a hundred people. There was the little altar and a canvas backdrop behind the altar for protection from the wind and dust.

All the villagers were present for Mass. Three families traveling together had stopped at the store and found there was a Mass scheduled. They decided to attend. First order of the day was the blessing of the totem cross. At my request, the villagers had donned their traditional attire. Following the blessing we moved in procession back to the church. I could see some of the cars on the highway slow down to look at the 'totem cross' and the odd procession before moving on. I hoped soon, some of them would stop to attend services. The villagers had brought blankets, which were spread on the floor of the church.

I had decided early on that this was a native mission and church services would definitely have a native flavor. Before the start of Mass, twelve members of the tribe performed the stomp dance to the accompaniment of drums and flute. It added an interesting twist to the ceremonies.

We had a nice barbecue lunch after Mass. The visitors were invited to stay for the free barbecue lunch and they did. We gladly accepted the $30 donation they gave. I handed it over to Doug in support of the barbecue.

Doug wanted to return $1000 as the total collections for June had exceeded the target, although not by much. I had other plans. I told him to use the money to invest in the icemaker and the cooler they wanted. They could repay me later. There were other pressing issues too. There was every reason to believe they could run out of merchandise to sell. If sales continued to pick up, there was no way they were going to make things fast enough to meet the demand. They should scout around and buy items from other reservations and re-sell them. They would have to invest more and more if the store was to remain successful.

It was very important for me that the Sunday services were well attended. Without fail, every member of the tribe who could come attended. I wanted more than that. I wanted non-native participation and repeated attendees. That would spell success for the mission. I placed a collection box, another one of Freddie's creations, at the entrance to the church. There would be no formal collections during the service; it would be voluntary.

One day I asked Doug if anyone could remember why the mission was built where it was. It was a protected spot but a church or a mission would not have been built so far off the trail or so far away from the native village without a reason. He mentioned hearing from his mother that the village was situated on the banks of the Little Bend River. The mission was built close to the village. Indeed, the natives had lived in the valley of the Little Bend for ages and that's how the tribe got its name: Paiutes of Little Bend. The Little Bend was more like a lake than a river, a small tributary of the Virgin River that ended here

Why had the river gone dry? In these canyon lands, it was conceivable for a river to change course, go deeper into the soil, and do all kinds of strange things. Such events usually happen over thousands of years. Cataclysmic events can of course impact things quite suddenly and drastically. But then, there would be some record of it. No one knew why the river had dried up or when. The demise of the Little Bend was a mystery. But, it had to be a fairly recent event because the mission was not that old. It looked strange that the river had dried up and the tribe that lived around it didn't know how or why.

Why hadn't the Paiutes taken to cultivating the land when water was available? Or had they? I hadn't seen any signs of cultivation around the village. Natives in general were not farmers. At various times during the tumultuous history of the native nations, the US Government had attempted to encourage them to take up agriculture. Most natives looked upon these attempts by the government with suspicion.

There is the story of a native tribe that was forced into a reservation with the promise of federal assistance to help them settle down. They were provided assistance and taught to farm the lands and raise cattle. In a strange twist of fate, the natives rose up to the challenge and became rather successful. They became good farmers and ranchers and achieved a high level of self-sufficiency. Unfortunately for them, the success proved to be a curse. As soon as the white settlers saw the thriving farms, they connived with unscrupulous and corrupt agents of the Bureau to drive them out of their lands and into other inhospitable reservations under some bogus treaty. The settlers became the new owners of the developed properties.

Well-known Christian groups were complicit in such dealings, and were often the beneficiaries directly or indirectly. I'm sure many a mansion and place of worship across the country sit atop such ill-gotten properties. Every time the poor natives were driven into further misery, many starved and died. Christian charity at its most benevolent best.

An unbiased observer looking back in time can easily recognize the strategy employed by the agents of the US government to swindle the native tribes. It was brilliant in its simplicity, really. By deceit, coercion or any means possible, get the natives to sign a treaty they couldn't read or understand. The agent would read aloud what was acceptable to the natives but the written word of the treaty would be altogether different. As soon as the treaty was signed, the terms of the treaty were enforced, with the help of the military, if needed.

Needless to say, the majority of the treaties involved the natives giving up their lands in return for something. In most cases, these treaties were illegal. The wording was intended to defraud and manipulate the unsuspecting natives, or they were coerced to sign under threat. No sooner than the ink had dried on the paper, the federal agents rushed in to occupy the lands ceded by the natives.

The 'something' that the natives were supposed to get in return never materialized. The treaty had to be approved by congress. Under the constitution, only congress could enter into treaties with native nations. That would take years. In most cases, congress would delay or never ratify the treaty. Congress could come up with all kinds of reasons for objecting to the terms of the treaty. While congress debated, the natives had lost their possessions. If congress finally passed the treaty, there was further threat of a presidential veto to complicate matters. In the end, the natives lost what they had to lose and got nothing in return. This cruel game was so successful that it became the government's strategy in dealing with natives. The shocking truth is, the practice continues even today in some form or another. It may be a little more sophisticated or subtle, but the strategy is the same.

Almost every administration in US history has made attempts at Native American Reform. It has been a circus. When you look at these attempts at reform, past or present, it's very difficult to accept the sincerity of the administrations. But nobody cared. Deceit against natives wasn't a crime.

The attempts were called reforms—but they were not. The native people were not in need of reform. They were doing just fine. They just needed to be left alone. How does one call these tactics reforms? When the reforms are enforced upon the natives against their will and when in every instance the natives are the losers, you don't call them reforms. When these actions drove the natives into further deprivation, famine and deteriorating populations, you don't call them reforms.

From what I had read, it was soon after World War II that the idea of assimilating the native people into mainstream American society gathered momentum. The idea had been tried before and failed. What was with another attempt? If it failed, who would suffer? The natives.

As America established itself as a superpower in world affairs, Washington think tanks started to believe that being American was a very desirable dream. If so, why should the nation allow the existence of sovereign native nations within the United States? Why should native nations be given the privilege of holding on to their sovereign status? Thus began the process of elimination of special status for natives and their integration into regular society. It was argued that these special privileges gave the natives a false sense of identity. If the special status were eliminated, by necessity, the natives would be forced to assimilate into American society. Doesn't everybody want to be American? Americanization of native people became the next big reform agenda.

In one of the saddest ironies for local tribes, a Utah senator sponsored the bill that sought to abolish special rights for Native Americans and integrate them. He wanted to show the world that he would set the example. He offered to eliminate the recognition of most Utah tribes. What a sacrifice. What a noble gesture. What did he have to lose?

The ill-fated integration policy was a dismal failure, leaving almost the entire native community destitute. With the enforced loss of status and deprived of whatever little protection they had, their fate was sealed. It was not merely the elimination of status that was initiated; it paved the way to the elimination of a race of people. Another experiment and another disaster for the natives. Who benefitted? Special interests. Native lands and assets were plundered. Why did the policy fail? Was the outcome predictable? No one had expected it to succeed in the first place. Was it a conspiracy?

Congress knew or should have known that the integration initiatives didn't have the least chance of success. History of such attempts all had headed in one direction, failure. Leaders who push for these reforms know that the public has a negative opinion of the natives. The media kept fueling the fire with their unfair characterizations. The natives were the enemy that needed to be subdued. There would be no sympathy, no tears shed over the demise of the native race.

Yes, America, whose shores beckoned with welcoming arms people from every part of the world had no place in her bosom to embrace the native sons and daughters, the original inhabitants of the land.

Native people were ill equipped to survive the onslaught of disintegration and they didn't. Finally, the government was forced to confront its blunder and reversed the integration policy. Congress reinstated recognition of native nations. Their numbers had severely declined in a very short time and their level of poverty was far worse than recent immigrants who had arrived here with nothing in their hands.

In another cruel twist of fate, Utah nations were left out of the reinstatement process. Further sacrifice or oversight by the Utah Senator.

It took another thirty years before Utah nations were reinstated. By then most of them had approached near extinction. Looking back on the sequence of events, I couldn't help but feel that this was nothing more than an ill-scripted conspiracy to steal what the natives had and leave them destitute. When all was said and done and sovereignty restored, most nations had lost lands that had been held in reserve for them. The Paiutes of Little Bend was a small example of the irrevocable harm done to the natives. Here, the tragedy continued because they were not recognized and had no reservation to lay claim to. They were irresponsibly thrown into the mix with the Cedar City band, thus destroying their identity and chance of survival.

I surprised myself how cynical I was starting to become when it came to the treatment of native people by the US Government and her agents. I guess one has to live among them to comprehend the extent of abuse they've suffered and continue to suffer. Yet, when you live among them, you recognize how noble a race of people they are. It was not surprising that as days went by, I started questioning whether the Little Bend River went dry by natural causes.

The Little Bend was not like most tributaries of large rivers that originate somewhere and flow into the dominant river. Here, the Virgin River fed and supported its small tributary. The Little Bend ended here in the valley, forming a lake. The Virgin River was alive and well and was going strong. How did the Little Bend then dry up?

One day I asked Doug why they had not tried to find out what happened to the Little Bend. Characteristically, he showed little enthusiasm. He had come to accept the reality that the Little Bend had dried up. What else was there to investigate?

After some coaxing, probably to please me, he offered to take me to visit one of their oldest living relatives. This lady, he told me, had moved in with the Koosharem Band when her only daughter had married someone from that band and they both went to live with the husband.

It was impossible to gauge the age or sex from looking at the individual we met. She was so wrinkled up and bent over; she seemed to move on all fours. She was over ninety, they said, but could have been well over a hundred as far as anyone knew. She was astonishingly sprightly, but a little fuzzy in her speech and vision. When she smiled a welcome, there was not a single tooth visible. We had been warned she liked her Jack Daniels straight. That and some chewing tobacco could get her going. We came prepared. She spoke the native dialect but managed to mess it up with a few choice English words used out of context. Doug had to translate—or tried as best as he could—until he finally gave up and promised to summarize it for me later.

A couple of generous swigs from the bottle and having stashed half-a-can of tobacco into some remote recesses of her mouth, she was ready to roll. I watched Doug, usually a very stoic individual, look exasperated as he tried in vain to keep her focused on what we wanted to know. He gave up after a few feeble attempts to rein her in, and with a resigned expression, sat and listened. It ended suddenly when she fell asleep right in the middle of a sentence without any warning. We were at a loss what to do. The old lady's great grandniece who was present, motioned to us it was over for the day. We had no choice but to leave.

On the way back, I drove and let Doug digest what he'd heard and put the story into plain English. What had taken two hours of storytelling was whittled down to about five minutes of relevant material. There indeed had been a thriving Paiute colony on the banks of the Little Bend River. They cultivated corn, alfalfa, and sundry vegetables for their daily use. They also kept a herd of cattle. Then one summer the river just choked and stopped flowing in. A few years later, the water was gone.

There had been recent incidents of trouble. White settlers had repeatedly raided the native village, destroying crops, shooting cattle, and setting fire to teepees. The harassment continued for several months during which time they lived in a lot of fear. Some white folks wanted to buy the entire valley and convert it into a cattle ranch. The Paiutes refused. There were rumors that some religious sect was after the Bend Valley to establish a commune. They claimed they had bought the land from the Big Father. They brought all kinds of papers to prove they were the new owners. They offered to move them to a new settlement at the outskirts of the town of Joseph. The Paiutes had had enough of these forced relocations and decided to stay and perish rather than move and perish. They would lose everything, anyway, and why not stay and lose it with a show of defiance? The attacks ended, but soon the river started to dry up.

Within a few years the Little Bend was totally dry. Without the water, the farms disappeared, the cattle were sold, and little-by-little the encroaching desert laid claim to what had once been a fertile valley.

What the white settlers couldn't grab by force, the desert was only too happy to devour without a fight. It was a reservation all right, but like many other reservations, it became inhospitable. The benign spring they found in the hills allowed them to remain and eke out a threadbare existence.

How did the river dry up so quickly and in such a dramatic fashion? I suspected foul play. It was becoming a habit now. The timing and the sequence of events as explained had me wondering that human hands were behind the death of the river. I vowed to get some answers and find out what really happened. There had to be some records somewhere. A river, even a small one, does not just disappear without any mention of it in some documents. I voiced my concerns to Doug on the drive back. Here we go again.

A few days later when Doug and Sarah came to visit, I brought up the river issue. Doug was non-committal. He even looked a little uneasy I had brought it up again. Before he could say anything, Sarah jumped in as I had hoped she would. Sure enough, she was all for finding out the truth. Doug offered a feeble protest. Sarah silenced him with one of her patented looks, and Doug was willing to support the investigation, albeit as willingly as a lamb being led to slaughter.

Our first order of business was to follow the river upstream to the point it ended. Doug and I set out in his pickup truck along the southern rim of the empty ravine. As we drove along, I looked around to see if there were any remnants of past human habitation to authenticate the storyteller's tale about the colony. There was nothing and I started to doubt if it was anything but a story. The desert was dry as a bone as far as I could see except for the occasional thorny bush.

"Father Tosco, you must be working on a theory about what happened to the river. Can you share it with me?"

"Sure. Any number of things could have happened. The more I think about it, the more I tend to believe something sinister took place to change the fate of the river. Cause and effect, if you will. The death of the river altered the fate of the native people living here. If someone wanted to punish the natives, what better way to do it?"

"Even if something sinister happened, what can we do about it now?"

"We can only answer the question after we find out what happened."

"You must have a plan you are working on. You want to get the river restored, is that it?"

"Let's say it is, wouldn't that be great?"

"Of course. It would mean everything for us. I can't even imagine how great life would be if the Little Bend is alive and well."

"If it can be a life-changing event for you, is it not worth fighting for?"

"It is, no doubt. However, the obstacles are insurmountable."

"I won't kid you; they are. Remember what we talked about a few weeks ago. For a people who have been beaten down by fate and everyone else, failures are expected, even anticipated. That mindset must change. We must look for small successes, every little success is part of a big victory."

"I wish I could share your optimism. I am sorry if I sound cautious. I am that way. If it were Sarah, it would be a different matter. She would dive in with both feet up."

"That's all right to be cautious as long as you don't stop trying."

"You won't let me. She won't let me."

"A river won't suddenly die unless something catastrophic happened to it."

"It's not impossible. The river may have changed course. Canyon walls may have collapsed."

"That's what we are trying to find out. It's a short river. It shouldn't take us too long to find out what happened."

"Let's say there was foul play. What can you do about it? Who was responsible? Can the responsible party be brought to justice? Whose responsibility is it to restore it?"

"I have no idea what we can do about it."

"Aren't we wasting our time then?"

"Let's take it one step at a time. There's nothing we can do until we know what happened. Then we search for solutions."

"How likely is it that we will get to the bottom of the story, if there is one?"

"You never know until you start digging. Even if we don't find the cause, we can find out if what nature or human hands did can be undone."

"The Little Bend back to its old glory. That would be a dream come true!"

"We can't dream until we know the facts. Nothing may come of it. I don't think people are going to line up to restore the river even if it's possible."

"Father Tosco, pardon my saying so, I think you are crazy."

"You're right. Often, I believe crazy ideas seek me out with a vengeance."

"We call it fate or destiny, when things of this nature happen. The supreme power ordains how each of us must live our lives on this earth. My fate, like that of my tribe is to wait for things to happen and then react to them. You on the other hand are forced to seek out and make things happen. You don't accept the hand of fate."

"I don't know for sure what fate has in store for me. That's my problem."

"I think that's the curse of the white man. You can never sit still. You're never satisfied. You don't let nature take its course. You want to set the course."

"The one thing that bothers me most is injustice, by humans on humans. I came into contact with native people by accident and it was a defining moment in my life. As you say, fate brought me here for a reason. I had the good fortune to be accepted and live among you as one of you. Fate has a purpose for me. I can't walk away from it. It's my destiny."

"We natives are like the Neanderthals, an understudy and expendable in the process of evolution of the white man's race. Our lifestyle, our beliefs, our social institutions and our values, can't survive in a world where the white man's policies reign supreme."

"In this country we abide by certain fundamental principles, a belief that all humans are created equal and that the rule of law applies to all citizens equally. That applies to native people as well as non-native people. The native people of this land must not be sidelined to accommodate the advance of the white man."

"Isn't that what's happening to indigenous people all over the world?"

"That does not make it right. What is not right can be and should be corrected or at least challenged. If not, it becomes a policy by default. We can't change past history. But we can set it straight for the future."

"I am afraid it's too late."

"Not so! Look at all the people who support human rights! They risk life and fortune for what is right. There are good-hearted and principled people out there. If animals, plants and insects are worth preserving from extinction, are not whole masses of indigenous people deserving of protection?"

"Our ancestors taught us that the Great Spirit ordains the fate of each of us. If it's our fate to succumb and perish, then that's by his will."

"I have one problem with that. We have no way of knowing what that destiny is until it happens. Getting into an accident may be in your destiny. Getting treatment to survive is your choice. If you refuse treatment and you die, you can't call that fate."

"Father Tosco, you do not understand. We have lost the will to fight."

"There is nothing like a little success to rekindle the will."

We came to where the hills curled around in front of us from our right to the left. The riverbed ran right through the heart of the hill. Driving further was not possible. We got out of the truck and walked to the edge of the canyon. It was not too deep at this point; no more than a ten-foot drop. From where we stood, we could see where the river had flowed out of the hill in a gentle slope into the valley. There was a dark tunnel extending into the hill. We dared not go in but couldn't see any obstruction. With some persuasion, Doug agreed to climb to the top of the hill for a look on the other side.

We climbed until we reached a point near the top from where we could see for quite a ways on the other side. To the east we could see green pastures and farmlands extending far and wide. Far-and-away to the south, I could see glints of lights from a large body of water. The hill we were standing on was part of a large range, snaking its way in a southwesterly direction.

The contrast was not lost on me. Before us lay a large and fertile valley, dotted with large ranches surely owned by white settlers—

whereas the arid lands behind me were part of the Paiute reservation.

I was surprised to see no trace of the Little Bend on this side. Where was the river? To our left, we could see an outcrop of rocks and directly below should be where the river tunneled its way through. Looking closely we saw the landslide where the hillside had collapsed. It was not obvious at first sight. The landslide was so massive it had formed a small hill of its own, and over time nature had refurbished the whole area with an overgrowth of shrubs. Once you visualized the landslide, it was easy to trace the contours of the slide. The landslide must have completely blocked the entrance to the tunnel and choked off the river from passing through. So where was the river on this side and where did all the water go? There was no river and no dry riverbed visible anywhere. I was puzzled. I wondered if this was an underground river that emerged from inside these hills. That was not possible. When the hill collapsed impeding the flow of water, it would have found a way out somewhere.

After careful scrutiny, we could see signs of what had once been a river, the dry bed hugging the sides of the hills. Through millennia, it had burrowed its way deeper into the hillside making it almost invisible. Trees and shrubs had grown all around further hiding it from view. But it was dry. The mystery was deepening. The collapsed hillside had not cut off the river. The river was obstructed further up. I looked out toward the glittering lake in the distance. Did it have something to do with the dried up river? Did the Little Bend originate out of the lake?

Could the hillside have collapsed due to natural causes? Of course, it could. Landslides were not uncommon in these canyon lands. All anyone had to do was drive toward Moab. One could feast one's eyes on breathtaking canyons, intricate designs carved by nature, and awesome arches suspended precariously and held up by unknown forces. Numerous collapsed structures and landslides were all over, some small and some really large. Could human hands have caused the landslide? All it would have taken were a few sticks of dynamite.

"What do we do now? Did you get the answers you were looking for?"

"Not all of them but I definitely have a few more questions. We must find the spot where the river was cut off."

"Today?"

"Good idea. Let's go."

"That's not exactly what I meant."

"Are you tied up with something? We can do it later."

"Let's go."

"Are you sure?"

"It'll be done so why not now?"

"They have done a pretty good job here."

"The lake looks beautiful."

"I want to see the other end of the lake."

"We will have to walk. No vehicles are allowed on the levees."

"We both can do with the exercise."

"Sure. Of course."

It was easy to understand what had been done. There was a rocky ridge forming a steep wall along the Northern bank of the Virgin River. The Little Bend originated from a depression in the rock formation allowing water from the Virgin to flow over and down an embankment. It wasn't a very large depression. Water to the Little Bend would be cut off when the water retreated below the depression in the parent river. In times past, the water would have flowed over and down, traveling north until it reached the hills. After meandering along the side of the hill, once it found the tunnel, it had burrowed through and flowed to the other side into the Little Bend valley. That flow of water had been interrupted to create the lake. Traps had been built along the Virgin River to control the flow of water.

It wasn't a natural lake and not very large, but it looked pretty deep. A dam visible from where we stood blocked off the far end. The sides of the lake were fortified with an impressive levee with a wide trail, and trees planted on both sides of the trail. It was evident the dam was built to create the lake. I looked out over the lake. On a beautiful day as today, I would have expected a few boats out there with people fishing, or just enjoying themselves. There was no one on or around the lake, except us.

It was a nice looking dam, like a miniature Hoover Dam. The trail went over the dam and around. Standing in the middle, we could see where the river had tumbled down almost twenty or thirty feet, and then had disappeared through a narrow gorge. Large volcanic boulders lay strewn all along the path of the Little Bend. Once the waters had negotiated the gorge, it took a direct and northerly path toward the hills. The sides were overgrown with trees and some seemed to grow from within the wide and shallow riverbed. If you looked from afar, there didn't appear to be a riverbed at all, but a line of trees. No wonder we had trouble locating it from the top of the hill. The traps and the dam must have been built when the hillside collapsed to control the flooding that must have followed.

"What happened to the conspiracy theory, Father Tosco?"

"Conspiracy or not, nobody bothered to take into account what happened to the natives living in the valley beyond."

"True. But would they have known?"

"I wonder what your people thought happened to the Little Bend when water started receding."

"They may have been surprised. But, rivers do recede and flood over the course of time. When the river started receding, people would have anticipated the end. They probably had no idea what happened or what to do about it. Like us, they too must have accepted what was."

"Let me work on my conspiracy theory a little more. Assume someone or some group was behind this. What would they have expected when the river was gone? What did they want?"

"Normally, our people would pack up and leave to find another, more hospitable location and rebuild."

"Or sell it to whoever was crazy enough to buy a wasteland."

"Possible."

"At a bargain price."

"Or none."

"In one knockout punch, the individual or group achieves total victory. The natives are punished and flushed out. They lay claim for the land with a cooperating Bureau of Native American Affairs. All that remained would be to remove the landslide and restore the river. Everything gets back to normal. It may take a few years but the prize was more than worth the wait, don't you think?"

"When you put it that way, certainly."

"There was one little glitch. Your people were too stubborn to leave, even after the river dried up. Eventually a dam was built to create the lake. Traps were put in place on the Virgin River. End of story."

"I can see how that scenario could have played out."

"Don't you think it's time to do something about it?"

"Like what? After all these years."

"Get the river restored."

"Who would do it? Nobody living is responsible, even if the story is true."

"The State of Utah."

"The State won't."

"There must be a way."

"Why would anyone want to reverse what happened a long time ago?"

"Because what happened a long time ago was wrong and threatens the livelihood of a group of people who have nowhere else to go."

"Many an injustice has been done to native people. Does anyone care? Can we go back in time and correct them now?"

"Not all of them. But, what can be must be. Here is a specific injustice that can be rectified without hurting anyone."

"There is no river now and I don't think we'll get it restored."

"Removing the landslide would be difficult but not impossible. Restoring the Little Bend would also be difficult but not impossible. Release water through the lake during winter months when the Virgin River is flowing at full capacity. In a few years, the Little Bend will be fully restored. The lake remains intact."

"You make it sound simple. But it won't happen as long as it's for us."

"Doug, think of what a restored Little Bend would mean to your people."

"It would be awesome. We can raise cattle; we can farm the land. We can go back to our way of life, like we want to. We can do all kinds of things."

"That's what this is all about. This is not about global solutions to world's problems. This is about the life and future of a small band of native people. This is about fairness. This is about the rule of law. This is about standing up and challenging those who have denied you your rights. This is about human rights."

"I didn't mean to get you all worked up. Yes. I see the injustice but what can we do. I feel inadequate."

"I am here today and tomorrow I may be reassigned elsewhere. This is not about me. It's about you and the future of your people."

"I want to do what's right. It's just not my style to confront and fight."

"Make that two of us. Yet it must be done when the need arises."

"Father Tosco, do not misinterpret my lack of enthusiasm for lack of desire. When I think of the struggles it'll take I am overwhelmed by it all."

"It's only natural to feel that way. There is a saying that a cat that has been scalded by boiling water is afraid of any water."

"That's exactly how I feel."

"But you have not been scalded. There's no need to be afraid."

"I know you have already thought about the next step. What is it?"

"We approach the State to demand restoration of the river."

"Sounds so simple."

"It's not. To learn to drive, you must first get behind the wheel. To get anywhere you start somewhere."

We took turns narrating what we had found. I watched with some level of fascination as Doug discussed animatedly the tragic end of the Little Bend. He wanted to restore the river. I had hoped for the transformation. It had to be Sarah. Doug must have recounted the day's events to Sarah as soon as we returned. He must have also expressed his reticence at doing anything to get the river restored. It was then time for Sarah to work her magic. Quietly and skillfully, she must have turned him around and his doubts and hesitation became clear action plans.

"We can sit around and curse our fate or we can do what we can to get the Little Bend restored."

"We should be focusing energy on the store and not waste time on this."

"The store is proof it's not a waste of time trying to get our river back."

"It's not the same. We didn't need outside support to get the store going. We need help to get the river flowing."

"What's the worst that can happen? That we don't succeed. What would we have lost? Time and effort."

"We have plenty of both. The goal is worth the effort!"

"We must get the Little Bend restored. It can be done!"

"If the Little Bend is restored, it will ensure our future."

"Father Tosco, where do we start?"

"With our local congressman and the senator."

"They won't help. We know that."

"They don't need us and they don't care!"

"We must do it because it's the right thing to do! We will force them to do something!"

"We are too small and powerless."

"Have you seen how the little blackbirds protect their nests from large predatory rooks? They gang up and attack until the rook is driven to distraction and decides it's not worth the trouble. We will have to be pretty pesky too until they get tired of us and do something about it."

"Restoration of the river, recognition of the tribe and reservation of these lands for us. That's what we want."

The store was improving steadily. It was an energizing factor for the whole village. Everyone had taken ownership of it. Those who lived and worked away from the village visited frequently. They'd hang around the store and help with things. On Sundays they came early to clean up the church before the start of services. Afterwards, they sat around and talked and talked. Sunday afternoons were set aside for relaxation and fun. Visitors to the church or no visitors, they made sure they had a party. Who could blame them? They deserved it.

Sundays were special. It became the busiest day of the week. The store saw the highest number of customers. During services, it became a crowded place for a few hours. The stomp dance became part of the routine before Mass. It started by accident but there was so much interest generated that I incorporated it into Sunday services. Visitors were thrilled. It became a form of advertisement. So what!

After Mass there was the barbecue lunch, which was a smash hit on its own. It was a moneymaker too. People attending Sunday services were mostly travelers coming from far off places. There were no restaurants, not even fast food places, within twenty, thirty miles of the mission. The barbecue lunch was offered free of charge to Mass attendees. Visitors were welcome to contribute something. And most did. People contributed willingly and generously. It is common practice at most churches to offer free coffee and donuts after Sunday services. We offered free barbecue.

The strategy proved to be sound. It became so successful that soon we added to the sign:

ST. JOHN THE BAPTIST CATHOLIC MISSION
MASS ON SUNDAYS AT 10:00 A.M.
FREE BARBECUE LUNCH

The church was the only place where people could find some shade to stand around and eat. As soon as services were done, the church became an open-air restaurant.

We were learning the fundamentals of market economy. The concept of 'free' brings in customers. If some people were attracted to the services because of the free lunch, it was fine with me. The more the people attending, the greater the opportunity to spread the good news. The more the people attending services, the greater the success of the mission. Even Jesus fed the people for free. Being who he was, he could work a miracle to do that. He could make water into wine, and feed thousands with a few loaves of bread. I couldn't. I had to be sure we had enough voluntary contributions to justify the free lunch. We tracked the collections and it confirmed the theory that we made more by not charging a specific amount.

As weeks passed, we realized how successful the Sunday program was. I didn't want the mission to become part of a commercial enterprise but right now, it was impossible to separate the mission from the store. I knew there would be closer scrutiny from the diocese as the mission became successful. Although most members of the tribe attended the Sunday service, I was yet to baptize and 'convert' anyone. That didn't bother me, but I knew it would raise concerns with the diocese.

By 4:00 p.m. on most Sundays, the customers would thin out. They would close the store, put up a "Closed" sign at the entrance, and then relax under the tent. I had bought a couple of large floor fans which gave some relief from the heat. They would have a couple of beers and talk.

Doug and Sarah would come over and spend some time with me before leaving for the village. It was our private time. It had a purpose for Doug. He used these conversations to sound off ideas and pick my brain on issues that bothered him. It helped clarify issues in the presence of two people he trusted most so that he could more effectively communicate them to other members. Sarah sat quietly at his side, providing eye contact when he sought her opinion. She would talk and argue when needed. It was marvelous to observe the synergy between the two. She could almost enter his thought process subliminally.

"Sarah, I tell you, we should start saving up for the winter months. We need to put away some money."

"Doug, I agree, we need to start saving. But, we need to allow people to enjoy this time of prosperity. We are not getting carried away. We must experience some plenty to want to maintain it. We have never had any fun before. Let's enjoy this moment before tightening our belts."

"I am not saying we shouldn't have any fun. I don't want the fun to end. If we start saving a little bit at a time, we won't have to sour the spirit of excitement while learning the importance of saving. We must open a bank account. We must start keeping proper accounts. We must run this as a business."

"Doug has a point. Store sales will decrease as seasons change. I am hoping attendance at Sunday services will remain strong even in winter. That will ensure we have a somewhat predictable income year round. That will also bring people to the store."

"Father Tosco, I think it's time we separate funds generated by the church from the store income."

"Why? The mission needs no income. The voluntary contributions are for you."

"That's not right. The mission needs money to make improvements. I am sure if all goes well, you'll want to build a real church."

"Bishop Scanlon's goal when he established the mission was to help improve the welfare of this native community. That's what I am doing. There's a lot more to be done."

"We need the mission. We won't allow the mission to fail. We will become Catholics if we have to, to protect the mission."

"That would not be the right reason to become a Catholic. That would be a matter of convenience. Conversion comes from God. When the call comes, you will respond."

He showed up one evening at my trailer and introduced himself as Malcolm Donahue from the Utah Herald. He was a freelance writer and had a weekly column with topics ranging from politics to religion and everything in between. He was currently doing a series on native tribes in Utah and had observed the birth and rise of the little colony here. He had been intrigued about the church and what it was doing here. I had a natural aversion for reporters and the media ever since my experience at St. Bonaventure's. My defenses were up instantly. He was white.

"Father Tosco, I hope you can spare a little time for me. I can come back at a more suitable time, if now is not a good time. I want to ask you a few questions about this native tribe."

"Is this an interview?"

"If you agree. I am hoping you can provide me some information for my project on Native Americans, particularly this tribe."

"I am neither an expert on the subject nor a spokesperson for this tribe. I wouldn't want to be quoted about native people. They can help you with whatever information you need."

"They won't talk to me. I tried."

"They fear media attention. They're convinced it'll hurt them. They trust reporters no better than the cops."

"I'm not surprised. A lot of people look at us as the scum that feed on people's miseries. It's true sometimes. There are reporters who try to grab attention any which way they can by creating controversies and conflicts. Sleaze sells. I am not one of them."

"What makes you different?"

"I am after serious stuff, not some sensational stories. I am doing a series on Native Americans and I'm biased toward native people. I am hoping I will be able to help native people by telling the real story."

"Malcolm, you must respect their fear of media. Media's controlled by white people. They don't expect the media to be fair to them. They have been victimized so often they don't trust you."

"But they trust you."

"I hope they do. It was not easy and being a priest may have helped. They sent you to me. But I know they expect me to send you on your way."

"That's too bad. I think there's a story here and it's a story worth telling. It's long overdue. The American public should understand the true predicament of our native people."

"Malcolm, tell you what. Why don't you come for Sunday services? It's open for all. You'll get to meet and observe the people. They are at their most relaxed on Sundays. They host a wonderful barbecue. Maybe once they get used to you, they will be open to talk to you."

"I am not a Catholic."

"They are not either."

"Why do you have a Catholic Church on a native reservation?"

"Hold. Hold. Just like that, this is turning into an interview."

"Sorry. It's involuntary."

"Come for Sunday services, and hang around afterwards. You will learn a lot more by observing than asking questions."

"I will. I don't give up easy, not once I put my mind to something."

Doug and a couple of guys came over to my trailer a little later for a chat.

"What did the newspaper guy want?"

"He's a reporter and wants to write about your tribe as part of a series on native people of Utah."

"I don't like reporters."

"Me either."

"As he was leaving he said, 'See you on Sunday'. Is he coming back?"

"If he's serious he will. Who knows? If he's sincere and interested in the truth, we could use him to our benefit."

"How do we know he'll tell the truth?"

"We don't—that's the dilemma. Only time will tell."

"I know you are apprehensive. I know you prefer to remain anonymous and unknown. I respect that. But, I want you to know my project is a serious look at the plight of Native Americans today. Native Americans today are facing far worse conditions than ever in their history. The indifference shown to native people by the US government is unacceptable. We fight to change the world and make it a better place but won't raise a finger to save native people."

"Why are you different? We don't know your true motives."

"I'll let my actions prove who and what I am. I've brought samples of what I have done so far. You are not the first native tribe I have worked with."

"In other words, you will write about us with or without our cooperation, right?"

"Yes. The presence of a mission and the beginnings of a business make your story different. It may be a small story, but still different."

"If you print misinformation it will hurt us."

"I tell the truth and if truth hurts, so be it."

"Why not go after larger nations? They would welcome your attention."

"They don't represent the average Native American struggling to survive."

"What do you want from us?"

"I want to have the freedom to visit and be around you as much as possible. I want to have your permission to meet and talk freely with anyone willing to do so."

"What do you have to say that's different?"

"We are all biased one way or another by what we see and hear as we grow up. Most people know about native people from movies, books and comics. I want readers to have a fair evaluation and appreciation of the original inhabitants of this land. I want to write about how you live and survive today."

"The very people that plundered our lands and destroyed our culture are the same people to whom you are telling our story. Why would they listen to you? Do you think they'll change their minds?"

"There are fair-minded people who want to know the truth. Will I make a difference? Will attitudes change? I don't know. I really don't know!"

"We know it won't. I feel you are wasting your time."

"It's not true. Look at Father Tosco. He believed. He has become a passionate supporter. I am sure he has helped you immensely."

"If it were not for him, we would still be living on the hillside."

"He gave you hope and a vision. You are doing the rest. All it needed was a little spark. Even one person can make a change."

"There are not many Father Tosco's."

"True. That's what makes your case fascinating. If my article hits the right nerve with one or more Father Tosco's, just imagine the difference it'll make. We're not talking about your tribe alone. There are numerous other tribes just like you that need help. Your story will be an inspiration to them. It's important for other tribes to know what you are doing. Father Tosco, how long will you be here?"

"I can't tell. If and when the diocese reassigns me, I'll leave."

"What happens then?"

"If I leave, the chances are, the mission will be closed. The diocese has little interest in this mission."

"The mission may close but this nation must prosper."

"They have shown they can and they will."

"That's why I want to write about this nation. They have found the means to survive. Why did you decide to come here? What is in this for you, Father Tosco?"

"That's a long story and I don't understand it myself. It's God's will."

"Most readers are non-natives. Most if not all, have had very little or no interaction with native people. I must piqué their interest. If I can capture your passion, I can make the reader see what you see and feel what you feel. That is my role. It's your decision."

The Paiutes needed Malcolm. I needed him. He was using me to connect with the natives. I could use him too. Instinct told me that the VG was going to lose interest in the mission sometime soon unless it served to enhance his image. I wanted to keep the mission open. The one strategy that would keep it open was to make it succeed beyond all expectations. That's where Malcolm had a role to play. Certainly, his interest was with the Paiutes and he was going to write their story. But, their story would include the mission smack in the middle of it. The mission would figure prominently in any news of the tribe. The mission would be depicted as the miracle of the Little Bend Valley. As long as the role of the mission was positive, the diocese could take credit. That would force them to keep it open. Malcolm was an unexpected, but welcome, ally.

Doug remained skeptical. Again it was Sarah who in her unique way spoke to him with gentle persuasion and the magic worked. What she said made a lot of sense. Malcolm was offering free advertising for the tribe. Indirectly the store would get free publicity. Intuitively, she had seen the potential benefits of controlled exposure as a marketing tool.

"The Lord's Prayer is a prayer for all people, of all religions, anytime in history. It's a prayer for anyone who believes in God, who looks up to him as the Great Father, the Creator, and the Supreme Being. It's so simple a prayer, even a small child can understand it and repeat it. It needs no interpretation. Jesus taught it to simple and uneducated people.

We are all children of the same Father and he's a father to all. That makes us all brothers and sisters. No color, race, nationality, religion or way of life can differentiate us before the Father.

The Father provides for the children and the children trust in him. A child before a father is confident, affectionate and respectful. That's the fundamental relationship of love. We must love God and equally we must love our neighbor. In other words, love of God is measured by our love for our neighbor.

With love comes respect. Love without respect is a hollow

sentiment. Love is the glue that binds us to God and it must be demonstrated by our love for our neighbor. God so loved the human race that he sent his son, Jesus, as a sacrifice to redeem us. Jesus said: 'Go; love one another as I have loved you.' Jesus makes it clear that to be worthy of his love, we must love our neighbor.

We can loudly proclaim our love for God. It's easy. We do not see and feel God's physical presence. Loving another human is not that easy, especially, when that human is different from us in many ways and whose presence before us may not be pleasing to us.

There's one commandment we must obey: 'Love your neighbor as yourself.' There's one prayer we need, the prayer Jesus taught us, the universal prayer, the Lord's Prayer."

"Here's a quick update on the mission. It's good news by the way."

"A success story. That's what we need. I hate to start with the dismal details of our cathedral."

"Monsignor, give us the good news about the mission."

"I can state unequivocally that the mission is a success."

"In such a short time. That's remarkable."

"Father Tosco has done some great things. He has helped the tribe achieve financial success. The mission is doing well and he has a good following."

"Last Sunday I was taking some friends down to Grand Canyon and we stopped to make a restroom break at a little store where 15 meets 17. It's one of those native stores selling carvings, blankets, baskets, and other trinkets. Next to the store I saw this odd-looking cross on a totem pole, and further back a large tent. I realized then it was our mission, Church of St. John the Baptist. Mass was about to start and so we stayed. The place was full. Mass was followed by a free barbecue lunch."

"How can they offer free lunch?"

"People contribute. We did too. It was worth it."

"The collections must be pretty good."

"There was no collection."

"Why? How can that be?"

"I don't know why. There was no collection taken."

"Did you meet Father Tosco?"

"No. There was no time."

"Who would have thought it would succeed like this?"

"He has turned this mission around in a way none of us anticipated."

"People travel in the winter too. If we provide them what they need in the winter, it'll allow us to keep the store open throughout the year."

"People may not buy soda in winter but they will buy coffee."

"People buy cigarettes all the time."

"We can sell snow chains."

"We can install them too."

"We can change tires and sell tires."

"We can sell engine oil and auto accessories."

"We must become a convenience stop for travelers."

"We should consider opening a gas station. There's none within thirty miles."

"We have enough people to do these things."

"Doing business from a tent won't work during winter."

"We need a permanent structure for the store."

"It'll take time and we need lots of money to build a store."

"What if we build a log cabin store?"

"We can harvest timber from the hills."

"We don't have to pay for labor."

"We know how to build with wood."

"It shouldn't take long to build the store."

"We can actually build around the tent and not interrupt sales."

"It doesn't have to look beautiful."

Doug had stayed back. Sarah had left early to the village

"Life is strange. We get cast into roles we don' expect. We get pushed around like a log in floodwaters. Even as you toss and turn, you must focus on going forward. It scares me. I don't know if I'm feeling any more confident now than when we started."

"When self-doubt creeps into your mind, remember, there is a community of people who are backing you up. Be aware of your shortcomings but focus on your strengths. Sarah loves you and is totally dedicated to you. You have qualities she and others respect."

"You always make it sound simple. That's a skill you have I wish I had."

"You have skills but you don't recognize many of them."

"I wish I could handle conflicts and confrontations calmly. So far there have been no serious conflicts. There will be in the future. I don't know how I will handle them."

"Oftentimes, conflicts define the leader. In time, you learn to anticipate conflicts and try to dissolve them before they can rear their ugly heads. Dealing with young people always poses a challenge. They bring to the table intensity and passion, and they tend to be impetuous and over-react. You must channel their energy in the right direction."

"Our lives are changing, and there's no turning back. While trying to reclaim our traditional way of life, we seem to be giving birth to a new way of life?"

"You are adapting to the new world order, that's all. When you seek to preserve your way of life, it does not mean you get stuck to the ways of the past."

"Father Tosco, I want to take you into confidence. It's been bothering me for some time. You must not talk about it to anyone, not even Sarah."

"Not even Sarah. That important? Okay."

"Do you believe in dreams?"

"Yes. I believe dreams are relevant."

"You are a Catholic priest. You don't take dreams seriously, do you?"

"Take any religion and there are numerous references to dreams or visions or revelations. The Bible recounts the dreams of Joseph in Egypt, Jacob's ladder, the angel visiting Mary in a dream, the angel visiting

Joseph in a dream, the apocalyptic writings of St. John."

"I've been having this dream for over a year now. It's the same identical dream over and over again. It happens at least once or twice a month."

"Most dreams are forgotten before we wake up. Are you able to recall the details? Do you recall the people, the colors, and the landscape?"

"I can describe my dream in detail. I have seen it so many times."

"What's the dream? Tell me about it."

"I see a fast-flowing river, and I am standing on the bank looking toward the setting sun. On the other side, I see trees and fields of rich, golden corn. My side of the river is totally barren, sand dunes stretching as far as I can see. There are no sounds. The sun is slowly setting. Above me it's dark and foreboding as black clouds billow across the sky. As I watch, I see on the opposite bank a big buffalo standing on a bluff overlooking the river. He is old, but the majesty of his silhouette is unmistakable, framed against the crimson rays of the sun peeping through the clouds. He stands there motionless, looking at me for a long time. Then as the sun starts to descend, he slowly turns and walks toward the setting sun. I stand rooted to the spot unable to move. The sun drops below the horizon. The buffalo disappears; there is total darkness. I wake up bathed in sweat, with unease and apprehension."

"Dreams are considered important among your people, aren't they?"

"They are. It's part of our beliefs and religion."

"Don't you have shamans among you who can interpret dreams? Why don't you go see one and find out what it's all about?"

"The only person within our tribe who could be called a shaman is Sarah. I have been reluctant to approach her or anyone else. I want to find the meaning of the dream and at the same time, I fear what it may imply."

"I am sorry, Doug. I can't think of an explanation. I think you need to go to someone who is knowledgeable about native symbols and their meanings."

"It's okay. I had to tell someone. Now that I have talked about it, it's like a load off my mind. Thanks for listening."

Doug went into a reverie, which lasted almost until we reached the city. I was used to these periodic bouts of silence and let him be. I was driving. His face revealed no emotion. He had assumed the classic posture, his face frozen into an expressionless pose that revealed nothing. It reminded me of the awesome sculptures hewn into the canyon walls all over this vast landscape by the hand of nature. It was almost like he had dropped a mask over his face and now the whole world was shut out. But I knew he was anxious. He was a reluctant inductee into the world of activism. Unassuming by nature, he was forced into a role he was not comfortable with, even though it was for the good of his people. When the level of discomfort reached a critical point, the mask was lowered, blocking all.

We had no appointment, which meant we had to wait in the lobby. Finally, the Senator's Secretary for Community Affairs came out to meet us and led us to a conference room. He was a nice young man with a cherubic face and a twinkle of a smile that seemed to come and go with no particular rhythm. He listened intently to the story of the native band. Doug did the talking as had been agreed upon earlier. He was a man of few words and his presentation didn't last long. I watched the young man's face closely while Doug was talking. He was in his late twenties or early thirties and it wasn't easy to get a read whether he was well versed in the complexities of native nations and their history. He seemed genuinely interested.

He told us the senator was on a fundraising trip to California and would be flying back the next day. He would be spending the rest of the week in Utah, but he had back-to-back commitments. He said he was keen on setting up an appointment for us but the calendar for the next several months was full.

He spent a good deal of time poring over the calendar. I wondered why. He picked up the phone and made a few calls. Then he came up with a small ray of hope. The senator was scheduled to participate in a charity golf tournament in St. George on Saturday, tee off time 9:00 a.m.; inaugurate a community center at 12:30 p.m. in Cedar City before driving back to Salt Lake City. It was possible, just might be possible to stop by at the reservation around 2:00 or 3:00 p.m. Perhaps he could squeeze in a half-hour stopover. Of course, he had to confirm this with the senator and he could call us to confirm this. The problem was we had no phone. We told him it was okay. We would remain prepared to meet the senator. If he couldn't, we would try another time.

Congressman Conway was in his office, but meeting with a business group. We had no appointment and the secretary had been told not to take any further appointments for the day. Emboldened by our previous experience, we told her that we would wait until it was closing time in the hope we could get a few minutes with him. Once it was clear that we were going to sit in the waiting room for as long as it took, things changed. In about fifteen minutes, we were ushered into the congressman's office. We apologized for barging in unannounced, but explained that without a phone, we had no way of calling his office for an appointment. He said that he didn't want to trouble us with another visit and could spare a few minutes.

His father, William Conway, Sr. had been a congressman and had died a couple of years ago. Jr. had first been appointed by the governor to complete the term and then ran and retained the seat vacated by his late dad. In no uncertain terms he made it clear that the Native American restoration was a closed chapter, for better or for worse. Doug and his band would have to take up the issue with the bureau. As far as he was concerned he would not waste any more of his time. The Paiutes should be thankful for what his dad had done to get the Cedar City band the 60,000-acre reservation.

I had never seen Doug snap, not even close. I did then. He reminded the congressman that he had a responsibility to correct the wrongs done to native people. Was he proud of his dad's efforts to allocate 60,000 acres for the Paiute reservation? His dad was no saint and what he did was criminal. How did what started out as a 170,000-acre reservation suddenly get pared down to 60,000 acres with most of the desirable land carved away? His dad and his cronies sabotaged the restoration to legitimize what they had fraudulently stolen from native tribes.

The congressman's face went red and his eyes blazed with fury. I was afraid for a moment that he was going to get physical and throw us out of the office. He recovered his composure quickly and said that he would ignore the insult, explore the situation, and do what he could, but not to expect much. Washington and the rest of the country were in no mood to take up the native issue when there were many more pressing problems to deal with. In plain language, it was a blunt repudiation. There would be no point in returning to his office in the future.

Doug was enraged. He was not cowed down by the congressman.

He had a few choice words for the congressman before I dragged him out of the office. He reminded the congressman that he and his fellow politicians were playing poker with their lives and their future. He threw in a final verbal punch that the congressman had not heard the last of his band of natives, and he would live to regret this day.

I decided to remain quiet for as long as Doug chose to rant and give vent his feelings. He was fuming and he was not making any efforts to camouflage his feelings. It took a while before he ended the monologue. Finally, he was spent and done. This was a new side of his character that I was witnessing for the first time. Had my perorations gone too far?

"Did I put you in an embarrassing position, Father Tosco?"

"No."

"They are all hypocrites, the whole bunch of them. He and his kind won't move one finger to help native people. What loss can there be to the US government to recognize us and reserve for us the area we live in now? It is well known how the Congressman's father and his friends had plundered and stolen native lands. They drove us out of our ancestral lands like cattle. Can we rewrite history now? The natives were short-ended but it's all in the past and what good would it do to rake up those embers now. The native people were hoodwinked and cheated out of their birthright. It's too late for redemption. Easy for him to say that restoration is done and a dead issue."

"Doug, they won't give in to your demands, if they can. You must force them to come to the table and concede."

"Congress terminated our native status because they said it prevented us from becoming part of the mainstream citizenry. But they never gave us a chance to survive. They took our fertile lands. They run their herds of cattle on them now. Are we less important than cattle? Without our lands, how can we feed our children? Corn does not grow on rocks."

"They do not care."

"We will demand retribution, not just restoration."

"Right is on your side but might on theirs."

"We will teach this Congressman a lesson. He can't get away with this."

"Doug, you remember the reporter from the Herald, Malcolm

Donahue, who we met a few weeks ago? I want to contact him. Maybe he can help."

"He is a white man. He won't."

"So am I."

"You're different."

"No. I'm not. There are people out there, white or whatever, who have a genuine interest in native people."

"What can he do?"

"Your story needs to be told. It must be presented to the public. Exposure, any kind, even negative, will help bring the issue into the public's eye."

"You think the public cares about us?"

"Let's find out. Some things you must give it a chance; you must test the waters and wait for the results. It's a small ripple that becomes a tsunami, a tiny breeze that develops into a hurricane, a little spark that becomes a wildfire, a little speck of snow that rolls into a giant snowball. The public has the capacity to convert a non-event into an overwhelming big bang. It's the reporters that fuel the firestorm."

We stopped at the offices of the Herald. Malcolm was out on assignment. I left him a note about the senator's visit.

"Let's look at the bright side of things and forget about the Congressman. We really are lucky the Senator will stop by. What the young assistant did is refreshing. Let's hope the Senator will be more accommodating than the Congressman."

"Should we do something to prepare for his visit?"

"You should tell him what you want."

"Restore, recognize and reserve."

"Senator, we welcome you to this small native community of Paiutes. We thank you for stopping by. I know you are on a tight schedule and therefore I will come to the point without too much elaboration."

"Thank you."

"You were instrumental in restoring the status of several native nations of Utah and establishing reservations for them. During the restoration process, we were overlooked. We were included as part of the Cedar City Band of Paiutes. We are a small band of Paiutes but we are not part of the Cedar City Band. We want to be recognized as what we are, Paiutes of the Little Bend Valley."

"You said you are part of one of the recognized bands of Paiutes. You are covered under the restoration."

"We want independent recognition as a separate band."

"I studied the history of the tribes of Utah extensively and held multiple hearings before proposing the Restoration legislation. I heard from leaders, advocates, and even detractors, but nowhere did I hear about your band of people."

"That doesn't mean we don't exist. Nobody asked us."

"How come you were not represented at the hearings? Why did you not speak up before?"

"Sir, nobody informed us. Our voice was not heard. We knew nothing of restoration until after the implementation of the changes."

"But you are represented. You are part of the Cedar City Band."

"No, Sir. We are an independent and separate people. We want to be recognized as a separate nation—and we want these lands we live on reserved for us. We'll not give up our identity because it would be convenient."

"I don't see what other choice you have. There is little that can be done now. You can certainly submit a formal application through the Bureau of Native American Affairs. The problem is they've been given strict guidelines what to do to recognize a nation and I'm afraid you'll find it hard to qualify."

"We are caught between a rock and a hard place. We are forced to be a part of the Cedar City Band. Cedar City Council won't allow us to break away because it will affect their status."

"Can you not work out some form of accommodation with the Cedar City Band without forming a separate band?"

"Accommodation is not what we seek. We want recognition."

"That'll be tough. You don't realize how much time and effort it takes."

"Does not the plight of our people mean something?"

"Of course it does. All right! Tell me, what is recognition as a separate nation going to do for you? What exactly are you looking for?"

"Three things. One—we want to be recognized as a separate nation and restored to official status."

"How can you prove you are a separate Paiute band?"

"The very fact that the five official bands treat us as separate."

"That is weak."

"Senator, I am Father Tosco of the Catholic Diocese of Salt Lake City. We have a mission here and I am in charge of the mission. From the information we have been able to gather, this band of Paiutes had contact with Dominguez and Escalante. During the time of the Reverend Scanlon, there is recorded proof of contact with this nation, the result of some extraordinary circumstances, which I won't go into now. This mission has been in existence since 1881. There is a copy of the covenant signed by Reverend Scanlon and this tribe. There is a church to the southeast of where we stand as testimony to this history."

"My question, Reverend, is not the existence of sundry Christian missions around these parts. The issue is: Are the Paiutes of Little Bend Valley, as they call themselves, a sovereign native nation and not part of another?"

"Senator, do you have any doubt that we are Native Americans or that we are Paiute?"

"I have no reason to question that."

"But we have no proof to show that we are Paiutes and not Anasazi or Shoshoni. The five recognized bands can't prove that they are who they claim to be. You took their word for it. We all share customs and a common language with other bands of Paiutes but we are separate bands by tradition and history. The other five bands will confirm this."

"I am not disputing your arguments. What you are up against is the criteria we have set up for recognizing tribal nations. Let me study the issue some more. What are the other two demands?"

"The Paiutes of Little Bend have lived in this valley for centuries. This valley was included and is currently a part of the reservation of the Cedar City band. Nobody has bothered us here because it is a desolate area with little water to support farming or cattle. With the help of Father Tosco, we have established this store and we are making a living. We want to expand the store and maybe open a gas station so that we can have a source of income throughout the year including winter months. What we fear is that as soon as we establish ourselves, the Cedar City Band will lay claim to this land and force us to share in the profits. We have suffered plenty at the hands of everyone. We want to ensure that the land we call our own is made an indisputable part of our heritage which we can pass on to our children and their children. We want this parcel of land we call home to be reserved permanently for us."

"I can assure you that I will do my best to bring this parcel of land under your control. We can talk to the Cedar City Council and see if we can get an agreement from them. That may be a quicker solution. The third one."

"Our people lived and flourished in this area because there was plenty of water from the Little Bend River. That's where we get our name. This river no longer exists due to suspected human involvement. We believe the river was purposely destroyed."

"We want the river restored."

"The river has since been dammed."

"To us, that river is our life and our future."

"You are going too fast for me. This is all new stuff."

"Sir, we believe someone caused a hillside to collapse and shut off the flow of the river to this valley."

"A landslide. That's not uncommon in these parts."

"Sir, if you ask for proof that human hands were responsible for the destruction of the river, we have none."

"Regardless of who or how, we want the river restored."

"We can take you there and show it to you in person."

"That's not necessary. I can assign someone from my office to meet with you and study the matter. We can then decide what we can do."

"How long will it take?"

"It will take time, but how long, I can't say. One thing I can tell you for sure. Nobody's going to force you out of this parcel of land. Please stay in touch with my office."

"Thank you, Senator."

"Folks, I wish I had more time. The restoration and re-settlement of Native Americans have been very important to me. I will continue to do everything in my power to set right the wrongs done to native people."

"Thank you, Senator—and thanks for stopping by."

"You are welcome. Good luck with the store."

He left with his motorcade heading north. Would he do something? My reading on the Senator had been fairly accurate. He was all business right from the start. It would be great to have a friend like him.

"Father Tosco, do you think that the senator will make any effort to help?"

"I think he will. To what extent, I can't tell."

"He does not need our political support. He certainly knows that there will be no money coming from us for his political action committees. So, what's in it for him?"

"He may not be looking for something. He may want to finish the task he took on many years ago."

"He has made a name for himself as a crusader for native rights. He does not need to do anything more to advance his reputation."

"There are politicians who look beyond their self-interest. He could be one of them. Let's give him some time. He may surprise us."

"He showed enough interest, stopping by."

"It's good to seek out and get the support of powerful politicians like him. But, in the end, it's really your fight and you must lead the charge."

"What more can we do?"

"You must decide how far and how long the struggle should go. If the senator decides to do nothing, will that be the end of it for you? Will that be the end of everything?"

"That's not what I meant. We have very limited options at our disposal and we need outside help. We can only go so far."

"We must keep the fight going. Time can't be a factor."

"Do we have the will to keep it going until we get what we want?"

"If we don't, then we'll become another one of many nations that are no more. That's the choice before us."

"If we truly believe we are an independent nation and we want to preserve our identity, then we must keep fighting, no matter what."

"We Paiutes have always shown a soft chin to the aggressor. When the Spanish and other conquerors stole our women and children, we didn't stand up and fight. When other nations took up arms against the greedy settlers, we remained compliant. What has been the result? We do not even have official status. We do not get invited to represent our interests as a nation. We are not ourselves anymore but a part of another."

"We can't remain passive. We risk our existence as a nation and we take away the true identity of our children forever."

"Restoration, Recognition, and Reservation. There must be no compromise."

The construction of the store was proceeding as well as could be expected. There were suggestions made and changes adopted along the way. One interesting modification was the shape of the front of the store. It was divided equally into two parts, and each part was constructed like the entrance to a teepee with its triangular shape. This gave the store an interesting and unique appearance. It was truly a native store. They had some heated arguments about the roof and how to make it leak-proof. They finally decided to use lumber and cover the top with metal sheets. It would be hot during the summer, but it would provide protection from rain and snow during the winter.

Building around the existing tent structure allowed them to continue running the business without too much disruption. The project was a defining moment for the tribe, demonstrating to themselves a newfound determination, a desire and a hope for a better future.

I had my own issues to deal with. During my last visit to the diocese, there was a letter from the Monsignor that he wanted to visit the mission and would it be convenient for him to come over on August 18, the Sunday following the Feast of the Assumption. I left him a reply inviting him to the mission and confirming that the date he indicated was fine with me. Mass was scheduled for 10:00 a.m. as usual, and if he could arrive early, we would concelebrate.

The villagers greeted this news with enthusiasm, and they decided to make every effort to finish the construction by then and have an official inauguration by the Monsignor. They wanted to put on a show for the VG and the diocese.

Business continued to flourish and they started adding new items for all types of travelers—tourists and non-tourists alike. The construction work was tough in the hot sun, and they had limited tools and resources. Often, they had to improvise. There were times when every member of the village was present, helping out.

The women and children would hang out inside the church to get away from the sun. While the men worked on the store, the women continued with their basket weaving and other artwork that tourists found attractive. Some of their creations, particularly with the beads, were exquisite in design and shape. They seemed to be experiencing a revival of their ancient traditions and art. It's one thing to make things to sell to other stores, but totally a different motivation when it's being done to sell in your own store, as your own creation.

I would go help with the building work whenever I could. I wanted to show my solidarity with their efforts, without being a distraction. They objected but seemed to appreciate my presence.

I had gone with Doug to meet with the telephone utility again. It wasn't an easy sell because the company was reluctant to put in several miles of lines or build a transmission tower for one small customer. After exploring several options, the company came up with the idea of putting up a relay tower. They would use the tower primarily to expand their communication network. They would sublease the tower to satellite, radio and television companies. We would get our connection. The company would send out a team to investigate. The tribe would have to sign a long-term lease agreement for the site where the tower would be erected.

A group of engineers and technicians from the telephone company arrived on Friday before the Monsignor's visit. They spent a good part of the day taking measurements and looking at locations. They would build the relay tower far enough away from the store so as not to be intrusive. They would build it close to the freeway and the total needed would be a 50' x 50' area. They would need access to the tower. They could begin construction of the tower in about three months. It would be a pretty tall structure, and they had some pictures of similar towers. They also made an offer that was attractive. They would construct the tower, and provide free installation of the phone connection to the store, in exchange for a permanent lease of the location. They would reserve the right to sublease it to radio and television companies to transmit their signals.

In a sign of the growing business awareness of the tribe, they made a counter offer. The lease would be valid for a total of 99 years. The tribe would be paid 10% of gross revenue from sub-leasing the tower and services. After some discussions, the company agreed to a 5% split. It was a win-win situation. The telephone tower would prove to be a source of income too.

Monsignor Mark Cavanaugh, Vicar General, Catholic Diocese of Salt Lake City, arrived early accompanied by three members of the Diocesan Pastoral Council. By 9:00 a.m., members of the tribe had assembled at the church. Non-native attendees started trickling in. Doug welcomed the Monsignor and the council members and thanked them for their support of the mission. He invited them to stay for lunch after Mass.

The Monsignor expressed his happiness at the progress being made and proclaimed the diocese's intent to continue support for the mission. Council members also spoke reflecting the same sentiments. I was glad to see that we had roughly one hundred people in attendance. I had been debating whether to have the stomp dance as usual and finally decided to go for it. The VG must know we were doing it and it was a regular feature of the Sunday services. There would be more questions raised if we didn't have it. The natives put some extra energy into the dance and the Monsignor to his credit appeared to enjoy it.

I introduced the VG and the council members to the congregation and the Monsignor gave the homily. Following Mass there was lunch; and as had become the custom, most everyone stayed and participated and contributed. It was a joyous occasion.

After lunch and after everyone had left, I met with the Diocesan team in front of my trailer. They all expressed admiration for the work being done and the mission's role in all of these. I was invited to join them at their next council meeting, three weeks from today. I watched them leave feeling a little smug that we had done as best a job as possible to make them happy.

There was a lot we had achieved together in the course of a few months. The store provided the tribe with a reliable economic base. They had found a way to put to use their traditional skills and make a living out of it. They had electricity, and soon they would have telephone service and possibly radio and television. The community appeared to be coming together and working together for the common good. Hopefully, the enterprise would become large enough to provide jobs for all of them. But more important than any of the material accomplishments, they now had a sense of purpose and hope. In their mannerisms, in their talk, in their planning, there was determination and confidence.

Where did the mission fit in? I hadn't baptized one single person, native or non-native, since my arrival at the mission. I may have succeeded in advancing their material stability, but what about the spiritual? Was there something I was doing or not doing that was stopping the people from seeking the faith? I knew the villagers would probably agree to be baptized if I put some pressure on them. But that would be a phony conversion. The diocese would want to see a fair number of conversions to declare the mission a success. No. Baptism would only be initiated when an individual asked for it. My job was to preach the good news. It was up to God to open their minds and hearts to the faith.

I had always read with distaste, the stories of the great missionaries, traveling to unknown and faraway lands and indiscriminately baptizing people, sometimes with genuine zeal but often by coercion or with the promise of material benefits such as food, housing, and clothes. Some of these missionaries lost their lives in the process, and a few were canonized as saints for their troubles.

I believe many of these so-called martyrs didn't deserve the recognition given to them. Most of them were religious and political agents with a joint agenda for their European colonial sponsors. The process of evangelization had a political component. One may call it religious zeal—I call it arrogance—to walk into a foreign land, ridicule their customs, insult their beliefs, call them pagans, and then threaten them with hell if they didn't convert. If some of these zealous missionaries got killed in the process, well, they asked for it; they deserved it. How did that make them martyrs? That decision should have been made based on the opinion of the native people and not some cantankerous old cardinals in Rome. How about the innumerable natives who were murdered for refusing to be baptized? How about the poor souls who were physically and mentally tortured after they were baptized? Should they be canonized too?

I had read about Junipero Serra and his California missions. A brave man, a zealous missionary, he is alternately credited with bringing

Christianity to the West Coast of America as well as helping annex the region for the Spanish Crown. Regardless of either, most native people condemn him for destroying the indigenous population. He is credited for having baptized over 6,000 natives and he established nine missions. He fought for native rights and protected them against military abuses within the missions. Yet, if you're a Native American, it's hard to hold the Blessed Serra in high esteem. Serra's actions, directly and indirectly, led to the decimation of nearly one half of the native population of California through disease and the enforced change of their way of life. Converts were forced to live around the missions and adopt an alien lifestyle which made them totally dependent on the missions for their livelihood.

In my desire to help the native villagers attain financial and material stability, was I perhaps doing what Serra did? Would the native people start equating Christianity with material prosperity? No. It was different. There was a huge difference. The material progress was important to the tribe, for their survival. It was necessary to hold the members together and it was the result of their own hard work. I provided encouragement and inspiration, that was all. I made sure that they worked within a moral framework fashioned by Christian principles. But I didn't demand that they become Christians. It was a sound approach; sustenance for the body, and food for their souls, but no forced conversions.

The next day, we had a visit from Malcolm. He had been to Washington on assignment and had just got back. He got the note about the Senator's visit too late. Too bad he missed it.

"What do you think? Was the visit helpful?"

"I think he understands our dilemma."

"At least he seemed open to the idea we may be a separate band."

"Honestly, I don't expect him to do anything."

"Maybe he will. He didn't have to come and visit you."

"That's true. But, what can he do and why should he?"

"I think he will do something. He's genuine and he has clout."

"There is no time to worry about what he does or what anyone else does. We must do what we have to do."

"The natives were here before the white man came. We are still here despite the white man. Our future generations must be here even when the white man is gone. We must pave the way."

"People don't care what happens to us. We must take care of ourselves."

"Each year this country welcomes thousands of people from all over the world, immigrants, legal and illegal, refugees, asylum seekers, you name it. We embrace them, give them food, shelter, money, medicine and jobs. We give them free education and welfare. What about the native people of the land? We didn't come from anywhere. We are here. But, we are treated like pests. We are locked up in reservations out of sight and out of mind."

"Malcolm, can you help us find out what happened to the Little Bend River? There must be some record of it somewhere."

"I'll do my best. It won't be easy. The farther back in time, the fewer the records. If it's in our paper's archives, I'll find it."

"Should we build a regular church for the mission?"

"A church is not the immediate need of the people."

"If the attendance stays high, why would we not consider building a church there?"

"We should start looking beyond the natives. There are more non-natives attending—correct? May be we should start thinking beyond a mission."

"True. We should be looking out for our interests too. The location has great promise. A church there would look great, if we can afford it."

"We don't have to plan anything big right away. Father Tosco has shown he can make it work with a simple church."

"It's too early. Let's see how things develop. It's a native reservation. They must allow us to build a church."

"I'm sure Father Tosco only needs to ask. The natives owe him their livelihood."

"They owe me nothing. They didn't come looking to us for help."

"You know what I mean. Where would they be without your leadership?"

"Father Tosco, is there anything else we can do to help improve things?"

"What they need more than anything is water."

"How do we get them water?"

"They had a river flowing into the valley at one time. Tragically, it was destroyed by the local settlers. I am hoping the diocese can assist them in getting it restored."

"What can the diocese do?"

"Never heard of such a thing before. We can't get involved in such things."

"I was hoping we could use any influence we have with elected officials to get it done."

"Politics is bad news. We should stay out of politics."

"It would end up in bad publicity for the diocese especially if it pits us against local people"

"These things get messy and we'll end up with egg on our faces."

"The river is more important to the Paiutes than a mission. The mission was built when there was a river. The mission died when the river dried up."

"Yet, you brought the mission roaring back to life without the river."

"Without the river, the mission will meet the same fate as before. It's that important for them."

"It's unfortunate if they see it that way. We need to stick to our real goal, and that is to evangelize them and bring them into the fold."

"Do they really expect the diocese to help get the river restored? That's too much."

"You know how the bishop hates unwanted attention. This can get very nasty, very quick, if we stick our finger into it."

"Let the politicians handle such matters. Tell them to talk to their elected officials. Our role is to minister to their spiritual needs."

"They will have no need for our spiritual ministry if they have no place to sleep, no food to eat, and no water."

You make it sound like a dire situation. They survived before we were there. You made things better."

"It is dire. I live among them; I see their daily struggles; I hear their stories of abuse and exploitation; I feel their yearning for survival. They have made a few strides toward progress. But, it's fragile and can collapse easily. A restored river will allow them to farm and raise cattle. That is sustainable."

"Look at it objectively, Father Tosco. The diocese is a religious entity. We have limitations. We can't extend ourselves beyond our limits."

"I recommend we stay out of it."

"We can only do so much. We must stick to our mission."

"No good can come out of it. It'll get us a lot of negative publicity."

"Let the natives take care of it. Don't they have a department or bureau to deal with their affairs? Let them do it."

"If it's about collecting clothing or furniture, I am all for it. Restoring a river is a whole different matter."

"We could end up making enemies all around us. You said the river was destroyed. That means there are people out there that don't want the river there."

"It verges on political interference. We'll get dragged into controversy."

"Once they all convert and we build a permanent church, we could raise it to the status of a parish. We can get involved at that time."

"How many of these folks are Catholics? Do we have a count?"

"None."

"That's incredible. I thought they were all Catholics."

"Why do we have a mission there if there are no Catholics?"

"Do they want to become Catholics?"

"I don't know."

"We have a mission for the Paiutes. But none of them are Catholics and they have not shown an interest in getting baptized. I don't get it."

"We must give them time. We can't stuff religion down their

throats. They must hear the word of God, see Christ in action and experience the power. Then and only then will they want to be followers of Christ. They must experience the love of Christ and then they will answer the call. The mission was not started with the premise they would become Christians."

"Isn't that obvious? Isn't that a fair assumption?"

"We don't need to be shy about our expectations that we want them to become Christians. If there's ambivalence on our part or theirs, let's dispel it now."

"The Paiutes are benefitting handsomely because of the mission. They should be lining up to be baptized and not complaining about a river."

"Sounds like they like the money but don't want to make the commitment and convert. That's not a just reward for our efforts."

"We should give Father Tosco more time. Within a matter of months he has worked miracles. He can't force them to be baptized and become Catholics just because the mission is doing well. These things take time."

"All right. Maybe it's too soon to be making demands or setting goals. We should keep building on the good we are doing. However, we can't lose sight of the missionary obligation of the church to spread the word of God. Father Tosco, we must convert them. Our goal is evangelization. We are proud of what you have done Father Tosco. Let's try and take it to the next step. We will keep you in our prayers."

"Thank you. I appreciate your support of the mission. Bye now!"

"Do we know what's really going on at the mission?"

"We must establish some measure of control. What he does there affects the reputation of the diocese."

"He has changed. He's not the same person who left for the mission. He has an agenda. I didn't sense he was very forthcoming."

"He seems very sure of himself. If we are not careful, we may regret that we restarted this mission."

"Success can breed arrogance and that's what may be happening."

"We could become helpless bystanders. We may end up having to clean up any mess he creates. We can't lose control over the mission."

"The mission has become a presence and Father Tosco has

become an integral part of the Paiute people. Unfortunately, the diocese is becoming irrelevant. If we don't act quickly, it could become Father Tosco's mission."

"It may be too late already."

"It may appear we are not on top of things at the mission. I must confess we have not paid much attention to how things are being done there. We gave Father Tosco a very difficult task and we trust he'll be true to the goals of the diocese. Unfortunately, we have no guidelines on running this mission. He's reacting to the demands of the moment rather than following a scripted policy. Now that he has succeeded, we need to monitor closely what's happening and set guidelines"

As I drove back to the mission, I reflected on my meeting with the Diocesan Board. They wanted control but couldn't quite figure out how to do it. The VG was another story. Behind his kind and parting words were warning signals in plenty. I had often wondered about the passive neutrality professed by the bishop. I didn't know the man very well. Either he was hiding behind a self-imposed veil of secrecy or the VG was like a shield denying access to him. It was common knowledge among the clergy that the VG was the one wielding the real power.

The bishop seemed consumed with the desire to complete and consecrate the cathedral. That would be his crowning achievement, his legacy. His professed low-key policy was probably intended to divert attention from the huge sums of money being poured into the project. It was like quicksand, swallowing money faster than it could be found.

I knew I had secured a spot on the VG's radar. There would be a close watch on every move I made. That didn't bother me. I had nothing to hide. What I was doing and what I was preaching were all out in the open. They demanded clarity on my future plans. They were troubled they didn't get it. I had no plans.

The construction of the store was almost complete. They were nailing down the final logs on the roof. It was a primitive structure. They hadn't had the time to scrape and polish the logs. The tarpaulin would be pulled over the logs, thus, covering the roof and protecting the inside from rain and snow.

The guys were really proud of what they had accomplished in such a short period of time. They had found the will to come up with an idea and bring it to fruition. They had become proactive. This was a remarkable achievement for a people who for centuries had allowed themselves to be led by circumstances. This definitely was a key step in their growth as a nation and as a people.

I was amused to see a couple of banners they had strung next to the freeway. One read: 'Save the Spotted Owl! Save the Paiutes too.' The other was more direct: 'Restore the Little Bend River.' I've always wondered what effect roadside banners had on people who saw them and what the long-term benefits were. I guess the display had greater significance for the tribe than the passers-by. They were demonstrating the will to express themselves. That itself was a sign of assertiveness, a definite change from the past.

The newly reconstructed store was inaugurated with pomp and ceremony. There was the tribal dance and invocation of the spirits followed by a feast. People pulled over to the side of the freeways and a few parked in front of the store to watch the action. The drums kept rolling. What began as a tribal dedication soon took on the air of a full-blooded celebration. They even invited the public to join them in some of the dances, and a few folks did.

People who stopped to watch often became customers.

They did brisk business that day. Some of the visitors wandered around, and a few stopped by my trailer and talked to me. Most were surprised there was a Catholic mission here, and there were services on Sundays.

They took note of the interest visitors had in their tribal rituals and dances. Ancient traditions of indigenous people generate lots of interest. People will come to watch if they feel it's safe. Most native nations are reluctant to expose themselves to outside scrutiny, probably for fear of misinterpretation or ridicule. I'm not a fan of commercializing spiritual traditions. But, done properly, it can be an educational tool to enhance understanding and acceptance.

There was great demand for native garments and they could literally have sold the clothes off their backs that day. It was a good time for the tribe. Everything seemed to be going well.

Success was doing wonders for their morale. As their confidence grew, their resolve strengthened. More than ever they decided the Little Bend had to be restored. Their future depended on it.

How quickly things can change. Such, indeed, is human nature. When one group grows in stature, others feel threatened even though there are no rational conflicts between the two. How could a band of Paiutes inhabiting a piece of native land pose a threat to anyone? They didn't have the numbers or the resources to challenge anyone. Was I wrong?

It happened suddenly and without any warning.

The morning following the inauguration, they found both banners cut and slit into shreds. The couple living at the store was the first to take notice. At first they were shocked, and shock turned into disbelief, and then finally to anger. After the euphoria of the celebration and the crowds that had gathered the previous day, it was a setback. News traveled quickly back to the village, and within an hour Doug and the rest of the men were at the store and looking at the vandalized banners trying to make sense out of it. They then came marching to my trailer with the torn banners.

"Father Tosco, what do you make of this?"

"I am as baffled as you are about why anyone would do such a thing."

"There was nothing offensive on the banners."

"Is someone trying to send us a message?"

"Some people don't like what we are doing here."

"It could be the work of pranksters or a random act."

"This is not a prank. This is malicious."

"It is not a random act. It is intentional and purposeful."

"If it's a prank, it'll be repeated. If someone's trying to send a message, we'll find out soon. There'll be further attacks. We must be prepared."

"We should be extra vigilant from now on. We need more people living here at night to keep an eye on what's happening around the store."

I knew they were uneasy, even though they seemed to quiet down after they had voiced their immediate outrage. What happened had been shocking. They had no enemies they knew of. They weren't a threat to anyone, be it another native nation or the settlers around. They weren't about to put anyone out of business by opening the store. Could it be, then that this was a threat against the mission?

They wasted no time in making and putting up the banners in the same spot. Tuesday morning came and I was relieved to see the banners in place with no damage. All the men of the village arrived early at the store and decided to stay well past sunset. They were upset and angry. Around 2:00 p.m. two officers from the Utah Highway Patrol showed up at the store. Doug brought them over to my trailer.

"Good afternoon gentlemen. What brings you out here, in this heat?"

"We received complaints about a wild party here on Saturday resulting in traffic jams on the freeway."

"Who made the complaints?"

"Concerned citizens."

"These citizens apparently had no idea what was going on here."

"That's what we came to find out. What was going on?"

"We were inaugurating the store."

"Nobody contacted the UHP regarding permits to hold celebrations on the freeways. You are running a store and there's the mission. None of these have permits as far as we know. Is that true?"

"This is a native reservation. They need no permits from the state."

"You need permits. That is the law. You also caused traffic disruptions."

"There was no public gathering. No one was invited. We didn't create traffic problems. We were having a ceremony to mark the opening of our store. If people stopped to watch, we had no control over it."

"That's why you get a permit or inform the UHP so that we can be around and prevent traffic problems."

"There were no traffic jams. A few people slowed down to see what was going on. That can happen when there's an accident or even a deer or an animal on the side of the freeway."

"The complaint we got states there was extensive traffic disruption."

"Whoever sent the complaint is lying."

"I will have to shut you down until you get the proper permits to run a store here and even to have a church."

"We need no state permit to operate a store on native territory. You have no jurisdiction here."

"We shall see about that. And you must be the Reverend Tosco. Sir, you should know you can't pitch a tent and call it a church without permits."

"You'll have to take it up with the Diocese of Salt Lake City. They operate this mission. It's been here for over a century."

"I am going to refer the matter to the DA's office. In the meantime, if I were you, I would pack up and go back to wherever you came from. That goes for you too, Reverend."

Was this a coincidence or a conspiracy? The message was getting clear. There were people who wanted the natives and the mission out of here. It couldn't be the work of an individual. Was there a link between the vandalism of the banners and the UHP visit immediately after? Both had to be viewed as intimidation. Putting up the banners again and temporarily neutralizing the UHP were not going to scare them off.

Intimidation, harassment, and threats often tend to solidify a group's determination or sense of purpose. Violent persecution of the early Christians only served to rapidly expand the nascent religion. Such is human nature. Of the many native nations I had read about, the Paiutes had shown the least militancy throughout their history. But, given their current level of frustration, there was no saying how they would react. I was sure they were feeling as if they were being driven into a corner. The younger members of the community kept voicing strong opinions for defiance. I hoped and prayed that the community could go about their business without further provocation.

Labor Day came and went with a big rush of tourists trying to make the best of the last few days of summer. Schools reopened and there was an immediate drop off in tourist traffic. The weather remained good. Business was fair but signs of weakening sales were evident. We had several ongoing discussions as to what should be done once the snow started falling. The villagers decided to keep the store open unless it got really bad. I would do likewise with Sunday services. The tent had been pitched so that it could be taken down quickly in inclement weather, much like sails on a boat.

There were no further incidents and as time went on we decided that what happened was a random act. The banners were intact and the UHP hadn't shown up again. Malcolm stopped by, and we reviewed the letters that would be mailed to Utah Senators and members of Congress, the Secretary of the Interior, and the Bureau of Native American Affairs. There had been no response from the senator's office. I had little expectation there would be any.

The villagers were uniform in their belief that the letter writing campaign was a waste of time. They looked at me quizzically when I told them that we would send a second round of reminder letters to the same folks. We got some responses but nothing to crow about. The Department of the Interior had forwarded the letter to the Cedar City Office for review. The Bureau of Native American Affairs cited their records to reconfirm that there were only five bands of Paiutes, and no new Paiute band would be recognized. A couple of congressmen's offices acknowledged receipt of the letter; they would study the matter.

Interestingly, we found out that the Cedar City Band of Paiutes operated the Cedar City office of the Bureau. Was this conflict of interest or a confluence of interests? Would the Bureau act against itself when the dispute was with the Cedar City Band of Paiutes? They promised to look into the restoration of the river but didn't sound too hopeful. Rivers and lakes came under state jurisdiction. They would write to the Governor of Utah in support of the restoration.

The younger members wanted aggressive action to get things done. There was talk of a sit-in at the offices of the senators and congressmen or occupying the office of the Bureau in Cedar City, like what AIM had done in Washington. There was talk of taking the Bureau to court.

As days went by, there was growing frustration with lack of progress on the restoration of the river. I could feel the tension among them. Having tasted success, they wanted success to come quickly every time they pursued an objective. The generational gap was also evident. The young people were not satisfied with the status quo—and as it is with youth all over, they wanted immediate results. Generations of Paiutes before them had taken to the path of adaptation rather than confrontation. It wasn't a point of pride among the younger members. They were restless and impatient; they showed it. I could sense the conflict brewing and wondered if it would spill out into the open.

How does a small tribe with limited members and resources

challenge powerful establishments like the state or the bureau? I sat with the elders on weekdays and discussed this quandary. The tribe had no choice but to take some action or they would have to face internal strife. But you don't want to do something for the sake of doing something. Actions must lead to success or it would make it worse. Many great leaders had led their people to victory by pursuing the path of non-violence. Gandhi, Martin Luther King, Mandela, and of course Christ, were just a few. They succeeded because they were persistent and right was on their side. Of course it helped that they were powerful motivators.

I don't remember who voiced the idea or when, but it was casually mentioned they should block the freeway to call attention to their cause. It didn't catch anyone's attention—or so it seemed. Being a major junction, it would have immediate and devastating impact on traffic. It would attract a lot of attention that was for sure. Who reignited the idea or why was never identified. When it did, it came back with such force that there was no time for rational introspection. Why was it embraced with such intense enthusiasm when it came up a second time? All caution was thrown to the winds. All on a sudden, the idea caught fire and they started hotly debating it. Soon it was not a question of if they should do it, but how and when. There weren't the usual words of caution. I was taken aback by the sudden show of emotion, the whooping, the shouts, and the spontaneous demonstration of aggression.

The idea of a freeway blockade was soon the only action of choice. There were no alternatives even vaguely considered. Doug, characteristically, was stunned by the speed with which the idea sprouted, built up steam, became a storm, and then mushroomed into a tornado. It gave him no time to procrastinate. Everyone was energized by the idea. It had to be done. Even the women were very vocal in support. I could only surmise that their frustration with their own inaction had reached a boiling point and something had to be done. That was it.

They could accomplish it with a few people. The women probably saw an opportunity for them to contribute equally with the men because it didn't require leaving the vicinity of their homes. There would be an immediate response, all right. The state and federal authorities couldn't afford to have two vital freeways blocked off, even for a short period of time. The tribe was so engrossed with what they wanted to do, they didn't even bother to consider the aftermath or plan for it. What would the response be? Would they get arrested and cited or thrown into jail? They would be breaking state and federal laws. Who would have primary jurisdiction? It would raise complex issues. But then, these complexities could work to their benefit.

Every cause, right or wrong, attracts supporters and detractors from the public. There would be little empathy toward the tribe from the traveling public who would be caught unawares. What would the response of the locals be? There were very few around and they were what one might call conservatives with right-wing leanings. They definitely would not take kindly to the distraction and unwanted attention to their habitat, let alone the inconvenience. There was no way to predict what the fallout would be.

It would be Columbus Day. Native people have always objected to honoring someone responsible for the destruction of indigenous civilizations in the American continent. It would be an exclamation point to their act of civil disobedience. The more I thought about, the more I concluded there would be severe repercussions. If white people did it, it would be interpreted as "freedom of expression." When done by any other ethnic group including Native Americans, it would be a criminal act of subversion.

Should I be an active participant or keep my distance? Should I be like the National Geographic photographer forbidden from intervening in a natural event, however tempting it might be? Should I be nothing more than an interested witness to the unfolding events as the tribe struggled to establish their own rendezvous with destiny?

I felt strongly I couldn't stand idle and be a mere spectator. At the same time, the stakes were high. My participation in a native protest would bring universal condemnation. The bishop, the diocese, and probably folks further up the ladder would be shocked and dismayed and certainly react. It would definitely be contrary to the wishes of the diocese and the bishop. I couldn't dream of seeking permission from the diocese to participate. I couldn't let them or anyone else into what the natives were planning. It must remain a secret.

In my heart I knew the tribe needed my support. They wouldn't request it and would probably object loudly to my participation. How could I not be a part of their struggle? No. That was impossible. The villagers would think no less of me if I chose to remain on the sidelines. How would I feel about myself if I stayed away? I would despise myself. In some ways, was I not partly responsible for their nascent aggressiveness? There was no hesitation. It was part of my mission to be with them, to be part of their struggle, regardless of the consequences.

My present and future were inextricably intertwined with this small band of natives and I would not back out. There would be a backlash, for the tribe and me, but the worst could be reserved for me.

The plan was simple. Women and children would be kept out of the action much to their displeasure. They would remain in the village. It was a three-way intersection with 17 ending and merging into 15. On the morning of Columbus Day, around 8:00 a.m., three teams would drive about one-quarter of a mile down the freeway approaches and set up flares narrowing the roadway until it was fully blocked about a hundred yards from the junction. Meanwhile, the remaining men would walk onto the junction, and sit in a triangle blocking access and exit. The teams who set the flares would return and join in. So would I.

They would hold three banners—one for each side of the triangle showing the three demands: Recognition, reservation and restoration. It would be done in silence. There would be no slogans and no interaction with the public. Everyone would wear masks over their mouths to emphasize the plight of the silent minority.

To the traveling public, they would be left to figure out for themselves what this was all about. Word was sent to Malcolm to be at the store early on Columbus Day with his camera, and to not let anyone know where he was. An impartial witness was needed to document whatever transpired. I knew my life was about to change, and it would never be the same again—ever. The tribe was on a mission unknown. Where would all this lead us to? There was growing anxiety but there was tangible excitement in the air. Nobody even breathed a word of backing out.

In the days leading up to Columbus Day, they drew up plans and each knew what he was going to do. A few women including Sarah would run the store. There was great anticipation and apprehension. Excitement grew to a fever pitch as the day approached. It was so intense nobody would even venture to voice what the following day could be like. That aside, they were of one mind, and there was no dissent. For once, there was no self-doubt.

The sheriff was not a happy man. He had been roused from sleep with the biggest headache of his career. He had been on the force for nearly thirty years and never had to face such a thing. Most members on the force were veterans, and it was one big family. New additions to the force were mostly children of past or present officers or close relatives for the most part. It was Columbus Day, a holiday. He could care less what Columbus had done, but it was a holiday. It was a day to sleep in late, have a mid-afternoon barbecue with kids and grandkids, and watch a game. It allowed him to double his daily intake of vodka the previous night. Needless to say he was totally unprepared for what happened.

By the time the sheriff showed up at the scene, the traffic had backed up for miles in each direction. The flares had brought cars at the front to a stop, and vehicles pulling up at the back had no clue what was going on in front. Some of the more adventurous folks drove through the flares and when they reached the front, but they too were brought to a halt with nowhere to go. Soon, the freeway was one huge parking lot with cars packing the entire roadway, leaving very little space on the curb.

It was nearly 9:00 a.m. before the Utah Highway Patrol arrived on the scene as well as members of the sheriff's department. Officers on bikes were able to maneuver between cars to the front, trying to figure out where the problem was. The sheriff's deputies, like many of the other officers, had to park their cars quite far away and walk to the front. This was no easy matter. The force was made up of men who were past their prime, and few could be described as being in shape. Some had tried to drive alongside the freeway and ended up stuck in the sand, their spinning wheels throwing up heaps of dust. It was a mess.

The sheriff arrived panting and sweating. He had hitched a ride with a UHP officer to the front. By then, people were getting out of their cars and screaming and shouting, demanding answers. People further back vented their anger by honking incessantly.

I had waited till the "flare party" had returned and taken up their positions before joining them in the middle. They looked up in surprise but didn't say anything. We had agreed there would be no one to answer questions. People would have to come to their own conclusions, the banners the only clue to what this was all about. I hoped Malcolm was there taking all of this in. I hadn't seen him. Maybe, he hadn't got the message. Somewhere above the din of the honking and the shouts of the people, I heard the noise of a helicopter circling around. News media or police, which was it?

We couldn't have choreographed a better scenario or worse, depending on whose perspective you were getting. It was total pandemonium. All of us, twenty-seven to be exact, were arrested, handcuffed, and marched off to patrol cars. How they sorted out the traffic mess or how long it took them, we would never know. None of us had spoken a word to the police before, during, and after the arrests. That seemed to aggravate them more. We were taken to the sheriff's offices in St. George, cited, booked, and released on our own recognizance. The Paiutes refused to give their names and carried no identification papers. They were cited en masse.

The court was on holiday. We were told to appear on Tuesday, the 22nd. We had no way of getting back home, and refused to leave unless they transported us back to the village. We sat down on the floor of the office. The sheriff had had it up to his ears by then. He was ready to do anything to get rid of this unwanted nuisance and get back to a house full of guests. He managed to get someone to drive us back in a sheriff's transport bus.

I was relieved we'd all been released. I found a note from Malcolm at the store. It had two words: Good show. I wasn't sure what he meant by that. Hopefully he didn't take it as a mere show. He must have been as shocked as the general public and the police were. He, however, had the advantage of making a reasonable guess what it was all about.

The whole village was waiting at the store to welcome us back. There was no rejoicing or gloating over the success of the plan that had been enacted to perfection. There was in every eye a sense of pride and fierce determination. I knew there was something set into motion that day that no one would be capable of reining in, not that anyone wanted to. There were no speeches, no spontaneous expressions of victory. There were a few customers milling about the store, some of them media personnel. We refused all interviews. We drove to the village to meet and discuss our future course of action in privacy.

We decided not to appear in court on Tuesday, forcing the judge to issue warrants. It was civil disobedience with a slight twist. There would be more police action. There would be media coverage and with each event, word would spread to the general public. Soon, it would reach elected officials. That's when we could expect action. It was a plan they had conceived and completed. They knew of no better.

It made a splash indeed. It was front-page news in the Herald and other major newspapers Sunday morning, but the Herald alone had pictures to go with the article. It was their helicopter that made it in time to cover the story and get some good pictures. Other reporters were too late by the time they'd arrived on the scene. TV stations made mention of the incident during the nightly news and radio talk shows and news anchors ran commentaries of the trouble brewing at the Little Bend. All of them were left to come up with their own conclusions with no help from us.

As expected, local response was very negative. I knew the reporters would be there en force for Sunday services, and they would latch on to each and every word I uttered. My sermon would serve as a public statement and would be studied and interpreted to suit each one's angle and storyline. It wouldn't be long now before I heard from my superiors, the bishop to the VG, and all the way up and down. I had received significant attention in the media for my role in the blockade. Too bad. There was no turning back now. Everyone would have to play the guessing game. There would be no help from the tribe or me. The drama was playing out better than expected.

"The Pharisees wanted to test Jesus and asked him which the greatest commandment was. He replied without hesitation: 'Love God with all your heart, soul and mind.' This is the first and greatest and the second is like it: 'Love your neighbor as yourself.' Jesus made it clear that the greatest commandment was actually a fusion of two inseparable components. You must love God, but that love will be measured by your love for your neighbor.

'Go love one another as I have loved you,' says Jesus on another occasion. 'Love one another as my father has loved you,' on yet another. The message is clear. Love for God must be evidenced by love for one another. He does not say who or what the 'another' is. He gives us no room to make a distinction who we can love or how. It's everybody, regardless of color, beliefs, ethnicity, or nationality. He sets the bar high for how we must love. He equates it to his love, his Father's love for us.

We are all equal in the eyes of God. Jesus tells us: 'Not a hair of your head shall fall without God's knowledge.' That 'you' is each one of us and every one of us.

There is no chosen race. The human race is the chosen race, including each and every one of us without distinction. Jesus gives no preferential treatment to any race or group. It is the height of conceit to claim that one class or group of people is different or superior to others.

Native Americans have lived in this land for centuries before the arrival of the white settlers and the Christian religion. The settlers were received with kindness and given food and shelter. The settlers showed no inclination to embrace their neighbors and resorted to building walls and barricades around themselves, excluding the natives from their midst. The settlers took all they wanted from what once belonged to the natives. The settlers claimed rights given to them by a king or queen in a far off land. The settlers soon drove the natives further and further away. The settlers were Christians.

The Paiutes have lived in in this little valley long before the white settlers arrived. They have known nothing but misery since then. The Christian settlers haven't shown them the compassion and love that Jesus demands of his followers. The Christian settlers have not loved the native people of this land, as Jesus commanded. The Christian settlers have broken God's commandment to love these neighbors. It's not too late to change. But, you must change and love them as Jesus loves them. Beware my Christian brothers and sisters. On the day of reckoning, you won't be able to look up and say, 'Lord, Lord, these people were less than human and therefore I didn't treat them as neighbors and love them.' The Lord won't be pleased or appeased.

It is easy to love God who you cannot see and feel. It is not easy to love the neighbor that stands before you. Love your neighbor whoever it might be, unconditionally and without judgment and God won't judge you. Amen!"

Catholic Priest at the heart of Native Uprising. The story continued to get top billing. Having no authentic source for much of the information they were forced to carry, the reporters gave full freedom to their imagination to run rampant. Every story must have a villain; the lot fell on me. I was the mad priest inciting the poor natives to revolt against the country. There was hardly any information on the Paiutes of Little Bend and few understood their demands.

There was one winner in all of this. In a strange twist of fate, with all what was happening, business at the store actually improved. The store became a celebrity of sorts, a hangout for news reporters and their vans.

Tuesday came and went. Nothing happened. It must have been a big disappointment to the reporters who had camped out at the courthouse waiting for us to show up. We had no idea what action the judge would take, but we were certain that something would happen soon. Wednesday and Thursday went by without incident. Friday 8:00 a.m., there they were a whole posse of sheriff' deputies and highway patrol, with two large buses.

I went out to meet the officer in charge. Of course I knew the purpose of the visit. He had one warrant for me and a second for the natives. I explained to him that the majority of natives lived further inland. I would send word to them to come and answer to the warrant. The officer was instantly suspicious. Was I was planning to tip off the natives so they could disperse and disappear? I managed to convince him there was no foul play intended. They wanted to be arrested. They would comply.

I made sure he knew I was doing him a favor, as he had no authority to arrest natives on their reservation without a federal warrant. He didn't argue. It was better to get them on the buses and into the courtroom rather than get into an argument over jurisdiction and return empty handed. They had come with a show of force, probably for the benefit of the news cameras that had accompanied them. The posse and the media followed us all the way into St. George. There was an even bigger group waiting for the buses at the court.

No visitors were allowed inside the courtroom. It was clear from the attitude of the judge that he wanted this over quickly and he pretty much had decided what he was going to do. The charges were read aloud: disturbing the peace, unlawful trespass, disobeying a peace officer, resisting arrest, and failure to respond to a summons. I wondered where the 'resisting arrest' came from. But what was one more?

"I have decided to deal with the tribal members together because you all face the same charges. What do you have to say to these charges? Do you have a chief or leader, someone in charge?"

"Sir, I dispute these proceedings and your authority to try us."

"Who are you?"

"I am Doug Wilson and I am the President of the Council. We are Paiute, and we are a sovereign nation. The State of Utah and its courts have no legal jurisdiction over us. We can only be tried in federal court."

"You committed crimes on Utah State property, and you will be tried within the state's legal system."

"We conducted a protest on property that belongs to our people. The freeways sit on native lands. We didn't deed easement rights to anyone to build the freeway. We committed no crime."

"Are you trying to teach me what a crime is?"

"We are not here to teach anybody anything. But, Sir, you should be aware of the limitations of this court when dealing with a sovereign nation. We will submit to federal authority and to federal authority only."

"It shall be as you wish. I am adjourning the court until 2:00 p.m. today. All parties to the conflict, including all of the accused, shall be present. All except Peter Tosco may leave."

"Sir, we wish to remain."

"Very well! You may stay but you must remain silent."

"Yes, Sir."

"Reverend Tosco, you have chosen not to have legal representation. Is that correct?"

"Yes, Sir."

"Do you understand the charges against you?"

"Yes, your Honor."

"Do you dispute any or all of the charges?"

"I dispute all of the charges."

"Why? Is it not true you joined the natives to block the freeways?"

"I have charge of the Catholic mission for the native tribe. I live among them and I minister to them. I support them in their struggle."

"That gives you no special privileges under the law. Your commitment to the Paiutes does not make you immune to the laws of the State of Utah."

"I can't fulfill my commitment to the native people without being an active participant in their struggle for justice."

"I am here to administer justice. You broke the law."

"They have a right to protest peacefully for their rights, and so do I."

"The charges do not reflect restrictions on the right to protest. The charges stem from the manner you chose to protest. Do you dispute that you participated in the freeway blockade?"

"I joined them in their pursuit of justice."

"You do then acknowledge that the charges are true."

"I will leave that decision up to you, Sir. I joined the Paiutes when they blocked the freeways. We wanted to draw attention to their demands for recognition as a sovereign nation, to have the land they live in reserved for them, and for restoration of the Little Bend River. It was peaceful."

"Are you a member of the native tribe?"

"No Sir, I am not."

"The native people may dispute my authority and the legality of the proceedings against them. They may have some protection due to their special status. Your situation is different. You have no excuse for your part in this. Worse reverend, you didn't appear in court as appointed. You are held to be in contempt for disobeying the court's directive. I find you guilty of all the charges. I can impose the maximum penalty and sent you to jail if I so choose. However, I shall take into account your fervor in serving these people, misguided though it is. Do you have anything further to state in your defense?"

"No Sir. I am fully prepared to face the consequences of my actions. I did what I did in support of the people I serve."

"I will be lenient with you as you have no previous record, and I do not find the presence of criminal intent. However, the consequences of your actions can't be ignored. You are determined guilty of a misdemeanor on the charges filed against you. You shall pay a penalty of $1,000. You may serve thirty days in county jail in lieu of paying the penalty. In addition, you shall be on probation for one year starting today. During your probation, further charges and conviction of a misdemeanor or higher shall constitute a breach of the terms of the probation, and you shall serve the remainder of the sentence in a state penitentiary in addition to the penalty imposed."

The gavel came down with a loud thud. I signed the paperwork and paid the fine. This didn't sit well with my native friends. They wanted me to appeal the judgment. I reminded them it was important to keep the focus on their demands and not get sidetracked with what was happening to me. We went back to court at 2:00 p.m. The case against the natives was transferred to Federal Court. They were asked to appear when ordered.

There was no time to celebrate or even treat this as a victory. It was important to keep in focus the main issues. It didn't matter what the news media had to say. We didn't buy or read newspapers except the one Malcolm dropped off. Like in any conflict, some people would agree and many wouldn't. It was imperative we steered clear of both views. It was important not to react to public opinion nor be influenced by it. No interviews were granted. Malcolm alone was allowed access and he was our source of information about what was going on outside.

Saturday brought a surprise visitor from the diocese, a surprise because of who it was. I had anticipated a visit from someone at the diocese ever since the freeway blockade. I found it hard to hold my anger in check when I saw who it was. I had no problem recognizing him the moment he showed up in front of my trailer. Yes. This was the person who had betrayed me and nearly led me to my death. It was Brother Francis, Father Francis by now. I reasoned, maybe, this was all part of God's plan for me. Francis was an instrument in His master plan. However, it was difficult to demonstrate much warmth. A not so charitable thought came to mind. Had he been sent here to spy on me?

Francis seemed overjoyed to see what had taken place at the mission. He told me he was an Associate at St. Florence Mission in Huntsville, some fifty miles north of Salt Lake City. He had come for a meeting at the diocese, and was surprised when the VG asked him to deliver a letter to me in person. My guess was right. He was sent down to investigate and report back on what was going on. I was getting more than a little annoyed by his behavior. He acted as if nothing had happened. If I was cold and unresponsive, he didn't seem to notice or care.

It wasn't long before the question had to be asked, and in spite of my resolve, it came out sounding much harsher than I had wanted.

"When we last talked, you were to come back to the Mission fourteen days later to pick me up. How come no one showed up to take me back? If you were assigned elsewhere, why didn't you make arrangements with someone to come and pick me up?"

The shock and surprise on his face were too spontaneous to be connived. He was speechless, and he looked at me as if he had been struck by lightning. Guilt, shame, and embarrassment were evident on his face as he kept looking at me in disbelief. I knew right away that something had happened and he was not to blame.

"Peter, I had no idea. I was sent on a pre-ordination retreat, and then for parochial work in Mexico a couple of days after I went back. I had asked the VG to send someone to pick you up on the day you and I had agreed on. He promised. What happened?"

"That's what I want to know."

"That can't be. I had given a full accounting of our trip to the VG in person when I returned and why you had stayed back. He knew you had no car as I had driven your car back. I left the keys with him and it was parked in the chancery lot. Could he have forgotten?"

"I wouldn't be surprised. The VG has more important things on his mind. The fate of Father Tosco is of little consequence."

"I am sorry Peter. I feel terrible. Please tell me what happened."

I was reluctant at first. But the more it became obvious he had no role in the near fatal fiasco, my resentment abated and I told him the whole story. I had to get it off my chest.

"You could have been killed."

"I know. But things have changed. Now that I have told you about it, it's not important anymore. Maybe it was part of God's plan for me."

"That's not an excuse for what happened. Does the VG know? Have you told him?"

"No and I don't plan to. It's over. I am glad you came and we got to talk about it. I had been harboring real bad feelings about you."

"I am sorry Peter!"

"Let's put it behind us. It was not your fault. I survived. It has led me to something meaningful. For the first time in my life I feel I'm doing something worthwhile. In that sense, it had to happen. It's interesting the VG remembered all of a sudden that you'd been here before. It's no accident he chose you to hand deliver the letter to me."

"He didn't tell me anything other than to deliver it to you in person."

"Let's find out why it's so important."

Dear Fr. Tosco:

I am very much perturbed by news of your arrest and arraignment. Your actions and the resulting notoriety have placed the diocese in an unenviable position. You have a difficult task working with the natives and developing the mission there. However, we can't lose sight of our goal which is to administer to the spiritual needs of the community. Your actions as a priest of the diocese affect the diocese as a whole and the Catholic Church in general. I view your involvement with the natives in their social and political unrest as contrary to the goals of the mission.

The following order goes into effect immediately:

1) The diocese can't be directly involved in nor seen as an accessory to or sponsor of native unrest. There is talk in the media that you are the instigator of the native unrest. This is of grave concern. Such media attention can only serve to damage the reputation of the diocese and the church. You shall not involve yourself in such activity.

2) The mission has specific goals. A Catholic mission exists to spread the word of God and provide spiritual support to the faithful. However worthy the cause, the mission shall not be part of politically motivated activities.

3) It is conceivable that one can't fully separate the spiritual needs of the community from their social needs. However righteous you may feel about the plight of the native tribes, it is the policy of the diocese to pursue the path of non-intervention. You shall abide by this policy.

4) You do not function as an individual person acting in a personal capacity. As a priest, your actions have a direct bearing on the role of the diocese. Therefore, the goals of the diocese and the mission must always take precedence over personal preferences. This is inviolable.

I have had several discussions with the bishop ever since news of what happened started appearing in the media. I have received numerous complaints from members of the clergy and the faithful expressing their dismay and displeasure over your actions.

As directed by his Excellency, I am ordering you to cease and desist immediately from any and all activities that may be interpreted as political involvement with the tribe. You must put aside personal sentiments and remain bound to the vow of obedience to the bishop.

We will keep you in our prayers.
Sincerely in Christ Jesus,

Monsignor Mark Cavanaugh
Vicar General, Catholic Diocese of Salt Lake City

"How about that? I have been given my marching orders."

"You are making them very nervous."

"It's nothing but a hoax, this policy of non-intervention. They are trying to hide and remain inconspicuous. They have the cathedral hanging like a noose around their necks. They don't want any attention focused there."

"But, they have the authority and we are bound to obey orders."

"The church can't be a bystander and run like a dog with its tail between its legs whenever there is a controversy. The church must support and champion the just cause of oppressed people. Otherwise, the church has no relevance and we might as well close the mission."

"That must sound like music to their ears."

"Then, let them do it. I can't preach the gospel to these people and not be unconcerned about their welfare. I would be a hypocrite."

"Do what you do but do it quietly! Maybe that's what they want."

"I am not trying to draw attention to myself. What I have to say, I say during my homily. What I do is what I preach."

"Peter, you are doing the right thing! It's your deeds far more than your words that will bring the message of Jesus to the people. I wish to have the courage one day to do what you are doing."

"You are welcome anytime, Francis. There is a couch in the trailer."

"I might take you up on your offer."

"No Francis. You are new. You are young. You can't afford to get into their bad graces. They won't be as tolerant of you as they are of me."

"Young or old, I too have my convictions."

"Take your time. If you make noises now, you will be branded as a revolutionary. Your time will come. There is a saying: 'Do not stretch your legs until you sit down.' I got into this by accident. But this is where I am and I am not about to back out. I am not going to cozy up to the bishop or the VG and try to win them over. But your case is different. You can't afford to take a stand, yet. I do not want to see you accused as my accomplice."

"I will be quiet and bide my time. But, I am with you in spirit. Is that okay if I stay tonight and celebrate Mass with you tomorrow before I head back?"

"Of course Francis. It's nice to see you and have your company. More importantly, I am glad you cleared up my misunderstanding."

It was a relief to have Francis with me for a little while. My good feelings for him were restored. I enjoyed his company. I introduced him to the natives when we met in the evening. Later, Francis and I strolled through the store. They had been slowly fixing up the interior and it was starting to look really nice. It was large enough to contain a lot more stock, but what they had was displayed cleverly to make it look full.

I found I could talk with ease with this young man, and he had an air of eagerness to listen that was unaffected. During my meetings with the tribal members, I preferred to be a listener and let them express their views. Here with Francis, I found myself talking aloud about my dreams, my goals, and the many obstacles I foresaw. Not surprisingly, they all centered on the future of the Paiutes of Little Bend.

I thought it fitting to have Francis deliver the homily. He was taken aback by the media presence but once he got going, it didn't seem to bother him. If he was here to experience the real meaning of mission work, there was no better way to do it than by taking it on, front and middle. Francis ended eloquently weaving the role of the mission with the humanity of Christ.

The barbecue lunch was a success as usual and sold out a lot sooner. It was my custom to hang around and converse with people after services. Not surprisingly, today, most of the discussions centered on the freeway blockade. I talked about the importance of restoring the river. A small minority expressed support for the Paiutes; most expressed outrage and felt the church should stay out of such issues. The media circus was finally gone, disappointed and frustrated that they couldn't engage anyone of the natives or me in some discussion on the freeway blockade. They took pictures and wandered around taking more pictures. Most of the villagers were present, but chose to ignore the media and treated them as nothing more than customers to the store. Francis and I sat in front of my trailer and watched the goings-on. Doug and a couple of others came by and sat with us for some time.

We sat quietly, enjoying the peace and serenity of the early night. It's really fascinating to look up at the heavens on a clear, desert night. The sky appears a lot closer, and there is a greater clarity and sharpness to the stars and other heavenly bodies. It was after eleven o'clock before we decided to call it a day. Francis would be heading back early next morning.

Something woke me up with a start. I heard loud shouts and cries for help. It took a split second for me to realize it wasn't part of a dream and it was coming from the direction of the store. Before I had time put my feet down, Francis was up and fully alert. I grabbed a flashlight, and without any hesitation, we both dashed out of the trailer.

There was a fire spreading quickly. With a sinking heart I realized the store was on fire, spreading quickly, rearing and crackling into life. There were the shrill cries of women mingled with the hoarse shouts of the men. Above it all, I could hear the honking of horns and the sudden screeching of tires. We saw a large pick-up speeding away in a southerly direction, tires trailing smoke. It was too far away to identify the make and color of the truck.

The fire was spreading rapidly. There wasn't anything we could do to put it out and save the store. We raced around in helpless despair, knowing all was lost, and all we could do was watch. The wood of the structure had dried completely in the summer sun and it burned with cruel ferocity. There was the unmistakable smell of gasoline in the air. Whoever had done this knew what they were doing.

It was hopeless. We managed to pull everyone away to the safety of the church. The heat was intense and we had nothing to even make a feeble attempt to put out the fire. The natives were in total shock, unable to comprehend the tragedy that was unfolding before them. Devastated, we watched as the conflagration engulfed and consumed the entire store. With a great display of sparks and smoke, the roof collapsed. We watched in horror as the hopes and aspirations of a community were reduced to a heap of ashes. It had taken no more than fifteen minutes to obliterate months of hard work and planning.

No one spoke. The feeling of helplessness was too much to take. The women sobbed and moaned quietly while their companions stood expressionless and watched. The unexpected shock and the total destruction had numbed every one and we stood and stared. No one could find anything to say. Even Francis, the only one who could be detached from the happenings of the last few months, was totally stunned. He sat there clutching his fists in a fierce knot.

The searching headlights lit up the column of smoke giving it an eerie look. The villagers had sensed something was wrong, and they were crowding in to the front of the store—or what had been the store. They must have seen the glow of the fire and instinctively realized it had to do with the store or the church. We still didn't move, huddled together, unable to feel anything or say anything.

The villagers ran out of their vehicles, and then came to an abrupt stop as realization sank in and the reality of the tragedy stared at them. I have no idea how long they stood watching the now smoldering rubble, horror and disbelief written all over their faces. Eventually they came to the church to where we sat. As if driven by some unseen primordial force, they joined together in one embrace, like players in a football huddle—and in slow motion, they started to rock back and forth moaning or mumbling in their native dialect. The tragedy had pulled them together and they sought comfort as a group. It was like someone had died within the community and they were expressing their grief. Here, they were faced with the death of their dreams and hopes.

They were native Paiute, shorn of all affectations of civilization, children of the soil, seeking refuge in time-honored rituals in the hope they could overcome the senseless tragedy. They went on in this way for a long time until, as one, they were spent. Then, they sat on the ground, hands clutched together, and with their faces turned toward the heavens. In their own way, they were seeking help from the Great Spirit to provide meaning for the evil they had been subjected to. There were no expressions of anger, only anguish. There was no call to battle or revenge. Who was the enemy?

We sat there, Francis and me, separate from the villagers. Finally two of them were dispatched back to the village to report on what had happened. The rest of us waited, each lost in silent thought. Words would have been superfluous; words would have appeared silly, unable to capture the despair and the agony. Silence was the only remedy. It was a strange scene. As other members came, the scene was re-enacted.

The embers of the fire had completely died down and even the somber glow was gone. Dawn came piercing the darkness with slivers of golden light to illuminate the now-unfamiliar landscape. There was nothing left of the store. Some smoke could be seen rising from here and there, probably the dying gasps of a horse or a buffalo sculpture that had perished. The church and my trailer suffered no damage, being too far away from the fire. The trailer behind the store suffered some damage to its front where it had been seared and singed by the intense heat. Luckily, it survived.

Once there was enough light, we got up as one and walked around the burned-out store. We then walked slowly back to the church. We were oblivious to the honks of intermittent travelers who wondered at the strange assembly and the tell-tale signs of a fire.

There were decisions that had to be made, but no one was willing to break the silence. Where does one start—and how, when you are confronted with such unfathomable feelings? It was unclear how long we sat there. Finally, I broke the silence and addressed them as a group.

"The work we have done over the last several months has been turned to ashes today. Never in our dreams could we have envisioned such hatred. We have become targets of bigotry. We have become the object of human nature at its worst. But, we are alive. We breathe, we walk, and we raise our eyes to God. In our sorrow we ask God, we ask the Great Spirit, why? There is no answer. There will be no answer.

God has not abandoned us. God is with us even now. God won't offer us solutions. We must come up with our own solutions. We must choose to respond to this hateful act in our own way. We must overcome this tragedy. We have come too far to be beaten down. The spirit burns within us, even stronger than the fire that consumed the fruits of our labor. Those who perpetrated this heinous act, they want to defeat us; they want to drive the stake deep into our will so that we will never rise again. It is they that must be defeated. They must understand the futility of their folly. We will not be defeated.

We shall not be driven to act in anger. We shall not give in to despair and certainly we shall not fall prey to fear. To those who are responsible, we shall stand up and say, 'You can't defeat us. We won't let you find satisfaction in this hateful act.' They shall not see us bite the dust and crawl away. We must overcome their hatred. We must rise again.

We built our dreams from nothing. We have nothing again. But we can and we will rebuild. We shall rise again. We can. Thus shall we defeat and shame their evil hearts and souls. The spirit is strong within us. The spirit shall not die. My friends, a new day is upon us. We shall live again. We are not cowards. We shall overcome this tragedy. Yes, we shall."

"How can we rebuild? We have nothing left."

"We have us and that's what's important."

"So much work, all gone in a flash."

"We can't give up. We must not give way to despair."

"We must rebuild. We owe it to ourselves."

"We achieved much in a short time. We proved we could. We'll do it again."

"Yes, we can."

"Somebody out there wants to destroy us. They will do it again."

"We were lucky this time. Nobody got killed or injured. How about next time?"

"We can't turn tail and run. That's what they want to see and that's what they hope will happen."

"We have shown what we can do. We can do it again."

"We must rebuild."

"We are Paiute. We won't be defeated."

"We must rebuild."

"We are here and here we are to stay."

"We must rebuild."

"Our bodies are strong, our souls are pure."

"We must rebuild."

"We must be vigilant. They will attack us again."

"We will be prepared."

"Evil shall not be rewarded with evil."

"We will defend ourselves. We have the right to do so."

"They have might, but right is on our side. We shall conquer might with right, and we shall prevail."

"We shall overcome."

"We shall rise again."

"We shall rebuild."

"We must rebuild."

"We will rebuild!"

I looked around and saw a mixture of emotions—confusion in some, disquiet and anger among the younger members, an uncharacteristic level of passion among the women, and hesitation among them all. The elders who, in the past, would have gone into withdrawal mode, appeared to embrace the prevailing sentiment to act. It was a welcome sign. They were stepping out of their centuries-old habit of withdrawing into a shell in the face of threat and making a resolute decision to move forward.

In a spontaneous spurt of excitement, they rose as one and went into the Bear Dance, chanting and moving in circles. The women, though not dancing, joined in the chants, and beat their chests with both arms. It was an expression of solidarity demonstrated in their traditional way. The dance, usually reserved for sending braves into battle was taking on a new meaning. Maybe, symbolically, that's what they were doing. They then sat down in a circle swaying from side-to-side, still chanting with occasional shouts. The meaning of the utterances was unclear, but what mattered was they were acting in unison with a common purpose.

Francis watched the unfolding drama, totally incredulous, at a loss what to make of it. I saw before me a small tribe transforming itself into a nation with a new sense of purpose and a determination that would not be denied.

"How much do we have in savings?"

"About $3,000."

"That's not much."

"That's more than what we had when we first started."

"Let's do what we did at the beginning. $2,000 to buy merchandise, $1,000 to rebuild the store."

"We will need a lot more than that to make the store like it was."

"That's true. But we don't have to. What we lack in funds, we will replace with our effort. Starting today, everyone who can, must pitch in to make things we can sell."

"We should have the same groups go scouting for merchandise, collect the lumber, and buy materials. Everyone pitches in to rebuild."

"We reopen in two weeks."

Malcolm showed up the next day with a camera crew. He was angry, and didn't try to hide it beneath a veneer of professionalism. He was an objective reporter, accustomed to seeing all kinds of tragedies. Yet, he was human and he couldn't but be touched by the injustices these simple people were subjected to. When he left, he gave parting words of encouragement to the people to hang in there and fight for their rights.

The ash and debris were shoveled off and heaped to one side forming a mound visible from the freeways. A sign was made and planted in the middle of the mount facing the freeway that read, "You burned down our store, but re-kindled our spirit."

A load of lumber and a tarpaulin for cover were brought in later that day, and they began setting up the tent exactly as it was before. We were back to the tent store until the log walls could be built around it. Over the next two weeks, merchandise was brought in by the "foragers" and set up inside the tent and hung from the ceiling.

I wrote a letter and sent two of the members to the thrift stores of Goodwill, St. Vincent De Paul, and Salvation Army to pick up used furniture and appliances. They came back with a few donated items, a midsize old refrigerator, a microwave, a jukebox, and other odds-and-ends they could use in the store. Electricity had to be reconnected as the original connections had been burned out. An extension from my trailer would take care of it temporarily. Most of the tools they had bought earlier were safe, as they were stored inside the trailer. If the trailer had caught fire, it would have been a total disaster.

I sent a letter with Francis to the VG explaining what had happened and sought his support to help the tribe maybe through a special collection. I wanted to make sure I left no stone unturned to find help to rebuild.

There was a large crowd for the Sunday service. There was the usual contingent of media types that was becoming a regular feature of the services. The area was becoming a hotspot. The Herald must have published another piece about the recent suspicious fire.

In my homily, I touched upon the struggles of the native tribe. For the first time, I asked the congregation to support the tribe financially. People could see for themselves what the tribe was doing to rebuild.

There was the usual barbecue lunch after services. When the proceeds including the collection were counted, we had a total of a little over $1,500. Even the media people contributed. It was all going to be used to rebuild the store. The following Sunday a total of $900 collected.

On Wednesday, Malcolm showed up. He had brought along copies of the paper. The front-page article had a picture, actually two pictures juxtaposed to form one. The pictures were taken at an angle that showed the cross on the totem pole in the background, the one on the left showing the store as it had been, and the one on the right showing the smoldering ruins of the burned out store. The article was titled, 'Why in God's Name?' It was a probing article recounting the struggles of the native tribe, the role of the mission, and my involvement with the tribe. Malcolm told us the editor was so touched by what the tribe had to endure that he had set up a fund with the help of a local bank to support them. So far the fund had brought in $2,000, and he had brought it with him. They would continue to support the ad for a few more weeks. Three churches, two in Salt Lake City, and one in Provo, had run collection drives and that netted a little under $1,000. More was expected.

The natives were deeply touched by Malcolm's efforts, the support of the paper, and people from far away who had never met them. It helped restore some of their confidence and repaired a little of the damage that had been done to their psyche. There were a few Letters to the Editor, some expressing outrage and a few bad ones condemning the natives for sparking the problems with the ill-fated freeway blockade. A couple of them even went so far as to allude that the tribe had done it themselves to generate sympathy. Prejudice and ignorance often go hand-in-hand and in the hands of irrational people, it's a toxic brew.

Francis came back for a quick visit and was thrilled to see what had happened since his last visit. He had called on the VG before leaving and told him where he was headed. The VG was indifferent, but had asked him to inform me that there was no chance of making an appeal for money. The parishes were already inundated with too many demands for help and it was not an opportune time to ask for more. I was disappointed, more so since the churches that came forward to help after reading about it in the paper were not Catholic and had no connection with the native tribe. The diocese had the capacity to do something for the tribe and had a vested interest in the mission. They chose to ignore their mission.

I found it hard to swallow. Exactly one week before the fire, the diocese had its annual mission drive. Priests from the Congregation of the Sacred Heart had gone around the parishes talking about and seeking support for their missions in Central America. I was mortified by the blunt hypocrisy of a diocese burying millions into the renovation of a cathedral, asking the faithful to support missions in faraway lands, and preaching about compassion while refusing to look at the needy in front of their eyes. Supporting foreign missions is a noble thing. How about a mission within its borders?

The days were shorter and the nights were colder. The work on the telephone tower had begun. They were laying the foundation, and final construction would begin sometime mid-spring. Another thousand dollars was collected and delivered by Malcolm. There could be more in the weeks ahead.

It looked exactly like the original tent store. Filling it up wasn't easy. The villagers were busy, especially the women, working night and day, weaving and making trinkets. There were two families living at the store now. I knew they had firearms with them, but decided not to express my personal opposition to weapons at this critical stage.

It was the Sunday evening after the store was rebuilt. We met in front of my trailer as we often did. The store looked no different but I could sense a change of attitude among the villagers. They were angry. As Doug spoke, there was no wariness or defensiveness. You could sense suppressed anger. His opening statement came as a shock though.

"We will blockade the freeways again. We'll show them we are not scared. Father Tosco taught us to be persistent if we want to succeed. We must continue to strike and force the issue. We have limited options but blocking the freeways is one of them and effective.'

"Once the authorities understand that there will be no lasting peace at this location, they will sit down and negotiate with us."

"They may put us all in jail. But, they can't keep us in jail forever. When we are released, we will block the freeways again."

"How will other nations react to what we are doing?"

"It's not our concern. They can join us or stay away."

"We will keep the women and children out of trouble. They will have to run the store in case we are arrested and get thrown in jail."

"The governor will want it resolved. He can't allow this to continue."

"We must expect force, violence and intimidation before they decide to engage us in serious discussions. We won't be intimidated."

"We must find out who is behind the burning of the store."

"It could be the work of white ranchers from the south. It may have to do with the demand for the restoration of the Little Bend."

"They may be warning us to back off from the demands."

"Like vultures that wait for a weak animal to die, they have waited for our demise. A thriving native nation is not what they want to see here."

"There are Klan elements and the brotherhood is alive and well in these parts. They could be behind this."

"Father Tosco, you must be careful. You are at great risk. You must stay away from the protests."

"The police won't show restraint in dealing with you. The diocese and the general public have been harsh in their condemnation of your role."

"Let me make sure we all understand this the right way. I am in this with my eyes open. I am under no compulsion to join you. It is by my choice. It's something I want to do. I'm not afraid of the consequences."

"Father Tosco, you can help us immensely without putting yourself at risk."

"We deeply appreciate what you have done and what you continue to do. Without you none of this would be possible. We need you, your advice, your judgment, and your support. We don't want you in jail."

"We have a responsibility to protect you and your reputation."

"I understand and appreciate your concern. But, remember, I am here to serve you. The mission can succeed only if you succeed. That means we are in this together. Only you can stop me."

"We need you a lot more than you think we do. We won't stop you from what you want to do. We don't think it's fair to put you at risk, that's all."

"Our purpose is just; we have nothing to fear. Our actions are guided by pure principles. Nothing can stop us. Only we can stop ourselves!"

There would be serious repercussions. The state and local

authorities would act decisively and forcibly. There would be a loud outcry from the public. Those were predictable. People in power resort to use of force because they can, they have the tools, and it's easy. But the truth is, it fails. Even though you enslave a whole race of people and suppress their aspirations, it'll not bring lasting peace. You can force people into compliance through physical, spiritual, or psychological torture and you may feel you are in control. Yet, one day, the spirit will shake off the manacles of restraint and strike back at the oppressor.

Police have weapons and they claim it's not for show. That's the beauty of power. Power creates a false sense of strength that blinds people from reason and compromise. It was unclear whether my friends knew what awaited them. Will they be like concrete that hardens under the sun, or like butter melt under the heat? Time alone would tell.

The blockade was total. It was a Monday morning just after 8:00. Lumber was laid across all the lanes on all three forks of the freeway. A tepee was set up in the middle and to the rear of the junction. The men sat in an upside 'V' three people deep, facing the teepee. The three demands were pinned to the front of the teepee. They chanted and swayed to some rhythmic beat. Even with reduced traffic on the roads the backup lengthened quickly in all directions. I knew it wouldn't be long before the police arrived. I watched from the front of the store.

It wasn't the police that showed up first. It was a helicopter from a TV station. It circled fairly low overhead, creating an infernal din and kicking up swirls of dust.

The first batch of patrol officers came screaming down from the north on their bikes, sirens blaring, and lights flashing. I could see them from a longs way off. It was then I made my move. I walked slowly toward the middle of the group. They didn't notice me until I walked right through them and took a seat in the middle. They looked up, wavered for a second, but continued the chanting. Quietly, I sat down facing the teepee. The patrol officers arrived, their radios snapping on and off. Sheriff's deputies arrived a short time later.

Out of the corner of my eye, I could see them group together with batons drawn and the visors on their helmets lowered. Soon others arrived and positioned themselves on all sides, surrounding us. A few took up positions behind the teepee so that we couldn't escape that way. They outnumbered us four to one. They had their riot gear on and the formation was tight so that no one could pierce their ranks from inside or out. We were completely caged in. They had come prepared.

No one on the ground could see what was happening as we were sitting on the ground and the cordon of officers was standing. An officer got on a bullhorn and ordered us to stand up and turn around to face the officers. We didn't comply. We were advised we were under arrest for breaking the peace and disobeying a peace officer. He informed us of our Miranda Rights. There was no response from us. The chanting continued.

The cops moved in close and we could feel their presence even though we were not looking at them. If we had expected to create a scene, we couldn't have planned it any better. I could hear a second chopper, and soon a third. The noise was deafening. The news cameras were taking all this in and a crowd of travelers had gathered around pushing and jostling each other and the news crew for a better view. They were prodding the officers on to take action.

There was no resistance from any of us as we were roughly hauled to our feet and handcuffed behind our backs. All of us were turned around and made to face the officer in charge, the one with the bullhorn. A dozen or so officers were lined up behind him. They had the baton in one hand and the other was at the holster.

Doug led the cry: Recognize the Paiutes; Reserve the Bend Valley; Restore the Little Bend. Every one repeated the refrain. They did that over and over again. The officer shouted to them to shut up and listen, but nobody paid any attention. They kept shouting the same slogans.

People were getting restive and screaming at the officers to clear the freeways and get the people off the roads. Verbal abuse was being hurled equally at us as well as the officers. Doug and company kept their slogans going without a halt. Various objects, soda cans, water bottles, and various fruits came flying in from all directions. Dust was swirling around as well. Amidst the din, confusion and chaos, the police were struggling to keep their composure and get a handle on the situation.

The officer in charge was red in the face from trying to shout through the bullhorn, angry, frustrated, and at a loss for what to do. It was comical. Here we were standing less than three feet in front of him, and he was shouting orders using the bullhorn. He must have observed me standing in the middle of the group, and realized that I wasn't a native. He ordered me to come forward, and demanded to know what was going on. There was no reply from me. I stood where I was.

"I know who you are. You are the Catholic priest. I see you are at it again. You should be ashamed of yourself."

I didn't respond.

"I don't care if you are a priest. You are breaking the law and instigating these people into breaking the law?"

There was no answer.

"Get him out of there."

A young officer stepped forward. He grabbed my shirt and yanked me forward from behind a couple of our people. I was unprepared for the suddenness and the force of the pull that tore my shirt and popped the upper buttons. We were standing in a tight knot. My feet got tangled up and I fell clear of the protesters, almost at the feet of the officer. With my hands tied behind my back, I had no way to check the fall or regain my balance. I fell hard, face first, onto the asphalt. It all happened in the blink of an eye before anyone could react. There was hardly any space for all of us; we were so tightly grouped together. I tried to turn over, but the same officer grabbed the back of my shirt and tried to haul me back on my feet. That didn't work. I was trying desperately to get my footing right. The shirt came loose into his hands and I fell back hitting my head on the hard surface with a loud thud.

There were loud shouts all around followed by expressions of shock. I could feel and taste blood flowing down my face. My glasses must have splintered and I could feel the searing pain where shards of the lens had embedded in my face. There was blood in my eyes and I couldn't see. Without the freedom of my hands, I couldn't wipe off the blood. It was a mess. I wasn't sure if my eyes were okay. Blood was flowing into my nose and mouth and as I gasped for breath, I snorted blood through my nose and started to choke. I coughed violently splattering blood all around.

I struggled helplessly, and slowly got to a kneeling position and finally managed to stand up, unable to see at all but aware of all hell breaking loose around me. I was half-naked and there must have been blood all over. There were cries of shock. Then came the hail of objects being hurled from all around hitting us and the officers alike.

The officers were losing their cool and shouting orders that no one was heeding. I heard shouts of anger from the natives and the rush of feet toward me. I heard the shouts of the officers, the swish of batons, and the unmistakable crack of wood on bone. In my blind state, I was expecting the batons on my head at any moment but didn't have the freedom to protect myself with my hands. It was chaos around me with the situation totally out of control.

Suddenly, there was the sickening sound, the unmistakable sound of gunfire. With all that was going on around, it was impossible to say how many shots were fired. There were cries of pain. People had been shot. An eerie silence, and then the sound of people running and stampeding.

I was knocked to the ground a third time. I was getting trampled, but could make no effort to help myself. I could feel heavy boots crushing my bare skin against the asphalt. What was happening? Where was I? My face was burning and the pain in my head was excruciating. If only someone would free my hands. Let me wipe the blood out of my eyes. The pain was relentless.

I felt myself slowly passing out. No. I couldn't lose consciousness now. I fought hard to stay awake, but my head was swimming and the pounding pain in my head was unbearable. I wished the copters would go away. There were odd shouts and sounds of people groaning and women wailing. The sounds slowly faded as I sank into oblivion. The last thing I heard was the distant wail of sirens, and then darkness took over.

How long I remained unconscious, I have no idea. As if coming out of a deep sleep, I became aware of distant sounds, like muffled thunder. It was all darkness, and I couldn't feel a thing, my hands, my feet, or any other part of the body. The sounds seemed to clear up momentarily and I was aware that they were human sounds. It was impossible to gage the direction of the sounds or what was being said and by whom.

Where was I? What was wrong with me? Confusion, panic, anxiety and anger were all welling up inside. There were people, at least two, somewhere near me. How can I communicate to them that I'm awake? I couldn't feel anything. All on a sudden, a wave of nausea hit me without warning. I couldn't move, I couldn't breathe and I couldn't open my mouth. The next thing I knew I was convulsing uncontrollably, racked by spasms and bouts of coughing. I wished I could pass out again but was denied that luxury. I had never felt so sick and miserable in my life.

There was a rush of feet around me, multiple incoherent voices, hands gently but firmly holding me down. And then that welcome feeling of calm nothingness.

❦

"What do we do with Father Tosco?"

"He will survive!"

"Last I heard he's able to tolerate the pain for longer periods of time."

"He sure was lucky. A little deeper and he would have been history. The bullet didn't miss by much."

"His eyesight has not suffered, has it?"

"No, the eyes are okay and he should have his vision intact once the swelling subsides and the stitches are removed. The injury to his skull will take longer. They say the bone will grow back in time."

"There is no damage to the brain, is there?"

"No, thank God. Escaped literally by the skin of his teeth. The bullet took a glancing blow and knocked off a piece of his skull."

"When's the last time a Catholic Priest has been shot and killed by police?"

"I don't think ever. Not in this country."

"The physical scars will be the lesser of the problems."

"What do you mean?"

"The doctors don't know how he'll react to the death of the natives."

"He does not know?"

"No. They've kept him sedated. Whenever they try to keep him awake, he goes into spasms and convulsions. It's getting better though."

"He should be able to recover fully, won't he?"

"That is the prognosis. The psychological scars are difficult to predict?"

"This whole incident is bad for the diocese."

"The bishop must be steaming in his shoes."

"What's he going to do about this? What can he do?"

"He is gravely troubled. The image he has worked up so diligently to cultivate has been shattered."

"The diocese is in the news every day."

"The press has been attacking him and the diocese."

"Father Tosco has become a magnet for trouble."

"People like Father Tosco can never stay out of trouble. Trouble follows him like a shadow."

"We still have to deal with the situation."

"It must be handled carefully. The media will scrutinize our every move."

"Father Tosco must be removed from the spotlight as soon as possible."

"Let's get him someplace where the media has no access to him. Once he's recovered, transfer him to the Seminary or to a retreat house where he won't have much access to the public."

"Sending him to the mission was an attempt to take him off the spotlight."

"Wherever he goes, he'll find a way to become the spotlight."

"I think he likes the attention. He must enjoy the exposure."

"We must put a lid on how he conducts himself in the future."

"I do hope he'll recover intact to have a future."

"What kind of restraints can we put on him?"

"I sent him a letter asking him to refrain from political involvement and stick to mission activities. It made no difference."

"What exactly can a diocese do if a priest does not obey orders? Can you not discipline him?"

"This is no time to talk about disciplinary actions. We need to let him recover fully."

"He must not return to the mission."

"He won't be ready to return there any time soon."

"We don't need this mission anymore. It's been nothing but trouble. Let's close it once and for all."

"We'll move him to Holy Cross in Salt Lake City as soon as he can tolerate it. They have a really good rehabilitation program there. More important, he'll be far from the media crowd."

"How is Father Francis doing at the mission?"

"I haven't heard back from him. He volunteered to go and I agreed. It would have looked bad if we closed the mission and abandoned the natives in the face of tragedy."

"Father Francis must be told what he can and can't do. I suggest all he does is say Mass on Sundays and then return."

"What about the natives?"

"They won't care. The Paiutes have been traditionally very compliant. They may not want to continue on a confrontational campaign. Maybe, they are regretting they got themselves into this mess. They lost two of their members. They probably are convinced they made a bad move for which they've paid a heavy price. They may resign themselves to their old ways."

"What they do, that's their problem. We have to be clear on what we do. Close down the mission."

Book of Sarah

By unanimous choice, we have selected Sarah Wilson as the new president of the Paiute Nation of Little Bend. As the senior member of the council, and as required by tradition, I personally met with all adult members of the tribe. The president and a new council have been selected by majority opinion. Sarah, we know it's a time of immense personal tragedy for you. You have lost your husband and we are barely done with the funeral ceremonies. But we are facing a critical period in our life. We need to ensure we have leaders in place to guide us through these dark days. We ask you to accept the new responsibility."

"The loss and sorrow I feel can never be wiped away, and I will carry the pain with me until the day I take my last breath. Doug was a good man, a loving husband, a friend, and a companion. He was a cautious man. But he believed in this cause. I am honored you have put your faith in me and chosen me to be the president of the council. I accept, for the sake of Doug, for the memory of Stan, and for the future of our nation. We shall continue what we started, what Doug and Stan gave their lives for. I accept and together we shall fulfill the dreams of a man who lies in a hospital battling for his life, a life he dedicated for our future. I accept knowing if we work together we can achieve what we set out to achieve."

"Sarah, we are confident the Great Spirit who is everywhere, will guide you. The spirits of our forefathers and the spirits of our fallen brothers will counsel you. You will lead with grace and dignity and won't allow anger and hatred to influence your decisions. We have confidence in you."

"The struggle must continue. We shall not falter or veer off course."

"Father Francis, we appreciate your presence with us in our time of need."

"We are very concerned about Father Tosco's condition."

"Do you have an update on him?"

"The good news is he should recover fully. There is no permanent damage to his eyes and to his brain. Part of the skull that was blown away will heal but will take time. What we don't know is how long it'll take."

"Please tell him when you see him that he is constantly in our thoughts."

"We haven't visited him as we were told he was not ready for visitors; it would be too much for him right now. We know you've been to the hospital almost every day. When you can, tell him we care about him deeply."

"Visitors won't be allowed for a few more days. I am there in case he asks for someone when he wakes up. He has no family we know of. When I see him, I'll tell him. He has a tough road ahead of him. He'll have to deal with his physical issues and also deal with the media, the public and the diocese."

"The media has not been kind to him or to us."

"The media is not going to make a saint out of him. He's more valuable to them as a villain."

"We learn what we know from you and Malcolm and from the newspapers you both bring with you."

"He's not a deranged demagogue as the media portrays him. He's not the leader of an uprising or rebellion by the natives."

"We have all lost much for this cause. Our loss is irreparable."

"But, we won't back down. We will continue until the goals are met. We owe it to our brothers who gave their lives for this."

"Father Francis, they were family. We have two widows and two children without a father. We lost two of our brothers. Who can replace them?"

"Look at the frequent patrols. We are under siege. All we did was ask for some consideration of our basic rights to live with dignity, and have a decent existence as a nation and as a community."

"We did what we could to draw attention to our plight. Look at the response. Look at how little they value native lives."

"I am not Father Tosco but I will be here when you need me, until he's back."

"Father Tosco spoke highly of you. He told us we could trust you as we trusted him. That's enough for us. You shall be accepted as warmly."

"Thank you. I am greatly honored."

"Many nations were represented at the funeral. They are slowly waking up to the struggle going on here."

"There were expressions of outrage and messages of solidarity."

"Are they willing to do something more? Will they join us in our fight?"

"We will continue our struggle with or without their support."

"The locals are angry. There have been calls to drive us out of here and shut down the store and the mission."

"Doug had expressed concern about a group of ranchers down South who are opposed to the restoration of the Little Bend. He suspected they were behind the burning of the store."

"They'll try again but they won't succeed. We will be ready."

"They are not rational people. Hatred is in their blood; our destruction is their religion. We must be on guard."

"We will be prepared."

"Weakness and meekness won't serve us. We must strike back."

"Violence will only breed more violence. We must forgo the path of violence except in self-defense."

"We must not remain passive. They must know we can and will retaliate with force and cause harm. That will discourage their brazenness."

"They will be less brave if they know we'll fire back."

"What about the future of the mission? Will the diocese shut it down?"

"It's too early to tell. Many within the diocese are angry at what you did. But, I don't expect anything will be done until Father Tosco recovers."

"Here comes Malcolm. He'll have the latest news."

"Thanks for stopping by Malcolm."

"The FBI's investigating because the shooting involves a native nation. The state, I am sure, will order an investigation too. The police are desperate. They claim the shooting was in self-defense when attacked by a mob of angry natives."

"A group of unarmed natives with their hands cuffed behind their backs? What violence are they capable of?"

"The police opened fire. Only the police fired the shots."

"No amount of proof will win us justice. We are still the ruthless barbarians that need to be tamed by force, if needed."

"We should look beyond investigations. We should look beyond public opinion. We must stay focused on our demands."

"The investigations will prove nothing. We don't need to prove anything and we don't owe an explanation. Ours was an act of civil disobedience. It's not what we did, but what was done to us that deserves attention."

"Greenpeace climbed the towers of the Golden Gate Bridge and brought traffic to a standstill. It was a protest. They broke the law. Did the police shoot them down?"

"The investigation will be a mockery. We shouldn't cooperate."

"I think you should tell your story, which is the truth, the real truth."

"There's only one truth. The police shot and killed two of our brothers in cold blood. There's the video and there are the witnesses. If that doesn't convince anyone, what we say will make no difference."

"Ultimately, people will believe what they want to believe."

"The investigation will get us sidetracked. Our focus is not police brutality. Our focus is our demands: recognition of our nation, reservation of this land, and restoration of the Little Bend River."

"Father Tosco, I am Agent Thompson from the FBI. I am investigating the shooting at the native village. I know you were just released from the ICU and I understand you are very weak. But we need to talk. It's real important for the investigation that I get your side of the story. I need a statement from you. It won't take long."

"I have nothing to tell you."

"That attitude won't be helpful. I need all the facts I can get to reach a fair conclusion. We need to talk and soon. I see you are not ready now. I'll leave my card with you. Call me as soon as you feel ready to talk."

"Go away."

"There's no need to be rude."

"Leave me alone."

"I'll be back."

"Go! Leave me alone! Leave me alone!"

"Calm down! I am just doing my job!"

"I said, go away!"

"Sir, didn't we tell you he's not ready to talk? You wouldn't listen!"

"I am sorry Ma'am! I didn't realize he's that sick!"

"Francis, Is that you?"

"Yes, Peter."

"Lord, my head feels like it's ready to split apart."

"Take it easy Peter."

"What else can I do? Couldn't that guy wait a little?"

"We tried to stop him."

"What day is it?"

"Thursday."

"How long have I been here?"

"Two weeks."

"That long?"

"You are lucky to be alive."

"What happened? I don't remember anything."

"Why don't we wait awhile to discuss all that?"

"I am feeling better. It's just the headache. The guy just barged in and started talking. I don't remember anything. My mind is blurry."

"You have a nasty head wound. It's pretty bad."

"How did it happen?"

"Peter, you should wait until they feel you are ready to receive visitors. They let me in because you kept insisting on seeing me."

"Francis, I must know what happened. Am I all right? I have no feeling in any part of my body. You talk and I'll listen."

"You're okay. You should get your feeling back soon. They've kept you sedated all these days because of the convulsions. It could have been much worse. The bullet took out a piece of your skull. A little deeper and we wouldn't be talking today."

"I got shot! Who? Why?"

"Nobody knows! At first they were concerned about your eyes. I heard you had pieces of lens all around your eyes."

"Why was I shot?"

"It happened during the freeway protest. It's under investigation."

"Was anyone else hurt?"

"Let's talk about it later. I am over the time limit I was allowed. I will come back later. Get as much rest as you can."

"Francis!"

"Yes, Peter!"

"Tell me!"

"What?"

"Who else was shot?"

"This is what I was afraid of! We will talk about it when I come back!"

"No! Francis, tell me now! I must know."

"Later!"

"Now! Please!"

"The news isn't good."

"Tell me! I can take it Francis!"

"Let's wait."

"Tell me Francis! For heavens' sake, tell me!"

"Peter, take it easy. What did I tell you? You are coughing. Coughing is not good."

"Tell me."

"All right! Don't talk!"

"I won't talk. I'll listen."

"They don't know yet who fired the shots or how many shots were fired."

"I got shot. Who else?"

"Several people were injured, two seriously."

"Was someone killed?"

"Two didn't survive."

"Doug was one of them?"

"Yes. Stan was the other."

"Oh my God! Why? Why?"

"Shot at point blank range and died on the spot. They had no chance."

"Why? Why? Why?"

"Peter, Peter! Good Lord! Doctor! Nurse!"

"What happened?"

"We were talking. Then all on a sudden, his face went white and his breathing changed."

"Get him back into ICU and get the O^2 going."

"I am sorry. I shouldn't have been talking."

"This is what happens when you don't listen."

"He was stubborn!"

"They're all stubborn! No more visitors!"

"Father Francis, how are you? I had no time to let you know we were coming. This is Sr. Margaret Mallory, Superintendent of Schools and Agnes from the chancery."

"Yes, Monsignor. Hi Sr. Margaret, Hi Agnes! Good morning. Have you been here long?"

"No! Just a few minutes! We wanted to visit as soon as we could. I guess we didn't time it right. Nobody's allowed to see him today."

"I was told you talked to him earlier today."

"Not much—but more than I should have. He had a little setback and they put him back on sedation and back in the ICU."

"I talked to his Doctor. They think that he still has some swelling in the brain that is causing the convulsions. They have scheduled an MRI."

"We brought some flowers and a card from the bishop and the staff at the chancery. His grace wants to visit as soon as Father Tosco is ready."

"Francis, how long will you be staying?"

"I was planning on staying all day."

"Good. Can you do me a favor?"

"Yes."

"Call me once you have the MRI results."

"No problem."

"Here's my card with the direct number. Call me if anything comes up."

"I will."

"I am glad you are here. How are things at the mission?"

"They are doing okay, given the circumstances. The funerals are over. They are getting back to normalcy, little-by-little."

"Tell them we are with them in this hour of tragedy. If there is anything we can do to help, let me know."

"Thanks, Monsignor."

"We will get going. When he is awake, tell him we are praying for a quick recovery and return."

"I will, Monsignor!"

"Francis?"

"You are awake! How are you feeling?"

"Better. See, I can wiggle my toes."

"The MRI came out okay. Thank God!"

"Francis. I want to get out of here!"

"I'm not sure I want to start a conversation with you again."

"I'm sorry Francis. I'm all right. Really."

"You said the same thing last time. You had me fooled me completely."

"I should have been more careful. It set me back a week. I don't remember what happened, but I couldn't take it when I heard that they had died. Doug was like a brother to me."

"I know."

"Tell me. How are the villagers doing?"

"As well as they can under the circumstances. They're a determined lot. They won't give up the struggle. There's been a fair amount of support from other nations. Some of them were present at the funerals."

"What are your plans?"

"The VG wants me to stay until all this settles down."

"Good."

"That does not mean until you return."

"Why do you say that?"

"There are rumors they will close the mission as quickly as they can. They are probably waiting until the media attention dies down."

"Did the doctor say how long I'd be here?"

"No. But, as soon as you're discharged, the VG wants to move you to Holy Names in the city. You need rehabilitation and there's no better place around."

"No."

"Peter."

"I am not going there. I will go back to the mission."

"Full recovery could take months. You'll require lots of medical attention."

"That's all right."

"Who's going to take care of you there?"

"They need me now."

"Are you out of your mind? They won't be able to take care of you. You will be a burden on them."

"I won't be. They are fully capable of providing the care I need."

"Come on Peter. Don't be stubborn. How can they take care of you? You need a lot of treatment still."

"The treatment I need I can get there. I won't get that anywhere else."

"They have lots of issues they are dealing with. You'll only add to them."

"No."

"You are being unreasonable."

"I know what I am doing. But keep it to yourself, though. I don't want anyone at the diocese to know about my plans."

"You are putting me in a tough spot, Peter."

"I am sorry, Francis. I have no choice. Do you think I'll be better off with people who once forgot about my whereabouts and me? I could have been dead, remember!"

"That's then. This is now. You have a serious head injury. You need care."

"I need peace of mind more than medical care. I can get that only with the people I care about and who care for me. My friends are dead because of me. I'm responsible for what happened. Don't you understand, Francis?"

"There you go again. I was warned not to talk about anything that would excite you. I'll leave and come back later."

"Francis! I'm sorry. Please don't go! I promise! I'll be careful!"

"Sarah and company wanted to visit. I discouraged them."

"Did the VG ask you to go to the mission, or did you do that on your own?"

"A little of both. As soon as I heard the news, I went to the VG and told him I wanted to go and he agreed."

"I am grateful and I am sure the villagers appreciate your gesture."

"I get there on Saturday and return to my parish on Monday."

"Be careful, Francis. For your own good, don't get too involved."

"The people have been very good to me."

"I am not talking about the villagers. I'm talking about the diocese. I know the bishop and the VG will come down hard on me. I don't want you to be hurt by trying to stand by me."

"How about you? You feel you can take the hits!"

"I am damaged goods already. I'm never going to get back in their favor."

"I know what I'm doing. Yes. I'm doing it of my own free will."

"That doesn't make it safe."

"Thanks for your concern. But let me tell you something. Use some of that concern on yourself and go to Holy Names. Go and get your health back. Then, come back and preach to me. I don't think you understand how serious an injury you have."

"Francis, the Lord has given me another chance at life. It's for a reason. I intend to make full use of it. I don't think it was given to me to whittle it away in obscurity. The diocese wants to send me to Holy Names because they want to keep me under surveillance. I will be a prisoner at Holy Names. No! I'm going back to the mission. God has a plan for me."

"I don't think you are being prudent."

"You think I'm crazy. Maybe I am. But, I know the Lord is calling me and he has a mission for me. What happened was not mere coincidence!"

"What are you talking about?"

"There were times the past couple of weeks when I was awake and I saw my life flash before me. There's a lot I have to do and there's not enough time. Francis, I must get back."

"Why don't you take a little time off to reflect on things, maybe go on a retreat, and think things through?"

"That's what I've been doing, ever since I set foot at the mission. It's been a long retreat. I've had lots of time to reflect. I had an idea what I wanted to do. What happened has made it clear to me. Now I know what I must do."

"I think he's sleeping. Maybe we should wait outside for some time."

"Oh. I am sorry. I didn't hear you come in. I am awake. Come on in!"

"How are you feeling Father Tosco?"

"A lot better. A whole lot better. Thanks for coming. It's good to see you."

"We wanted to come sooner, but you were not ready to receive visitors."

"You know these people. Always cautious."

"That's a good thing, right?"

"I know. It's really frustrating, lying here and doing nothing. Sarah, I am so sorry about Doug and Stan."

"It's destiny. They sacrificed their lives for a cause. You nearly did too."

"Their sacrifice must be accounted for."

"The cause for which they gave their lives won't end with them."

"The struggle will continue."

"We shall not back down."

"I want to ask you for a favor. When I'm discharged from here, I wish to return to the mission."

"Certainly. You don't have to ask"

"It'll be some time before I'm well enough to take care of myself fully. I don't want to be a drag on you."

"You won't be. Why do you ask? What's the alternative?"

"The diocese wants to send me to Holy Names Hospital for rehabilitation and therapy. I don't want to go there."

"Father Tosco, you are welcome back anytime. You'll never be a burden to us. But all we can provide you is rather primitive care. Don't you think you could use the rehabilitation and therapy?"

"Father Tosco, we need your guidance and your support, especially now. It would be a relief to have you. But, is it wise to take the risk?"

"There's very little risk. I know I'll be better off with you than any other place on earth. But, I'll have to wait and see how I feel when I'm discharged. I will let you know as the time approaches.

Please keep it to yourself for now."

"We'll be ready for you, Father Tosco, if and when you so decide to come back."

"Thank you! What's new at the village?"

"We are getting some support from other nations."

"That's good to hear."

"Native blood has been spilt. That seems to have woken some of them up."

"It's us now; it could be them tomorrow."

"The FBI is conducting an investigation."

"An agent was here as soon as I was awake to take a statement. I couldn't talk then. He'll be back any time."

"Must be the same agent. He's been trying to get us to talk. We won't!"

"I don't remember much about what happened after I slipped and fell. Why did the police start shooting?"

"It all happened so suddenly nobody was prepared. The officer appeared ready to strike you with the baton. Doug was the first to leap forward, followed by Stan, to ward off the blow. The other officers then charged and started swinging the batons. Then shots were fired. We do not know who fired the shots or how many shots were fired."

"That's not what's going to come out of the investigation!"

"They will investigate and reach the same conclusion. Police fired in self-defense."

"We have invited representatives of all five bands of the Paiute for a meeting. In addition, we have sent word to all native nations in Utah and Colorado and asked them to send representatives for the meeting. The Chairperson of the Navajo Nation has confirmed she will be there."

"When are you having the meeting?"

"Two weeks from today."

"They are watching our every move; they know something's brewing."

"So much the better. When people see other nations joining forces with us, it'll give them something to think about—we are not in this alone."

"We, the Paiutes of the Little Bend welcome you, great Chiefs and Council Members of nations. You have answered the call of your Paiute brothers and sisters in the time of their need and for this we are forever grateful. We welcome you and invite you to participate in our humble hospitality.

We were once a self-sufficient nation living on the banks of the Little Bend River. We cultivated the land and raised cattle. We were never rich, but we depended on no one. Then one day the river started to grow smaller and smaller until it dried up completely. We believe someone dynamited the path of the river and killed it. We want the river restored.

When native nations were restored to full status, we were included as part of the Cedar City Band of Paiutes. Nobody asked us for our input, and nobody gave us a choice. But we know we are a different band and we want our identity back. We want to be recognized as a separate nation and we want the Little Bend Valley reserved for us and for our children.

We approached state and federal agencies for help. No help is forthcoming. We decided to block the freeways to draw attention to our demands. You all know what happened. We have been touched by tragedy. We lost two very valuable and brave warriors. We hurt nobody, we threatened nobody, and we never dreamed it would come to this. There are those who will disagree with the method we adopted. We couldn't come up with an alternate course of action. Father Tosco, a Catholic priest, who has charge of the mission here, joined us in our efforts. He has been the inspiration behind this movement. He nearly lost his own life in this struggle. He is present here today as the only non-native, and I seek your permission to have him attend."

"Our dear sister Sarah has spoken well and we share in her sorrow at the loss of her husband and a fellow brother and we share in the sorrow of this community that has lost much. It's not often that a non-native person shows the courage to fight for the rights of our people. I welcome the presence of Father Tosco. We need you and people like you, and we express our deepest gratitude for your sacrifice."

"Thank you."

"We are here to show solidarity with our brothers and sisters. Your cause is our cause. Your future, our future, and the future of the indigenous people of this country are all closely knit together. An assault on one member is an assault on the whole people. We join you in this struggle for justice."

"This struggle must not begin and end here. Every day, governments all over the country, States, Counties and Cities are usurping the autonomous freedoms of native nations."

"There are evil stories being spread around, conceived in bigotry and nurtured in prejudice. There is the un-informed public, educated by fiction and Hollywood, unaware of reality, perpetrating the same old myth of the savage native. All this has and continues to inflict great harm to our nations and our status in this country."

"We must get our message across to the people of this country that the natives have been wronged and their status should be restored."

"We must protect our heritage, customs, religion, and our way of life."

"Times have changed, but attitudes toward native people have not. There are forces seeking the destruction of indigenous people. We must resist."

"The murders of our two brothers show the callous disregard authorities have for the lives of native people. Would the murders of two white men have met with this same level of apathy?"

"Strength comes from numbers. We have numbers if only we could unite. United as one, our voices will be heard. Separately, we shout in vain like the howl of the lone coyote on the vast prairie lands. No one takes heed!"

"We must bring politicians to the table to negotiate with us in good faith. They will when native people speak with one voice as one nation."

"The Bureau of Native American Affairs (BNAA) was created ostensibly to safeguard the interests of native people. Truth is the BNAA is the single worst enemy of native people, responsible for the destruction of the community they were entrusted to protect."

"They stole our lands and our birthright. They dumped us into reserved lands that are inhospitable and incapable of supporting cultivation and the raising of livestock. Our people struggle to make a living. Yet they claim that natives have been protected and rewarded."

"When a few fortunate nations find natural resources like oil or minerals in their lands, the government moves in to take away those lands by force or other unjust means. They argue that natives do not utilize the resources and they don't need them. They use the 'principle of better use' to steal lands from us."

"Will they do it on white man's land? They won't!"

"In this land of prosperity and plenty, the majority of native people live in poverty and near starvation. Native people are the poorest of the poor of this land, including immigrants and illegal aliens."

"More than 80% of native communities have no electricity, running water, or health care. They want them. They lack the means to get them."

"The Bureau creates divisions among nations by bribing and backing rival factions. They broker agreements dissipating assets and sovereignty."

"The government seeks the total disintegration and dissolution of our heritage and way of life. They will stop at nothing to do it."

"If our nations unite, we will be a force to reckon with. Governments will be forced to come to us and negotiate terms."

"A united Native American nation should have happened a long time ago. We must unite and resolve our disputes within ourselves."

"There are very few rights remaining; we must fight to stop further erosion of our rights and protect what is left."

"State and local governments pass initiatives with no regard for native rights. When challenged in court, we lose because judges are ignorant of our constitutional rights or they are unscrupulous. Most nations lack resources to fight for rights or seek legal protection."

"Our youth suffer from widespread alcoholism and substance abuse. Generations of neglect and disillusionment have left them bereft of hope."

"They have few educational opportunities and unemployment is sky high. They have low self-esteem and in despair they self-destruct, enslaved by drugs and crime. They have little pride in their heritage."

"Our elderly suffer from malnutrition and lack of health care. Their communities are splintered and they have nowhere to turn. They are forced to live out the waning years of their lives in misery."

"We can go on endlessly with the problems we face. There's no one who will come to our rescue. It's up to us to find the solutions. If we don't, we as a people will be extinct as early as in our lifetime. Look not to the federal government to resolve these problems. They never have and they never will. We must provide for ourselves."

"We must gather together all nations as one into one fold. We each may have to give up something so that we don't lose it all. We must form a united nation of native people. That's our only hope for survival. We must unite or we will become a footnote to history sooner than later."

"Brothers and Sisters, I want to bring us back to focus on the crisis at hand and decide how we can help the Paiute nation."

"There are several investigations going on to review the shooting and death of our brothers. We have decided not to cooperate with any."

"There is some merit in cooperating with the Governor's Commission. You can bring to the table all of the issues you are fighting for."

"I feel that you should at least meet with the Commission and say what you have to say, whether they take it seriously or not."

"We will heed your advice! Let the Commission come here without cameras and the media. We will meet them then!"

"We are here to support you. What can we do for you?"

"Cedar City Council can resolve two of our demands. You can recognize we are a separate band of Paiutes and reserve the Little Bend Valley to us. We and only we have lived there for millennia."

"That's impossible. That is a Bureau decision. As we have discussed many a time, Cedar City Band is a consortium of big and small Paiute nations banded together as one excluding none and including all in this area. It is wound together as a rope, and secession by one will unravel the whole."

"You claim that it is a bureau decision but you are the bureau for this area!"

"Our inclusion was not of our making. You had the option to alert us or clarify our status before the Reorganization Committee. You chose not to. This was something that was forced upon us without our knowledge or consent. Our status outweighs your concerns."

"If you are concerned about the loss of funds, rest assured, we don't want any. We have refused them so far and survived. We will manage without them in the future. You will suffer no loss of income."

"Why is recognition and reservation so important?"

"Our independence! Our identity! Our future as a nation! We will get our Little Bend River restored. We want undisputed rights to this land and the restored river. Without recognition, all that we have sacrificed so far, including the lives of our brothers will all be for naught."

"Maybe there is an alternate solution. Would the Cedar City Council be open to a binding agreement allowing the Little Bend band to hold exclusive rights to the Little Bend Valley in perpetuity without having to recognize them as separate?"

"It's a wise suggestion. It'll amount to a bi-lateral agreement between Cedar City and the Little Bend bands of Paiutes. It'll keep the Bureau out of our internal affairs."

"We will consider it in council. It has a lot of merit."

"This is how we must resolve differences within ourselves."

"We must adopt the concept of a national unified body to represent all native people; something like the United States or the United Nations. We could call it the United Native Nations of America (UNNA)."

"Sheriff, the governor had to do something to appease the public. He has appointed a Commission to look into the incident at Little Bend. Nobody's going to take the police to task over this. They understand what's at stake. The last thing they want is a police force on the defensive. I expect the commission to say the evidence is inconclusive. They may throw in some feel-good recommendations for good measure."

"Thank you, Mr. Conway, for your support. The public must understand that police are human, too. I can't send my men into battle with a handbook of rules restricting their every move. We might as well disband our force. These are not out-of-control mercenaries. They are well-trained and disciplined peace officers. They come from good Christian families. They have spouses and children. They have lived here for generations. They are not out to murder people."

"I don't think the public has been critical of the police for how they reacted. Polls have been uniformly supportive of the police action.

The natives were clearly out of line. The shootings and deaths were unfortunate. Keep in mind there will be an FBI investigation since it involves a native nation. Again, I don't expect anything drastically damaging there."

"There is nothing people want more than peace and quiet. We have delivered. We will continue to deliver. We won't allow some little tribe to disrupt the lives of the people around here."

"I am with you, Sheriff."

"Congressman, you know you don't have to face a re-election challenge worth mentioning. You have no serious contenders to unseat you. But, that's not the case with me. I have to face the voters every so often. I have been lucky so far. I don't want this freakish incident to throw a monkey wrench into my plans. I want to retire in this position, soon. This is the only serious incident that has tarnished my reputation since I took office. My department has never faced an enquiry so far. I may need your help in case something bad creeps into the commission's report."

"Nothing will happen. Everyone around here supports you and will continue to support you. Your reputation is intact, and may have been enhanced somewhat by this incident among the people of this area. What we all want is a stable, firm, and decisive police force that'll keep the people safe and keep the criminals out. That's what you and your department have done for as long as I can remember."

"I heard there's some criticism in the media about the use of excessive force by the police."

"They were not at risk. You were! That's to be expected. Two natives were killed. There will be some tears shed in sympathy. Some liberal crazies in the media will feel obligated to support the cause of the natives. I would not pay much attention to it."

"Maybe you could make a statement in the press or do a couple of interviews in support of the force. As the local congressman, your words will carry weight and take the edge off the negative press."

"You are right. I will. I didn't want to draw too much attention to what happened here and make a big deal out of it. But, silence can be risky, too, as if we have something to hide."

"Thank you. I appreciate that. I hope we get the same support from our other state representatives too."

"They have to be a little cautious there. We have quite a few native tribes in our state and they have remained surprisingly silent so far. It's better not to arouse their passions with some ill-timed statements."

"I don't think these tribes care for each other that much."

"Maybe. Maybe not. Let's not try and find out. But there is another factor that would worry me locally; the Catholic Church. A priest was bloodied up pretty badly and nearly killed. I expect some backlash."

"From what I have heard, the priest was not very popular among his peers, or with the diocese. They may be reluctant to review in public the role of one of their priests in a distasteful native unrest."

"I don't trust them. All it would take is for some priest to take to the pulpit in some church and rant about religious persecution. Everything would change in a hurry, and even those that don't like this Tosco guy will be forced to toe the line."

"Can you maybe talk to the bishop? He will listen to you."

"I don't know him at all. He's rather reclusive. But I may have some luck with his second in command, the Vicar General. He seems to be the one holding the reins of power. I remember him vaguely from when we stayed in the same dorm at BYU."

"We do have a fair number of Catholics in our state. They have always been a quiet bunch. But, you never know what they will do."

"I don't think there is much the bishop or the Vicar General can do about it. They are not going to condemn one of their own in public."

"I am hoping you can get a pulse on how they will react. Thank God they haven't said anything publicly so far. But you never know."

"There is no way we are going to buy their silence or intimidate them."

"Maybe they'll listen to reason. This can reflect badly on the diocese and the church. Maybe you can suggest that this is not about human rights but about law and order. The priest had no business being part of this."

"Let me talk to the Vicar General, and see what he has to say."

"Why do they need a mission in the middle of nowhere?"

~

"Thank you for agreeing to meet with us. As I explained to you earlier in the week, the governor appointed this commission to review the incident at Little Bend and submit a report to him within thirty days. Your contribution is extremely important, and I am grateful to you to scheduling this meeting. Why did you decide to express your protest by blocking the freeways?"

"We have made attempts to contact elected representatives from the governor all the way down. We wanted to get some resolution to our demands for recognition as an independent nation, reservation of these lands and the restoration of the Little Bend River. These are vital to our existence. No one has paid attention to our demands so far."

"These things do take time and need the involvement of many agencies. I am sure you can appreciate that."

"We don't have the time. Not anymore. We've waited centuries for the white man to correct the wrongs done to us."

"Our people starve. Our communities are falling apart."

"The action by the police is nothing more than a brazen disregard for native lives. I was one of the people wounded; hit on the head by a baton, while my hands were cuffed. I was one of the lucky ones. My two brothers weren't so lucky. They were shot at point blank range."

"We were all handcuffed behind our backs. Father Tosco was getting roughed-up by a young officer. You should have no problem identifying who it is—he has a tattoo of a black panther on his right forearm."

"Doug tried to intervene and push the officer away with his shoulders. There was little else he could do."

"Why did the police open fire? We were unarmed and handcuffed!"

"Who gave the order to fire? How were we a threat to fully armed police?"

"Who fired the shots? Do you know how many shots were fired?"

"We were thrown to the ground like rags. We heard them shout: 'This should teach you a lesson, you filthy dogs!' Are we nothing but dogs?"

"There were obvious lapses in procedure and a lack of proper chain of command. Those issues will be addressed."

"Will that bring our brothers back to life?"

"No. Nothing will bring them back to life. But, we can make sure such things don't happen again."

"If it were white people would the police have opened fire? If white people blocked the freeways, wouldn't that be constitutionally protected freedom of speech? When native people protested, it's a rebellion, sedition, anarchy, and a crime that can be crushed with force."

"Can we keep race out of it?"

"Why? We are the victims of racism! Why do you shy away from it?"

"You don't want to complicate it any more than what it is. We will review and analyze what happened as best we can. Only then can we make a determination of what went wrong and where!"

"Will you bring the police to justice?"

"This is not a judicial enquiry. That'll be up to the governor to decide."

"And that will be the end of that. You'll submit your report, more discussion will follow and then nothing! Back to square one!"

"There will be action if needed. You can be sure of that. We want to study the problem in depth so that we can offer recommendation and prevent such incidents in the future."

"You want to study the cause of the problem. I'll tell you what it is. It's poverty; it's hopelessness; it's despondency; and it's lack of respect. You want to find the cause. We seek solutions."

"What is the solution you seek?"

"Restore the river and we will take up the other issues with the BNAA."

"We will recommend that the river be restored if at all possible. But you must exercise restraint and be patient until due process is done."

"Don't tell us to be patient. Our patience has run out!"

"Matters of government are not done in haste. There are processes you can't circumvent especially when you are dealing with an issue such as a river. Environmental issues need careful review. There's more!"

"You are not creating a new river. Restoring the river is how you protect the environment. Just release the water back into it!"

"We protected the environment for centuries before the white man came!"

"Monsignor Cavanaugh, I appreciate your willingness to meet with me at short notice. It's good to see you. It's been many years. How are you?"

"Forget the title Bill; it's Mark to you."

"All right, Mark."

"I am doing all right. How about you?"

"I'm okay. Being in Washington can get lonely sometimes. But it's politics."

"You grew up in a political family. It should come as no surprise."

"When congress is in session, you lose touch with family and friends. Still, it's a great honor. I'm grateful and blessed to serve my country this way."

"I am happy for you. I wish you continued success."

"Thanks! What made you choose priesthood? I was surprised when I heard about it."

"It surprised me too. Being what I was in college didn't make me an ideal candidate for this life. Then, one day suddenly, it hit me and I said to myself, this is what I want to be."

"God called and you answered 'yes'!"

"Pretty much! And, I have not regretted it."

"I am sure! And you commitment shows. It didn't take the church too long to recognize your worth."

"The position of VG does not mean much, really!"

"As the Bible says: You do not light a lamp and put it under a bushel. I am sure there are greater things lined up for you!"

"It's God's will. Honors and titles are irrelevant. I am enjoying what I am doing. That's all that matters to me."

"That's important. I am hoping we will get to meet more often. If you are ever in Washington, look me up, especially when Congress is in session."

"I'll do that. Was there something you wanted to discuss with me or is this purely a social visit?"

"There's something I want to talk to you about. I'm sure you have been following the events at the native village where you have your mission."

"Yes!"

"It's part of my District. I've never had any problems there until these recent events. I was shocked! It was so unexpected!"

"Are you referring to the police shooting and the deaths of the natives?"

"About the natives blocking the freeways and the shooting that followed!"

"That was very unfortunate!"

"We need to keep the natives off the freeways. I don't want this to develop into a bigger problem. What's happened can't be undone. But no more!"

"I can't believe it happened! Worse, the diocese got pulled in!"

"The diocese has been dragged into the mess because of Father Tosco."

"That too is unfortunate. It's put us in a delicate position."

"I want to talk to you about him, if I may."

"Sure! I'm limited in what I can discuss with you though."

"I understand! And I know there's not much you can do about the natives. But I am sure you have some control over what Father Tosco does."

"Some, yes. Not a whole lot."

"There's general consensus Father Tosco's the man behind the native unrest. From what I have seen and heard, I have to agree. The tribe has lived quietly, almost unknown and unnoticed until the mission reopened and he showed up. If he wants to energize them and improve their well-being, that's great. It can be done in so many peaceful ways. They didn't need to block the freeways and get into a confrontation with law enforcement. Father Tosco could have used his influence to direct them toward a more civilized form of protest."

"Frankly, I was not happy with what happened. We don't want the diocese in any kind of controversy. We like to remain anonymous when it comes to political activism!"

"I fear Father Tosco does not agree. He must have his own agenda, then!"

"I don't think he and the tribe thought it through. They couldn't have dreamed of the consequences of their action. I believe they miscalculated and it was a gamble that backfired."

"They don't seem contrite about it. They seem even feistier than before!"

"The diocese has no control over the actions of the native tribe. I can only review the church's involvement and how to prevent further conflicts."

"Yes, of course! I don't want to be presumptuous but I must say that things won't improve, not as long as Father Tosco's there!"

"He has some influence with the natives. The life of a mission is different from a regular parish."

"He and the mission are synonymous as far as we are concerned. He *is* the mission."

"What happened and Father Tosco's role in it are not reflective of the goals of the mission. We want peaceful co-existence with people around us. The mission is not intended as a social or political forum. I believe his emotions got the better of him."

"If I may express myself frankly, Father Tosco's ambitions are political in nature. If this were a correct statement, why would the diocese operate this mission?"

"It's a good question and one we are debating internally. As soon as his health improves, I will address the issue with him. The diocese does not want to be part of a native unrest. If there's a contradiction between our goals and his actions, I'll close the mission. I'll do it in an orderly and dignified manner."

"There is a sense of urgency. Even without Father Tosco, the tribe has embarked on an ambitious agenda, one that does not give much attention to the rule of law. I fear it'll only get worse when he returns. It'll be much easier to diffuse the situation before Father Tosco returns. I want to make a personal request to you to close the mission before he returns. He's the catalyst. With him gone, the natives will settle down."

"I am troubled with what's happened and the furor it has generated. I am almost at the point of deciding to close the mission."

"Interstate Freeways are the lifeline of our nation. They must remain free of obstruction at all times. When there is disruption of any kind on a major freeway such as 15, it has a rippling effect all along the north-south corridor. Utah and the states around us depend on these freeways for our tourism dollars. That's a big part of our budget. I have had calls from the governors of states all around us wanting to know what's going on here. What do I tell them? That we have a bunch of natives behaving like a herd of stampeding cattle?"

"It's been all over the media. It even made national news."

"If I tell them it's all about restoring a little river, they're going to laugh at me. This ruckus over a small river. Give it to them! That's what they are going to say."

"They don't understand the dynamics of the dilemma we are facing."

"I don't either. Why can't we restore the river?"

"Governor, not unless you want a full-blown local rebellion on your hands. On one side, you have a group of suicidal natives who will stop at nothing to get their demands met. You have a Catholic priest prodding them on as if this were some kind of a crusade. On the other side, you have a well-organized group of ranchers who have sworn never to allow the restoration of the river. You need to proceed cautiously if you want to avoid further bloodshed."

"Just what I need in an election year!"

"You and me both, governor!"

"Has the FBI come up with anything new?"

"Not anything more than what everyone knows."

"The truth is the deputies panicked and the firing was unwarranted. But we can't acknowledge it publicly."

"You're right! We can't charge the officers involved in the shooting, truth or no truth. We'll end up alienating a powerful group of supporters and get nothing back in return."

"It's a no-win situation."

"We got to believe the police acted appropriately given the circumstances. I don't want to make judgments based on hindsight. I was a law enforcement person myself. We can sit around and talk all we want how it could have been handled differently. The officers caught up in a highly explosive situation had to use the best judgment possible."

"Bill, your situation is different than mine. You can go on record in support of the police. You almost have to. You have to worry about your constituents. You have to secure your vote bank. I have to take into consideration the entire state and the US Justice Department."

"You bet I'll stand by my constituents. The natives don't vote. They don't count. Don't expect my support if you decide to fault the police."

"If I take the wrong step, the whole thing will explode out of control. If I side with the police, every activist in the country will be on my case for abetting police brutality. If I refuse to restore the river, the natives will be up in arms again. Other tribes can join in. Already I am hearing rumblings."

"In the end, you have to be mindful of the people who vote for you, governor! You have seen the polls. People are disgusted with the freeway disruption. The public wants action. They want the natives punished!"

"I can't be led by public opinion and polls only. You have to do what you think is right! I can't disregard the rights of minorities."

"Minorities have no special rights to block freeways. If this happens again, you'll be put through the wringer. Don't expect me to come to your rescue. I have made my position very clear."

"That's what's unfortunate about public service. You can't satisfy all the people all the time. But, we are elected to make tough decisions."

"If you make the wrong decision, the voters will make the final decision and kick you out. You can preach fairness and end up on the bench."

"I see here an opportunity to do something constructive for the natives. Look at what the river will do for them! It'll give them a future!"

"It'll destroy my future and yours too. I'll be branded a traitor. My people don't understand political compunctions. They'll dump me without a second thought. I won't agree to the restoration of the river."

"Try and make your people understand. We have to play by the rules!"

"To them, they make the rules. They are the law! What they decide goes. What they want happens. They'll fight to the bitter end on this issue. They would love nothing better than a fight. If there is conflict and violence erupts, they'll love it. If the fight's with the natives, it would be the icing on the cake."

"A restored river will appease the natives and keep them off the freeways!"

"The river can't be restored. My people won't go for it. I won't either."

"As governor, I have an obligation to protect and safeguard the rights of all the people of the state. If the river can be restored, within reason, I will order it. I won't deny justice where it's due. That's where I stand!"

"The restoration of the river is non-negotiable."

"The Bureau of Native American Affairs is made up of Washington bureaucrats and political appointees. They don't represent our interests."

"Historically they've worked as agents of the US Government to squeeze and extract more and more concessions from our people. The Bureau's philosophy and method of operations haven't changed. It's still made up of mostly non-native people and anti-native people. Their goal remains the same, dissolution of native rights."

"They meddle in the affairs of nations. It's a page taken out of British colonialist tactics, divide and rule. They create factions within nations and then support the factions against lawfully elected councils. Once the rebel factions are in power, they demand concessions that hurt the long-term interests of the nation. The BNAA is a curse to native people."

"The Bureau must be reorganized to include native representatives. They must adopt the principle of advocacy for native people. We natives must have a say in who's appointed to the bureau."

"Presidents appoint the Commissioners of the Bureau. Which president has been friendly to native people?"

"Presidents and the Congress will take us seriously once native nations unite and speak with one voice."

"We must forgo differences and embrace the bonds that bind us together. We are one people and now's the time to unite or never."

"We are a people under threat of extinction. What happened at the Little Bend can happen anywhere, anytime, over and over again."

"The blacks in this country joined together under a broad rainbow coalition and see what they have achieved. We must do likewise."

"We will be taken seriously if we can show the numbers and demonstrate unity of purpose and the resources to back it up. We must unite as one."

"United Native Nations of America, UNNA! There lies the solution."

"We must first convince our nations to join together to form one union. Some nations may balk initially, but will eventually come around once they see the benefits. Nations must join not under compulsion, but by recognizing the benefits."

"Some of our larger nations have well-established governments. They are wealthy and have influence in high places. They may see the concept of UNNA as an intrusion rather than a benefit."

"UNNA is not about sharing wealth. UNNA is not about native power. It's all about survival of the native race."

"We have smart and talented leaders among us, but not the kind with national recognition. We need to support and elevate them on to the national stage."

"Politicians and society in general are sensitive to offending blacks and other ethnic communities. A news anchor making a derogatory statement about blacks was summarily dismissed. When we objected to the use of native symbols as sports mascots, no one took us seriously. Native people are not accorded the same level of recognition because we are splintered with no unifying goals."

"There are thousands of native remains stored in the Smithsonian and numerous labs around the country? Why? Are native people such anthropological oddities that they deserve scientific research? The remains must be returned to their final resting place."

"Why is Peltier rotting in jail? What crime is he guilty of? Is he a criminal or is he a political prisoner? Did the US courts establish beyond reasonable doubt that he was guilty of the murder of the FBI agents? Isn't that the cornerstone of our country's jurisprudence? Why is he imprisoned for life without parole, when at best his guilt is based on suspect circumstantial evidence?"

"Puerto Rican Nationalists tried to assassinate President Truman. They opened fire inside the Capitol Building in Washington while Congress was in session wounding several lawmakers. President Carter pardoned them as political prisoners. But not Peltier! It's hypocrisy! It shows a lack of respect for native people."

"We are to blame. It's our disunity that's to blame. We will be taken seriously if we stand united as one. Peltier will be freed if we cry out with one voice for his release."

"We are losing reserved lands at an alarming rate. Our sovereign status as enshrined in our constitution must not be compromised. It's not for congress to give us what's already ours. We must unite and protect what's lawfully ours."

"Our heritage and our way of life must be preserved for posterity. We must unite to survive."

"If we unite as one, this land shall see the new light of dawn and recognize the sacred markings on the face of native people. This country shall witness a new native awakening, a new spirit of determination among native people."

"We must not let this opportunity slip away. Brothers and Sisters, let us forget our differences and call to mind what binds us together as children of the same destiny."

"Let those here present take a solemn oath on the sacred pipe to work as one, work toward national unity."

"Let us create one nation that stands tall for us all. Let us create the United Native Nations of America, UNNA!"

"Tom, what's this about a freeway shooting in Utah?"

"Why? What happened?"

"A reporter popped the question during my press conference yesterday in Wichita. I knew nothing of it and had to resort to the fall and roll tactic; we are concerned; we are monitoring the situation; we will take necessary action."

"It happened near a native reservation. The Paiute natives blocked the freeway to protest for something. The police tried to remove them. Violence erupted. Police opened fire killing two natives."

"You knew about this?"

"Of course! I do my homework, Mr. President. It's my job to keep an eye out for hot spots, wherever they may be."

"Why wasn't I briefed?"

"It's a local issue. I don't think we need to be concerned."

"I don't like surprises and I don't want problems involving minorities."

"The FBI is monitoring it. The governor has appointed a commission to look into it."

"Keep an eye on it and let me know if something comes up. If the question was raised once, it'll come up again. These reporters are like sharks. A slight indecision and they smell blood. They'll come after me again. They know my answer was weak."

"A catholic priest appears to be the troublemaker there. He was also shot, seriously—but not fatally."

"Great! Just what we need! I don't want the church on the offensive!"

"Luckily this is not a priest well-liked in his diocese, and the general sentiment is he had no business in this affair. The church has been muted in their response."

"I'm running behind in the polls. I don't want any new fires erupting and taking us by surprise. Let's have a quiet and uneventful campaign. I don't want to give any ammunition to my challenger."

"We won't let this escalate out of control."

"This is getting out of hand. We need to act, now!"

"There are a few who accuse the diocese of supporting Father Tosco."

"If only they knew! We need to end this charade."

"Recall Father Tosco and close down the mission. Enough is enough."

"Let the tribe fend for itself. They are not Catholics. We are wasting our time. Father Tosco is not keen on converting them."

"It seems Father Tosco has one goal and the tribe has another. They are both using the mission to advance their separate agendas. The diocese has become a helpless bystander. We can't tolerate this any longer."

"I had a meeting with Congressman Conway. Politically, they're taking this very seriously. We have to do the same on a diocesan level."

"Father Tosco has shown no signs he plans to back down."

"He's become a celebrity. I fear he'll be difficult to bring under control."

"He knew you wanted him to rehabilitate at Holy Names. He thumbed his nose at you by going back to the mission. That's disrespect!"

"Let's close the mission, reassign him, and bring this sad saga to a closure."

"What about the covenant?"

"It's irrelevant!"

"Sarah! Father Tosco does not look good. Is he okay?"

"He's not! He needs lots of care. But, he wants to be here with us. He says he'll have peace of mind only among us."

"It's good to have him back with us. But, his health is a concern."

"Malcolm, you had a chance to meet with and talk to him. Has he told you about his future plans?"

"Physically, he's weak but his mind is clear. He feels responsible for the deaths of Doug and Stan. He's determined the struggle must continue."

"It will continue! It's only started!"

"I was at a news conference with the sheriff and Congressman Conway. They have vowed that the public won't be inconvenienced again."

"If they think they can scare us off, they'd better think again."

"We must dispel any doubt anyone has and show them we mean

business. Threats won't work."

"We want Little Bend restored. We won't rest until it happens!"

"Should we wait and see what the Commission says in their report?"

"We can't wait for things to happen. We must make things happen. If they're serious about restoring the river, our actions will hasten it. If they are stalling for time, inaction will weaken our advantage."

"When shall we do it?"

"Veterans' Day, Nov. 11?"

"In Canada they call it Remembrance Day. Let us dedicate the day by remembering and honoring the brave native men and women who fought and suffered while resisting the settlers."

"We'll dedicate the day to Doug and Stan who gave their lives for us!"

"The women will lead the blockade this time."

"It's too dangerous, Sarah! You could get roughed up."

"So much the better! Can you imagine how it would play on national TV, police brutalizing native women? It won't happen. They'll be very careful."

"I don't like it. If they lay hands on you, I won't stand by doing nothing."

"I don't think it's a bad idea. It'll add a little twist to the plot. Police will come prepared to use strong arm tactics. They'll be taken aback when they see only women. The little element of surprise won't hurt."

"You will get arrested. They may use you as hostages to negotiate."

"Such tactics don't work in a non-violent struggle. We do not negotiate under whatever terms. We want the river restored."

"If we want results, there can't be a let up. Men or women, it doesn't matter. Let the women do it."

"There are risks but if we are afraid of risks, we shouldn't be in this."

~

"We now switch you live to a press conference by Governor Berger from the Capitol Rotunda in Salt Lake City."

"Utah is uniquely blessed. It is one of the most attractive places in this country and home to great natural wonders which we have in abundance. It is also a desirable place to live. The State of Utah stands out as a great success story not only for its vast and storied history, but because we have been a model of strength and prosperity. We have supported our citizens and businesses through great infrastructure development and providing an economic climate which has been carefully crafted over the years. But more than all these, what makes Utah truly great are the people of this state. We have a diverse cross-section of society here and we take pride in how we treat every citizen regardless of who they are, where they come from, what they believe in, and what they practice. We also are blessed with the greatest concentration of Native Americans in the USA. That is not by accident. It is a testament to how we have worked together to live in harmony and peace as brothers and sisters of one race, the human race.

We are one of the few states that have a fully operational and effective Department for Native American Affairs to supplement the federal Bureau of Native American Affairs. We are at the forefront when it comes to respecting and caring for the people of native origin. Utah senators and congressional representatives have proven themselves as champions of reform for native people. It is extremely unfortunate that such a state has come under criticism for the events of the last few months.

I deeply deplore the loss of native lives during the conflict at Little Bend. It is an unfortunate tragedy that should never have happened and I firmly declare, never will again. Why it happened shall not become irrelevant. The native lives that were lost demand that we examine fully our commitment and resolve to support our native citizens.

Any incident where human life is lost is of extreme consequence. Yet, this incident shall not tarnish the long history of cordial relations we have cultivated with our native people. The nation of the Paiutes of Little Bend Valley is demanding recognition as an independent nation, reservation of their lands, and restoration of the Little Bend River. I have appointed a commission to fully investigate the incident and submit a report to me without delay. I promise I will take appropriate action based on the findings and the recommendations of the commission.

It was an extremely shocking incident to me, personally—and I am sure to all of you, as it goes counter to our policy of inclusion. We live in a democratic society that allows all citizens to enjoy the fruits of freedom our forefathers enshrined in our constitution. An integral part of that democratic freedom is the right to express our dissent and disagreement when we feel our pursuit of freedom and happiness is imperiled. It is an extraordinary commitment and promise.

We can express our disagreement and displeasure in many ways, labor strikes, protests, and the ballot. We respect the right of citizens to express their dissatisfaction and protest. However, it must be done in a manner that does not compromise the freedom of other citizens. Acts of civil disobedience must be within the context of the law of the land. Blocking access and transport on freeways is not an acceptable form of protest, and can't and won't be tolerated regardless of the intent. The Paiute nation caused great chaos by blockading the freeways. It was wrong. It must not happen again, and as governor of this great state, I won't let it happen again. At the same time, I will do everything in my power to resolve their concerns in a civil and legal manner.

Peace and prosperity can endure only if our citizens act in a responsible manner and resolve issues within the boundaries of civil liberties. Utah will never be a police state, but it will be a disciplined state. It's a state where every citizen will have freedom to express themselves and where every citizen respects the rights of others. Utah will remain forever the great State we all love so much. Thank you and God bless!"

"Arrest and remove every one of them to the county jail."

"Sir, they are all women."

"What?"

"The protesters are all women!"

"What about the men?"

"They are standing in front of the store but they are not participating in blocking the freeways."

"What a mess! All right! Arrest them and move them off the freeway. If anyone, I repeat, anyone tries to intervene, arrest them too. I will dispatch buses to take them to jail. Hang tight, I am on my way."

"Sir, there's only the two of us here. There's nothing we can do until there are reinforcements. Highway Patrol is on their way. But we need backup real quick. The situation is deteriorating fast. People are mad."

"I understand. There will be plenty of backup. In the meantime, can't you move a few people and open up at least one lane?"

"Sir! Things are getting nasty. People are getting out of their cars and appear ready to take matters into their own hands. We are trying to keep them separated from the women."

"Tell UHP to keep the public away from the women. Order people back into their cars or start writing citations. Back-up is on its way!"

"Yes, Sir!"

"Sarah! Do you see the officers standing around to our left?"

"I see them. They don't seem to know what to do."

"There is trouble brewing on the Southern side. There's a group of guys making their way toward us. They look like trouble."

"They are trouble. They are screaming and some of them are kicking the sides of the cars as they come."

"Listen, everyone! Regardless of what happens, do not get up or move. Hold your spot. On no account, make any kind of response."

"Get off the freeway; NOW!"

"Are you deaf or what?"

"We will move you by force if we have to."

"Where is your leader?"

"Where are your men?"

"Guys—return to your vehicles! We will handle this."

"Officer, you won't. You are too chicken to do anything."

"These people don't understand reason."

"We'll show you how to deal with these filthy natives!"

"I am ordering you to get back into your cars. You will be cited for disobeying a peace officer."

"Why are you protecting them?"

"Dudes, we have no quarrel with the police. All right guys! Clean this up quickly, will you? We are losing our patience."

"Let's go by the store and get some coffee!"

"Let's go talk to the men and get them to pull the women off the road."

"Where's the backup? Those guys are up to no good!"

"What'll we do if trouble erupts at the store?"

"We can't leave the women alone!"

"Get your women out of there now and go back to where you came from."

"We will teach you a lesson you won't forget for a long time!"

"Do we have to burn you down with the store?"

"I am asking you to leave the store!"

"And what if we won't?"

"This is native property and you are trespassing."

"This is a store and we have every right to be here."

"If you want to use the store, get your stuff and leave."

"That's poor customer service."

"We reserve the right to refuse service."

"We have rights too—to be treated with respect."

"You don't deserve any respect. That's enough! Leave the store, now!"

"I dropped the vase. Sorry!"

"Get out! Leave, now!"

"What are you going to do if we won't?"

"Let's throw these bums out!"

"You want to pick a fight? Come on!"

"Cool it guys! Let's go! They are pulling out guns!"

"This is no way to treat your customers."

"Get out! Now!"

"There are at least a dozen of them back there and they have guns. Let's get out of here!"

"We'll be back. Watch out! We'll be back!"

"We'll be waiting!"

"This is the police! Everyone inside! Come out with your hands in the air."

"Either you come out on your own or we come in."

"Let's go guys."

"Hold it! What's going on here?"

"We came to get some coffee. All on a sudden they pulled guns on us."

"We'll take care of it. Leave now and go back to your cars."

"Stop playing games officer. This isn't how you deal with this scum!"

"Teach them how to behave! You know what I mean!"

"This is a final warning. Leave now or you will be arrested."

"Let's go! Be careful! Those guys are armed."

"Everyone, step outside the store with your hands above your heads."

"Why don't you come inside the store?"

"We are not coming in. I want everyone out. It's an order!"

"Let me show you what they did to the store!"

"Later! I'll take a look at it later."

"Anyone else left inside the store?"

"No!"

"Tell you what! Do as I tell you and we'll forget this mess and go home! Go, tell your women to get off the freeway and we can all breathe easier. You go your way; we go ours! No hard feelings. If not we will arrest the whole bunch of them. You make one false move and you'll go with them."

"Officer, we don't take orders! You do what you have to do."

"So be it! I thought you'd listen to reason. Guess not!"

"We want to search the inside of the store."

"Show me the warrant!"

"I hear you have weapons inside the store."

"Show us a warrant, officer!"

"You want to play hardball! You are a threat to public safety. This is no game! I don't need a search warrant!"

"Officer, we are not here to play games with you or anyone else!"

"You are on a native reserved land. You have no authority here!"

"We shall see!"

"If you think you can barge in here and order us around, you are mistaken. You let those guys go! They came in to do damage to the store. That doesn't bother you, is that right?"

"We don't have the time for that now. There are more pressing issues!"

"I'm sure!"

"Where is that Catholic priest who is behind all of these? Maybe, he can talk some sense into you folks."

"You'll find him in his trailer next door."

"Look at the people caught up in the jam. You should feel lucky people have been so patient with you. Don't expect it to last!"

"We have been patient for centuries. Our patience has run out."

"This is the third time they have blockaded the freeways this year, Mr. President."

"I heard another tribe in New Mexico had a sit-in in front of the federal building and had to be removed by the police."

"What's their problem?"

"They are demanding the release of the women arrested in Utah."

"Why were women arrested?"

"The women led the protest this time and blocked the freeways. The judge said she wanted to send a clear message that the freeways are not to be tampered with, regardless of who is doing it or why. She ordered the women to jail without bail."

"She didn't have to put them in jail."

"If every group that protests takes it to the roads and freeways, the results would be disastrous."

"This has every chance of backfiring. I got calls from leaders of some native nations. They are threatening nation-wide agitation if the women are not released immediately."

"Will the judge rescind the ruling?"

"I don't think so. There is a lot of anger in the communities around. The judges' action has been uniformly praised."

"They are going about this the wrong way. The judges' action may be popular locally, but it's not going to sit well with native people around the country. This will only serve to galvanize them. We need to get the women out of jail."

"Should they cave in because the natives are threatening more protests?"

"No! We are the ones doing the threatening by locking them up instead of listening to their demands. We haven't learned from history, have we? Can't you see the racial implications? When people of Nevada blocked trains carrying nuclear waste, nobody shot them or put them in jail."

"There's another issue that could be more serious! The women are on a hunger-strike for as long as they are in jail. That includes medications. If anything happens to any one of them, it could spell disaster."

"Can you get the Interior Secretary and the Attorney General on a conference call, please?"

"Ted, Ralph, did you know about the native women arrested in Utah?"

"Yes! They are in jail!"

"I know! How do we get them out?"

"Let the courts deal with it!"

"They are in county jail by order of a state appointed judge. What's the governor saying?"

"He's caught between a rock and a hard place. He is sensitive about the native issue but he has to ensure that the freeways stay open."

"This involves a sovereign native nation. We can't stand idle."

"I can get a federal judge involved. We can overturn the Utah judge's order and get the women released pending a hearing in federal court."

"Do it then! The governor can save face by requesting a hearing before a federal judge as it involves a native nation. He must act quickly. You think I should put in a call to him."

"Let's give him a chance to resolve it. Let's see what he does."

"All right! I want updates if something comes up."

"You seem to be unnecessarily alarmed. This is a local matter."

"I got a call less than an hour ago from Secretary Camden. She's threatening to resign if the women are not released immediately."

"What's her problem?"

"This as an affront against women! They didn't commit murder, they didn't blow up trains, they didn't hold up a bank! You get the idea!"

"That's not fair! She shouldn't do that to you!"

"Easy for you to say! All on a sudden, this thing has become the news! No sir! We have a big problem coming if this doesn't get resolved quickly. Bigger nations have been silent so far. They won't stay that way for long. NOW, NAACP and every other group will come out with statements. National news media is going to pick it up soon."

"Agent Thompson, you understand we have a very delicate situation on our hands. There's a lot at stake here. People at the top are getting antsy. Nobody wants these problems, not with elections coming up. Are you certain you can handle it?"

"Yes, Sir! I have the perfect plan. I need a few more details, that's all!"

"There's no time for too much planning. People want results—not bad results, mind you, but amicable solutions. Do you understand?"

"Yes, Sir!"

"Unfortunately, we are forced to deal with several elements that disagree on almost everything—the natives, the police, the white ranchers including elements of the Klan, and the Catholic Church to top it off."

"I'll work it out."

"Do you need more help? I can ask the Bureau Chief in Salt Lake City to send a few more agents! The FBI has lots of resources in the area."

"No Sir, not yet! In my opinion, it's the Catholic priest who is the real problem. If we can get rid of him, things will calm down quickly. The natives will crawl back into their teepees and the ranchers will go back to doing whatever it is they like to do."

"Be careful when you deal with the Catholic Church. They are an unpredictable bunch."

"Yes, Sir! Do you want me to call you with weekly updates?"

"I will call you when I want updates."

"Congressman, Agent Thompson, from the FBI."

"You are working on the Little Bend case, aren't you?"

"Yes I am."

"What can I do for you?"

"I need your help. We need to prevent further escalation of trouble."

"I agree. We can't allow any more unrest. The natives must be brought to heel. They must understand they can't get away with such behavior."

"I need your help on a very important issue."

"Shoot!"

"We must get the ranchers and farmers down river to stay put and allow law enforcement to take care of this matter."

"Good luck. You don't know who you are dealing with."

"They are your constituents, your supporters. They will listen to you."

"They should. But, they won't. You don't know these people."

"Congressman, I do. They are different and it's a challenge. But, we got to make sure they don't cause problems. They're not helping themselves or anyone else by taking the law into their own hands.

Vigilantism may sound appealing. It'll only complicate matters and put them in the cross hairs of the FBI. You must get them to lie low so that I can concentrate on the main culprits, Tosco and the natives!"

"They listen to nobody. That includes me. If you are here to talk to me about the river, forget it."

"I am not from these parts."

That's pretty obvious!"

"I don't understand why the river is such a big deal."

"They won't allow it to be restored. My constituents don't care if the Paiutes are declared a separate nation. They don't care if they are given a reservation. But they will let no one mess with the river."

"The river is not my concern. Law and order is."

"Your lack of concern is not their concern. Here's the deal. The river won't be restored. The natives can have their store. They can do whatever they want on their reservation. Leave the river alone. And leave the freeways alone."

"Natives were shot and now they are protesting. Their women are in jail. I am under orders to investigate what happened and resolve it quickly. Your people must let the FBI handle this or they'll have the Bureau breathing down their backs. They don't want to do that."

"They could care less about your threats. They won't listen to you."

"Tell them to trust me. I have a plan."

"Why should they trust you?"

"They won't be disappointed."

"That won't be enough."

"I can't say anymore. I am hoping you can get them to lie low for a few weeks. I need some time to put my plan into action."

"I'll try to talk to them. But, don't expect much."

"Buy me some time."

"Controversy is not a bad thing for a newspaper; it sells copies. I have put through every piece you have done on the native uprising. I'm getting a little nervous though, not about the paper, but about you. You read the Letters to the Editor, don't you?"

"If you are referring to the personal attacks on me, yes, I do read them."

"Malcolm, I am referring to them. They are not mere criticisms. Some of them are downright 'death threats.' They are not to be taken lightly."

"Dave, I understand and appreciate your concern. I don't take it lightly, nor do I take threats against my life nonchalantly. You were a reporter yourself; you understand the dangers we face. You risked your life among the Contras. You knew the risks but you didn't let that stop you. I am not doing anything different."

"A dead reporter gets a free obituary in the paper; that's all."

"I could have died many a time in Vietnam. I am lucky to be alive. Maybe, the exposure to constant danger has made me numb to it. Danger has no special effect on me. It neither thrills me nor scares me."

"Maybe I am being selfish. I need you. The paper needs you. I don't want you knocked off by some crazy lunatic."

"Dave, what do I have to lose? I have no wife or kids and no dependents. To me life has meaning when I am doing something I feel passionate about. I have found that something as a reporter. I have found passion in reporting the story of this native people."

"The cause must be worthy of the sacrifice."

"My question is, am I worthy?"

"You are making enemies, some in high places. Law enforcement can make life difficult for you. The congressman is someone you should keep an eye on. The Catholic Church and the Mormons don't always follow the practice of turning the other cheek."

"I report objectively, truthfully, and professionally. I do not offer solutions, but I like to see justice done. I will pursue truth and when I find the truth, it will appear in my column in its stark-naked form. I have been working on this story of the native tribe for some time. It will continue. It's your decision whether you want to publish it or not."

"We are a great paper because we report fearlessly and our founder preached one word: Truth. Truth. Truth. People have come to accept, if it's in the Herald, it's trustworthy. Reporters like you keep that trust alive. I can't afford to lose you."

"These groups that threaten anonymously are playing mind games or are plain stupid. I am not swayed by either. It's not always the big stories that need to be told; sometimes these small stories make sense and they are worth the attention. Or, maybe I am just plain naïve."

"You are anything but that."

"This story has piqued my interest and there's no turning back."

"It's been received with a lot of interest. Reactions may differ, but either good or bad, response has been good. It's got a lot of attention. It's good for the paper. My concern is you."

"There are many Americans who still ask what we were doing in Vietnam. Why did we take on the commies in Korea? What was our problem with the Soviets? What did the people of Cuba do to deserve our blockade? Why did we jump into the World Wars? Other than Pearl Harbor, has one bomb fallen on mainland USA? Why do we send our young men and women and sacrifice them in unknown lands? Stranded in the rice fields and the muck in Vietnam, with the constant noise of bombs exploding all around and wondering if death lay hidden behind every bush and knoll, I asked myself that question many a time. I know now why we were there; at least I think I do. There is a truth lying hidden behind the madness."

"I understand where you are coming from. But, do not let caution be sacrificed on the altar of your altruism."

"We are a nation of destiny. We have a moral obligation to protect the people all over the world from the grips of tyranny and totalitarianism. We have a mandate that is larger than us. We can't help it. It can't be measured in victories and successes. We honor, we remember with pride our role in the Second World War. We made victory happen. We won it for the world and the future of mankind. That was a decisive victory. We are proud of our role. Vietnam and Korea are not as easy to accept because there was no clear victory or maybe we have lingering doubts we were the losers. As a nation, we find it hard to accept failure. But, we did win in Vietnam and Korea. It was a more subtle victory. We stopped the new terrorists. We slowed the spread of a new fascism. With the Cold War we kept the Soviets preoccupied thus preventing the rapid spread of their morbid propaganda. Religious and ideological terrorism are not easy to eradicate because the concept of suffering and death is garbled. It is an awesome responsibility we shoulder, one we are finding harder and harder to carry alone. People often fail to consider what would happen if we refused to wield our immense power to root out rogue nations and their arrogant tyrants. The world would degenerate into chaos. It's unfortunate that often it is the beneficiary of our sacrifice that shouts the loudest insults against our so-called imperialistic designs."

"Wow. That's the longest speech I have heard you make in all the years I have known you. This native tribe has really transformed you."

"I hope they did."

"Mr. Goldstone, Agent Thompson from the FBI. I would like to have a word with you in private."

"Why do you want to talk to me? What did I do?"

"I didn't say you did anything. I just wanted to ask you a few questions."

"Why me?"

"It's not just you. You're one of many. I'm talking to people of this area."

"What if I refuse?"

"You can remain silent if you like. You can have an attorney present if you like. That's not the nature of my visit though."

"What is it then? Is this about the native unrest?"

"That's it. What do you know about it?"

"Nothing. Are you going to arrest me or something?"

"I don't have any reason to. No. I didn't come to arrest you."

"Am I a suspect?"

"You are not a suspect. Should you be?"

"Why would I be?"

"Exactly. I just want to talk to you about some of the things you may have witnessed or heard about. If you so choose, I can issue summons and have you report to my office. Then, you can invoke your rights."

"I don't like this. Maybe I should get an attorney."

"Your choice, certainly. I had hoped I could talk to you informally."

"I told you I have done nothing wrong."

"I didn't say you did. I am conducting an investigation into the shooting deaths of natives by the police. I have nothing on you or against you. Like I said, I want to ask you if you had heard something about what happened at the native village."

"I had nothing to do with the shooting of the natives."

"I didn't say you had anything to do with it."

"Why pick on me then?"

"I am not picking on you. You are one of several people I plan to talk to. Sir, you make up your mind. If you want to talk to an attorney first, go ahead. I will want to talk to you one way or another. I can talk to you here and now informally. There won't be any record of it. If you don't want to talk to me now, I will send you the summons to appear at FBI offices in Salt Lake City. What's it going to be?"

"If I talk to you now, will you promise not to summon me to your office?"

"I can't make that promise. I am trying to avoid summons and formal questioning. It all depends on what information you have."

"Why do you think I have any information?"

"I don't. I want to ask you a few questions not as a suspect but as a local person. I won't make you come down to my office, if possible. Look, I prefer to work with people who are willing to talk rather than force people to appear. What'll it be?"

"How long will this take?"

"Maybe an hour, unless you decide you want more time."

"That's not intended as a joke, is it?"

"I seldom find the time to joke when I am on duty."

"All right. We can meet at the barn you see against the hillside. I will ride with you in your car, if you don't mind. You can drop me back as you head out. For anyone that asks, you are here to buy a gelding."

"Why the cover?"

"You think I want it known I was questioned by the FBI?"

"As you wish. Can we talk as we go?"

"Might as well and get it over quickly."

"You signed a petition along with several other ranchers to Congressman Conway, stating strong opposition to the restoration of the Little Bend River."

"We strongly object to any messing around with the Virgin River."

"You signed that petition, did you not?"

"I did. It was not really a petition. It was more a letter from constituents to their congressman."

"How did you guys decide to do the letter? Was it at a meeting?"

"I don't remember."

"Where did you sign the petition? At home? Alone? With friends?"

"I don't remember. Probably after church."

"Do you meet regularly after church?"

"No. I think one of the guys circulated this letter and everyone thought it would be a good idea."

"That makes sense. Do you guys belong to a guild or commune or organization or something?"

"No."

"Do you ranchers meet often other than at church?"

"Most of us guys meet Friday evenings at the Rosy Glow Bar and Restaurant to have drinks and shoot pool. We meet at church on Sundays. That's about it unless there is a wedding, a baptism, or something else going on."

"Did you mail the petition to the congressman or deliver it in person?"

"I don't know. One of the guys passed it around. That's all I know."

"Was the Congressman present at that Sunday service?"

"No. Why are you so hung up on the petition? Isn't that the kind of thing you would do if you were concerned with something important? Maybe you don't understand the importance of the issue."

"Was the river issue discussed at one of these get-togethers?"

"These are no formal meetings. We discuss many issues whenever we get together. The river issue is very important and we discuss it all the time."

"Was the decision to burn the native store made at a get-together?"

"I had nothing to do with the burning of the store."

"Do you know who did it?"

"How should I know? That is a job for the police to find out."

"You are right. It is part of my job. That's why I am here."

"I had nothing to do with the burning of the native store and I have no knowledge of who may have done it. For all I know, the natives could have done it themselves to gain sympathy from the public."

"That's a thought."

"Is that it?"

"Did you rip up the banners the natives had put up next to the freeways?"

"What banners? I never ripped up any banners."

"Do you know what happened at the native village early this morning?"

"No. What happened?"

"A group of people raided the village and torched it. Were you with them?"

"No."

"Do you know who did it?"

"No."

"Did you hear anyone talking about setting fire to the village?"

"No. I told you I had nothing to do with these things."

"I know. I am just asking you if you know something."

"No."

"There is speculation in the press that local white ranchers are behind the attacks on the native people."

"It's not true. They can write what they want. They are liberal leftist communists. They'll write anything to create controversy. I am not surprised they are siding with the natives. They are always against us."

"Are you a member of the Klan?"

"Of course not."

"Are you a member of the Brotherhood?"

"Are you crazy?"

"Are you?"

"No. I am not."

"Are you a sympathizer of a white supremacy group?"

"No."

"Have you donated to any group that supports race-gender superiority beliefs?"

"No."

"Where were you this morning between 2:00 a.m. and 6:00 a.m.?"

"At home with my family."

"You went out for dinner last night? Is that correct?"

"Dinner. Last night? Oh yes."

"At the Atherton's, correct."

"So you know?"

"Answer the question."

"That's correct."

"You went home after dinner?"

"Yes."

"What time did you leave?"

"I am not sure. Probably around 10:30."

"Did you leave by yourself or did you leave with your wife and son?"

"Of course we left together."

"And you went straight back home or did you stop anywhere?"

"We didn't stop anywhere."

"Who else was there at the Atherton's?"

"Five families altogether. Jack and his wife, Todd and Rachael,

Jim Stafford, my family, and the Atherton's."

"What was the occasion? Isn't that unusual for a weekday?"

"It's rare, but it happens. One of their calves broke a leg and had to be put away. He decided to do a barbecue. We do these kinds of things when the occasion arises."

"Which car did you drive back home from the Atherton's?"

"The same car we drove over."

"Which car was it?"

"The Cadillac."

"Your wife and son will corroborate this information, right?"

"Keep them out of this."

"I want to. Will they?"

"Of course they will. Are you saying I am lying?"

"I am investigating a crime. I want to find out who burned the native store and who burned the native village this morning."

"Why suspect us folks living around here?"

"Nobody is a suspect and therefore everybody is a suspect."

"Why would we have anything to do with these events?"

"Because you could have. You objected to the restoration of the river."

"Writing a letter to our own congressman is not a crime. It's about something that affects our livelihood."

"You could also employ intimidation to scare the natives from their demand to restore the river."

"If people are intimidated because we wrote a letter to our congressman, then, they have a problem."

"A letter may not intimidate. Burning down a store and village can."

"That's their problem."

"They have a problem, all right. They have reason to feel intimidated. Many could have been killed this morning. It's my problem now."

"I assume nobody was hurt."

"I didn't say nobody was hurt. I said nobody was killed."

"Why do you suspect we had something to do with it?"

"Who else would have a motive?"

"The natives are not very friendly people. There are a lot of people who are upset with their antics. People don't have much sympathy in these parts for those who shut down the freeways."

"I'm trying to find out who was upset enough to burn down the native store and the native village."

"Good luck, agent."

"Have you ever been inside the native store?"

"A few times."

"The old one or the one rebuilt after the fire?"

"Both."

"Did you purchase anything?"

"I may have. I was more curious to see what they were selling."

"Did you ever destroy property inside the store?"

"Why would I? Come on."

"Did you?"

"I didn't destroy property inside the store."

"Do you know of anyone who did?"

"No, I don't."

"The police identified four people that went into the native store on Veterans' Day and started a fight. It was on the same day the native women blocked the freeway. I talked to three of the four and I am talking to the fourth person now. Is that correct?"

"What did they say?"

"You are the fourth person, correct?"

"I didn't destroy any property."

"You would know who did it if you were inside the store."

"We didn't destroy anything. I remember one of the guys dropped a vase and it broke. That was an accident."

"Was that person you?"

"No."

"Why did you go to the store that day?"

"We got caught in the back-up. We went to the store to get something to drink. Those guys at the store were horrible. They were rude. They threatened us and ordered us out. When we objected to the way they were behaving, they pulled out guns."

"Without provocation."

"Just like that."

"This should never happen. This is extremely disturbing."

"There are dangerous people out there opposed to the native presence."

"Governor, the FBI is conducting its own investigation. The Sheriff's Department and the UHP are cooperating with the FBI. They should find out who's behind all these very soon."

"Time is not on our side. I had a call today from the Secretary of the Interior. That's how serious it's become. He was offering to help. You know what that means. What that means is they doubt we can handle it on our own."

"I wouldn't jump to that conclusion. Native nations are the responsibility of the Interior Department."

"We must get the women out of jail."

"We will."

"How?"

"Refer the matter to federal courts and get them released."

"Do it now. Priority number one."

"It won't sit well with the public."

"We can't always act or react based on popular opinion."

"If it's perceived we are favoring the natives, whoever is behind these attacks could intensify the attacks."

"Commissioner, I want 24/7 patrols in the area. It's a tough task given the location. The freeways must remain open and the natives must be protected. The highway patrol must be ready to respond within minutes of any suspicious activity."

"Yes, Sir."

"Contact the Paiutes again and offer assistance to rebuild the village."

"They won't accept assistance."

"No matter. I want it known that we tried."

"Governor, we need to come up with a lasting solution. We can't let this fester and linger. It's taking up a lot of attention."

"I agree. But what can we do. Will they quiet down if they have the river restored? Or will that lead to more demands? Will the settlers take it on the chin and look the other way? Or, will they sabotage the river?"

"It's impossible to predict what will happen. Yet, we must act. One thing we can't do is do nothing."

"What is our best course of action?"

"Restore the river. That is the right thing to do. It'll satisfy the natives. The settlers will be ticked off. But, their stand is not justified. The Virgin River will be unaffected by restoring the Little Bend."

"How about the dark horse behind all this—the Catholic Priest, the Reverend Tosco? We have to do something. Either he's with us or he must go."

"He should be happy once the river is restored. That's what he wants."

"Maybe, maybe not. He may have other ideas. Will this be the start of something else that he's going to conjure up?"

"He's a maverick. There's no telling what other actions he's plotting."

"We don't know much about him. He's kind of a loner. He has no confidants and he keeps things close to the vest."

"The diocese will deal with him soon. They don't tolerate dissent."

"They are being very careful; too careful I would say."

"Keep an eye on his every move and every person he meets. Monitor him closely. If something's brewing, we should know immediately."

"Yes, Sir."

"Back to the river. Can we restore it?"

"Yes. But I would caution you not to act in haste."

"How about cost and the environmental impact?"

"Shouldn't be a big issue. There will be political fallout, though."

"We need to buy as much time as possible."

"Let a little water flow under the bridge, so to speak. We can then test the waters and take it from there."

"Let's get the Survey Department do a feasibility study? That'll buy time."

"The ranchers won't like it. A survey will be an indication we are leaning toward restoration."

"We need everyone to settle down a bit. We need at least three months."

"Do we have an alternative? If the natives take us to court, they probably will win. If we delay, Washington could step in. The Interior Department could decide it's about a river and involves a native tribe; therefore, it's their problem. I don't want them getting into the act. It's our problem. Let's take care of it."

"Reverend Tosco, I am agent Thompson from the FBI."

"What can I do for you?"

"I am sorry to barge in on you like this. I need to talk to you. Is this a good time, or should I come back later?"

"We can talk now. Visits from the FBI are not always by appointment I would imagine."

"That's true. The element of surprise is often needed, although that's for people who might be a flight risk or have something to hide."

"I appreciate the implied suggestion that neither applies to me."

"Do they?"

"Why would they?"

"I take it the answer is they don't."

"I am going nowhere. What I do and what I say are in public."

"What about what you think?"

"What I say and what I do evolve from what I think. So, there is nothing to hide there, either."

"I like that. I wanted to talk to you about what's been happening here at the native village."

"It involves the Paiutes. I think you should talk to them."

"I will. But, I want to talk to you about your role in it."

"My role is irrelevant."

"Most people wouldn't agree."

"And you."

"Me neither."

"You are convinced that I must have a role because I should."

"Correct. That's a logical conclusion."

"What do you want to know, Agent Thompson?"

"You instigated the native uprising? Why are you doing this?"

"I didn't instigate anything. And it's wrong to call it an uprising. It's a protest to draw attention to the needs of the natives."

"Semantics, Father Tosco. Nothing more than semantics."

"To you maybe. Not to them."

"Well, all right. What part do you play in this protest movement?"

"I am a supporter. An active supporter."

"Nothing more."

"I choose not to sit on the sidelines."

"That's not what's normally expected of a Catholic priest."

"No one has told me what's expected of me."

"As a priest, I am sure you know what's expected of you. Is it not safe to assume that active support in a native protest would not be expected?"

"It's not unheard of for priests to be actively involved in protests. I am sure you have heard of priests participating in pro-life demonstrations, immigration reform, and so many others."

"True. But, still, it's not what you normally expect of a priest."

"Are you trying to say that I am not a normal person or that I do not fit the mold of a normal priest?"

"How about both?"

"Both are wrong. As the head of the Catholic mission, a mission established for the well-being of the Paiute tribe, my primary role is Christian ministry. I live and work among them. I share in their sorrows and joys. I am one of them. If I can help them in their struggle for survival, then that's part of my responsibility to do what I can."

"Is that why the diocese sent you here?"

"You don't—and you won't—understand my role unless you have a good grasp of what a Catholic mission is all about."

"I thought I did. But, maybe not. Tell me."

"You're willing to listen, but I'm not sure you're willing to understand."

"I will keep an open mind."

"The mission is not just a structure where religious services are conducted. It is part of the community it serves, in every sense of the word. The success of the mission depends on the success of the Paiutes."

"The diocese does not want a mission. They have made it clear in no uncertain terms. They told me so. What's happening here and what you are doing are on your own are against the wishes of your superiors."

"A mission's primary concern is spiritual, but the social and economic welfare of the people are extremely important. You can't separate them."

"Your superiors obviously can and they have. You have chosen to ignore their wishes and what you are doing leading this native revolt is in conflict with the goals of the diocese."

"Mr. Thompson, if the diocese wants to express concerns about me or my actions, they will contact me directly. They would never use you as a proxy. What's happening here is a legitimate protest. If this were a revolt against the United States, I would have no part in it. This is nothing of the kind. This is a struggle for survival by a people who have been trampled underfoot for ages by hordes of stampeding settlers. They are human, just as we are. They have rights, equal to all of us. That's why I am in this struggle with them to fight for justice."

"I can understand that you are passionate about what you do. You have your own perception of your goals. But, not many people share your views or agree with what you are doing. They can't all be wrong."

"Have you talked to the natives?"

"Let them fend for themselves. They are capable of doing it."

"Yes. But, the rest of the world won't let them. When I first came here, I found a proud people, deprived of their lands, their heritage, their way of life and their dignity. I made a commitment to do what I can to help them get back on their feet. Today, they are a different people. They have a purpose. They have a goal."

"I had a hunch you were the brains behind this. Now, I am quite certain, by your own admission. Why? What's in it for you?"

"I didn't start anything and you can't stop what they started. They found it in themselves, the will to survive and succeed. I wish I could do more."

"You are doing a lot more than you should. The public is not too thrilled about what's happening here. Law enforcement knows that you are fueling the unrest and fanning the fires of rebellion. You are disrupting the peace in these parts. I am here to stop it."

"The brief disruptions are nothing compared to the endless tragedy these natives live under. It's the non-native public that made it happen."

"Father Tosco, you may feel justified in encouraging them to violence to correct wrongs. The natives have tried violence and failed miserably forcing them into where they are now. You are prodding them to fight the US Government again but the results will be no different."

"Love God and love one another. That's what I teach them."

"There's no love lost here, for the natives or by the natives. You are sowing the seeds of hatred between them and the people around them."

"Civil disobedience is not a new concept. It's how citizens protest in a democratic society. Where's the evidence of violence in what they did?"

"Reverend Tosco, don't kid me. There's a lot more going on here. You can hide behind platitudes. But, I don't buy it. I will get to the bottom of this and when I do, you won't be able to hide from me anymore."

"Is that what you came here to tell me?"

"My job is law enforcement. I am sworn to protect the country from threats internal and external. I take my job seriously; very seriously. I won't let you or your native friends endanger national security."

"Mr. Thompson, the police fired upon the natives during a peaceful demonstration. Two of them were killed. The natives have been attacked. Their store was set on fire. Their village was torched. Where were you when these criminal acts were perpetrated? What did you do to protect them? What will you do?"

"You forget what happened prior to these acts. Violence was answered by violence. Blockading the freeway is an act of aggression. It has bred more and more violence. I am here to put a stop to it."

"You are in the wrong place, Agent. Why did you want to meet with me?"

"To stop whatever it is that you and your friends are plotting. You'll face a very harsh response otherwise. I will guarantee it."

"Agent, you're wasting your time here. You should be going after those responsible for the hate crimes against native people."

"You don't need to remind me what my job is."

"If you believe that putting me on notice and threatening action against the natives are part of your job, I think you should re-examine your role more fully."

"You started it and you have the power to end it. Do it now. You and the natives disrupted interstate commerce. That is a federal crime. I can charge you now and arrest you. The collar won't protect you. But, I want to give you a chance and end this madness."

"They'll continue their agitation until their demands are met. When they decide to take action, I'll be right there with them."

"That sounds like a challenge. I do not back away from a challenge."

"Agent, this has nothing to do with you. This is about their survival."

"I have studied human behavior. I can see through the shroud you have thrown around you hoping to conceal your secret agenda. You can fool the natives. You don't fool me. There is no social agenda here. There is something more sinister playing out. I can smell it. I will root it out."

"Sir, I am not interested in your analysis and conclusions. If you want answers that'll prove your theory right or wrong, I don't play that game."

"You are playing a dangerous game. I will end it for you and extinguish the fire you've started before it spreads any further."

"You can't extinguish the yearnings of a race of people. You can slow them down, but not stop it. Remember Wounded Knee. I'm sure you know the FBI's role in it. It set the natives back. But they're back now because their survival is at risk. You can't suppress by force the hopes and prayers of a whole race of people."

"Wounded Knee posed a threat to national security; it was suppressed. Little Bend will become another Wounded Knee if you persist."

"There are reporters who are in it to make a living; there are reporters who are in it for the glory. Then there are some crazies like me who get smitten by the pursuit of truth and justice. But we all share one passion; a willingness to take risks, even risking life sometimes, in search of a story. The story of this native tribe has caught my fancy."

"You are the lone voice in the desert, Malcolm."

"But, it's you who nearly got killed."

"I knew the risks I was taking."

"I'm no stranger to risks. I've crossed swords with death many a time."

"They need you Malcolm. They need you alive to be of help to them."

"That puts both of us in the same boat. Don't worry, Father Tosco. I plan to stay alive. I have no desire to become a sacrifice."

"Malcolm, were you in court when the judge released the women?"

"Yes."

"Why is it taking this much time for them to get home?"

"They demanded that the sheriff drop them back here as they were illegally removed by the police. The women refused to leave the courtroom otherwise. Left the sheriff with little choice."

"Sarah knows how hard she can push the buttons. The police won't want a confrontation with the women. It won't look good in the media."

"There have been a few demonstrations against the jailing of the women. It even made the president's news conference."

"The vigilante groups have me worried. The police and the FBI won't scare them. They burned the village down and they fire bombed the store. They won't hesitate to do it again."

"They know that law enforcement will look the other way."

"It took America over two centuries to start changing their attitudes toward blacks. I hope it doesn't take another two for the indigenous people to be recognized as true citizens of this country."

"News must spread nationally. Urban communities generally follow humanitarian causes with greater passion. They are accustomed to traffic jams and protests. They don't view the blockade of a freeway as a catastrophe. It's people of the northeastern states that spearheaded the emancipation of slaves. They owned no slaves themselves, but they recognized the evil of slavery. The native issue must be funneled into urban enclaves. That'll make the difference now."

"Native nations must unite and become one nation. That'll make the difference for their future."

"Monsignor, agent Thompson from the FBI."

"Have a seat."

"Thank you. I really appreciate you finding the time to meet with me."

"What can I do for you?"

"I am investigating the events at Little Bend where you have the mission. I'm sure you realize Father Tosco figures prominently in our investigation."

"I'm sure it does. I'm not surprised."

"It's my opinion that he's the instigator of the native unrest. Is he doing this with the blessing of the diocese?"

"We are responsible for his actions."

"I understand. My concern is whether his actions at the mission are sanctioned by the diocese, or is he acting on his own?"

"There's no established protocol. However, he knows what the parameters are. Every priest of the diocese does. But, it's a mission. Father Tosco has a certain leeway to do things the way he sees fit."

"Not only is he involved with the activities of the native tribe, I now have evidence he's in contact with known domestic terrorists. We can't tolerate his actions much longer."

"It would not be against church policy for a priest to be actively involved in social justice issues. He must decide the extent of his involvement. He must not cross the line and compromise the interests of the church."

"These are not merely social justice issues. It has to do with national security. He's breaking the law."

"We won't intervene or interfere with due process. We won't shelter criminals."

"The Bureau has no quarrel with the church and doesn't want to start one. We want to maintain a constructive relationship with the church."

"Agent, the bishop and I are not pleased that the diocese got dragged into this conflict. We are keeping a close eye on things and we are concerned. We want to minimize the church's exposure. But I want to make it clear he has broken no laws of the church."

"He certainly is breaking the laws of the people."

"Then, deal with him as you see fit."

"If we take punitive action against Father Tosco, your faithful will interpret it as an attack on the Catholic Church. The Bureau is very sensitive about such perceptions and the public relations damage it can do."

"If Father Tosco has broken the law and you have proof to convict him, there will be no protest from the diocese. If you're framing him, that's another story. Right now, I'm not convinced he has broken any laws by participating in a native protest."

"I don't want to get into what constitutes unlawful activity. Let the courts decide that. There's more to it than breaking the law."

"What are you referring to?"

"I suspect Father Tosco wants to establish his own church. His efforts to unite Native Americans may be prompted by his desire to start an independent church. Natives don't have a solid religious basis and would be open to support a religious community that borrows from native practices and philosophy."

"I think you are overreacting. He's not capable of such grand designs."

"He must have undergone a dramatic transformation."

"I've known him for a long time. I'm not convinced he has such plans."

"Getting shot and getting nearly killed are pretty serious—a near-death experience, if you will?"

"Agent. What are you asking me to do?"

"There is danger. If you don't contain him quickly, there'll be disastrous consequences. It won't be good for you or the church."

"Please be more specific."

"We suspect the hand of the local ranchers behind the burning of the store and the native village. They are fed up with the freeway disruptions and they are very angry with the demand for the restoration of the river. If the natives don't back off, the attacks against them will escalate. If Father Tosco promotes confrontation, things will get ugly at the mission."

"You make it sound ominous."

"You think I'm exaggerating. But, you're closer to the truth than you realize."

"What do you want from me?"

"I have strict orders to ensure peace and prevent further hostilities. I will ensure compliance by the local ranchers. The natives don't trust the FBI and won't interact with us. Father Tosco can. He's the key. We want him to tell the natives to back off, at least for the time being."

"If restoring the river can placate the natives, why not do it?"

"It's a lot more than the river, now. Native leaders are meeting regularly to push for national unity. He's meeting regularly with AIM and Red Power members who are known terrorists. There will be more bloodshed if something isn't done quickly. Only Father Tosco can stop it."

"How?"

"By his absence. Remove Father Tosco from the mission. Close it and remove Father Tosco from there. With him there, danger lurks."

"Without him?"

"We will find a way to pacify the natives. We'll get them the river and that's where we want the unrest to end."

"Frankly, Agent, I do not agree with your conclusions. He's not the revolutionary firebrand as you depict him."

"I hope you are right. I just want to protect all of us in case you're wrong and I'm right"

"I can tell you one thing though. We are strongly considering closing the mission because it does not meet our goals, not because of Father Tosco's actions. It's only a matter of time."

"Time is an issue. I want to minimize his access to the natives. The sooner he's pulled away, the lesser the damage he can do. I suspect he will resist. That'll be your proof."

"I'm not talking years, just a few months, maybe weeks even."

"I have observed closely the progression of events that catapulted Father Tosco into prominence. I have studied closely the histories of 'God-Men' or cult leaders as we know them. Father Tosco fits the image of a cult leader."

"Impossible."

"I know the phenomenon. I see it taking shape. Father Tosco didn't go to the mission to start a cult. A sequence of unanticipated events has changed all that. He feels he's indestructible. Did you know he nearly got killed when you originally send him out to the mission?"

"I know that he nearly died from a gunshot wound."

"I am talking about the first time when he went to dissolve the covenant. The natives cared for him back to health. Yes, he was nearly killed a second time in the police shooting. The natives cared for him again. He survived two times. Death and danger don't scare him anymore. He knew of your wishes to send him to a care facility. He decided to defy you and went back to the natives. Would it not sound logical if he feels he is chosen for a higher calling, a man of destiny, a new Messiah, to save the natives?"

"It all sounds too far-fetched to make sense."

"He has a cause now, the restoration of native power. He's willing to die for their cause and he's proven it. He's already convinced the natives it's honorable to die for the cause and two did. It's tough to deny reality."

"Father Tosco is not a cult leader and never will be. He could be described as reacting or overreacting to circumstances."

"Every cult leader starts out quietly and they fool everyone around them until it's too late. Once they gain psychological control over the followers there's no escape from the clutches of their hypnotic power. How about Waco? Did anyone identify Koresh as the monster hiding behind the religious fervor? He called himself a Messiah and convinced everyone that he would be hunted down and persecuted. Then he went about fulfilling the prophecy. How about Jim Jones? How about the Doomsday Cult? Remember Ruby Ridge? To the society at large, it seems insane they can have such mind control. That's the evil beauty of it. They pick a limited group of followers and brainwash them thoroughly until they believe absolutely. Now you have the core of a cult; others soon follow. It ends in disaster, death and destruction. Do you see some parallels?"

"Those are extraordinary people with incredible capacity to manipulate their followers. Father Tosco does not belong in that league."

"It's a story we see all too often, unfortunately. These prophets of doom succeeded because society ignored them and rejected their power to manipulate, until it was too late. People who know them refuse to believe they are capable of the delusional fantasies they preach until they subject their followers to unimaginable horrors. Father Tosco is no different. He's led the natives to the brink of the precipice. He can't turn back now and he won't allow them to turn back. That is the power of the cult."

"Agent Thomson, I am not sure if you are the victim of the same delusional fantasies you accuse him of."

"Most of us are rational people. Therefore, we think rationally and look for rational behaviors in other people. We refuse to neither believe in extremism nor understand its inner workings until we are hit in the face with their hideous actions. We refuse to acknowledge evil exists even though it's around us in plenty. We are shocked when the friendly neighbor Timothy McVeigh blows up the Oklahoma federal building."

"It requires a quantum leap of faith on my part to perceive Father

Tosco as anything other than an average priest in a mid-life crisis who happened to be in the wrong place at the wrong time."

"Yes, Monsignor, every cult leader is an average person. It's when they become a passionate disciple of their own diabolical machinations that trouble erupts. It's their infectious passions that make partial truths become magnified wrongs. What set Hitler off? What happened with Lucifer? What's worse is how followers support the horrors they prescribe."

"You make a compelling argument for all the characters you mentioned. I still fail to picture Father Tosco in that league."

"Assume I am exaggerating. Maybe I am delusional. True, Father Tosco is nowhere near the explosive flash point yet. But signs are pointing in that direction. But ask yourself the question: Is there potential for trouble? If there is, why take the risk? Why allow it to get to the point of no return?"

"That I accept. Cult or no cult, the diocese wants no part in native unrest."

"Thank you. It's wise to act now than be sorry later. Recovering alcoholics must be removed from the source of the addiction, including people who may be innocently contributing to the addiction. With Father Tosco removed from the mission and banned from further contact with the natives, I can go about the business of resolving the real problems."

"I will take all this into consideration. Will that be all?"

"Will Father Tosco obey your order to close the mission?"

"There is no home Sarah."

"I forgot."

"We set up teepees behind the church; it's somewhat hidden from the freeways but close enough to the store."

"From now on, here's home."

"Our biggest problem is getting enough water here."

"If only we had the river."

"We will."

"It's good we can stay together in one area."

"What do we do about the village?"

"We left things as they are. The burned-out tepees, the pickups, and the charred remains of the horses will be a reminder of our struggle."

"Were you able to salvage anything?"

"Nothing at all."

"They must have driven into the village sometime after midnight and tossed gasoline soaked bales of hay into every tepee and then set fire to the whole thing."

"We were lucky there was nobody at the village."

"It was a blessing you were in jail. Otherwise we would have been at the village. Not everyone may have got out in time if the women and children had been there."

"They must have known there was nobody at the village. This was intended as a message and there will be more."

"I don't think it would have mattered. They couldn't have been absolutely sure there was nobody there and they did it. Our lives don't mean much to them."

"How's Father Tosco?"

"I don't know if I am imagining, but he seems to have changed a lot. He looks different. He has let his hair and beard grow."

"He spends a lot of time by himself."

"He does not seem to smile much anymore."

"He has lost weight."

"He takes responsibility for the death of our brothers."

"I think the pressure is getting to him. The media is hounding him. The diocese is no source for comfort. The FBI is hard on his heels."

"We must stand by him."

"It's good to have you back, Sarah"

"It's good to be back. How are you feeling?"

"I'm fine. Did they treat you okay?"

"They were very careful with us."

"You showed mental toughness Sarah. That's what we need."

"I don't know if I am tough enough. It was easy standing in the shadows and whispering to Doug. It's different now. I feel so inadequate."

"You just need a little time. Your natural instincts will come through."

"Here comes Fr. Tosco!"

"How's our fearless leader doing?"

"You are gifted with natural leadership skills, Father Tosco. I don't have it."

"It's a matter of recognizing what you have. You always had the ability to articulate things clearly. You are a good listener. You're a good healer."

"It's a comfort having you around. How's the wound on your head? Can I take a look?"

"It feels all right. There is some tightness as if my scalp is getting pulled to one side."

"It's healing well. I will make some more of the herbal oil and massage the area for a few more days. Whatever I had in stock must be burned and gone."

"I can manage with a little discomfort."

"The skin can get knotty and gnarled. That can permanently pull and stretch your facial skin and create other problems. I'll take care of it."

"Love God and love your neighbor. These are the two commandments Jesus taught us. It's easy to love God who you can't see and feel. It's not so easy to love your neighbor who often hates you or hurts you; is envious of you or looks down on you; treats you with mistrust or indifference. It's not easy to love your neighbor who looks different, behaves differently, and practices customs you consider strange. Loving God is meaningless unless you can love that neighbor."

"God is present in the neighbor. Look not for God in the great and opulent palaces built in his name. Look not for God among the great princes of the church, sitting on gilded thrones, and adorned in foppery. You won't find him there. God is not hiding behind bulletproof barriers. God is among us, visible in the neighbor standing next to you. God is

you. God is you and I. God is your neighbor. That is the essence of Christian values."

"Baptism is a ritual act binding the human to Jesus Christ in an act of faith. But baptism is not a freeway to heaven, and baptism alone won't save you. A baptized Christian with no love for his neighbor is no follower of Christ and won't be saved. An unbaptized individual who loves his neighbor is a true follower of Christ and will be welcomed into his embrace."

"You can recite the Bible front to end and back and have the ability to quote every book and verse. That does not make you a Christian. You can carry the Bible with you all day and sleep with it under your pillow at night. That does not make you a Christian. Christ is a living presence and he lives in your neighbor."

"Remember the parable of the talents. The master severely punished the servant who buried his one talent for fear of losing it. The talent we are all given is the gift of life. It's not to be hidden and buried for safekeeping. We are not temporary tenants of this human form, eagerly awaiting for the day when we can free ourselves from a world full evil and misery and fly to the bosom of the creator. This life is the greatest gift God has given us. Live it."

"There is inspiration in Mother Theresa who used her talent to alleviate human suffering. She didn't cloister herself in a cell and pray for them. Father Damien brought comfort to the abandoned lepers of Molokai. He didn't find glory switching places with another on the way to a Nazi death chamber. God has no shortage of angels and if he needs more he can create more. We humans are given the opportunity to live. We were not created for his great glory. We were given the gift of life and it is the greatest gift of all. It is an insult to God to keep the gift hidden and unopened. Live life and glorify him through your life."

"Stop feeling sorry for Jesus and the agony he endured. Stop feeling sorry for yourself that you are burdened with the sin of Adam and the sins of others. Stop trying to be a martyr and start living life. Peter was pretty smart to deny Jesus and live to spread his message."

"The Son of God was born in a manger and lived a life of poverty. When he died on the cross as a common criminal, all he had was nothing but the tunic he was wearing. Almighty God took the form of a simple human to demonstrate his love for us. His representatives surround themselves with symbols of wealth and prestige, pomp and power, adorn

themselves up in vainglorious foppery, claim infallibility, and act as anything but human. These God-Men sit on gilded thrones wearing bejeweled tiaras and crowns forgetting they are human while reminding everyone else what sinful humans we all are."

"What you've just heard is a compilation from several sermons. The FBI has been secretly recording every word he utters in public."

"I am shocked. Is he turning against the church?"

"This is unacceptable. He's mocking the Pope and the bishops."

"He seems to ridicule the laws of the church and imply that teachings of the church are irrelevant as long you love your neighbor."

"This is heresy. It must be stopped. It can't be allowed to go any further."

"This is going too far. Is he saying baptism is not important?"

"If you listen closely, there is an arrogance that defies church authority."

"He is trying to establish an alternative following. The message is resonating with crowds that flout church authority. No wonder they gather in increasing numbers to the 'desert church'."

"It sounds like he's addressing a larger audience than the people attending Mass each Sunday at a mission."

"He knows he's being monitored. He knows what he's doing."

"There are radical elements everywhere, in search of a cause. They are like some frogs that wait, sometimes for years, for the right weather conditions to emerge out of hibernation."

"Father Tosco is targeting the anti-church elements of society."

"He has a definite agenda. His message is directed toward people who challenge the church's institutional structure. He wants to establish a church of his own following."

"All this started with a simple appointment to a defunct mission."

"Why is the FBI documenting his sermons? These utterances are anti-church. They are not anti-government."

"The Bureau is trying to make a point. I was skeptical to their argument that Father Tosco is trying to establish a cult, his own church. They are very concerned about the political fallout. They believe he is championing the cause of the natives to establish a native-based cult. The radical challenge to church hierarchy helps gather around him a following of elements that question any and all authority. It's only a first step in a calculated plot. He is slowly but steadily building a platform from which he can launch his cult-based church."

"What is his agenda?"

"That is the unknown. The FBI believes the natives are nothing but a vehicle for his long-term goals. They are concerned about a native uprising. If you follow history, native people and the FBI don't see eye-to-eye. It's easy to pit the natives against the Bureau. Father Tosco knows that—and that may be the ace up his sleeve."

"How do we get out of this mess?"

"We should close the mission, now."

"Father Tosco should be moved out of there. He should be reassigned."

"The bishop and I are very concerned. We know we must act. Unfortunately, we have to move very slowly and cautiously. It's a touchy situation."

"He's created enough trouble already. Why wait any longer."

"We can't take any kind of disciplinary action without attracting public attention. There will be speculation in the media. You know what the bishop's feelings are. The diocese wants no part in the notoriety the mission has generated and certainly don't want to feed into it. But we can't act hastily. We can't fault the bishop for wanting to do what's proper even if it takes time."

"I think it's time for you to act and we're with you."

"Is this a punitive action?"

"Is the diocese retaliating because of your support for us?"

"Maybe, the diocese wants no part in what we are doing."

"This has nothing to do with you. It's me they're after. I came here, and trouble erupted. Move me away from here and trouble disappears. The diocese has carefully crafted a strategy of staying out of controversy. They feel the diocese is getting dragged into the mess as my name gets battered in the press. With me gone, there'll be no problems."

"If they were after you, they could have recalled you. They didn't have to close the mission."

"They are being clever. They know what I've done and they know it's just and right. But they don't want to acknowledge it. By closing the mission, they can eliminate the need to have me here and solve the problem with one swing."

"When does this become effective?"

"It has. The order is with immediate effect. I have been asked to report back to the diocese. I will be given my new assignment when I get back."

"It's so sudden."

"I have been anticipating this for some time."

"We hate to see this end this way. You made the mission relevant. You made our lives relevant."

"What are your plans?"

"I haven't made any."

"When are you leaving?"

"I am not. I am not going anywhere."

"What do you mean?"

"I will leave only if you ask me to leave."

"That'll never happen."

"We will never ask you to leave."

"What about the order from the bishop?"

"I've had the order for over a week. I've spent hours on end praying for God's guidance. I made my decision. I can't leave."

"Father Tosco, we're deeply grateful for your decision. But, you risk so much."

"We can't expect such a huge sacrifice from you. That's not fair."

"I've made my decision to ignore the order. It's final."

"What'll the diocese do next? They are not going to take it kindly."

"I know there will be repercussions. There will be more punishment. The diocese, like anyone in power, will look weak if they allow disobedience to go unpunished."

"As a tribe, we are going through unprecedented upheavals. Compared to what you are facing, that's nothing."

"My mind is at peace now that I've made the decision to stay."

"I would hate to see you suffer on account of us. Your future is at stake."

"Father Tosco, please reconsider for your own sake. We know our struggle won't be the same without you, but we will continue as best we can."

"You can help us even though you are not here physically."

"I'm convinced you're capable of directing your own future with me or without me. It's not that. There's a lot of unfinished work for which two of your brothers gave up their lives. I feel I'm responsible. I must see what we started lead to fruition. Their lives must be accounted for."

"We won't forget the blood of our brothers that was shed for this cause. We'll not give up the fight. But, we can't expect this sacrifice from you."

"My departure can divert attention from you and the goals you want to achieve. If I leave, they will focus attention on my radicalism and the disgrace that follows. The media will turn their focus on me and away from the movement. This just isn't the right time for me to leave."

"We have no words to express our appreciation of your sacrifice. It makes us even more determined to carry on."

"Fear not for me. My conscience is clear."

"We will all become Christians then. Baptize us all. Maybe that will help them change their mind."

"This is not a business proposition. Baptism is a rite of initiation. It is based on faith, faith in Jesus Christ. My role is to bring you the good news. It's God who grants you faith. If he calls, you will answer. I pour the water, but God gives faith. It is he who will baptize you with the Holy Spirit. That's the right reason. Baptism for keeping me here and keeping the mission open is the wrong reason."

"Father Tosco, you have taught us what it is to be Christian by your example."

"You are all Christians as far as I am concerned. When native people swear on the sacred pipe, it's a holy covenant. White people insist on written and signed contracts. Which has greater value, the promise made on the sacred pipe that is honored or the signed contract that is reneged? Your ancestors developed a belief system in a supreme being, the Creator, Wakan Tanka, the source of life. It is belief in a supreme God. God is not the birthright of any one people or any one religion. God directs us to be good and follow the path of righteousness. More than baptism, more than becoming Christian, more than the rituals and symbols, the conduct of our life is what's important. We are all, each one of us, called to obey God's commandments. He only demands two simple things: love God and love your neighbor. You obey those two commandments; you are in God's grace."

"It was amazing. It's really hard to explain the visual impact unless you witnessed it yourself. It was organized by the Paiute Nations. The objective was to draw attention to the plight of native people and the neglect they suffer and endure. We now take you over to Salt Lake City which today witnessed one of the more colorful demonstrations this great city has ever seen. Standing by is special correspondent, Carla Murphy, of our affiliate KSUY. Carla, it must have been a sight to behold."

"Yes, indeed. I have never seen anything like this nor do I think I will ever again. Viewers on television can only guess what it really was like—you had to be there to experience the intense feeling. This demonstration by the native tribes was no surprise as it had been announced weeks ago. Law enforcement was out in force, although they remained strategically inconspicuous. There had been rumors that white supremacy groups would try and disrupt the demonstration. Thankfully no such thing happened."

"From the pictures I have seen, this was no ordinary demonstration, to say the least. Tell us what happened and how."

"As you can see in the video, native warriors rode into town from all directions on horseback, in full native attire with face paintings and feathered capes, as they used to in the past when preparing for battle. The women folk came later in pickup trucks and cars, also dressed in traditional attire. Once they arrived in front of the Federal Building here, the men on horseback took up positions facing the main entrance outside the concrete barrier."

"How many were there?"

"We counted seventy warriors. There were about fifty women."

"What happened next?"

"The women set up two teepees on the grounds inside the barriers and they sat in front of them weaving baskets and beading necklaces. They unfurled a banner between the teepees. No entrances were blocked."

"Carla, what does the banner say? I can't see it very well from this angle."

"Proud to be Real American"

"Does it have any particular significance, I mean, the choice of words."

"It has. The wording is clever. They are proud to be American citizens and they are proud to be the real Americans, meaning the original Americans."

"Interesting."

"They arrived at the Federal Building at 10:00 a.m. At precisely twelve noon, three of the men walked up to the main entrance and delivered packages to the guards."

"Do you know about the contents? Who were they for?"

"I understand they were addressed to the president, the two US senators, and the three representatives from Utah. No information on what the packages contained."

"Any response from the recipients?"

"We're waiting for a response from their respective offices, and as soon as we get something, we'll let you know."

"Thanks. Anything else?"

"They left just as they came. Not a word was spoken. No slogans. Nothing."

"Were you able to interview any of the natives?"

"They paid no heed to the public or the media. We tried, but they said nothing and didn't even acknowledge our presence. They didn't speak amongst themselves. The men sat on their horses stony-faced, and the women went about their business until it was time to leave."

"How about the public? What was the crowd reaction?"

"There was a good crowd of onlookers. The windows of buildings around were packed with employees trying to get a good view. Then slowly people quieted down into an uneasy silence. Everyone seemed to be waiting for something to happen. Nothing happened, leaving confused looks all around."

"Unbelievable."

"That sums up the whole demonstration. I had seen natives in full attire only in the movies—and to be able to see it in real life was indeed a treat."

"They came, they demonstrated, and they left."

"He has requested a one-year sabbatical."

"Do you have to approve it?"

"No. But I have no reason not to. It's pretty standard practice to grant such requests especially from senior priests."

"That takes care of the problem, at least for the time being."

"It doesn't. It compounds it."

"What do you mean?"

"This is only a ploy. He'll remain at the mission and continue as if nothing happened."

"Are you certain?"

"Am I certain? No. Do I believe that's what's going to happen? Yes."

"Why do you suspect that's what he's going to do?"

"People take a sabbatical because they have plans, to finish studies, travel the world, or to do missionary work, to name a few. Father Tosco didn't give a reason other than he wants to take some time off."

"If that's what you suspect, you can deny his request, right? You can say his services are needed elsewhere in the diocese. His absence will create a hardship."

"How can his sabbatical create a hardship for the diocese? If we were that badly in need of his services, we would not have sent him to the mission in the first place. The word request is nothing but a formality."

"If he chooses to live with the natives during his sabbatical, there is nothing we can do about it, can we?"

"No. We can express our displeasure but we would not be able to compel him not to remain there."

"You bet he's going nowhere. He will stay at the mission and continue to torment us."

"The mission is closed. That's your order. How can he stay there?"

"He's pretty much living in a trailer among the natives. By declaring the mission closed, we no longer have a say in what goes on there. It's up to the Paiutes. If Father Tosco conducts services during the sabbatical, the diocese is powerless to stop it."

"Will the diocese be held responsible for his actions?"

"We will always be held responsible for what he does. Do you think anyone will make a distinction?"

"What do we do now? He may be approaching this as gamesmanship. He may think he is outsmarting us."

"What are our options?"

"Ignore his request."

"I am afraid things will keep happening and they won't be to our liking."

"The more we try to gain control of the situation at the mission, the more things seem to slip through our fingers."

"Christ always stood in support of the poor, the oppressed, and the downtrodden. The Diocese of Salt Lake City has failed to respond to the needs of the people of their own mission."

"We are grateful to the Diocese. We have benefitted more than we could've dreamed of, when they sent you here."

"A benign interpretation."

"We hate to see you at odds with your own diocese."

"They sent me here. They know what's going on. They have an obligation to support the mission. Instead, they are resorting to bullying and pettiness. I will stay and I will continue the Ministry."

"What more can they do to you?"

"I'm sure they'll enforce even more rules. They think they have the power. They will try and force me to bow down before them. The church demands obedience. They won't tolerate challenges to their authority."

"Father Tosco, we don't want to see you get hurt on account of us."

"I thought they would recognize how important this mission and this ministry are. I requested a sabbatical so that I could continue this ministry. So, what do they do? The diocese has retaliated by ordering me not to conduct religious services at the mission."

"What's wrong with conducting services?"

"It's an abuse of power. They think they can and therefore they do it. I don't have the time to play these mean-spirited games."

"What'll you do?"

"I'll continue with the ministry, as I have done up until now. There's something happening here that is of great importance to you as a tribe and as a people. It is about the dignity of the native people; it's about who I am as a Catholic priest; it's about what Christ stands for, and what the Catholic Church should stand for"

"We will never ask you to leave."

"They will direct more punishment unless I capitulate to their wishes. I've made up my mind. I know God has a plan for me."

"What plan?"

"The mission will stay open. Sunday services will continue as usual."

"What further action can the diocese take?"

"Against you, nothing. This is your property and you can do what you want on your property. If you allow me to conduct services here, there is nothing the diocese can do about it."

"How about against you?"

"Several things. They can suspend my religious privileges meaning I can no longer function as a Catholic priest. If that fails, they can excommunicate me, and expel me from the Catholic Church."

"Are you planning to break up with the diocese?"

"I don't want to."

"Will the bishop be open to compromise?"

"The issue of compromise does not arise. My job is to obey. I can repent and request forgiveness."

"They sent you here to take charge of a mission. That's what you did and you made it work. Why are they punishing you for it?"

"Have I done anything against the Catholic faith? Should we close the mission and quit because the bishop doesn't like the negative publicity? I can't submit to such cowardice. I won't undo what we have achieved here. I am bound to obey Christ. I will submit to Christ's commands. What I do is consistent with Christ's commands. What I did, I did according to the dictates of my conscience."

"Father Tosco, this is a tremendous sacrifice. You're risking your security, your future, and a lot more for us. I hope we're worthy of your sacrifice."

"I am nothing but a tool in the hands of God. I submit to his will. Yet, it is not about me; it's about you. He has a plan for you. I am honored he chose me to assist in that plan."

"The genie is out of the bottle. How do we put it back?"

"We can't. It's too late now."

"Why not give them the river?"

"You want to cave in because they blocked the freeways a few times. Let me caution you. You do this, you can rest assured every group that has a demand or an axe to grind will end up on the freeways."

"Who said we are caving in? It's a legitimate demand. It's very true the river was cut off to destroy the native lands. We have a moral and a legal obligation to restore it."

"Let the BNAA handle it."

"We should take care of this on our own, quietly and quickly. No feds."

"Let's at least give it some more time. Maybe, the natives will lose interest. Maybe they'll see the futility of it all. Maybe they don't want to risk public animosity and resentment."

"That's too many maybes for my comfort. No. We can't afford to dilly dally around any longer. We must take care of it?"

"Why the rush? The commission faulted the natives for what happened. I quote, 'All indications are the natives aided by the Catholic Priest, helped escalate the situation resulting in the police opening fire.'"

"Laying the blame on the natives for the police action is lame. I don't think the commission's report should be released."

"I think it was pretty courageous to acknowledge that the police opened fire. The report is daringly objective pointing out the field officers' lack of proper training to handle such situations and the supervisors' unpreparedness for effectively coordinating resources when faced with such an emergency. Lack of a chain of command, due process, and proper procedure were all highlighted. What more could we expect from the commission?"

"Police action must be justified irrespective of the circumstances. Police must follow proper procedure. This is the kind of stuff minorities, especially blacks, have been bemoaning for ages. It is wrong."

"It's politics. The natives created an explosive situation. It got out of hand. It didn't go the way they wanted or anybody wanted. I'm sure the police regret what happened more than anybody else. But when you throw fuel into the fire it can only make things worse, never better."

"The state must take full responsibility."

"The Utah State Sheriff and Police Associations have unwaveringly supported our campaigns. I won't mess with it over a native unrest."

"What's the governor going to do about it? How's he leaning on this?"

"I don't think he'll make it public. I am sure he'll release the feasibility study on restoring the Bend River, and then go ahead and restore it. That is a safe tactic. Restoring the Little Bend has no lasting impact on anything. Once the natives get the river, they'll be happy and settle down."

"How about the cost of restoration?"

"Three million if all goes according to plan."

"He doesn't want the Department of the Interior involved. It's a local issue and must stay that way."

"The State of Utah must be seen as doing this because we feel it's the right thing to do."

"You will pay a heavy price for this. You sold us out."

"Why don't you try and be reasonable? We don't want Washington to step in. We must keep it a state issue."

"How come the governor sent you? Why did he not talk to us in person?"

"He's out of town at the moment. But he wanted to inform you as soon as possible."

"We are the losers—and we don't like being losers."

"We have been over this several times. There will be no impact on the Virgin River."

"It's a matter of pride. We opposed the restoration of the river and that's the way it will be. The effect on the Virgin is no longer of consequence."

"You are risking a lot of goodwill to please a few natives."

"It'll not happen. The Little Bend won't be restored. We won't allow it."

"There is something called the rule of law. You and I didn't create that river. You and I didn't kill that river. But, we all know, the river didn't kill itself and we all know the hillside didn't collapse on its own. Human hands played a part. Those hands were not native hands. Those hands were the hands of white settlers. The losers were the natives. Their livelihood was severely imperiled."

"What are you trying to say?"

"There's a lot of buried past that's best left undisturbed."

"So let it be with the river."

"The decision has been made. The river will be restored."

"Is this what you called this meeting for, to tell us about the rule of law?"

"Why don't you stop pampering the natives?"

"Enough of this moral posturing."

"You have nothing to gain by supporting a bunch of good-for-nothing natives. You have a lot to lose by alienating people who contribute big bucks, vote for you, and keep you in power."

"It is the right thing to do and the governor has decided to do it. But he wanted me to explain the situation to you before he goes public with it."

"We should be pleased with that, and feel honored that he chose to reveal this to us ahead of a public declaration."

"You invited us to come and eat your cookies, listen to this nonsense, and go home like happy children."

"You want us to feel thrilled that the natives broke the law and will be rewarded for it. What if they blocked the freeways, severely inconveniencing the public, and provoked the police? Minority rights."

"We do care about the future of our Virgin River, and we won't allow anything to affect one drop of water in that river."

"The governor will regret this decision, if he goes ahead with it."

"No water will flow down the Little Bend."

"We are the true natives of the land. We made this land what it is—we're not a bunch of illiterate natives."

"We cultivate this land. We put food on the tables of the people of this state; we pay taxes. Can you say the same of your native friends?"

"We will make our wishes count, in the State of Utah."

"I want to make sure I am doing the right thing. I don't know who you are and I have no way of contacting you in case of an emergency."

"Agent Thompson, I am the chief and that's all you need to know. I will call you when I need to."

"Yes, Sir."

"Give me an updated report since our last meeting."

"The two natives died as a result of police firing. Ballistic testing proved that every bullet shell found at the scene was police issue."

"I am not interested in the shooting incident anymore."

"The possibility of further hostilities between natives and the white farmers remains very real. The governor's decision to restore the river has aggravated the situation."

"What do you plan to do?"

"Many of the white settlers are Klan sympathizers. I have concerns the conflict could expand in that direction."

"Any proof?"

"Nothing definite."

"Then it's fiction. I am not interested in fiction."

"Yes, Sir."

"How about the natives? What about the Catholic priest?"

"The tribe is getting support from other nations. Father Tosco is the real thorn in the side."

"Get rid of him. The priest is an easier target than the natives. I don't mean literally. Make him ineffective. Render him impotent from causing trouble."

"How, Sir? He's not an easy target."

"Any way you plan to neutralize him is fine with me. That's what your job is, to come up with a strategy to eliminate such threats."

"I don't think the Catholic Church will come to his aid. But you never know. I am taking it slow until I know what the sentiment is."

"It doesn't matter who he is, priest or no priest. If you feel strongly enough he is a risk to peace, eliminate him. Do it quietly, but make it quick."

"I do believe he's trying to create a cult following among the natives."

"All the more reason to choke out his influence. He may be no cultist. It matters not. But if true, the danger is too extreme to be complacent. If he is the source of the trouble, cut him off at the roots."

"I may be able to turn the tribe against him. I am working that angle. It would leave no after-taste. Without native support, he is useless."

"That will cause delays. Delaying action is never a wise tactic, not for law enforcement. Do we have to be absolutely correct before we take action? No. Do we have to be absolutely perfect in what we do? No. If we operate that way, this country will self-destruct. It is our ability to identify and eliminate threats before they materialize that makes us worthy of the trust the country places in us. Yes, what we do must be within a reasonable margin of error. Sometimes we do err, but that pales in comparison against the good we do. We accomplish things before they come under public scrutiny. It's what makes the bureau the unseen, but highly effective, national security instrument. We are under constant pressure to stop threats before they become threats. It is a tough mandate."

"I understand, Sir."

"The Bureau depends on intelligent agents capable of identifying and taking pre-emptive action. It must be done discretely, unobtrusively, but successfully. The nation is under constant threat from elements determined to destroy our freedoms and our values. That is the curse of democracy. People demand and enjoy the freedoms that are sacrosanct within our constitution, and yet they use those very same freedoms to undermine our systems. Freedom has its price."

"Yes, Sir."

"Countries with the worst human rights records are the first to cry foul when we punish criminal elements within our society. It's unfortunate but that's why we can't operate with total transparency. Most of what we do is covert. It may sound ludicrous. But the truth is—we are often protecting the public from its own foibles. Do you follow me?"

"Yes, Sir."

"For us, the end dictates the means. It may not always pass legal muster. We can't get caught in the act. What we do can't always be brought to light in front of an ignorant public that does not see the whole picture. How often have you seen naïve juries acquit a criminal or judges declare a mistrial on some flimsy technicality? We can't afford to let that happen in the cases we handle and risk loss of immense amounts of manpower and years of painstaking investigations. If we must act solely based on conclusive evidence, we might as well stay home. The maxim, 'not guilty until proven guilty,' doesn't apply to most targets we are after. I am not saying act indiscriminately, you understand."

"Yes, Sir."

"Congress recognizes our value, even though occasionally some left-wing members open their mouths out of turn. They continue to fund us without much hassle. Why? Because we are effective in fulfilling our mission. We win no Presidential medals of honor. We do not get written up as heroes in the media. We shun media attention. We seek out the enemies of the nation within and without and eliminate them. There is no publicity, no traceable footprints, and the security of our nation is our reward. We eliminate a threat that, well, never was one because we never allowed it to be one. We enjoy our successes in private."

"Yes, Sir."

"Our mandate is different. We follow a different code of conduct. We are given a wider berth and we can get away with bending the rules somewhat. With it comes a greater responsibility to use the power wisely and prudently. As an agent, you have a great deal of flexibility. If you get caught misusing it, there's not a whole lot the bureau can do for you. Use it wisely. You will err—and when you do, back off gracefully. Do not do anything out of spite, vengefulness, or vanity. If you're convinced your conclusions have met the requisite criteria of reasonableness, act quickly and decisively. In all things, keep the nation's interests above all else."

"At a time when we need to focus our attention on the crisis in the Middle East, it's unfortunate that the native issue keeps cropping up."

"Mr. President, these things take time to get resolved."

"Time is not on our side. We have a lot of ground to make up before the elections."

"The BNAA is under-staffed and under-funded."

"The same old argument. Tell me. What have they done in the last three years since we took office? More money and more staff to do more of nothing. Isn't that what they keep telling us: We won't do anything because we can't do everything. I am tired of this."

"The senate does not want to take up the issue. It's not a priority for them."

"I'm the one who has to answer the tough questions. Anytime there are reporters around, at least one will pop the native question."

"I heard the governor has decided to restore the river."

"Good. That's a good beginning. I wish he would get it done quickly."

"There's a lot of opposition. He's being cautious."

"I don't want to ruffle his feathers. His support is crucial to us winning the state. Maybe I should talk to him and give him a gentle nudge. Can you get him on the phone, please?"

"Sure."

"He is on his way to a commencement. Governor Berger, please hold."

"Hi Rudy, glad you could spare a few minutes. Will make it quick. You are coming up for the Governor's meeting next month, right?"

"I am planning to, Mr. President."

"Come on. No formalities, please."

"I am traveling with a group of dignitaries. Protocol must be maintained."

"All right. I am addressing the governors during the lunch session. Can you and Marlene stay back for dinner that night?"

"Sure. I would love to."

"Wonderful. One more thing. Rudy, this matter with your native tribe; what can we do? We need to get it resolved, quickly."

"It's a little tricky. I was just about ready to order the restoration of the river, and then ran into a little problem."

"What?"

"Congressman Conway; it's his district. He has gone on record opposing it. The people of his constituency, white ranchers almost exclusively, have sworn to block any attempts to restore the river."

"I don't know him. Would it help if I talk to him?"

"This doesn't merit the intervention of the President of the United States."

"If I can do anything to get this matter to go away, I'm willing to help."

"I want to get it done without confrontation with the local voters. Let emotions cool down a bit. The river will be restored."

"Another week or so won't hurt, I guess."

"I will have the National Guard on stand-by if I have to."

"The minority has the moral right; the voting majority has the absolute right. We are at the mercy of both. The perils we face."

"Wake up Sarah. There is something going on outside. There're cops all over the place."

"What's happening?"

"I don't know."

"Get everyone together and take the women and children over to the church. Everyone else meet me in front of the store. Alert Father Tosco."

"He's already here."

"They are setting up floodlights."

"It's so bright. I can hardly see anything."

"Father Tosco, do you know what this is all about?"

"No. Nobody has approached us yet. But I see a lot of patrol cars."

"We wait here."

"All right."

"What time is it?"

"It is a quarter past two."

"What do we do?"

"Wait. We will know soon enough what they want."

"Tell everyone to move to the front of the store where we can be seen. We won't give them any reason to do something stupid."

"I think everyone's here."

"Stand with your hands in front so they can see we carry no weapons."

"No movement until we know what they are doing here."

"I see someone moving to the front of the patrol cars with a bullhorn."

"Listen up. I want everyone to hold your hands up in the air where we can see them. You are then to walk toward me in a single file."

"Don't anybody move."

"Put your hands in the air and walk toward me, real slow."

"Don't move a step. Stay where you are."

"I am warning you. Do as you are told."

"Sarah, let me go to him and find out what this is all about."

"No Father Tosco. Let me handle this. Listen, everyone. I am going to walk toward them. Regardless of what they do, do not move."

"Okay."

"I am Sarah, President of the Council. Can you explain the meaning of this? Do you know what time it is?"

"I will do the talking. Keep your hands in the air."

"I won't. You can see well enough that I have nothing in my hands. Who are you and what do you want?"

"We are from the ATF. We are here with a search warrant."

"You have to wake us in the middle of the night to do this?"

"It is the middle of the night for us too ma'am. We have our orders."

"Let me see the warrant."

"Come on forward, real slow."

"I am not taking one step forward. Are you afraid of me? You have all these people with weapons drawn and I am an unarmed woman? What are you afraid of?"

"My men have orders to shoot at the slightest sign of trouble."

"We know how you operate. You can show me the warrant now."

"All right. We are here to search the area for firearms."

"Why?"

"There is a search warrant. That's all you need to know."

"All right. I will move everyone over there to the church. Please be quick."

"You stay where you are and tell your folks to stay out in the open. We will need to search the church, as well. Are these all the people you have? Where are the women and children?"

"They are in the church."

"Send someone over and tell them to come over."

"You can go and search all you want. I'm not going to move them."

"All right. You want to play hardball, fine. Go back to the group and stay put. Where's that priest?"

"I am here."

"Come forward.

"Do you need to do this? This is not right."

"Reverend, go with my men to the church. Gordon, do a thorough search. Run the metal detector inside for any buried weapons. Marty, take three guys and go through each teepee. Dave, get your men and go through the trailers and the store. I want every weapon of any kind back here. Be careful guys."

"Yes, Sir."

"Officer, why don't you come with me? I will show you around myself."

"No."

"You have nothing to fear."

"Stay where you are."

"We are not looking for trouble."

"I have men all around and they have their guns trained on every part of the store and surroundings."

"We don't want to put our lives at risk."

"Good. Don't try anything funny."

"Has there been a complaint? Why are you doing this?"

"We do what we're ordered to do. I don't ask questions."

"You are from the ATF, you said? Why are you looking for firearms?"

"Shut up and keep quiet."

"Give me five minutes and I will bring out all the firearms we have. That should save you time and we can all go back to bed."

"You stay where you are. We have our orders."

"Fine."

"Do me a favor ma'am. Hold your tongue until we are done?"

"You don't have to be rude. We are cooperating with you. Talking is not considered a crime in this country, is it?"

"If you don't shut your mouth, I'll do it for you."

"Go ahead and try."

"That priest is the cause of all this uproar. You natives were living here peacefully and not creating a problem for anyone, until he came along. He has taught you to be arrogant and cocky too. Too bad."

"You give him more credit than he deserves. Yes, we were not a problem for anyone until we decided to stand up for our rights."

"Get rid of him. He will only bring you more trouble."

"He's not causing any trouble nor are we. You are the ones making life hell for us. Where's your sense of decency?"

"My job is law enforcement."

"Law enforcement people live in a civil society too. You have families and friends. Look, we are not criminals or animals. We are human, like you."

"I do my job and that's it."

"What exactly is your job today?"

"There's a complaint you are hoarding weapons here."

"Who's spreading these tales?"

"That's not my job to find out. I obey orders."

"Why would we hoard weapons?"

"Sir, we found these in the teepees and some in the store"

"Ma'am, stay back where you are. Nobody move."

"Those are hunting rifles with permits. They are perfectly legal."

"My orders are to search and confiscate every firearm within the premises."

"There is nothing in the church."

"We have a right to own these guns."

"You can go and explain that to the judge who signed the warrant."

"This raid, search, and seizure of private property are illegal. This is a deliberate disregard of the rights of these people."

"You can explain that to the judge too."

"Morton, will you take a count of the weapons and ammunition, tag them and seal them for me please?"

"Yes, Sir."

"Give this lady a receipt for the items taken."

"Yes, Sir."

"Thank you for your cooperation."

"Father Tosco, what's the meaning of all this?"

"They're harassing us. They know we can't retaliate."

"I feel so helpless."

"This is only the beginning."

"If we don't stop them now, they'll keep coming back, whenever they want."

"It's a blatant insult. We can't let them do this to us."

"What can we do?"

"Sarah, I don't like the smell and sound of this. Tell everyone to be very careful. There's something in the works. Be very, very careful. Keep an eye on everyone that comes to the store."

"Police unearth a cache of weapons on Paiute reservation."

"Massive haul of weapons at native camp."

"Native American tribe's planned armed uprising foiled."

"Timely raid by ATF stops Paiute revolt."

"It's headline news in every paper.

"Except the Herald.

"What's going on Malcolm?

"I don't know. But, I don't like it. This story was leaked to every major paper, except us. The Herald was singled out and kept in the dark. We would have reported it differently, though."

"These papers got information on the raid, this late in the night and still could get it on their front page?"

"They must have been tipped off in advance of the raid."

"What is even more incredible, they have pictures and exact details as if they were at the scene."

"The pictures must have been given to them."

"Malcolm, any regrets for supporting us?"

"No. None at all. It only makes me even more determined to stick to the truth. We shall show them what we can do. The editor wants a full and detailed report on the raid and its aftermath—front page tomorrow."

"This is Marsha Dobbins with NPR, National Public Radio, All Things Considered, coming to you live from our studios in Washington DC. Today, we have decided to do something different, stray away from issues of global importance and focus our attention on a developing story from a small Native American reservation in a remote corner of Utah. Instead of using a telescope to look outwards, exploring issues of national and international importance, we are turning inwards as with a microscope to look at the small and often indistinguishable particles around us. When we turn our eyes toward the smaller picture, what we see is not a whole lot different from the big and scary world around us. In a sense it brings us back to the reality that what we see on a global canvas is nothing but blown-up images of the lives and legend of ordinary people. Therefore it is, that we bring you this story today. This is the story of a tiny native nation, the Paiutes of Little Bend Valley. Their story, their struggles, their future is a microcosm of the destiny of all the native people of this country—and in a sense—of indigenous people all around the world.

Joining me in the studio is Ray Mathews, National Correspondent for the Washington Post and Earl Murray, Professor Emeritus from the University of Pennsylvania, Department of Anthropology. And by satellite link we have Malcolm Donahue, Reporter for the Utah Herald and Monsignor Mark Cavanaugh, Vicar General of the Catholic Diocese of Salt Lake City. Welcome gentlemen."

"Let me start with you Professor Murray. Before we came on the air, you told me you have been following the events at Little Bend very closely. Can you give us a quick synopsis of what's happened so far?"

"Thanks Marsha for bringing me on. Recently, a small tribe, the Paiutes of Little Bend, which had hitherto been grouped together with another band of Paiutes, declared their independence and started an agitation seeking recognition and reservation."

"A reservation within a reservation."

"Correct. The BNAA, the Bureau of Native American Affairs has a detailed process for recognizing native nations as independent. The agitation for independence coincided with the reopening of a Catholic mission run by the Diocese of Salt Lake City within the Paiute reservation. I am sure Monsignor Cavanaugh can best explain the circumstances which prompted them to reopen the mission after nearly seventy years of non-existence."

"All right, let me ask Monsignor Cavanaugh. Why did you decide to reopen the mission—and why did you have a mission at the Paiute reservation at all?"

"The mission was opened at the Paiute reservation between 1887 and1889. As the story goes, the Rev. Scanlon, who later became the first Bishop of the Catholic Diocese of Salt Lake City, was traveling around in these parts, got lost, fell ill, was found by the Paiute Band of natives, and cared for until he was well enough to continue his journey."

"That sounds uncharacteristic based on the stories of atrocities committed by the natives on early settlers. Would you agree, Professor Murray?"

"That is popular myth. Of course, there were conflicts and violent interactions were commonplace. That is natural when you have strangers invading your lands. But, to come back to the point, the Paiutes were known for their peaceful overtures even in the face of aggression. I am not surprised by what the Paiutes did and history does back this up."

"Thank you. Go on Monsignor Cavanaugh."

"To show his appreciation and certainly with evangelization of the native tribes as a goal, Rev. Scanlon signed a covenant with the tribe committing the diocese to open a mission to promote religion, education, and healthcare. It was very successful for quite some time but since the turn of the century, with the world in turmoil and native tribes being relocated, the mission fell into disuse and disrepair. The tribal population fell sharply and the mission was abandoned but never closed. Recently, I decided to remove the mission from our list of ministries. The bishop insisted that since the covenant was still in existence, it should be dissolved by mutual consent before we officially took it off our books. Father Peter Tosco was appointed as emissary to meet with the Paiutes and get the dissolution signed. We were caught in the rare dilemma of having to reopen the mission in order to close it and that's what started this."

"Malcolm, you are a frequent visitor and if I may add, the only media person who has access to the Paiute people, and you are in contact with Father Tosco too. How did the reopening of the mission change the natives?"

"The Paiutes, as I understand, refused to sign the dissolution not because they wanted to keep the mission open; they just don't trust the white-man's documents. During his interactions with the tribe, Father Tosco realized there was a need and the mission could work for their benefit and welfare. He felt that more than anything, the tribe needed help in finding financial stability to go along with spiritual revival. Under his guidance, the tribe opened a native store and became fairly self-reliant. The mission became a success story."

"I know there is a mystery behind a river. Can you elaborate on that?"

"Sure. There is this tiny river, the Little Bend, an offshoot of the large Virgin River that once flowed into the Little Bend Valley. The Paiute tribe had settled and flourished on the banks of this little river, and that's how they get their name. Then, all on a sudden the river was cut off and in a few years dried up completely. The Paiutes believe that the Little Bend River was choked off at its origins by white ranchers who coveted the fertile valley. Their repeated efforts to force the Paiutes to cede the valley to them had failed, and they tried to flush them out by shutting off their source of water. The Paiutes want to get the river restored."

"The natives want the river restored but nobody wants to do it."

"Correct. The natives decided to fight for the restoration of the river and began a civil unrest to draw the attention of the authorities. They blocked the freeways as a form of protest. This got the attention of law enforcement all right, a lot more than what they had bargained for. There was a shooting incident. Two natives were killed. The white ranchers have vowed not to allow the restoration of the river."

"Let me come back to you, Malcolm. Ray, it sounds rather unusual for a small native tribe to confront and challenge the establishment; not in recent history."

"There have been periodic outbreaks of native violence here and there over the years. The actions of AIM, the occupation of Alcatraz Island in San Francisco Bay, takeover of BNAA offices in Washington, and the siege at Wounded Knee are some of the more prominent incidents. But, I agree, the actions of this tribe could only point to one thing; they are desperate; desperate enough to try anything. Attention for the sake of attention doesn't seem to be what they are after."

"They have caught people's attention for sure. What next?"

"From what I have been able to gather, they are not a militant lot. Their demands are not outrageous. Their protests, despite allegations to the contrary, were peaceful. They probably won't back down. They have tasted some success and they are gaining the support of other native nations. I have read that Father Tosco is extremely charismatic. The tribe is led by a female and from what I hear, she is special, a modern day Joan of Arc. I even saw a couple of cartoons calling her the Bandit Queen."

"Monsignor Cavanaugh, what are your plans for the mission? Obviously, what's been happening at the mission has drawn your diocese into the unexpected controversy."

"We have decided to close the mission, not because of the controversy, but because the mission is not achieving the goals we had envisioned."

"What were your visions for the mission?"

"The original goal of providing religious services, education, and healthcare are no longer relevant. We find that the mission is becoming more of a business and political enterprise. The bishop does not want the diocese to become embroiled in political controversy. Unfortunately, that was becoming a daily occurrence."

"Is that a reflection on Father Tosco and his radical approach, or the timing was just a coincidence?"

"I think Father Tosco's role has been grossly exaggerated. He certainly had an impact, but I would characterize his role as supportive rather than combative."

"The fact remains he was more than a spiritual advisor to the tribe. He took part in the first two freeway blockades and was seriously wounded in the shooting incident, correct?"

"The diocese does not support confrontation with law enforcement nor do we want to inconvenience the public. It is true the church's role is more than spiritual. We are concerned with social justice, human rights, poverty eradication, and lots of other communal issues. We operate several missions within the diocese. The Paiute mission was seen to wander away from core values of the church."

"Is it true the closure of the mission has led to strained relations with Father Tosco? I have this mental picture of him as this zealous renegade crusader who does not respect authority and wants do things his way."

"He has strong convictions. He passionately believes he needs to help the natives. He has shared some intense and very traumatic moments with them. I believe he's having a hard time separating the spiritual role from social responsibilities. We are working with him to ensure he understands his role must coincide with the expectations of the diocese."

"I hear he has been publicly very critical of you and the bishop. Has that had any bearing on his recent suspension from his priestly obligations? How does that affect him as a priest?"

"We are human; we are not beyond reproach. Yet, we are mature enough to face criticism. We accept what is constructive and ignore anything of a personal nature. He has criticized the diocese for not doing enough for the native people. We can live with that. However, when a priest of the diocese repeatedly ignores the orders of the bishop, the suspension is a warning to remind the individual of his obligations. What it does is stop the priest from performing religious ceremonies and provides him the opportunity to take a step back and reflect upon the commitments he made when he became a priest."

"Professor Murray, we are talking about this small tribe today because what happened there is taking on national implications. Is it true other native nations are talking about forming a united national federation?"

"Native people have never been famous for coming out in support of each other. The US government throughout history exploited it. It allowed them to destroy one-by-one the great nations that once roamed this land. They still have not joined forces to fight for common causes. That seems to be changing. The alleged atrocities committed against this small band of natives may have stirred them awake, made them realize the dangers of disunity, and the benefits of forming a union of nations."

"This is not the first time they have tried. Correct?"

"True; tried and failed every time—and the results may be no different this time. Only time will tell."

"Do you see it as a threat to national security as some claim, if they do organize and unite? Do you see them declaring war on the United States? Ray, what do you make of it?"

"Nonsense. Native Americans' loyalty and patriotism have never been in question. There are people who start hitting the panic button when there is a labor union being formed. There is absolutely no possibility of subversive activities. That's just propaganda. The native nations should have united a long time ago. It may prove to be an inconvenience to the government but should pose no threat. They are not talking about seceding or revolting or anything of the kind. Their biggest fear is they are becoming marginalized in this country, their numbers are dwindling, their influence waning, and their culture disappearing. They are an endangered species in their own land. It's a shame."

"How should the United States Government respond to this?"

"What the government has done so far has all been wrong. Take the case of this tribe. The official response to the agitation resulted in a police firing and the death of two natives. Subsequently, the tribe's store was firebombed; then the whole village was torched, and most recently there was a raid on their encampment by the ATF. There were news reports ATF confiscated a cache of weapons although we have information from reliable sources that all they found were nothing more than hunting rifles they have owned for generations. There is still a divide of distrust. The government must take steps to modify their attitude toward native people by recognizing them as the original citizens of this country and not as enemy combatants. A lot of wrongs have been perpetrated against them. We can't remedy all the damage done. Do the little things and allow them to live and enjoy the benefits others enjoy."

"We will keep a close watch over this story. That's it for now. Our thanks to Prof. Murray, Ray Mathews, Monsignor Cavanaugh, and Malcolm Donahue. What's been happening at this native reservation sounds like an old Western—except it's real and happening right here under our very eyes.

"Keep tuned to NPR news. We bring you news that matters because everyone matters."

"How's this possible? How's it we were not informed?"

"We should be getting some answers soon."

"How can such a thing happen in a civilized society? What country, what age are we living in? Who asked the ATF to conduct the raid? This is Draconian? A raid in the middle of the night with lights and sirens."

"I talked to the ATF Bureau Chief. She is trying to piece together what happened. She will let us know what she finds out. There was a breakdown somewhere."

"I want answers and I want them quick. To the public there is no difference if it was ATF or if it was UHP; whether it's federal or state law enforcement. The color of the uniform and the badges don't matter."

"It couldn't have happened at a worse time. It was flashed on national media before we even knew what had happened."

"How does that make me look? I am the governor. I don't know what's going on in my state."

"We need to do something quick to divert attention away from the raid."

"Why don't you call a news conference and go on the offensive before the media goes nuts?"

"If we order the restoration of the river now, it will appease the tribe and give the media something else to talk about."

"There will be more trouble if the river is restored."

"Be prepared to come down hard on anyone who attempts to obstruct."

"Let's say we go ahead and restore the river. They could destroy it after the work is completed."

"We will deploy the National Guard to protect the river during and after the restoration."

"We can't protect the river forever."

"We will if we have to, until the threat is no more. If these people think intimidation will work, we will respond in a manner that will discourage them from further misadventure. We will attack the slightest of provocation with force enough so that they'll soon get the message."

"Agent Thompson, did you make it clear to everyone, I mean everyone that the FBI won't tolerate attacks on the natives?"

"Yes, Sir."

"They must know it's best not to pick a fight with the bureau."

"Between us and the state, the ranchers should see the writing on the wall and lie low. There's one unfinished business though—Father Tosco. He and he alone can undermine the peace we have established."

"I thought you had enough to finish him off."

"I am now more than ever convinced that he is establishing a cult."

"Yes. I remember. What are you going to do about it?"

"I've questioned him a few times. The profile I put together is worrisome. I'm not getting the right answers."

"I thought I made my intentions clear the last time we discussed this. Deal with him as if a cult is real. Eliminate the threat."

"I will."

"What's the delay?"

"There's too much media attention at the moment. It's not what he's done, but what he hasn't done we must take note of. The diocese ordered the closure of the mission. He didn't close the mission. The diocese wanted to reassign him elsewhere. He didn't oblige and took a one year sabbatical. They ordered him to stop all religious services at the mission. He has not. The church suspended his priestly rights. He has paid no heed. That hasn't stopped his activities."

"The church won't tolerate such insolence. They'll kick him out."

"That remains the last resort for the church, to excommunicate him. But, I don't think that'll solve our problem."

"Let them do what they need to do. Don't let that stop you."

"I think Father Tosco wants the church to excommunicate him."

"There are dissident elements who question the authority of the church. It happens all the time. There are elements opposed to priestly celibacy; groups that support women priests; groups that challenge the church's rigid opposition to divorce, contraception, and abortion. There are groups that resent the church's stand on homosexuality. When it crosses the red line, the church will get rid of them."

"Once he is excommunicated, he can embrace these diverse elements and create a new ministry. Finally, he gets a reasonable justification to go out and start his own church."

"He does not have to be excommunicated to start his own ministry. Numerous dissidents have broken away from the church and started their own ministries."

"True. But excommunication makes him a victim of church excesses rather than a dissident. The natives are with him. Others will follow."

"It's possible but ne'er a sure bet. I'm not sure he has the charisma and the magnetism to pull it off."

"His approach is different. He's not a televangelist peddling religion. He's not a great orator and I'm not even sure he's a great communicator. Yet, he's got that something that rivets people to him and his words. He is a leader who can deliver. He doesn't stand on the sidelines and watch his followers get beaten up. He will unite the natives if he's given a chance."

"Let's say he succeeds. What then?"

"He will shape them into a political force."

"The blacks have tried to do it for decades. It hasn't worked."

"This is different. Blacks have fought for racial equality. They never could claim sovereignty. Native nations are sovereign. They have vast land holdings, which is theirs."

"What is in it for Tosco?"

"He would be their messiah and a prophet. The Ayatollah in Iran is hardly ever seen and does not rule; but nobody doubts he is the real power behind the government. I believe that's the kind of power Tosco seeks."

"Agent, remember what I told you earlier. The Bureau can't allow something terrible to happen to prove that we are right or wrong. If we err, it's better to err on the side of prudence."

"I won't err. I request permission to stay on the case for another year. The issue has not been resolved with the restoration of the river."

"Granted. If you are convinced the danger with this Tosco is real, take him out. To me, though, the native movement is the big concern. Keep an eye on the Paiute people. Make sure what started there stays there."

"Father Tosco, we three members on this panel have been appointed by his Excellency the bishop to address allegations of misconduct by you in the performance of your duties as a priest of the Diocese of Salt Lake City. You requested this hearing by the curia. We have prayerfully placed ourselves in the presence of God, reviewed available documents, excerpts of your sermons, and statements from people familiar with the mission and the ministry. As a final step, we will discuss the main areas of concern with you in person. The bishop may join in at any time if he chooses to. Upon conclusion of our face-to-face discussions, we will submit a report to the bishop with our conclusions and recommendations. As VG, I will act as the moderator. Father Benjamin Mueller is someone you know. He was the Rector of St. Patrick's Seminary, and is currently Visiting Professor in Scripture and Canon Law at Catholic University in Washington DC. Father Romero Espinoza is a Jesuit. He has a Doctorate in Canon Law and is a well-known author and theologian. He is currently working in the capacity of special counsel to the US Catholic Bishops Conference.

The church conducts these investigations of one of its own with reluctance and deep sorrow. We are all children of Holy Mother the Church. We are bound as members of the clergy to vows of obedience to follow the doctrine and teachings of the church. While we are given wide latitude in the expression of our faith and our devotional practices, the ecclesiastical doctrines of the church are inviolable. There's no room for personal interpretation on matters of faith and doctrine. It is absolute and sacrosanct.

Even though the church will go to the maximum extent and exercise restraint and patience, there comes a point when the church will establish its authority and root out repeated offenders. You have been given multiple opportunities to refrain from offensive actions and teachings that are in conflict with the fundamental principles of the church. It is unfortunate that you have chosen to disregard our attempts to help you fulfill your responsibilities. The church has established protocols that must be set in motion when a member of the clergy willfully advocates positions that are contrary to the teachings of the church. The proceedings we are embarking on today are of extreme importance and an indication that as arbiters of church doctrine we have few options remaining to hold you in compliance. May I remind you that you and we are bound by an oath of secrecy and details of the proceedings may not be released to any individual or group without the consent of the bishop. Is that understood?"

"Yes."

"You have requested these hearings of your own free will without coercion, threat, or any other form of persuasion. Is that correct?"

"Yes."

"This is a trial. But, unlike a civil trial, there is no judge or jury, and neither is there an accuser nor accused, and there is no determination of guilt. We will formulate an opinion to submit to the bishop who has the final say. We are not bound by time constraints. We intend to give you a fair hearing, following which we will submit our recommendations to the bishop. Is that clear?"

"Yes."

"The bishop has sole authority to act or not to act upon our recommendations. These proceedings are based on church law and practice. The results, the findings, and the recommendations have no relevance in a civil court. Is that clear?"

"Yes."

"We enter into these proceedings with a spirit of openness. Your concerns will be received with respect and your demands, if any, will be given serious consideration. We will individually or collectively offer constructive criticism and suggestions as we see fit. We will offer you prayerful guidance to help redirect your responsibilities as a priest, in accordance with the laws of the church."

"It is important you understand the potential outcome of this trial and the consequences that can result from it. The charges against you include: disregard of the vow of obedience, defiance of the authority of the bishop, and misinterpreting church doctrine. We may conclude that the charges are valid and significant enough to merit further disciplinary action. If so, such will be our recommendation. We may also set forth corrective steps that must be completed before you may return to the full embrace of the church. If the findings warrant it, we may recommend that the suspension in force now may be continued. It is possible that further constraints may be suggested including excommunication. Do you want to make a statement at this time?"

"No."

"The bishop informed you by letter of his intent to close the mission. You continued to operate the mission in spite of the order. Why have you chosen to disobey the order?"

"It was not my idea to reopen the mission. I did what I was asked to do—and against many odds, I made it happen and made it successful. The bishop ordered the mission closed claiming it was not fulfilling the purpose for which it was established. This is contrary to the truth. It has fulfilled its purpose and continues to beyond anyone's expectations. Having given them a ray of hope for their future, it is wrong to close the mission. A mission is about people and human dignity. I have concluded that the bishop ordered the mission closed based on erroneous and misleading information."

"I visited the mission. I have constantly monitored what has been going on at the mission. I came to the conclusion that our priorities for the mission were not being met. I made the recommendation to the bishop to close the mission. There was nothing misleading or incorrect in my report."

"Father Tosco, if every priest of the diocese obeys or disobeys the orders of the bishop according to the dictates of his conscience, there can be no effective administration. We believe that the Holy Spirit is working through our bishops, and that acceptance is fundamental to our religious hierarchy. We must unconditionally obey the dictates of the bishop in matters of faith and doctrine."

"Father Benjamin, I did what I believe is right. I am now more than ever convinced I did the right thing."

"There is only one right. The church demands that we take a vow of obedience to the bishop. We can't allow our personal convictions to override the laws of the church. There can be no rationalizations when it comes to obeying the bishop."

"You knew the bishop wanted no part in controversies and confrontations. You and I may not like his approach. You and I may not agree with it. But, you and I must submit to his wishes in such matters."

"Are we followers of Christ? Do we believe in the message of Christ? Do we have an obligation to clothe them, to feed them, and quench their thirst? Do we have a mandate to alleviate suffering, to liberate the poor, the frail, and the oppressed from the tyranny of their condition?"

"Let's keep liberation theology out of this. We are talking about the authority of the bishop. The order to close a diocesan institution does not create a conflict of faith."

"As a priest, my first and foremost obligation is to Jesus Christ, my Lord and Savior. You discuss dogma; I talk of reality. In my soul and in my mind I know I am doing what Jesus wants me to do. There is no ambiguity in my mind. We forget there are human lives that will be impacted if we shut down the mission. Please allow the mission to remain open and let me continue my work with the natives."

"The bishop has already denied the request. You must subject yourself to his authority unconditionally."

"I can't abandon them in the midst of this crisis. I have been granted a one-year sabbatical. Let me continue my work at the mission through the end of my sabbatical."

"It's not open for negotiation. The mission is closed and your priestly rights are suspended. By keeping the mission open and continuing with priestly functions, you are defying the authority of the bishop."

"If it's about me, I am ready to hand over the mission to someone else. Do not close the mission. I seek assurance that the work of the mission will continue and the support for the native cause will remain."

"You must submit yourself unconditionally. The bishop may decide to support the mission but that cannot be a condition for your submission."

"You must submit yourself in total obedience."

"I thought you would put aside your mantle of absolute authority and listen to my pleas on behalf of the native people. It is an insult and arrogant affront to the teachings of Christ to disregard their cry for help. I can't and I won't submit to your demands to close the mission and my ministry."

"Father Peter. Do you understand the consequences of what you are saying?"

"You may punish me. You may excommunicate me. But you can't defeat the will of God."

"I am really disappointed. You give us no options to resolve this in a positive manner."

"Father Tosco, it's the chosen few who are called to serve the Lord as a priest. Do not take your vocation lightly. I would entreat you to reconsider your positions and submit yourself to the authority of the bishop."

"Take heed, Father Tosco. A Catholic under excommunication lives in a state of mortal sin. You run the risk of eternal damnation. Please do not be blinded by conceit and self-righteousness. Repent and submit yourself to the will of your superiors. Return to the state of grace and communion with the congregation of the faithful."

"My decision is final. Be not concerned about my salvation or me. My soul is clean. God is just and merciful. I submit to his will."

"Do not get carried away by the adulation of your followers and their enthusiasm to the liberal brand of Christianity you preach. In the end, you may be dragging yourself and the innocent followers down the path of perdition."

"Let the Lord be my judge. He knows what's in my heart and soul."

"Our forefathers once roamed free like the buffalo on the plains; their children darted among the trees of the forests like the quick deer, and their hopes soared high in the skies like the winged birds. But we, their children, struggle for survival amidst an unrelenting and hostile world, able only to dream about what once was. Day-by-day, we see our values eroding around us. There has been nothing but suffering and sorrow for the native people ever since the white man set foot on this land. As our forefathers did before us, we must keep fighting for our survival. They fought with weapons. We must arm ourselves with righteousness in our fight for survival."

"The Supreme Being put us in this land and this is our birthright. We are the face of this nation; we are this nation. We must survive as a race."

"There is a will within us which refuses to be defeated, which ignores the temptation to surrender, and which gives us the strength to fight for survival."

"Today we come to lend our support to the cause of the Paiute people. Today we come to show solidarity with all our suffering brothers and sisters. Today we come resolved to challenge fear and rekindle hope. Today we come resolved to turn our faces to the east and receive the blessings of a new day, a new era, and a new awakening of the native spirit. Today we come resolved to shout with one voice, we shall overcome; we shall endure; we shall live again."

"Like a forest of great redwoods, we stand strong when we stand together. When one falls, many will fall with it. We may be strong individually, but we are stronger as a group. We must support each other so that we can remain strong together."

"Our forefathers left us a legacy of pride. We must hold our heads high and look beyond the barren wilderness toward a bright new dawn."

"We must be bold but cautious. We must be wise and patient. We must not resort to violence. We must not rise up in anger against our own country. We are true citizens. Our loyalty, just as our rights, is inalienable."

"Our Paiute brothers and sisters put up a peaceful and silent fight for rights. They hurt no one. They threatened no one. Yet, they were brutally attacked and harassed. They paid a heavy price. They didn't falter; they have remained strong. It is now our turn to support them."

"By supporting them, we are supporting the survival of many nations who face similar challenges."

"Day by day, our way of life is disappearing. We lack cohesiveness and unity. We have no sense of purpose and little vision for the future. It must change."

"Our nations struggle with lack of resources, unemployment, education, healthcare, substance abuse and despair. The younger generations do not value their heritage because the heritage has become a symbol of shame. We have the power to change it all."

"The message of unity has started to reverberate within the souls and minds of native people. It must take roots and grow firm. There will be trials and tribulations before they yield results. Little Bend and many such Little Bends must be restored."

"The attacks on native sovereignty will be relentless and constant. It won't stop. Lasting and enduring success will require native unity. There are seemingly insurmountable differences that we must overcome. We can. Let's embrace one another, as one race, one nation."

"We have lost much. We can't afford to lose anymore. The special status accorded to indigenous people in the constitution is not an act of charity. It is restitution for the atrocities of the past. Many seek to do away with these constitutional rights and would rejoice in the disintegration of native reservations. We must stand guard."

"Look at what happened to the Sioux in Badlands. When something of value is discovered on native lands, all treaties and promises are tossed aside and the government steals the land from us."

"Native reservations are becoming illegal dumps for toxic waste. Our waterways are polluted. The air we breathe is poison. Politicians with little or no vision are put in charge of native affairs. They sell us out."

"Christianization of native children in the name of modernization and forced sterilization of native women continue today. It must stop."

"We must seek representation at all levels of government, state and federal, in congress, the senate and the judiciary. States must recognize and respect native sovereignty. The judiciary must uphold and honor the sanctity of treaties and covenants."

"Revered leaders of great nations, the Cedar City Paiute Council and the Great Council of Paiute nations swear upon the sacred pipe, and recognize the Paiutes of Little Bend as a separate band and promise to hold in trust the valley of the Little Bend for them and their descendants in perpetuity."

"Thank you. It means a lot to us. We shall not forget this kindness."

"We will work with BNAA to further our decision and make it official. From now on, you shall be represented on this council as a separate Paiute Nation."

"On behalf of the nations represented here, I salute the Council of Paiute Nations for this noble gesture."

"Our hearts overflow with gratitude. We now have a place to call home. We now can look at a future that holds promise for us and for our children."

"Let us resolve as we take leave and return to our people, to reach out to every native nation and spread the word. We must unite as one nation. They must be part and partners with us in this struggle."

"Ladies and Gentlemen, it is a great privilege and an honor for me to restore the Little Bend River. As the waters flow through the dry riverbed, it brings hope of a prosperous future to the original children of

the soil, the Paiutes of Little Bend Valley. They are valued members of our society and their return to self-reliance is a goal we cherish with them. It is the first step in re-establishing a trust-partnership with the native citizens of our state.

We have proven again that much can be achieved if we put our hearts and minds to the task. That is the American way. That is the spirit that has propelled this nation into one of the greatest in history. It is the same spirit that will keep this nation and the people of the United States as the leading innovators and pioneers of change for ages to come.

Today we restore the Little Bend River. We are taking a tiny step toward restoring the trust of our native people in the American Dream. They are an inseparable and integral part of our past, present, and future. The restoration of this river is a testament to the resilience of the Paiutes of the Little Bend Valley. Their future contributions will make this state and this nation greater."

Malcolm Donahue

Special Correspondent
Utah Herald, Salt Lake City

"On a misty, cold March afternoon, the Governor of Utah flipped on a switch that released water from the Virgin River to a small tributary called the Little Bend. It is widely believed the path of the small river was dynamited almost a century ago to shut off and deny water to the small native tribe, the Paiutes of Little Bend Valley. They have lived here for thousands of years and survived along the banks of this tiny river.

The river flows again, and with it the hopes and aspirations of a whole generation of natives who have been sidelined and marginalized up until now. For our society and for the future of this nation it is of vital importance to protect and support the original inhabitants of this country. Our books, movies, and folklore have tarnished the image of our native people. It is time we as a nation put aside outmoded stereotypes and allow them to become part of mainstream American society while retaining their ancestral roots and traditions. The only crime committed by the native people is they resisted the encroachment of the white settlers into their ancestral lands and fought to protect their societies. Was that wrong? Who did wrong? It is time to right the wrong?"

"I'll make no bones about it. I want this man destroyed. Agent, I want him on his knees unable to rise up again. He's ruining my political career and he will, if he's allowed to continue his antics unchallenged."

"Congressman Conway, I understand your dilemma."

"I have lost credibility with my constituents. I promised them the river would never be restored. Now I stand helplessly by and watch while powerful forces beyond my control have intervened. I will go down in flames if he does not go down before me."

"My career is at stake. The bureau will have my scalp before long if he continues his merry ways."

"It's amazing how he has dodged the bullet so many times,—literally, too."

"Congressman, Tosco is a threat to you, to me, and to a lot of people around here. He is a threat to the Catholic Church and to the Diocese of Salt Lake City. His influence must be capped and sealed. It'll be difficult; but it must be done and will be done."

"The diocese will do nothing. They are a bunch of impotent cowards. We must do what needs to be done."

"He's learned to manipulate the native people. He's found success with his ministry. He'll continue and keep reinventing himself. Tosco is a festering wound. He must be stopped."

"Agent, I don't care how it's done. I don't like to take a licking from anyone, let alone a priest. If I get knocked out, I will take it fair and square. It'll not be because of some religious freak and a bunch of crazy natives."

"I will take him down. Please understand that such matters must be handled carefully. I ask you to be patient. Tosco will be stopped, not only to safeguard your credibility but because he's become a threat to national security. I need your help and I need a little time. You must trust me on this."

"My folks don't trust me anymore. I failed them. They may not try to sabotage the river. They don't want to pick a fight with the State. But, they're angry. They'll take it out on me. When the elections come up, they won't forget. I'm history unless I do something to regain their trust. It must be big and it must happen quickly before they pick my replacement."

"It'll be done. But, it has to be done with an appearance of propriety. We are not the mafia. We can't barge in and take Tosco out in a shootout. Those days are gone. It has to be done discreetly."

"A blow to Tosco is a blow to the natives. The blow must be clean and final. Neither must rise again."

"For the bureau, Tosco is presumed to be a threat until proven otherwise. I will eliminate this threat."

"The issue is not water anymore; the issue is not the restoration of the Little Bend. The issue is my folks lost a fight. I lost a fight."

"The real fight is just beginning."

"My folks are not used to losing; they get what they want, by force when needed."

"On no account should they resort to more violence. They must remain under the radar while I train my focus and attention on Tosco."

"Patience is not a virtue they care about. They act first and reason later. They don't care for subtleties. What they understand is intimidation. Use of force is in their blood. That's how they break a horse or subdue a bull.

"We must employ strategy. Lions are powerful predators. But, they prefer to isolate and hunt the weak or wounded. That's strategy. Let me isolate Tosco after I weaken him first."

"Tosco is not weak!"

"Not yet. But he's getting weaker. The church has kicked him out. That makes him a wounded dog, lot of bark and little bite. Even liberal Catholics tend to be skeptical of an excommunicated priest. Next, I'll separate him from the natives. That will leave him like Samson without his locks. If they come to believe Tosco is a liability, they'll dump him. They are pragmatic. Tosco will be made expendable."

"Sheriff, Agent Thompson from the FBI."

"What can I do for you?"

"I need a favor from you."

"Since when does the FBI come to local law enforcement seeking favors?"

"We live in a world of realities. Old paradigms must yield and be replaced with strategies that spell success. I prefer to work in tandem with local law enforcement. Together, we can achieve greater success and faster."

"In my experience, the FBI tends to look down upon local police and sees us more as a nuisance, bungling things up."

"Sometimes it's deserved and often not. I come with no such preconceived notions. We have our operational methods; you have yours. Resources vary but the goal is still the same. Most in the FBI come from police forces and we understand the limitations imposed on you."

"You said you wanted a favor."

"Tosco and his movement must be stopped."

"I thought it was kind of stopped once the Paiute got the river."

"Natives are talking national unity. Tosco is their spiritual leader. I fear we're going to see more of the same of what happened here but magnified a hundred times. The unity movement must not succeed."

"It won't happen. The natives won't forget past rivalries and mistrusts."

"Times have changed. New realities could forge new relations. Nations that couldn't stand the sight of each other are now meeting together. They feel they are facing a common enemy that threatens their existence. It may or may not work. Ironically, the police firings have provided them the spark. If they succeed, the blockade of the freeways will pale in comparison to the havoc they could create on a national level."

"We have been monitoring the tribe pretty closely. We have seen no cause for concern."

"The bureau works nationally and we have been shadowing the movements of certain persons of interest. Did you know that members of AIM are planning to meet with your native friends in the near future?"

"What's AIM got to do with the Paiutes?"

"We want to know too. We know who they are. What concerns me more is that AIM is planning meetings not only with your Paiute tribe, but also with other nations. If larger native nations entertain the presence of AIM, it can only mean one thing; the natives are willing to accommodate AIM's violent philosophy. It could only have happened through outside intervention, through the influence of Father Tosco."

"I see."

"This tiny nation has tasted success. They showed some guts and made the impossible happen. Tosco has made them believe in themselves. Now, they are thinking big."

"All right. What do you want me to do?"

"I must stop the native unity movement from expanding. But I need your cooperation. Please continue monitoring activity at the Little Bend, but on no account should law enforcement initiate action against the natives without consulting me."

"If we anticipate trouble, we'll let you know. But if it's immediate, we will take action."

"Call me before you do anything, if something does come up."

"All right, I will."

"They're planning a festival here. They plan to promote the Sun Dance and the Ghost Dance at the festival. You know what that means, don't you?"

"They have these strange dances all the time, even before Sunday Mass."

"Except the Ghost Dance remains banned and the Sun Dance is self-torture—a form of human sacrifice. I know what you're thinking. What's in a dance? I agree. It's stupid in this day and age to ban cultural expressions."

"I think we need to ignore such restrictions and bans. Makes no sense."

"That being said, you wonder why they are advertising their intent to perform these controversial dances. I see it as a challenge to the government to dare try and stop them. You and I won't oblige them and stop the dances."

"I still don't understand why you're so concerned. What's the big deal?"

"I see behind these moves a pattern of thumping their noses in the face of authority. I believe they have this idea that such acts of defiance will help unite them. A national agitation by natives will lead to unforeseen consequences. The natives are getting emboldened. I see the potential for armed insurrection. You and I are law enforcement agents. We are not politicians and we don't enact the laws, we ensure they are implemented."

"I think you are exaggerating the threat."

"Probably. We are contemplating preventive measures to counteract a threat the natives may not even have considered. That's the bureau's approach toward law enforcement. That's how we differ from you. We take steps fearing the worst to avoid the least. We act rather than react."

"We won a great victory. The price we paid is immeasurably steep for me personally and for my people. But, we've proven that the sacrifice was not wasted. This victory belongs to all native people reflecting our resiliency and determination. It was made possible because we, the indigenous people of this land, came together as one nation. It was made possible because of the support of great people like Father Tosco and Malcolm Donahue who worked tirelessly for us, even at great personal risk. I entreat my brothers and sisters to stay united and strengthen this bond so that we can achieve greater things in the future."

"Sarah speaks words of wisdom."

"We must keep alive the momentum we created here."

"This council must represent all native nations in the United States."

"We must be an integral part of this country's future. We cannot remain an asterisk to the history of this country, a forgotten footnote."

"We must exercise our right to vote. Few of us are participating now and the reasons are obvious. Whom do we vote for except the president and the vice president? Members of congress and other elected officials represent their respective constituencies. As sovereign nations, they do not represent us."

"We must have separate representation."

"The Bureau of Native American Affairs is a cruel joke."

"The time has come; we need a greater say in our affairs."

"The time is now; we must ensure representation at all levels of government. The Paiute nation showed us we have the power to make things happen. Our greatest threat comes from within us. Our disunity has destroyed us and allowed our enemies to choke our spirit."

"Like a snake that has shed its skin, our children leave their heritage behind them. They feel it's a hindrance to their advancement. Our children are ashamed of proclaiming who they are. They leave our teepees and hesitate to return. They show little interest in learning their history and culture. They raise their children as non-natives. If we believe in our heritage; if we believe it's a heritage worth preserving, we must unite as one and face the world as one."

"Some of the larger nations will survive longer while smaller nations will be lost and forgotten. Eventually, bigger nations will become small nations and suffer the same fate."

"We're different nations but in truth we're brothers and sisters, children of the same spirit. We believe in the same Great Mystery. We are one family."

"We speak different languages and dialects; we have customs and traditions that differ. But we have more in common than differences."

"We'll survive only if we join hands, as one people, one nation across the length and breadth of this land, and speak with one voice."

"The horizon is clouded with uncertainty. We can assure a future for us and our children only by standing united under one banner."

"We have taken a small big step. We must reach out further and farther to bring every native nation and every native person within one union."

"We are Native Americans, not Indians. We must be called as such. It didn't take long for the term African American to take hold."

"If our people unite to form a single vote bank, politicians will take notice. We'll have the power to make the difference. They'll listen to us."

"We'll support those who support our causes and oppose those who oppose us."

"It was not until 1929 that Native Americans were declared citizens of this country. It was twenty years later that native people got the right to vote. In all the years since then, we have achieved nothing with our votes."

"The people of Puerto Rico were granted citizenship and the right to vote before us."

"Puerto Rico is a commonwealth and they have special representation at the federal level. We are native citizens and we have none."

"We must have representation in Congress in recognition of our special status as sovereign nations. We can promote native candidates in viable locations. We can also get indirect representation by supporting candidates who will stand by us and for us. Voting as one bloc, we'll influence the outcome of many a race."

"We must become relevant once again. There was a time, when white people united and made us the common enemy. They took advantage of our lack of unity to defeat us separately and destroy us. Today, let us join together and win by electing those who will support us."

"We have the blood of our brave forefathers in our veins. They fought the white settlers knowing fully well their bows and arrows were no match against the guns and cannons trained on them. They fought and died because their lands, their families, and their way of life were under siege. They had pride. We must show the same resolve, the same pride."

"United Native Nations of America, UNNA must become the voice of the native people of this country. UNNA must become the fifty-first state of the union."

"Instead of cattle we should bring in buffalo."

"I hear Wyoming has a problem with an expanding buffalo population. Each year they are forced to thin the herds and send at least two-hundred to three-hundred buffalo for slaughter. I got in touch with the Wyoming Department of Wildlife and they are more than happy to donate as many as we want as long as we don't butcher them or resell them. All we have to do is pay for transportation. I think we can take in a hundred."

"That's wonderful news. The buffalo will be symbolic to our revival."

"The Fish and Game Department has offered to plant native fish in the river. Buffalo and fish. We are heading in the right direction."

"Father Tosco. Our fortunes are improving, because of you. But, fate has not been kind to you. What can we do to help?"

"Don't worry about me. I am happy doing what I love to do. I am at peace."

"I am surprised nobody stood up for you at the diocese."

"I'm not. I'm sure there're a few who support me. But, they may feel it prudent to hold their peace rather than invite the wrath of the diocese. I am damaged goods, the rotten apple in the bag. All those who come into contact with me can get tainted too."

"How can they disown you for doing what is right?"

"The church demands absolute obedience. My disobedience, regardless of justification, is unacceptable. They did what they had to do. I hold no grudge against them. But, I must continue the work of the mission because I believe the Lord wants me to do it."

"Gentlemen, thanks for freeing up your calendars so quickly to come for this breakfast meeting. I want to keep this meeting informal to allow everyone to speak freely and brainstorm in a bi-partisan manner. There will be no minutes and no official record of it, if that's okay with you."

"Fine."

"We can always go on record if we so decide, at a later time."

"Your message stated this had something to do with Native Americans. Does this have something to do with the shooting incident in Utah?"

"It got things started but it's become far more complex than that. Some of the large and well-known nations have joined hands with several lesser-known ones to push for national unity and new reforms."

"It's been tried and failed many a time."

"What is it now, five years since we went through months of hearings and testimony to come up with a reform package? Why do we have to deal with this again? We have huge problems facing the country? Why again?"

"I don't think we can ignore this. There is reason to believe this could spell trouble unless we address it quickly."

"Are they making new demands?"

"They want to be called Native Americans. They want recognition for United Native Nations of America, UNNA, as representing native people of this country and they want UNNA to have representation in Congress."

"That's absurd."

"Are they out of their minds? Are we going to rewrite history?"

"What's wrong with 'American Indians'?"

"Representation in congress. Give me a break."

"They want to become the fifty-first state."

"Good Lord. What else are they going to dream up?"

"Gentlemen, those were my first sentiments. But this is serious."

"How so?"

"Why now?"

"Who knows? Maybe they feel empowered. They have very lofty goals. They want to unite all native nations under one banner, UNNA."

"It'll never happen."

"There are too many nations and most of them hate each other."

"The big nations won't want anything to do with such a union."

"In the past, we tried to unite them so we could administer benefits uniformly. They resisted and fought it all the way. Now they want to unite. It's our turn to resist."

"I say, ignore their demands. They will cool off."

"Even if they manage to piece together a coalition of nations, it won't last. These are fiercely independent people and they won't work together for long. There are too many divisions and too much distrust among them."

"Secretary, is there more to the story?"

"Yes. They have elected a Supreme Council to represent them. I am told over one-hundred nations are signatories to the formation of a union."

"I don't believe it."

"Have they done anything yet, other than form the union?"

"It's not what they've done, but what they are capable of that's prompted this meeting. They could start a nationwide agitation and imagine what freeway blockades like those by the Utah tribe would do."

"Let them try, if they can. We'll meet them with force if we have to."

"If it's just talk and demands, we'll let them wander in the morass of political impasse—and in good, time they'll tire and go away."

"They won't dare block freeways on a national scale. They'll attract so much ill-will, it'll backfire on them."

"In such a case it's best not to do anything. By stalling or delaying you wear out their patience. Then, they either escalate the conflict or it ends in a slow death."

"Inaction is the best action. If the natives get aggressive with their tactics, let local law enforcement deal with it."

"It's well-known that Washington moves slowly. We can talk it up in the media and do nothing. Keep their hopes alive just enough to stop them from taking action. Eventually, they will tire and it'll just go away."

"If the media takes too much interest, we'll create a diversion. We can always pick on North Korea or the Hamas."

"We can even get a few native leaders to oppose the movement."

"The president is concerned by what happened in Utah. It got far too much attention than it should have."

"Tell him not to worry. It's probably election-year jitters."

"We can re-group the subcommittee on Native Affairs and deal with it."

"We can't play political Ping-Pong with this issue."

"The Secretary of the Interior listened, didn't reject our demands, but gave no indication he would do anything."

"The Under Secretary for the Bureau of Native American Affairs was there too. He was non-committal."

"They sat, they listened, they nodded their heads and it was over."

"I didn't get the feeling they took us seriously."

"We expected as much. But we'll change all that. They will take notice."

"We must force changes at the bureau. They always act as if they know what's good for us. They must listen and work to safeguard our interests."

"Not only the bureau, the nation as a whole must change the attitude toward native people. The March of Nations must be a spectacle the likes of which Washington has never witnessed. It must become the topic of conversation for a long time."

"At least one-hundred-thousand people should be attending."

"It may not be big compared to others, but it must be the most memorable."

"Millions of native people have suffered at the hands of settlers for no fault of their own other than they were here. Their spirits cry out for justice. Their trail of tears must be accounted for."

"We shall be a proud people once again. We shall walk freely on lands where there were no boundaries before the white man came."

"Our children shall carry on the great traditions of our people. They shall proudly proclaim they are children of the soil."

"He grows in stature day-by-day. The more they try to bottle him up, the more he seems to expand and flourish."

"Do you have any idea how many people attend his Sunday services? It's amazing to see all the people crowding into this crazy place. There's nothing but a tent; no heating or A/C and nothing but plain sand to sit or stand on."

"For someone who baptized not one soul while it was a Catholic mission, he is baptizing people by the dozen each Sunday. All you have to do is ask. He does not even ask if they have been baptized before. He keeps no records and issues no certificates."

"He knows full-well that what he's doing is invalid. He does not seem to care."

"He is practicing his own brand of Christianity."

"It must be driving the bishop and the VG crazy. What can they do?"

"Nothing. That's the worst part. They have no jurisdiction over him now."

"The VG must be furious. It was his idea to send Tosco out there."

"It may have hurt his chances for advancement. It was widely rumored he was in line to become the next bishop when the current one retires in a couple of years."

"Tosco has outwitted the VG time after time. Everything the VG has tried has backfired."

"Tosco seems to have the rare quality of dragging down and destroying anyone and everyone that comes into conflict with him."

"I warned the governor not to restore the river. He didn't listen. Now we have lost the goodwill and support of people but got nothing in return."

"Political contributions are down. My approval ratings have plummeted. I need to do something to regain the confidence of my constituents."

"The natives are untouchable at this point. Any attempt to discredit them will attract the kind of attention we don't want."

"Tosco is our best hope. You bring him down; you drag the tribe down with him. They won't risk losing what they have achieved to protect a disrobed ex-priest. But the case against Tosco must be significant to force such a reaction."

"I am sure the tribe will dump Tosco eventually. If they continue to be financially successful, greed and corruption will follow. When that happens, a moral standard-bearer like Tosco becomes a nuisance. Can you imagine a casino tribe having someone like Tosco around?"

"We can't wait that long for them to dump Tosco. I'll be history by then."

"You are not thinking of eliminating him, are you?"

"Good God, no. The last thing we want to do is make a martyr out of him. The formula is simple; destroy Tosco and the destruction of the Paiute tribe will follow. We must break up his unholy alliance."

"All across the Unites States of America, from the Eastern Atlantic shores to the far reaches of the West and beyond, there is a new awakening. Trees glitter in the sun displaying their tender leaves; new grass sprouts on the plains and the streams dance in joy feasting on the melting snow. The eagle cries from its high perch on the mountaintops. The lone wolf greets the rising moon in raucous joy. The elk, the deer, and the brown bear wander among the buffalo herds. The young trout leap out of the cascading waters in reckless abandon. The Great Spirit has walked forth from the ethereal realms and called upon the spirits to rise and stand with the living. Nations large and small, warriors, women and children, as brothers and sisters, have reached across this land in unity."

"O Great Spirit, from you we have all we have. To you we dedicate our whole being, and in you we find the strength to meet the challenges of our existence. The mountains rise and the rivers flow to proclaim your glory; the rich grasslands of the vast plains bow in homage to your great power; the herds of buffalo roam once again from horizon to horizon with the promise of hope and courage. We turn to you Great Spirit with uplifted hands. Turn not your eyes away from us. Breathe new life into our weary veins. With you before us and your blazing chariot guiding us, we shall overcome all obstacles."

"Children of the land, arise. Reclaim the land that the Great Spirit gave to you. Show to the world that you are many in body but one in spirit. Let the world take note and see the new resolve, the new spirit and the new life."

"It was a reminder of what it was like in this country at the time of the early settlers except for the backdrop of cars and trucks whizzing by. They stood as silent sentinels, some on horseback, most on their feet, reminding us that they were here first and they are still here. With their painted faces showing no signs of emotion, wearing their traditional attire, men, women and children stood shoulder to shoulder, seeing but not recognizing, hearing but not responding, motionless as the mountains and tranquil as a gentle breeze. There were no banners, no shouted slogans, and certainly no regard to the occasional honks of travelers going by. They stood with quiet dignity, the proud descendants of great nations. In their silence you could almost hear the fervent chants of the flute and the rumble of the drums, reverberating and echoing off canyon walls and tall trees. You could hear if you were to listen with your heart and mind the one message relayed endlessly around this

nation: We will be here till the end of time.

This was a fascinating display of solidarity by Native Americans. You have to recall the history of the bitter rivalries that separate these nations, the cultural and linguistic differences that raised insurmountable barriers among them, to appreciate the magnitude of this coordinated demonstration. They stood at key junctions of freeways, and important crossroads of cities, all across the country, offering no clues and causing no traffic disturbances. If there were minor problems they occurred when travelers stopped to take pictures or just to gape in wonder.

Precisely at noon EDT, they dispersed quietly, leaving no trace of their presence. One moment they were there and then they had vanished.

The demonstration was aimed at sending a clear message to Washington that they mean business. If they can stand along the freeways in such numbers, they can also stand on the freeways and bring the country to a standstill.

We tried but have so far been unsuccessful in getting a response from the Secretary of the Interior or the Under Secretary for the Bureau of Native American Affairs. There has been no response from the White House yet. We will have an update during our evening news hour. What a show. As the saying goes: 'It can only happen in America'."

"This was not a photo shoot."

"This was not a commercial promoting Native American tourism. The message is loud and clear: Watch out."

"They may not have overwhelming support, but they have enough to take it to the next step if and when they choose to."

"We can't ignore what they just did."

"We can't capitulate in the face of a demonstration. Yes. They made a great show. So what? We have to be careful with our response. If we are seen as caving in, you can bet there will be copycat demos from other groups. I say we do nothing now. Let's see what they do next."

"Whatever we do must have the appearance of an orderly process and not in response to such displays."

"The president is rather troubled. The natives have managed to grab news headlines again. It's well organized and orchestrated. We don't face questions at news conferences. He does. He wants to ward off trouble from native people. There's no good time, but now certainly is not the right time for divisive internal unrest. Inaction won't do."

"We can acknowledge the demonstration as just that. There's no harm in expressing publicly how impressive a show it was."

"I think the president should stay out of it and let the secretary or the under-secretary handle it. They should issue a statement, something vague enough to appease, but not detailed enough to raise hopes."

"I agree. Give the natives a hint that their demands will be considered."

"We could invite the Supreme Council for an informal meeting."

"Good idea. I can set something up in about a month. I'm sure they know nothing gets done in haste. A lot of things can happen by then."

"This is like a game of chess with checks, counter checks, and many a stalemate."

"Don't underestimate them. I don't think they see it as a game of chess."

~

"I wish I could get out of the office more often. But, I don't. I must be getting old. It's probably getting time to retire."

"I don't think you can or you will. You are a hardcore reporter. There will be no peaceful retirement for you."

"I guess you are right. Your story has kept me on my toes. I had no idea when I first showed up here that this would explode the way it has."

"None of us did."

"It seems to have taken a life of its own."

"Everything happens for a reason. It's futile trying to fathom the course of destiny."

"Sarah, your message said: 'Can you be here at 2:00 p.m. today?' Here I am."

"AIM wants to meet with us. You know what AIM is, don't you?"

"Yes. Of course. Why do they want to meet with you?"

"That's what I want to find out. I agreed to meet with them if Father Tosco and you would be allowed to join in."

"Just them and the three of us."

"No. As always our people are free to join in. I feel a lot more comfortable doing things out in the open."

"AIM's notoriety precedes them."

"I have heard plenty about AIM but unfortunately nothing good. Still, they are native people like any of us and should have a say in what goes on. They can contribute. We should at least listen to what they have to say."

"Do you think they will give up their militant behavior?"

"Assuming they want to work with us, they'll have no choice but to."

"Once word gets around AIM was here, there'll be a lot of talk. Do you want that kind of negative publicity? There's going to be whisperings you are planning some new trouble. There are native nations strongly opposed to AIM. They could misunderstand."

"I want no part in a militant struggle. I am no sympathizer of AIM's philosophy. But at the same time, it would be wrong to turn away from their overtures. They are the cream of our youth. We must engage them and figure out ways to direct their energies to the common good. They chose to contact me and I want to reciprocate."

"What's having us present going to do for you? You want us as monitors?"

"Sort of. That and more. I'm hoping you both can observe and act as impartial judges. I want you to participate fully and ask questions. Father Tosco has confirmed he'll be present. Your opinion will be important. But, if it makes you uncomfortable, you can leave. I won't feel bad."

"No. Of course I want to be present. It's an honor to be invited. I would not give up the opportunity to meet with AIM representatives in person."

"Thank you. Having you both provides me some protection that this is not some covert or clandestine activity."

"I understand."

"Malcolm, I have another request."

"Go ahead."

"Can you do a report of this meeting for the council?"

"Sure."

"Only for the council. You won't be at liberty to publish any account of the meeting without the consent of AIM and the council."

"That's a hard bargain. It goes against my professional principle to agree. You said it's a request. But if I don't agree, I can't be present. Is that it?"

"That's correct. That's how I sold your presence to AIM."

"All right. I agree. But why do you need me to do the reporting?"

"The council will accept your account. They trust you and Father Tosco, and you are the only two non-natives I trust. I am just being cautious."

"You have taken the precaution to cover all your bases. It begs the question: 'Is it worth the risk meeting with AIM?'"

"Father Tosco drilled this into us: Without risk there's no progress. This meeting is worth the risk. I want to hear what they have to say. I want to hear what they have to offer. They have the same goals for nationhood and native empowerment. They chose a different path. The path of violence has no relevance in the new struggle we envision. Will they adapt?"

"Do they think they can manipulate you to gain acceptance?"

"They'll find if they do, they miscalculated."

"They don't want to be left out. They are shrewd enough to recognize this movement has enough momentum and clout to effect changes. They have no direct access to the council. That's why they chose to meet with you."

"You could be right Malcolm. My very feelings. I sense they feel they will be rebuffed if they tried to approach the council. We have shown the resolve to challenge authority and it appeals to them. They may feel we would be more receptive because we need help. In turn, we could act as goodwill ambassadors to the council on their behalf."

"When do we meet them?"

"They are in the church waiting for us."

"I don't like it, but I will go along with it."

"What choices do we have?"

"Tell them flat out it won't work. Now is not the time to vacillate."

"Senator, we must be realistic. It could result in absolute chaos if they take to the freeways again."

"You are conceding to the threat of what they might do. That is weak. I would rather be upfront and tell them we can't do it. We are yet to recover from the protracted hearings we held not too long ago. But like I said, I will go along with the president's request. I can understand his concerns."

"I am sure the president will appreciate your gesture."

"I will convene a meeting of the sub-committee to discuss dates and issues. We have a Senate Sub-Committee for Native American Affairs but the house is yet to appoint one. I will talk to the House Majority Leader and try for a joint committee. That's the easy part. We also need to put together a panel of experts. That'll take time."

"Reasonable delays are to be expected."

"As long as we are moving forward, they'll accept delays. Once it's known we are scheduling hearings, the natives will quiet down."

"Sometimes I wonder if it's not better, to end, once and for all, these knee-jerk native reform exercises. We must eliminate their special privileges. We could use these hearings to build up public distaste toward native sovereignty and special status."

"No. No. Let's leave that alone. We can't entertain such thoughts now. Let's do it for what we planned it for. I will buy you time but we can't retreat from where we are now, even if we don't move forward."

"Agent, is there anything new we should be aware of?"

"Four AIM members visited the tribe. They had a meeting. Father Tosco was present as well as Malcolm the reporter guy."

"Tosco's at it again. The man is a maniac, an incorrigible troublemaker."

"What was the reporter doing here?"

"He is a known native sympathizer. An oddball. He's a Vietnam vet who supports Vietnam. He's an anti-war, anti-government communist."

"Any idea what AIM is doing here?"

"That's what I want to find out. It was expected although we didn't know when it was going to happen. I contacted the reporter and Tosco. They both refused to talk. The natives won't even meet with me. I'll track the AIM guys down to find out what's going on. I will, even if I have to drag them into prison on sedition charges."

"It's too bad these natives aren't satisfied with what they got. Someone needs to tell them to mind their own business and live peacefully here."

"They're animals. They're crazy. They taste a little victory and now this."

"This is Tosco's work. He is exploiting them but they don't get it. He wants to create more trouble. I bet he had something to do with it. AIM guys couldn't have just walked over."

"AIM's more to his liking. He probably thinks the Paiutes are too soft."

"What does he want now? What's he plotting next?"

"He's pushing the woman into the leadership role with the natives. He must find her easy to manipulate."

"What do we know about her?"

"Nothing much, other than she is the widow of the chief who was killed in the shootout. I hear she's well-respected for her healing powers; she's like a medicine woman. She's descended from some native sage. Some claim she has special powers"

"Nonsense."

~

Dear Mr. Secretary:

I am deeply honored by your invitation. I must respectfully decline, as I feel I have nothing of relevance to contribute.

I am glad the government is taking a proactive approach in dealing with the demands of Native Americans. I am confident that something concrete and useful will come out of these hearings. Native Americans are fully capable of expressing their needs and clarifying the issues. I would not presume capable of contributing anything more substantive.

Sincerely,

Father Peter Tosco

"He says he has nothing to contribute. We should be the judge of that. We must get him to testify when we start the hearings."

"He won't get away with a simple declination."

"With a subpoena, we will leave him no choice."

"Are we sovereign nations or are we slaves?"

"Many in government don't and few in public care who we are."

"We have, up until now, allowed the white folks to define who we are and chart the direction of our lives. That must change but won't until we take matters into our own hands."

"We were a splintered people. With no unity or common purpose, we allowed the white man to destroy us one nation at a time until we are nothing more than a shell of what we were. We must unite, and we must change how we think and act, if we are to survive. The white man's policy of dismembering and weakening us has not changed."

"Faced with superior weapons and coordinated efforts of the United States Army, our great leaders swallowed their pride and surrendered so that the people may survive. The leaders of today are challenged to come up with new strategies to ensure the survival of the native race."

"From top to bottom, the white man's government and his agents deal with us with treachery and deceit. They show scant regard for native life.

"Promises were made and treaties signed only to be shamelessly broken."

"Experiments and exploitation. That has been the history of Native American reforms. Some were not as brutal as the termination policies of the Truman administration, but uniformly, they have all been bad."

"Why blame only Truman? Which administration can we credit with having done anything for the benefit and uplift of native people?"

"The problem is systemic and unchanged since the first white settlers."

"George Washington compared us to wolves and referred to us as beasts of prey. The message was none too subtle. Wolves prey on innocent sheep. Wolves were a threat and so were we; therefore like wolves, we could be shot, trapped or exterminated any way possible. That was the father of the nation. He was no father to native people."

"Jefferson had no kind words for natives. He swore never to lay down the hatchet until an offending tribe was exterminated. He threatened to pursue natives to extermination or drive them away beyond reach."

"How about Clay who proclaimed that the disappearance of the natives from the human family would not be a great loss, and the race was not a race worth preserving?"

"Most famous statement of all was from the great General Sherman who declared that 'the only good Indian was a dead Indian.' He was referring to Native Americans and not people from India."

"Theodore Roosevelt's add on is an eye-opener. He wouldn't go so far as to say that 'the only good Indian is a dead Indian'. In his words, nine out of ten were and he wouldn't care to inquire into the case of the tenth."

"Here's a shocking statement from none other than Abraham Lincoln, the great Emancipator no less. It was his General Pepe who claimed that his 'purpose' was to exterminate the Sioux and they were to be treated as maniacs or wild beasts. Who gave him this 'purpose' if not his Commander in Chief Lincoln?"

"That's not surprising. Abraham Lincoln is infamous for ordering the largest mass execution in US history of thirty-eight Dakota Sioux. He ordered the execution to appease the white settlers who wanted to murder three-hundred Sioux. Lincoln was a lawyer and he knew the Sioux were not guilty of anything. Lincoln's rationale: it's better to sacrifice thirty-eight rather than three-hundred. He didn't have to act as King Solomon. As President he had the United States military at his command to protect the Sioux."

"When presidents make such statements and act in this manner, can you imagine what the general population is thinking?"

"Do not expect the olive branch from the executive branch. Their pronouncements may now be politically correct but their attitude toward natives is still the same."

"Presidents in their inaugural addresses talk about the importance of Hispanics, the welfare of Blacks, contributions of Chinese immigrants, and democratic aspirations of nations all over the world. There is never one mention of the native people of this land."

"We live in the shadows, out of sight. They seem annoyed and get paranoid when we show up."

"Our future is in our hands. No congress and no president will make a move to ease our misery. We must unite and force action."

"The United Native Nations of America and the Supreme Council must become the sole authority representing native people of this country. State and federal governments must deal with and through the council on matters affecting native people."

"UNNA shall have its own constitution. We are capable of doing it. Founding fathers of this country borrowed deeply from the Iroquois Confederacy when they penned the Constitution. Ironically, had they followed the Iroquois document even closer, we would have had a woman president in this country a long time ago."

"The federal government must respect the nation-to-nation principle. The federal government must henceforth interact with the council instead of dealing with individual nations. The federal government shall not intervene in matters relating to native people without the consent and concurrence of the council."

"Further depletion of native assets must be prevented. We can't allow small nations to cash in their assets, distribute the proceeds, and disband."

"The Senate Hearings gives us a great opportunity to propose meaningful reform. We must take advantage of the opportunity."

"However, it's about us and it must be conducted with transparency, integrity, and fairness. If not, we must withhold cooperation."

"We must continue efforts to encourage all nations to join UNNA; particularly the larger nations and bring them into the fold. We have assurance from several that they will provide behind the scenes support for now. They will send representatives to our meetings and to the hearings. They want more time to consider and decide."

"Most large nations have a system of government in place, efficient and functional. They may be debating if they would benefit by joining UNNA."

"The Navajo have run into a problem with an Arizona State utility company. They had signed a treaty with the utility for the use of their reserved lands. The utility is long gone and so is the ground water. The State has washed its hands of any responsibility because the utility and the Navajo had a signed land-lease agreement and the State was merely a referee. Navajo must fight the utility in court for draining and damaging the ground water. UNNA will work with the Navajo Council and pursue the utility and its subsidiaries wherever they have assets."

"No nation will be coerced into joining UNNA. They must see the benefits and come voluntarily. Nations must join because they believe it is essential to their and our survival."

"Members of the council, I seek permission to speak."

"Certainly, Sarah."

"I seek your counsel on a matter of significant importance."

"Speak and tell us what's on your mind."

"We had an unscheduled visit from four members of AIM."

"AIM. What do they want?"

"They want to be part of the new movement. They want to join UNNA."

"We don't want anything to do with AIM. They will sabotage our plans."

"They are trouble. We should keep them at bay."

"They must be up to something."

"Why did they come to you and not the council?"

"They know the council won't entertain their request to join UNNA."

"They guessed right."

"They offered to protect us against attacks. We declined."

"That was wise."

"They want me to act as their goodwill ambassador."

"The answer is no. They can't rid themselves of their past."

"They want to be given an opportunity to meet with the Supreme Council and offer their support. They want to explore how they can work together with the council. They don't want to be left out."

"The answer should still be no. They will derail this movement."

"They'll prove to be a distraction."

"We'll be subjected to unnecessary negative publicity for no reason."

"Their offer is unconditional. They will be subject to the direction of the council in all matters."

"I don't think they can or they will subject to anyone."

"Their intentions are good but their methods violent. There lies the problem. UNNA can only succeed by embracing a policy of total non-violence. AIM's past history does not reflect this. Yes, AIM and we share the same vision but our paths are different. We can't risk associating with them and self-destruct before we have found our footing."

"They may be sincere. But, no one will trust their word. Critics will pounce on AIM's presence and ignore the agenda we want to cultivate."

"I don't believe they can renounce violence."

"They make enemies; we don't want any."

"They may be trying to regain public exposure at our expense. They may try to infiltrate the council and take over this movement."

"Sarah. What are your feelings? Do you support them?"

"No. I have no personal interest in this. Not at all. I told them I would convey their offer to the council. That's all."

"Wait. Let's rethink differently. Their offer maybe worth consideration. They are young. They bring energy and passion. They bring certain advantages to the table. I don't think we should turn them away outright."

"It's true they can contribute. They can have a role to play, as long they are willing to play by the rules, our rules, and the majority rule."

"Will they channel their aggression and cooperate with us? It they do, it'll make them a great asset."

"They represent some of the best and brightest of our youth. We must try and bring them into the fold. We must not lose this opportunity."

"Aggression, yes. Violence, no. They must reject violence."

"Violence will do us in. We all know what happened at Wounded Knee. Given the slightest provocation, especially if AIM is around, the government will retaliate with excessive force. At Wounded Knee the president sent in tanks and helicopter gunships to end the occupation of a village by a few natives. They attacked as if they were battling insurgents and terrorists. Do you hear anyone criticizing the feds?"

"The FBI has a vendetta against us. Custer's regiments are still around. Goons are still goons. They are waiting for another opportunity. They know they have the power to destroy us and they will use it. They know they can do whatever they want with impunity. No. Violence will destroy us and win us nothing."

"Let's consider the possibilities. AIM and we share the same goals. We can make use of their zeal and their commitment if they pledge to adopt the path of peace and subject themselves to the council."

"We all want a better future for our people and I am sure they do too. They must accept the rule of law. They must adapt to the methods of the majority and the principle of peace. Then, they have a role alongside us."

"Prof. Stephen Villars, Dean and Professor of Anthropology at Florida State University, Dr. Leslie Munoz-Day, Professor Emeritus of the Native American University in New Mexico, Honorable Emily Barolo, retired judge of the Florida Supreme Court, Professor Ronald Schaumberg from the UCLA School of Law, Honorable Dan Wrigley, retired Judge of the Sixth Circuit Court and author of several books on nation within nation , and Attorney Barry Tillman, of Pastor, Small, and Tillman LLP, from here in Washington."

"That's an outstanding panel. I am okay with each and every one of them. How about Father Tosco?"

"We will issue a subpoena."

"Excellent."

"The natives are planning a March of Nations in Washington DC the last Sunday in April."

"Confirmed?"

"Yes."

"They are getting a little cocky, it would appear."

"Nobody wants a confrontation. They know that. They hold the cards now."

"They want the hearings to be concluded before the March of Nations."

"It's actually later than we had planned. Works to your advantage, though. You wanted to delay the hearings as much as possible."

"There's some risk holding the hearings so close before the event. If things don't go well, there could be problems during the march."

"How about if we plan for the hearings starting the week after the March?"

"Things are happening too fast. The demands being made on me frighten me. I am starting to feel inadequate."

"That's to be expected. In one year, you have gone from being a quiet housewife on a reservation to a prominent leader of a national movement. That's a huge transformation."

"I feel I've been thrown into the eye of the storm. I fear I'll disappoint you and bring shame upon my people."

"You've shown you can handle the demands. Sarah, instead of focusing on your inadequacies, focus on what you can contribute. The more you do, the more will be expected of you."

"I am one woman in the midst of powerful men who are accustomed to and like to be in the lead role. I am scared."

"They defer to you on many issues. That is evidence of your unique talents. They recognize your worth and respect you."

"You frighten me even more. I don't see in me the traits you talk about."

"It's best to let others see the qualities in you than you look for them. Be who you are. Keep the goals in your sights at all times. People fall and fail when they try to be what others expect of them."

"If only Doug were here."

"He is here. He's with you all the time. You're fulfilling the goals for which he and Stan gave their lives."

"When I lie awake at night and feel for him next to me, there's an emptiness that can't be wished away. I don't want to fail him and bring dishonor to his name."

"Nothing can replace the loss you experience. Nothing will. Transform your emptiness and fill it with action. Focus on the uplift of your people and the native people of this country."

"It's all happening too fast. I am not able to focus my attention."

"See Sarah. We do not come into this world with a beaten path laid out before us. As we grow, we see the footsteps of those who went before us. Sometimes the path they created is clear, sometimes not. It's up to us to stretch the path forward. And some day others will stretch it even further."

"The council has asked me to go with them to testify at the Congressional Committee hearings in Washington."

"That's wonderful. When do you go?"

"Never, if I can."

"Sarah, go. This movement took shape because of what happened in this remote valley of the Little Bend. No one can articulate the story better than you. It's real and personal. There's no loss greater than yours."

"They have asked me to be one of the speakers at the conclusion of the March of Nations."

"That's great. I am glad they recognize your worth. But it's more than that. You represent the smaller nations and the women. Without you, they would have no voice in this movement. Fear not Sarah. God is with you. He'll tell you what to do."

"I must give them an answer soon. They assume I will do it. I'm not sure I can do it. I have no experience and I have no skills."

"Be patient. The courage and confidence will come. The skills are there."

"I have done some thinking. I suspected you would support and encourage me to accept. I can't disappoint you. I'm being asked to do things that are not within me. I am asked to think in ways I am not accustomed to. I am asked to say things, as I have never done before. The responsibility is heavy. I feel inadequate. I know I can't flee from what's happening but I lack courage to do what's being required of me."

"The Great Mystery will give you courage. We can't always seek to understand his great purpose. Let him direct your steps. You Sarah Wilson are descended from the sage Wovoka. It's your destiny to carry on his message."

"I must seek the counsel of our ancestors and the guidance of the Great Spirit. I must know if they will speak to me. I must find out for myself if I can contribute to the cause."

"How?"

"I will go on a Vision Quest."

"The spirits are already working within you, telling you what to do. I don't know much about it but I've heard it can be physically and mentally taxing."

"If I can't face the risks, if I can't survive the rigors of the quest, then I am not worthy of the responsibilities placed before me."

"What if you do not receive the answers you seek?"

"The vision will be the answer. The vision will tell me if I must accept the role that is thrust upon me. If I have no vision then that too will be my answer. Without a vision, I must decline."

"You will have your vision. You will find the answer."

"Father Tosco, there's something I want to share with you. I do not know where to start and how to say it. Please forgive me."

"Speak Sarah without fear."

"It's about a dream I've been having ever since Doug was killed. I know not what it signifies or if it signifies anything at all. It troubles me."

"I do not know much about dreams. I believe they are significant but their relevance is often hidden within its interpretation. I can listen even if I am not able to offer any help."

"I need to talk about it to someone I trust."

"You can certainly trust me. I shall not discuss it with anyone."

"Actually it's the same dream, over and over again. It's unlike most dreams I have that are mired in uncertainty and confusion once I awake. This dream remains vivid in my memory, so much so my mind kind of anticipates the events and it never varies."

"Go on."

"I see myself standing on the shores of a fast flowing river. The sun is setting on the far horizon on the side of the river opposite to me. I am standing on a bluff with a clear view of a dry and barren valley on my right. It's rich pastureland on the opposite side of the river, with ripening fruits on trees and buffalo and cattle roaming freely. It's green as far as the eye can see. Suddenly, an old buffalo walks purposefully to the opposite bank of the river directly across from me. He stands framed by the setting sun and he is majestic in his bearing. He looks at me keenly for several minutes. I am unable to move and can't take my eyes of him. Finally, he descends slowly to the water's edge and amazingly, the waters part, making way for him to cross the river. He takes a few steps and the dream ends abruptly."

"What's a Vision Quest? I have heard about it but I must confess to my ignorance about its history and practice."

"It's a sacred and religious rite of native people. It is practiced among many cultures around the world in various forms. Many religions hold retreats that can also be considered a form of Vision Quest. However, it's mostly associated with Native Americans."

"I've heard it's becoming fashionable among corporate types to indulge in practices such as sweat lodge retreats and Vision Quests."

"They are different things. The sweat lodge is a cleansing ritual done as a group. A Vision Quest is more like a retreat one undertakes alone to seek guidance from the Great Mystery before undertaking important tasks. Many native tribes use the Vision Quest as an initiation ceremony for young adolescent warriors. In general it seeks answers to the questions: Who am I? Why am I here? What is my purpose in life? It's not much different from what Jesus did when he went into the desert to fast and pray before he started his public life. The Bible says he spent forty days and forty nights in the desert fasting and praying. The Vision Quest usually lasts two to four days. By then one has a vision or does not."

"Can anyone go on a Vision Quest?"

"Yes, although not everyone should unless they are in search of something of significant importance. It's not to be taken lightly. In native culture, the Vision Quest is celebrated and held in high regard because the results can have grave consequence for the individual and the community. In times past, a chief could undertake a Vision Quest before a battle. The timing, the strategy and even the appropriateness of the battle would be influenced by the quest. The chief could seek answers from the Great Spirit why the tribe is suffering through a terrible drought or famine. It may be undertaken when a tribe is faced with grave tragedy for which they have no obvious explanation. The tribe would want to discover if an individual member or the tribe as a whole has done something to offend the Great Spirit. The quest, the vision and the steps taken as a remedy, affect the tribe as a whole."

"I didn't realize it was that involved."

"It appears to have some similarities with Greek mythology. We read how nature responds in violent retaliation to unnatural behavior, particularly by the reigning sovereign, even unwittingly. Oedipus committed one of the greatest sins against nature when he married his own mother. He didn't and couldn't have known it was his mother. No matter. The sin was so perverse; nature subjected him to nemesis and not only him but also the whole kingdom. The King went on an extensive quest to decipher the root cause of the terrible tragedy. Gods had to be appeased before nature returned to normalcy."

"What's the role of the shaman in all of this?"

"The shaman acts as an intermediary between the Spirit World and the human world, as a medium of communication between the two worlds, interpreting signs and recommending corrective action. The shaman may not be privileged to see the vision, but is blessed with the power to interpret and recommend solutions. The shaman may perform the rites to propitiate the spirits. A Vision Quest has tremendous implications because so much rests on the outcome."

"How can you be sure, the vision is accurate? How can you guarantee the interpretation is correct? The shaman can make mistakes."

"No. That can't happen. A true quest is undertaken after careful and thorough preparation. The shaman recommends a proper regimen for the individual. Upon return from the quest, the shaman can assess from the description of the vision, whether it is true. While the quest is in progress, the shaman maintains a similar discipline, with prayer, meditation, and fasting. The shaman becomes part of the quest."

"What if there is no vision? Does that happen?"

"It can. It may be the Spirits are not willing to reveal the answers to what the individual is seeking. The spirits may be angry; that can lead to failure and no vision. It may be due to improper preparation. The spirit and the body must be cleansed through rigorous fasting, prayer, and self-denial. Like a field that is prepared for sowing, he or she must be ready to receive the answers. The answers come through visions, in visible or in spirit form. They may appear as signs or in symbols. An experienced shaman alone can provide the true interpretation of the vision."

"Sarah has chosen you as her spiritual guide, the shaman for her quest."

"I have been fortunate to learn and understand the ways of the spirits. I come from a long line of shamans who studied and practiced the art of medicine and observed the ways of the spirit world. I have had the benefit of drinking from the fountain of their knowledge."

"Does a Vision Quest always require the services of a shaman?"

"That would be the wise thing to do. Visions are complex and often hard to understand without proper interpretation. Like symbols, the meaning may differ vastly from what they appear to be. Visions are also influenced by time and milieu. The same vision to different people at different intervals may mean totally different things. The images, the colors, the smells, and sounds all have roles. One must know what they mean to give the vision coherence."

"A lot rides on your interpretation."

"Very true. Lives of people may depend on them. A shaman acquires credibility and acceptance through time. I must be prepared to admit my inability to interpret a particular vision if the spirits refuse to grant me the insight, rather than provide a fake or make-believe interpretation. You must practice only what you are good at."

"What happens next for Sarah in her quest?"

"She has requested my assistance, which is the first step. I will instruct and guide her through the process of preparation. She must be physically and mentally prepared for the rigors of the quest. Except in extreme situations, I won't interrupt or intervene during the quest. I will be here at the end to answer questions and interpret her vision."

"When will she start?"

"As soon as she is ready. She has already selected a secluded spot that's considered sacred. I know where it is and I have approved it. Once she is situated, she will be left alone. No one is allowed to visit her. She will pray and meditate, fasting to the end. I may check on her periodically to make sure of her well-being. I have the authority to end the quest under special circumstances."

"You mentioned it could last anywhere from two to four days."

"Usually. However, on rare occasions, it may be extended for another day or two although it is not advised. It's really up to the individual."

"Four or more days. That's a long time without food or drink."

"You must give yourself enough time to thoroughly cleanse your body and mind. You fast and relinquish physical comforts so that you can establish a state of harmony with nature and the spirit world. Then you begin the process of cleansing your mind, of all that is evil, all that is impure, your emotions, your longings, your sorrows, your hatred, your love, your desires, and everything else that may hold you hostage to the human world. Then and only then, can you seek communion with the spirit world. Then and only then can you look into your spirit, your inner being to find the meaning of your existence. You must formulate what questions you seek answers for before you can get them. You must cease to exist in real time to unlock the mystery of your existence in a timeless universe. You constantly pray to the Great Spirit to enlighten you through a vision or visions."

"She is fasting the whole time and she is exposed to the elements. Isn't that risky?"

"She may bring water with her. She may also bring a blanket to cover herself as protection from the elements."

"How about her safety? She could be vulnerable to wild animals."

"There is no record of anyone, anywhere having had a fatal attack during a quest. It is possible of course but we believe the person is on sacred ground, in the presence of the Great Spirit and thus protected."

"More time and money is spent protecting the spotted owl, salamanders, fish, snakes, and frogs than on a whole race of Native Americans."

"We must learn to protect ourselves. No one else will."

"Reforms must first begin from within. For over a century, the white man has been enforcing their reforms on us."

"It's genocide. That's what the white man has done to native people."

"A country that prides itself in freedom of expression and even tolerates racist and supremacist organizations flouting their bigotry was quick to condemn AIM as a terrorist organization. I am not condoning violence, but it's the attitude I find remarkable."

"We commend the Lakota Sioux. They have steadfastly refused to accept the settlement offer of the government for Paha Sapa, the Black Hills."

"The Black Hills is the sacred center of the world and must be returned to the Sioux. The United States Government must honor the Treaty of Laramie."

"The settlement fund offered for Black Hills has grown to over seven-hundred-million. It would make instant millionaires of current members. Yet they resist while living in near poverty because it is their sacred land and it is native land. That is the spirit. That is native pride."

"Washington has tried to break their resolve by deceitful means even creating and supporting a rebel faction. They have a renegade leader willing to dance to their tune. But, it hasn't worked because the Sioux have pride. We must all learn from them."

"We support the Sioux in this struggle. The United States Government must abandon the policy of interference. The Sioux must determine their destiny on their own."

"Federal mandates that placed nations under state stewardship must be annulled. No native nation must be under state control. It betrays the principle of sovereignty of native nations. Such stewardship must be within native authority. UNNA must assume such authority."

"The spot she has chosen is ideal as it provides unmarred view of all directions and the heavens. It has been used as a place of worship for centuries and the spirits know this place and acknowledge the solemn purpose for which it will be used."

"I used to come up here when I first arrived at the mission and stayed at the old church rectory. It is a wonderful location."

"The sacred circle has been marked and lined with specially handpicked, evenly sized rocks. Similar rocks have been placed marking the four directions from the center to the outer circumference of the circle. At the very center a bed of sage and sweet grass has been prepared for her. She will sit upon this bed during the quest and she may lie down on it during the night. She has prepared an altar of cherry twigs and covered it with a flannel cloth. Upon the altar she has placed the sacred objects, an eagle's feather, a conch shell, the four prayer flags, a single string with tobacco ties, the sacred pipe and offerings of tobacco, cedar, sage and sweet grass. In a small pit next to the altar, she has prepared a fire with cedar wood.

She will remain in the center of the circle throughout the quest and follow the path of the sun from east to west. She will begin the quest at sunset facing west. After the last rays of the sun have been swallowed into the great depths of the ocean, she will rise and sit facing east awaiting the rise of the morning sun. During the night she may lie down on her back facing the heavens. She may cover herself with the blanket she has brought with her to the quest."

"Is it true she has chosen not to bring any water?"

"That's correct; it's her decision. She wants a hard fast. And now, everything is in place. Sarah, are you ready to begin your Vision Quest?"

"Yes, I am."

"Dear daughter Sarah Wilson, you've chosen to undertake this Vision Quest of your own free will with no coercion and compulsion from any one. Is that correct?"

"Yes."

"The Vision Quest demands extreme sacrifices in personal comforts; it requires that you fast and be secluded within the sacred circle until the very end. Are you prepared for such sacrifices?"

"I am."

"From the moment you set foot within the sacred circle until the very end, you may not step outside except for personal needs. Do you understand?"

"I do."

"During the quest, you shall relieve your mind of all distractions, all human thoughts, and replace them with a pure emptiness, receptive to the communications from the spirit world. Are you prepared in body and mind to receive the word of the Great Spirit?"

"I am."

"Enter into the sacred circle and take your place in the center, facing west. Turn your eyes toward the sun, the source of all energy and give thanks to the Great Mystery, Wakan Tanka, for the gift of life, for wisdom and enlightenment. May the Great Spirit grant you the vision you seek so that you may better understand who you are, your purpose in life and your role in the new age."

"Sarah, pick up the string with the tobacco ties, which you have prepared for this event. The tobacco ties represent each member of your tribe, a specified number of people you want represented as your benefactors and patrons and a particular number of prayers you want addressed during the quest. Walk along the path to the west end of the circle and lay the string along the circumference of the circle as you move toward the north, east and south, and finishing at the starting point."

"You have now consecrated the place within the circle to the Great Spirit. Return to the center, pick up the four prayer flags, and walk along the path to the west end of the circle and plant the black flag. In the land of the setting sun dwell the spirits. May they open your mind and your spirit to a vision of your inner soul and the purpose of your existence."

"Return to the center of the circle and walk along the path to the North end of the circle and plant the White Flag. May the North Power grant you endurance, strength, honesty, and truthfulness so that you may fulfill your destiny."

"Return to the center of the circle and walk along the path to the east and plant the yellow flag at the east end of the circle. May the East Power endow you with wisdom and knowledge and the spiritual strength to face the trials and tribulations that await you."

"Return to the center of the circle and walk along the path to the south end of the circle and plant the Red Flag. May the South Power empower you with the ability to grow and expand your knowledge of medicine for the mind and the body."

"Return to the center of the circle. Pick up the Sukodawabub, the sweet smelling sage and make an offering to the West Spirit by placing it along the path to the west. Make an offering of Weengush, the sweet grass, the hair of Mother Earth, to the North Spirit. Make an offering of Semah, the native tobacco to the East Spirit and finally, make an offering of Keezhik, the sacred cedar to the South Spirit."

"Return to the center of the circle and stand facing west. Pick up the sacred Eagle Feather. The Eagle that flies high up in the skies, sees far and wide, and sees the minutest objects upon the land, shall carry your prayers to the Great Spirit who resides in the heavens and connect you to the Spirit World. Offer the Eagle Feather to the Four Directions and then return it to the altar."

"The Conch has been marked with the sacred clay in the shape of a circle representing the beginning and the end in a never-ending cycle. The Conch has been retrieved from the Ocean, representing the salt of life, our beginning. Offer the Conch to the Four Directions and return it to the altar."

"Place a small amount of tobacco in the sacred pipe and touch the pipe to the ground, the Earth Spirit while intoning: 'Mother Earth, by this act, I swear I will protect you.' Now, hold up the pipe to face the heavens, the Sky Spirit and repeat these words: 'Father Sky, by this act, I beseech you to grant me the life-giving energy.' Light the tobacco in the pipe from the sacred fire using the three-band braided sweet grass. The three braids represent the mind, body, and spirit joined together as one. Raise the smoking pipe to the Great Spirit, the Great Mystery, the unexplainable source of life and repeat after me: 'O Great Spirit, I thank you for the six powers of the Universe, the six energies. I thank you for the gift of life. Al I have comes from you and all I have I offer up to you. Bless my endeavor. Preside over me and protect me under the shelter of your mercy.' Now, offer the Sacred Pipe to the Four Directions."

"The pipe represents your prayers and the smoke represents the words you have uttered to express your prayers. May your prayers rise up high into the heavens as the smoke from the pipe, joining together the earth and the sky in a sacred union."

"Now, repeat after me: 'O Holy One, you who have been blessed with the ability to witness the mysteries, to you I offer this pipe as a sign of my faith. O Holy One, you who have been given the power to communicate with the spirits, to you I offer this pipe as a sign of my surrender. O Holy One, you who have the wisdom to interpret the ways of the spirits, to you I offer this pipe as a sign of my trust. O Holy One, you who can see into the future and open the doors to the destinies of individuals, to you I offer this pipe as a sign of my respect."

"Sarah Wilson, daughter of great chiefs, the Great Spirit has bestowed upon you the gift of leadership, the courage to face evil, the wisdom to understand the complexities of human nature, and the nobility of convictions to discern what is right and what is just. Trust in the mercy of the Great Mystery and he shall open your eyes to the future and anchor you deep to the values held dear by your people. They shall keep a constant vigil in your absence and offer prayers so that you may find the vision you seek. Be strong, be firm, and be resolute. You are in the presence of your creator who has given you life; be not afraid."

"Sit at the center of the circle facing west toward the setting sun. The fire will die out by itself. Do not rekindle it. For your personal needs, leave the circle always through the west direction and return by the same route. When you have had your vision or if you choose to end your quest for any reason, gather your sacred objects and walk down the mountain by the same path we took to come up here. Please repeat after me this final prayer: 'O Great Spirit, you who created this Universe and all living and inanimate objects within it, protect me. Spirits of our forefathers, who have gone before us, enlighten me. Give me courage to look beyond my inner self, to see and understand the vision of the future and fulfill the demands made of me.' We will leave you now. You are in the presence of the Great Mystery."

"Father Tosco is excommunicated."

"This is the first time ever that a priest of the Diocese of Salt Lake City has been excommunicated."

"Too bad it had to come to this."

"He doesn't care. There is no repentance."

"It remains to be seen how people respond. Are they going to keep attending his services?"

"The suspension didn't do much. I don't expect this to make a big impression either."

"Monsignor. Is there any further action the diocese or the Catholic Church can take to curb his activities?"

"I am afraid not. If it was church property, we could evict him. It is native property. What he does there with the permission of the tribe is outside of our jurisdiction."

"It's unfortunate."

"He's now free to do pretty much what he wants."

"We should ignore him, that's what we should do. He may have a following and he may look successful with his ministry. But, it's only a fad and like all fads it won't last for long. If it does, it does."

"It's confusing to a lot of people. He says the same Mass, the same prayers, and performs the same rituals. He has not declared a new church nor joined another. He wears the same vestments. To an outsider, he is just like another priest saying Mass."

"Can we organize protest meetings against him? We could disrupt the services and show people who he really is."

"It's on a native reservation and we would be trespassing."

"It would only attract more attention to him and advertise his renegade ministry. It would end up helping him."

"This is not going to end well. Mark my words."

"We must move on. Let God deal with him."

"Sarah, we were getting really worried."

"When you went past the second day, we were anxious. After the third day, we thought of coming up the mountain to check on you. By the fourth, we were in a state of panic."

"You had taken no food or water. Five days without water is dangerous."

"The shaman was unconcerned. He assured us everything would be fine."

"How do you feel?"

"I feel fine."

"Sister, there are things on your mind you want to talk about. I can see it in your eyes. I can tell you had a vision. But first drink this brew I prepared for you. It will make you strong."

"Thank you."

"We shall remain in the teepee here at the foot of the holy mountain for a little while longer. The quest is not complete until you have narrated to me all you have seen, heard, and experienced. Brothers and sisters, we will join you soon at the village. Leave us alone for now."

"Can Father Tosco stay?"

"All right. He's a man of God. He may have an insight into your vision."

"Thank you."

"Say what you have to say. May the Spirit who rules the universe, the sky, the earth, the far reaching oceans, and all that's within it be your guide."

"There are numerous images fleeting through my mind like deer on a meadow. I must not let them escape from memory."

"Talk sister. Tell us what you saw and what you felt."

"It was tough the first night. I sat with my eyes closed trying to shut out the outside world. It was cold. I resisted the temptation to cover myself with the blanket. As a child that is newly born I wanted to surrender myself entirely to the mercy of the Great Spirit. I felt miserable as the next day dawned and as the sun climbed to the roof of the sky and stood above me. I couldn't block out the heat and the sweat. I couldn't concentrate and meditate. I could feel the thirst and the hunger. When I closed my eyes I would get images of running water and inviting fruits. I made it through the first day. When night came, I lay on the bed of sage and sweet grass, searching the clear and starry heavens for signs. There were no signs. I may have slept a little. If I slept at all, I slept with frequent awakening.

I was awake and fully aware before the crescent moon had dipped below the horizon. I sat facing east as the rising sun, clothed in regal majesty, slowly climbed above the high mountains. I prayed for a vision and for direction. I prayed to the Great Spirit; I prayed to the spirits of our ancestors, and I prayed to the spirits of my husband and brother, Stan—martyrs for a cause. I prayed hard and I prayed fervently but there was no vision granted to me. I felt intense thirst and hunger.

By the end of the second day, I was in despair. There were no signs. I still couldn't eliminate the outside world. I was filled with self-doubt. Maybe I was not worthy of the quest. Maybe I was doing it wrong. I couldn't drive away hunger and thirst. I slept fitfully the second night. But I vowed to stick with my quest until some answers came.

As darkness dispelled and dawn arrived announcing the third day, my body seemed to have drifted away as if on a raft on a wild river. My mind seemed barren and I could hardly remember who I was or where I was. The sun seemed to have halted his journey directly above me but I could feel no heat. I couldn't feel my hands or feet or any other part of my body. Where was I? The day wore on. I didn't know if I slept or was partially awake. Nothing seemed to matter.

I heard a shrill cry, the unmistakable cry of the eagle overhead. I opened my eyes vainly searching the skies but I could see nothing and I could feel nothing, not even my surroundings. I could clearly hear the sound of the bird. I didn't know if I was imagining it. I couldn't remember how many days I had been up there. I knew I was fully awake but I seemed to have lost all my senses except hearing.

I don't remember when, but I heard the sound of retreating buffalo in the distance, like a slow-rolling thunder. At first I thought they were coming toward me and felt great joy. Then I realized that the sounds were fading. I cried and I couldn't control my tears. They were tears of disappointment. I couldn't see anything. Maybe the vision had come and gone and it had escaped me. Even the bird had become silent. All was still.

I awoke with the sun shining bright above me. I must have slept a long time. I felt guilty I had lost much time to sleep whereas I should have been awake and praying, calling for the vision. I could again hear the eagle somewhere above me and it was calling angrily. Was the bird angry that I had been so careless and surrendered myself to sleep? And then there was a bright flash of light like when lightning burns up the night sky, except it was day. I felt it more than I saw it. It was no lightning. Then I saw a long and intense shaft of flame coming straight toward me. But I felt no fear. It stopped a few feet from me, burning brightly, hissing, and crackling. Strangely, I didn't feel the heat. I could hear the distant wind, growing stronger and stronger. Then the flame and the wind faded away. I heard the sound of the buffalo. I looked keenly all around but I couldn't see anything. Sadly I realized that the sounds of the buffalo were again fading away. Silence returned. There was no light, no sounds and no vision. All was emptiness.

I was shaking as if with a fever. Then I heard the bird again. It sounded angry. I couldn't see it. The sun was bright and I knew I should be feeling the heat but it felt like I was in the embrace of old man winter. I wanted to cry aloud but no sound came to my lips. I wanted to draw the blanket closely around me, but my hands would not move. I couldn't think clearly. I couldn't remember anything. I heard the sound of the buffalo as if the herd was coming and going in an undulating rhythm. This time I was not sad. I didn't feel anything.

Day gave way to evening and then the night. The sky was lit up with stars and it looked like a full moon. There seemed to be some added glitter to the stars. On the ground there was a thick covering of fog enveloping the whole landscape. It felt like I was floating on a sea of clouds. There was a deep chill in the air. All on a sudden there was a burst of wind. Before my eyes, the fog cleared, and I saw this desolate valley with no trees, grass or water, just sandy, dry, and barren land. As my eyes became accustomed to the ghostly light, I saw the valley was strewn with bones, bones everywhere. They were bright and shining as if bleached clean by the wind and sun. I couldn't tell if they were bones of animals or humans. Then I heard the approaching storm, rolling in from the south. As I watched, the wind swept away the bones, with not one remaining. It seemed the bones were made of cotton, the way they lifted off the ground and flew away. The light was gone, the fog was gone, and the wind was gone. I was wide-awake. I was sitting facing the east and I could see the faint redness creeping up on the horizon, the markings of the sacred spirit.

I knew my quest was over. I was not sure what I had seen and I was not sure what it meant. I knew it was over. I was bereft of all feelings. I didn't know what day it was. It seemed as though it didn't matter what I had seen. I knew that I knew what it was, although I didn't know what it was. I was at peace with myself. There was a feeling of resignation. What I had experienced was more important than what I had seen and heard. It was more important than the meaning of what I had seen and heard."

"Sarah, you shall now return to the village with Father Tosco. Once there, you shall walk down to the water's edge and bathe in the river fully immersed. Then, you shall put on traditional clothing before you take food and drink. Let hunger be present at the end of the meal and let thirst be felt after you drink. Then, let your body rest. You shall sleep and no one shall wake you. Sleep until the North Star has faded. I will remain here to pray and meditate upon what you narrated. I shall seek answers to your quest."

"Tomorrow at sunrise, you shall pick twelve members of your people and you shall all bathe in the river, and then proceed to the medicine lodge that was built in your absence. You shall know whom to pick. I will meet you inside the lodge. There we shall offer prayers to the

Great Spirit and implore his mercy. Then, it shall be my honor to put into words the meaning of the visions you have seen and remember, and those that you saw but do not remember. I shall speak so that you and all may understand."

"Prayer Lodge or Sweat Lodge. Is there a difference?"

"I think it's one and the same."

"I have read about them and heard about them"

"I was there yesterday to watch them build it. It's a fascinating structure. I was down there this morning and it was done."

"They are usually built for a one-time event, isn't that right?"

"That's right. However, this is being built for long-term use. The shaman instructed them to build it that way. It is medium sized as I am told, and can seat up to twenty people."

"I understand they don't allow women to participate in prayer lodge ceremonies. This will be a break from tradition."

"The shaman says there is no such rule that women can't participate. Usually they don't for a variety of reasons but not because of taboos."

"These sweat lodges are getting pretty popular. They could make some money if they market it."

"At first I thought that's what they had in mind when it was proposed. But, I am told that it's intended for tribal use only and as a symbol of restoring native traditions."

"Makes sense."

"There it is. When I left yesterday, they had not finished the roof. They were going to cover it with animal hides, top it off with blankets, and cover the whole thing with tarpaulin to protect it from the elements. They have done a nice job."

"That looks pretty small and primitive. That's it?"

"It's more spacious inside than it looks."

"How're you going to stand without hitting your head against the roof?"

"You can't. You don't stand up inside the lodge. The floor is a couple of feet below ground level and strewn with fine sand. The entrance is a low tunnel and you crawl into the lodge on your hands and knees. Once inside, you crawl around and sit on the floor."

"I didn't realize you had to crawl around."

"Are you claustrophobic? You feel up to it, Malcolm?"

"Are you kidding? I wouldn't pass up such an opportunity."

"We are the only non-natives allowed in. Sarah had nothing to do with this. She was not aware a prayer lodge was going to be built."

"How did we get invited?"

"I was with the shaman on a daily basis during the quest. When he told me about the prayer lodge and its purpose, I asked him if you and I could join. He agreed."

"Thanks. It's rare you get a chance like this."

"I know Sarah would want someone to witness what goes on. This is a spiritual experience. I know she wants the world to know that native customs are genuine expressions of deep-rooted belief in God and nature."

"This personal experience has changed my views on native culture."

"That's the whole idea."

"How much do you know about prayer lodge ceremonies?"

"The shaman gave me a quick study on Prayer Lodge Ceremony. The lodge is like the womb, cramped but comfortable. When we are born, we crawl out of our mother's womb, totally helpless. Then as we grow, we fall prey to evil ways and acquire habits and manners that lead us away from the innocence of infancy. To be cleansed and become whole, we must be born again. We crawl back into the womb as we once crawled out. Remember what Jesus said to Nicodemus: 'Unless you are born again, you shall not enter the kingdom of heaven.' Same idea!

"The sides and the roof are completely covered. What do they do for ventilation?"

"There is none. There are four openings, including the entrance that faces the east. The three remaining openings represent the other three directions. These are exits only."

"What happens within the lodge? Can I ask now or should I wait to see what happens?"

"I will tell you what I know. The rest you can see for yourself. There may be changes depending on the decision of the shaman. In the middle of the lodge there is a gravel fire pit lined with river rocks. The shaman enters first and takes a seat in front of the pit facing east. The rest of the participants follow, crawling on hands and knees and as they enter they move in a clockwise direction and sit in a circle along the periphery."

"How are they going to fit the whole tribe inside this structure?"

"Only twelve members of the tribe will participate in the ceremony. Sarah will select the twelve. You and I are invited guests. Then you have the shaman and his helper, bringing the total to seventeen."

"What happens after people are seated?"

"I don't know. We will have to wait and experience it. But I do know one thing. There is a certain symmetry and pattern to the movements within the lodge. Nature behaves in an orderly manner. Heavenly bodies move in predictable patterns. Participants must also do likewise. All movements within are clockwise so that there is no confusion and there is minimal disturbance to others."

"What is the dress code?"

"It's a place of prayer and participants must dress accordingly. Participants wear loose clothing so that they are comfortable while sitting in a crammed position for a long time. No footwear is allowed within."

"Why is it commonly referred to as a sweat lodge?"

"That is a more recent and a corrupt term for the ceremony. The conditions within are hot and humid, inducing profuse sweating. That's part of the cleansing process, but not the purpose itself."

"Welcome brothers and sisters to the Prayer Lodge ceremony. We have with us two non-native friends who are closely associated with you. I welcome them. This ceremony will last up to two-to-three hours. During the ceremony, a good amount of humidity and heat will be generated. If it makes you feel sick or uncomfortable, you may leave at any time without interrupting the ceremonies."

"The Payer Lodge Ceremony is an age-old tradition of Native Americans. It is done with due reverence to the Great Spirit, the source of all life and to the spirits who govern every human act. It symbolizes all that is sacred in our culture. The revival of these rituals is vital to the survival of the native races."

"This is a prayer ceremony and as such our actions will reflect a prayerful and respectful attitude. A Prayer Lodge Ceremony may be conducted for a variety of reasons. Today it coincides with the end of the Vision Quest completed by Sarah. We shall offer interpretations of the visions she was granted during the quest."

"We begin with traditional chants and prayers to Waken Tanka, the Great Spirit, the Lord of the Universe, and the originator of life. Rattles may be used in accompaniment of the chants. We will then invoke the spirits of our forefathers to surround us with their wisdom."

"Specially selected lava rocks have been heated to a white-hot glow outside the lodge. Mike has volunteered to assist me during the ceremony. He will now bring in the heated rocks, one at a time, using antler horns. I shall arrange the heated rocks in the pit before me."

"O Great Mystery, you hold the secrets of our lives and the purpose of our existence in your hands; to you we make these offerings as a sign of our faith in you. Our lives, our joys, and our sorrows are dependent on your mercy. Please accept this offering of tobacco and as the tobacco burns on the hot rocks, let our prayers rise up with the smoke to your divine bosom. I offer to you offerings of sage, cedar, and sweet grass. May the fragrance produced by the sacred herbs, fill us with peace, and contentment. I place offerings of tobacco, cedar, sage, and sweet grass to the four directions and invoke their spirits to bless each and every one of us gathered here."

"This water was collected from sacred springs and brought here in buffalo horns. I shall sprinkle the water over the hot rocks. The water interacting with the hot rocks produces heat and steam and mingling with sweet scents of the burning herbs shall envelope us with peace and tranquility. We shall experience the bliss we enjoyed in our mothers' wombs. We are now once again in the womb, the womb of Mother Earth."

"Additional hot rocks will be brought in and placed in the pit and water sprinkled over them at intervals to ensure that the inside of the lodge stays hot and steamy."

"Our sister Sarah performed an arduous and difficult Vision Quest. She surrendered herself to the will of the Creator and put herself in his power and mercy. Her prayers were answered and she had a vision. As is often the case, what she saw and what she heard are hidden from her understanding, like a veil that is drawn over her head. The Great Spirit has willed that the message of the vision be revealed to me and through me to her and to you, her brothers and sisters.

"In her vision, Sarah saw a sandy and barren valley with no trees or grass. It was strewn all over with bones—animal, or human, or both. There were storms and strong winds. The eagle cried and seemed to rebuke her often. The sounds of the buffalo were clear but distant."

"The cry of the eagle is the sound of the Great Spirit, always heard, never seen. The Spirit calls us to remain awake and be alive. The Spirit calls us to be aware of his great presence in our lives. The Spirit is with you, Sarah, always. The Spirit is not angry and didn't rebuke you. The call of the eagle was a constant reminder of the presence of the Great Spirit over you. Call on the Spirit when you are in need and you shall hear the cry."

"You shall feel oppressed by the threats surrounding you and they are many. Storms, wind, heat, and flashes of light represent the constant dangers you must face. But they shall not harm you. The Spirit shall protect you. Even as the bolt of fire came barreling toward you, you felt no fear as you were with the Supreme Creator. You are under his protection. You shall not be harmed."

"The buffalo represent the spirits of dear and near ones who have entered the spirit world. They are around you, constantly on the move, unseen but near. They will chase away the powers of evil. You will be aware of and experience the dangers surrounding you but you shall not come to harm. The spirits will protect you."

"The bones you saw strewn all over the valley are the remains of your ancestors. They are also the sacred customs and traditions of native people that have been abandoned and allowed to fly away like autumn leaves in a storm. They lie forgotten and distant. They are being blown away by the winds of time and change. You must find shelter and refuge for their remains. It can only happen when the native way of life is restored."

"The valley lies barren and desolate and will remain so unless you regenerate it and bring life back to it. The Great Buffalo taught our forefathers the gift of regeneration and revival. Our people have forgotten the sacred rituals and allowed Mother Earth to go barren. Go and perform the Sun Dance, this year and every year. Bring new life to your people. Let the blood of young warriors bring new life to Mother Earth."

"The sky is painted in streaks of sacred red as a symbol of the enduring promise of a new day and a new beginning. Your vision ended with the beginning of dawn, a reminder that there will be a new day. You cannot see what it will bring; it is for you to make the new day what it will be. You experienced peace and tranquility at the end of your quest because now you know that the sacrifice of your husband and your brother were necessary and required by the Great Mystery. Their sacrifice was necessary to give life to the revival of the native spirit."

"The Sun Dance. Did the government not ban it?"

"It was—and for the wrong reasons until President Carter rescinded it. The white man's actions against the natives stem from ignorance of our culture and from an arrogant belief that the Euro-Christian traditions and practices are the perfect model others must emulate. Native people have practiced the Sun Dance for thousands of years. We can't let some narrow-minded bigots deny us our cultural traditions."

"Why was the Sun Dance banned?"

"Hypocrisy and arrogance. The white man was concerned for the safety of the young men who participated in the ceremony. It involved piercing of the skin. To the white man this was an act of self-torture. They cited health risks for banning this heathen practice. Yet, they had no compunctions murdering millions of native people and hunting them to near extinction to plunder their lands."

"That couldn't have been the real reason."

"I have not heard of anyone who suffered permanent damage or perished performing the Sun Dance."

"They wanted to impose their will and break the pride of the native people."

"They could have cared less if all natives suffered and died enacting the Sun Dance. If that were the case they would have encouraged it."

"There are so many practices from around the world that involve self-infliction of pain. Look at the many Christian societies that re-enact the crucifixion. During Holy Week there are gruesome rituals of devotees using self-flagellation and nailing themselves to the cross. But that is okay because it is a Christian tradition."

"Look at the practice of circumcision. Infants are subjected to so much pain in the name of religion."

"National Geographic graphically depicts rites of initiation from around the globe that include infliction of pain with risk of injury and death. If it is so bizarre, why show it? That is okay in the name of science."

"There is a Christian group in this country that handles poisonous serpents as an act of faith risking death. That is acceptable."

"How about polygamy? Plural marriage. Spiritual wives. They are tolerated because it is Euro-Christian."

"The US Government can accommodate such horrors but then turn around and ban the Sun Dance and the Ghost Dance. No more. No longer shall we relinquish our right to practice religious rituals because the white man does not approve."

"It is further evidenced by the lack of respect shown toward native people. We must not accept these slights any longer."

"The banning of the cultural traditions and practices of Native Americans is an affront to the sovereignty principle. It is a lack of good faith shown by the United States Government."

"This country spends millions of tax dollars trying to protect and preserve the cultural heritage and relics of people all over the world. We applaud the effort. It is money well-spent for a worthy cause. How about showing the same level of concern toward native people in this country and their customs and traditions? Stop these double standards."

"If we want to restore native unity and identity, we must revive the traditions and symbols that make us who we are."

"The Sun Dance is a rite of initiation; it is a ritual of regeneration and revitalization of the earth, our mother. We will revive it."

"Can we not modify the ritual without the self-infliction of pain?"

"Why should we? It has a purpose. We must cleanse ourselves through suffering if we truly cherish our traditions."

"We will perform the Sun Dance because it is an integral part of our being. There is nothing sinister about it. It is a spiritual ceremony."

"Is there a restriction on outsiders being present at our ceremonies?"

"No, there is not. The ban and the irrational bias shown by the white settlers forced our people to perform the sacred dances in secrecy. The bias is still alive and Euro-Christian attitudes have not matured enough to embrace our traditions. It is time we put fear of public condemnation behind us and become what we are and not what others want us to be."

"The great grandfather Wovoka gave us the Ghost Dance Religion. It was banned by the US Government and remains banned to this day due to the white man's paranoia. Wovoka taught us to live and work together in peace with the white people. He encouraged education. He condemned the abuse of alcohol. What an irony, they banned a religion that preaches these values."

"Is there any truth that the Ghost Dance led to the Pine Ridge uprising?"

"That is totally false. The prophet taught his followers that the Ghost Dance was so powerful it would protect them even from bullets. It was a metaphor no different from Jesus saying: 'They shall take up serpents; and if they drink any deadly thing, it shall not hurt them'. On another occasion, Jesus said: 'If you have faith enough, you shall move mountains'. The federal agents feared that the natives would be emboldened by the literal interpretation of the prophet's statement, and rise up in rebellion without fear of death. The Ghost Dance was used as an excuse by the government to wipe out the Pine Ridge protesters. The army riddled the Pine Ridge reservation with machine gun fire, killing men, women, and children indiscriminately, to prove to the native people that the Ghost Dance was no protection against bullets."

"We must break down the barriers of misconceptions by educating the public on the true meaning of our rituals and customs. We should allow public access to all our ceremonies. We have nothing to hide."

"We must challenge these illogical bans and restrictive policies.

We must not compromise with the white man in the practice of our religion, customs and traditions"

"We must reclaim our birthright openly and adversely by restoring and practicing customs that are culturally relevant to us without fear of rebuke or repression."

"We must encourage nations to study, understand and revive customs that are meaningful to us without fear of retaliation. If we unite as one nation, no government will dare again suppress our rights."

"That is the kind of defiance we must demonstrate. We must confront injustice wisely, armed with righteousness not with brawn."

"Violence can have no place in our future. We must show courage when threatened and tolerance when provoked. But, we must persevere."

"Acts of violence will be met with disproportionate use of force by the government. We can't run the risk of provoking the use of lethal force."

"This is our country as much as it's theirs. We are not traitors or anarchists when we fight for restoration of our rights. We are an integral part of the United States."

"We must fight for our rights with dignity and poise. We must force the change and it won't be easy. As separate nations, that task will be impossible. We must do it together. We must do it as one people, one nation."

"We can be independent and one at the same time. We can be unique in our variety. Like a mosaic or a collage, the several makes the final wholesome; the separateness adds vitality to the whole."

"There are treaties that have been breached by the government that must be remedied. There are unenforceable treaties forced upon native people under duress that must be invalidated. There are treaties signed by the government they had no good-faith intent to perform. United as one, we will have resources to seek reparation and challenge injustice in courts."

"Coercion, misrepresentation, and deceit were common practices of the US Government."

"There are plenty of treaties that are blatantly deceptive. They would not stand a chance in a fair court of law."

"UNNA as a single entity will have the strength to stand up to the bullies in government and demand justice."

"We are not treasure hunters. We want fairness and justice."

"We must do more to let the people of the country see what happens on our reservations. This is a new era, a new beginning. This is a new struggle for justice and restoration of pride. This is a struggle with no weapons."

"History must record the truth as it happened. Nowhere in the white man's history of what happened at Wounded Knee do you see that trouble began when a native failed to obey the soldiers' orders to hand over his gun. How many people know that the native person was deaf and had no idea why the soldiers were grabbing the gun out of his hands? How many people care that the gun was accidently discharged when the soldier wrestled for the gun?"

"But they used the accidental fire to mow down innocent natives. We must maintain a policy of non-violence not as a sentiment but as essential for survival."

"I was there during the Sun Dance Festival and it was indeed an experience. I came away feeling elated. I am getting together with my people to hold a similar festival."

"Were there non-natives present?"

"There were several reporters present as well as television crews."

"That was a bold thing to do. White people condemn our rituals as provocative. We should do them the right way, openly and publicly."

"How did it go? Tell me what happened."

"It takes a lot of work. That was evident. I am sure you don't do it unless there's a need for it. I can understand why."

"It's much more than a dance, then."

"Absolutely. Sarah Wilson completed the Vision Quest and the Sun Dance was demanded of her. They felt the time was appropriate for the ceremony and the dance. The Paiute are going through a transformation. They have achieved some success; they want more; they want to define who they are. They want to make sure that every member of their community is committed to the changes. Prosperity and growth of the tribe have relevance only if used to promote their values and interests. They need the Sun Dance to regenerate their lands that have been barren for long."

"I wish I could have been there."

"It is a religious ritual conducted under the supervision of an experienced shaman. The whole event was well organized and tastefully done. It was not a theatrical performance for the television cameras. Rather, they wanted to use the presence of the cameras and the reporters to educate the public. The shaman was very articulate. He explained carefully each step of the ritual and the symbolism enshrined in each action."

"I am glad. There is always the concern that such ceremonies could get depicted as savage or pagan rituals."

"No one could have come away with anything other than awe and respect. Every male member of the tribe between thirteen and thirty participated."

"A lot of the opposition to the Sun Dance stemmed from the fact there is body piercing and flesh offering to the Great Spirit."

"True. But, it's a spiritual ceremony and most of it is symbolic. Unfortunately it has been misinterpreted as a gruesome display of self-mutilation. It is so untrue. As a native person you couldn't but be intensely gripped by the spirituality of the final act of self-sacrifice."

"There was a whole lot more over two days preceding this; there were multiple ceremonies leading up to the ritual sacrifice."

"How do you think the non-natives reacted to it?"

"I watched for reaction on the faces of the attendees, native and non-native alike. I didn't see anyone turn away or appear shocked by what they saw. The ritual loses much of its emotional gravity in narrative descriptions. You have to be there to experience the spiritual intensity and the fervor of the participants. It was well-planned and executed. The shaman prepared the people for what would happen next and explained the meaning of the actions about to take place. They even had a medical staff and a fully equipped ambulance on standby in case of any unexpected medical incidents. There were none."

"One complaint about the dance is that participants are exposed to unacceptable medical risks. Is that true?"

"If there were any such fears, they were proven to be groundless.

No doubt it's a physical act. There is pain and suffering involved. There is piercing of the body; skin is ripped open, and some blood is spilled. However there is nothing gruesome about it."

"I wish we could ignore it but we can't. So here we are."

"Native nations as you know are in the process of organizing a national unity movement that they have named United Native Nations of America or UNNA. It was spurred into action following the success of the small Paiute tribe in Utah. We have had a few meetings with their leaders. They made some interesting demands. Some are reasonable such as the demand to be addressed as Native Americans. They want representation in the house and senate, a circuit court for Native Americans, and a Native American Day. There are more and the list keeps growing longer each time we meet."

"How serious do you think they are with their demands? Are they really united? Do you think they can pull it off or is it another one of those 'cry wolf' situations?"

"It may very well end up that way but they may be on to something here. We just can't ignore them. They had a national demonstration. They didn't disrupt public life but the message was obvious that they can ratchet up the pressure if they want to."

"What will the administration do now?"

"Nothing, if we can. There are many other important issues at hand. At the same time, we don't want this to be a distraction. To be honest, we want to do whatever we can to make them believe we are addressing their demands, but then delay any action until after the elections."

"We can't, even in our wildest dreams, consider demands like representation in the house and senate. I know they will bring up Puerto Rico but that was a mistake. We can't correct one mistake with another."

"An outright denial will be taken as an insult and then there is no saying what they'll do. Temporary appeasement would be the best option."

"Let's say the hearings are scheduled sometime in April. By the time they are done, it will be September-October. We'll submit a bill for the committee by December. The elections will be over and who knows what happens then. I don't think this national unity movement will last that long."

"The Sun Dance"

An eye-witness account by:
MALCOLM DONAHUE

Special Correspondent,
Utah Herald, Salt Lake City

It has been one of the greatest rewards of my professional life as a reporter to have witnessed the Sun Dance performed on the Paiute Reservation at Little Bend. I had my own apprehensions, not because of queasiness over witnessing blood and gore, which I have witnessed plenty during my days in Vietnam. Rather, my concerns stemmed from fear that the public spectacle could turn this ritual into an anti-native sentiment as has happened so often in the past. Thankfully, my fears were put to rest by the religious fervor with which it was done.

The Sun Dance was part of a three-day festival. I was there every day well before sunrise. I didn't want to miss any part of it. It was open to the public. On average, around eighty people attended each day, including members of the tribe. There were a fair number of reporters. On the final day, almost two hundred people showed up, mostly members of other tribes who wanted to witness the re-enactment of this time-honored— but once-banned—practice. The ceremony was performed under the direction and watchful eye of an experienced shaman called Art Godfrey or "He-Who-Walks-In-The-Rain" as he is known under his native name, an affable guy. I got to talk to him a lot.

The oldest woman of the tribe had selected 'the tree of life' with a trunk that is straight up for about fifteen feet with a fork at the very top. On the first day of the ritual at the first sign of sunrise, the tree was 'charged and ritually killed' by the young warriors of the tribe using their bows and arrows. The women of the tribe carefully peeled off the bark as high as they could reach. The warriors, making sure that it didn't fall down, cut the tree, carried and planted it in the center of a large clearing which had been previously prepared. The circular clearing represented the universe. The tree was planted deep and buttressed with stakes, strong enough to support the weight of many men. From above the fork of the tree, strong braids of hide were hung on all sides.

A young, bull buffalo was ritually sacrificed. The head, with a strip of hide running from the head to the tail, was placed on the fork of the tree facing the setting sun and bound to the tree with long strips of hide. Offerings of herbs and tobacco were placed in the fork of the tree and a sacred eagle feather was attached to the top.

After the 'tree of life' was planted on the sacred ground, the women and the men alternated and danced around the tree chanting and singing to the accompaniment of drums and rattles. The men and the women who participated in the Sun Dance ceremony fasted all three days.

The final day of the festival was the most important. Well before sunrise, seventeen young men of the tribe came forward and requested permission from the shaman to participate in the flesh offering to the Great Spirit. The shaman met with them individually to ensure they were doing this on their own and they were physically and spiritually prepared to endure the sacrifice. All seventeen were approved for the sacrifice.

They cleansed themselves in ritual bath and then put on traditional native attire including headbands, braids, and feather cloaks. They applied the sacred dye to their faces. Each took turns to touch the tree of life and made an offering of tobacco and sweet grass, which they placed around the base of the tree.

A few minutes before 9:00 a.m., all dancing and the music ended. There was total silence except for the incessant prayers being offered by the shaman. All except the seventeen sat on the ground forming a circle around the enclosure. The visitors and media people stood behind them. The shaman sat on a raised platform facing the east with the tree before him. He offered special prayers to the Great Spirit and entrusted each participant to the mercy of the divine protector. He made an offering of tobacco, sage, cedar, and sweet grass to all of the four directions. The sacred pipe was lit and offered to the Earth and Sky Spirits and finally to the Great Spirit. The smoking pipe was placed before him supported on an antler horn.

One by one he called out the names of the young men. As they were called, each young man stepped forward and stood motionless facing the tree of life. The shaman blessed each one of them. He approached the first warrior. He grabbed the flesh of the young man just above the right breast between his thumb and forefinger, pulled it up as much as possible and then pierced the outstretched flesh with a thin blade. A buffalo bone as thick as a finger was inserted into the cut and the blade was withdrawn. The braided hide that was attached to the tree was looped around both ends of the bone and tested to make sure that the bone and the hide could support the weight of the individual. The distance of the warrior from the tree with the hide fully stretched to its limits was measured and the circle of onlookers moved further back. One-by-one, the rest of the warriors came forward, were pierced, and then attached to the tree of life with the braided hide.

Amazingly, there was very little bleeding, just a slight trickle, where the piercing was done. It must have hurt, but not one of them flinched. Every young man was thus bound to the tree. The shaman returned to his seat. He gave the signal and the drums started along with the rattles. There was one lone flute adding an eerie melody to the raspy rattles. The women picked up the chanting and singing. The young men started moving to the rhythm of the chants and the drumbeat, swaying side-to-side, and to the front, and then to the back with their hands clasped behind their backs. They moved clockwise halfway around the circle and then reversed direction. They showed no signs of pain, maintaining a stony expression throughout with their gazes seemingly fixed on the head of the buffalo at the top of the tree. Occasionally one or more of them would join in the chanting.

As the sun moved to mid-day, the heat and the dust were having an effect. There was no cover for the warriors or those forming the circle around them. There were tents pitched further back and most of the visitors soon took refuge in the shade. The stress and the strain were now visible on the faces of the young men. There was a slight swelling of the outstretched skin. A few of them lost their footing, but they got up and continued to dance.

The shaman explained that the object of the ceremony was to break free from the bondage of the hide. By doing so, the young men were breaking free of the evil that surrounds us. By offering themselves as a sacrifice to appease the Great Spirit, they were atoning for the evil that has been committed. A dancer does not want to break loose too soon nor faint, both of which are indicative of cowardice. It was well over three hours before the first skin was ripped and the dancer fell to the ground. He was immediately gathered up and taken to the ambulance. The wound was irrigated and cleansed. Sutures were applied and antiseptic sprayed over it. In ten minutes, the warrior was back at the circle, to sing, and add encouragement to his friends.

The shaman followed their movements and watched closely. When he felt that the time was appropriate, he gave the signal. The drums picked up the crescendo. The rattles rang out faster and louder. There was the corresponding quickening of the dancers. They forced the action by moving forward toward the tree and then running fast away from the tree causing the bone to rip the skin and break free. It varied from person to person. Some broke free at the first attempt and some at the second. None had to do it more than three times. Then, they were all free. They were all attended to and then returned to the enclosure. Then as one the young men walked up to the tree, touched it with reverence, and then returned to sit along the inner circle.

The shaman explained that the drops of blood the young warriors had spilt on the hallowed grounds of the ceremonial site would serve to rejuvenate the people, restore harmony in nature, and regenerate their lands. I could see a glow on the faces of the young men, a glow of pride and purpose. It was a moving experience. The blood of the buffalo had mingled with the blood of the young warriors in one holy sacrifice.

The concluding rituals were enacted. All were invited back to the village where the buffalo had been cooked and a sumptuous feast awaited us. As a witness, I couldn't help but be moved.

You could sense an awakening among the people. There was nothing garish; nothing macabre or bizarre. It was done artfully and the spiritual quality of the ceremony was what gripped you.

It left me wondering what on earth prompted the US and the Canadian Governments to ban this dance. It is an initiation, a rite of passage, no different than what many cultures have practiced since the beginnings of human existence."

"It's not a subject most of us want to talk about, but I'm sure all of us are curious to know what's been happening at our famous mission."

"I would like to get an update too. We haven't heard a lot since Tosco was excommunicated."

"A lot has been happening and none we can be proud of. Monsignor Cavanaugh does not even want Tosco's name mentioned in his presence."

"Is Tosco still at the mission?"

"Oh yes. Jim and I went down there last Sunday and attended services. We wanted to get a first-hand look at what's going on there."

"How are people reacting to him, now that he's excommunicated?"

"I could sense no change. He attracts quite a following. He has services every Sunday as before. It's a regular Mass with some add-ons."

"Like what?"

"The Stomp Dance by the natives precedes the Mass. The bread is some coarse native creation. He does not use any vestments, but wraps a native blanket around his upper body to go along with the jeans and shirt. He wears his hair long and has grown a beard."

"He's probably trying to emulate Christ in appearance."

"Excommunication hasn't hurt him, it seems. The place was crowded."

"He's continuing his ministry in a state of mortal sin. I wonder if the attendees realize that the services do not fulfill their religious obligations."

"He mentioned at the beginning that the services would not fulfill

Sunday obligations for Catholics. He said nothing about the excommunication. If you were to judge by the reaction, the people didn't seem to care at all."

"He was holding services in a tent near the native store when I went there."

"There is only the store at the corner now. The native village and the church have moved back to the banks of the river, close to where the original mission was."

"There was a small church there."

"It's still there, although he conducts the services inside two large tents pitched close to the river."

"The river has changed everything."

"Things are looking up for the tribe, and for Tosco too."

"You have to admit it; he's done a terrific job. It's impressive."

"That whole junction has been transformed into a commercial center."

"If only he had agreed to live and work within the laws of the church."

"They promised it would be worth watching and it was. The March of Nations was not the biggest, nor the best, the capital has seen. But it was one of the most unique."

"Wave upon wave of warriors on horseback, with their faces painted, braided locks and tribal attire, marched down Pennsylvania Avenue. There were no signs or banners to announce which tribe they belonged to but it was obvious they belonged to different nations. Between the columns of warriors, there were floats with women and children depicting scenes of tribal life; there were teepees with women sitting in front weaving baskets while others ground flour or worked with beads and leather. At intervals they had teams of musicians playing traditional drums and flutes. No one paid attention to the onlookers that thronged the sidewalks. They went about their business without making eye contact with the people. Then, there were the members of the tribal councils, some in regular clothing, some with traditional attire with a few among them sporting a combination. They alone waved to the crowds and smiled."

"The Supreme Council of UNNA had predicted there would be over one-hundred-thousand participants. It doesn't look like they reached the target, but they were not too far short either. They made their way through the usual parade route and finally assembled in front of the Lincoln Memorial. The stage was set as we have seen it done so many times, in front of the imposing and stern-looking figure of the great emancipator. That's where a surprise awaited us. They had erected a huge backdrop that blocked out the statue of Lincoln. On the backdrop was a collage of native figures, legendary men and women, whose heroic deeds inspire Native American pride."

"If you felt a little uneasy that the statue of Lincoln was blocked from view, we were informed it was done on purpose. It may not be a well-known fact among the general public, but there is little regard for Lincoln among native nations for having ordered the execution of the Sioux."

"We witnessed a great display of Native American pride. But, was that the real goal? The leaders say 'no'. This was intended more as a convergence of disparate nations attempting to create a national unity. The people and visitors to the city witnessed a great spectacle, but for the natives who participated and the numerous that watched on TV or listened to the events on radio, this was a definite step forward, a big leap toward the dream of a united native nation. We listened to many speeches; we watched enactments of native music and folklore, and above all we saw hope in the eyes of the native people."

Sarah Wilson, Council President, Paiutes of the Little Bend and Member, Supreme Council of the United Native Nations of America, UNNA.

"For thousands of years we lived in this land we now call the United States of America. We were many people, divided by different languages, customs, and traditions, but united as one by a common way of life and the belief in the Great Spirit. We were children of the soil, living off the bounties of the land, its fruits, nuts, and seeds; and we hunted the living creatures that abounded, taking only what we needed for our food, clothing, and shelter. We worshipped the Great Spirit and the personification of God in his many images. We roamed free, with the animals of the land and the birds of the air. The land was vast and the inhabitants few. The land and we were one.

"Then came the settlers from far off lands and they brought with them a whole new way of life. We received them well and gave them

hospitality and showed them how to live comfortably on this land. We watched in wonder as they built homes and villages and cities. And they came in vast numbers and we found that they were as diverse as we were. They shared one common trait; they always wanted more and what they had they didn't share. There was a sense of greed in all they did. They parceled the land to themselves insensitive of the original people who called it home and had lived there for many moons. They hunted and killed far more than they needed for their daily life. From mountaintops and from across rivers, from the canyons and the shelter of the trees, we watched in awe as the settlers spread and changed the landscape of the land. We wondered why; the land was vast and the inhabitants few; why this greed?

"There came conflicts with the settlers over land when they coveted and used force to take whatever they coveted and there was never enough to satisfy their greed. They used superior fighting machines that could kill from far. They brought diseases for which our medicine men had no cure. They killed us or drove us off with the same intensity that they used to plunder the land and its resources. But still, we comforted ourselves, the land is vast and the inhabitants few. There is place for everyone.

"They found one fatal flaw in the customs of our people, which they took advantage of; the natives lived by an honor system where their oath was sacred. When the natives swore on the sacred pipe, it was an unbreakable covenant. The settlers gleefully entered into sworn agreements knowing that the natives would honor them and in their own hearts knowing that they would break them at will. Their wise men and leaders preached a religion that allowed them to use force or guile to convert all to their religion or kill them that refused. We turned to our leaders and they couldn't explain how a God could order the killing of innocent people who were not followers. We watched in growing fear of the reckless abandon with which the settlers exploited the land, but we believed that the land was vast and the inhabitants few; it could take in more.

"We started to feel the squeeze as waves of settlers moved in and we knew that their greed had no limits. For the settlers, we became an inconvenience that had to be removed. Like weeds in a bed of corn, we were uprooted and thrown aside. Like dangerous animals we were driven into the mountains and the forests. We were herded like cattle and locked up in pens they called reservations. We were hunted down like the

buffalo to the point of extinction. They placed a price on our scalps, men, women, and children. We were outwitted and stripped of prize holdings and subjected to restrictive laws. When the settlers wanted what we had, they just took it using any means possible and later justified the means by sanction of their big leaders. But in our hearts we held firm to the belief, the land was vast and the inhabitants few; we can all be one.

"There was no end to the humiliation. We became the evil villains of their stories and the object of hateful ridicule. Gone was the way of life we cherished most; gone was the pride and the dignity. We became despondent. The once-proud nations were reduced to the fate of starving dogs. Alternating governments competed with those who had gone before, to enforce upon us new and harsher laws veiled as reforms. With each such reform we were made even more miserable, deprived of the little that was left and shorn of any sense of pride and dignity. With each such reform, the natives perished in vast numbers and like the beloved buffalo, were pushed closer and closer to the brink of extinction. The white man preached they knew what was best for the natives. The land we once thought was vast and could accommodate many, no longer had space for the few native inhabitants.

"In the darkness of despair and disillusionment, we kept our spirit burning but ever-so-lightly. In confusion and anger, we tried everything in our power to recover our way of life. It seemed that the Great Spirit and the spirits of our ancestors had abandoned us. We were destined to be a thing of the past. Yet the native spirit would not be extinguished. It lives on in the blood, the sinews, and the souls of the remaining few. The few have today joined hands in one long embrace as brothers and sisters.

"Together we shall grow strong. Together we shall overcome the tragedies of the past and forge a new beginning, with perseverance, hope, and pride. Together we shall mingle with the millions of immigrants from all parts of the world that call this country home and make this an even stronger nation. This country is vast and its resources many, it has a place for us too. Yes, the native people of this country are here and here to stay. We shall overcome our misery. We shall rise again. We shall live again."

"Agent Thompson, how goes your investigation of Tosco?"

"The river has been restored and now Tosco is supporting the natives into nation building."

"I am aware of that. Go on."

"AIM members have visited the Paiute tribe a few times. Tosco was present each time."

"That's cause for concern. If AIM has been invited back, it would indicate a return to militancy."

"Tosco has been excommunicated but that has not affected his church following. His sermons have become more and more strident in their tone. He has dropped the name of Ernesto Cardenal a few times. He is associated with the famous Liberation Theology."

"A communist and a liberal. That's bad news."

"I have taped all of his sermons and compiled a dossier on him code-named 'The Baptist'. He does remind me of John the Baptist crying out in the wilderness."

"That's clever."

"He invokes the native saint Wovoka and his teachings."

"Isn't he the one who started the Ghost Dance cult?"

"Yes Sir. That's no surprise as the woman leader of the tribe claims to be a descendant of this sage. The tribe has started to openly perform native dances some of which are banned. He promotes them and has incorporated some of them into his Sunday services. It's easy to see what Tosco is trying to do. He's proving to the natives that he—and in turn, they—can dare the government and get away with it. Wovoka started a cult. It led to the incident at Pine Ridge. It's almost like Wovoka has come back to life through Tosco. They enacted the Sun Dance; now they are planning to host a Ghost Dance."

"The Ghost Dance. It's that wretched dance that set off the Wounded Knee disturbance. I am not concerned about the dance itself. Their decision to bring it back can only be seen as a challenge to Washington; it's a challenge to the bureau."

"We have the same set of circumstances here. AIM is present as they were at Wounded Knee. A Ghost Dance is planned and they are inviting members of other nations to send representatives. It's inconceivable the Paiute tribe is capable of these bold steps without Tosco's guidance."

"Tosco must be totally and completely neutralized? There is too much at risk."

"Yes, Sir."

"I want a clean operation."

"Yes, Sir."

"I don't care how you do it. No loose ends and no trails."

"Yes, Sir."

"I am not asking you to do away with him, you understand. That's old fashioned."

"Yes, Sir. I understand."

"Keep in mind what I told you earlier. The bureau must eliminate threats to our national security. Tosco is a risk. Remove the threat?"

"Yes, Sir."

"Don't get stuck on the cult theory. After all, does it matter if it's a cult or something else? He is supporting a native uprising that endangers our national security. Such a move can only lead to confrontation and conflict. It must end, and end it now."

"Welcome to National News Hour, this is Marsha Dobbins. Many a hearing takes place in Washington DC, most of them attracting little or no public attention. On any given day there could be three or more hearings in session on a wide range of topics. Such was the case this week with the Senate Native American hearings.

The hearings on Native American reform that had been in progress for a few days were considered inconsequential; so much so, even CSPAN didn't cover them. Then, as only it can happen in our nation's capital, things went berserk, the ordinary became extraordinary, and the mundane became the talk of the town. We too are now talking about it.

Details are sketchy. From what we have been able to piece together, representatives of United Native Nations of America, UNNA, walked out of the hearings in protest, after some rather heated and wild exchanges with two members of the Congressional Committee, Congresswoman Orwell from Kentucky, and Congressman Conway from Utah. We were not able to contact any of the participants, members of the committee, and the representatives of the native nations for their comments. But, we have an eyewitness report of what happened. Madeline Montalvin and Lisa Claire from Albany, NY, were in the gallery while the hearings were in progress and witnessed the concluding events. Tell us what happened."

"I was visiting Washington with my sister for the first time and thought it might be a good idea to see government in action. We had been there for about an hour before the fireworks started."

"I guess you got more than what you bargained for. In fact you witnessed history in the making. Did you realize that this is the first time ever that people have walked out of a hearing in protest?"

"No, I didn't."

"We were able to get a transcript of the entire hearing and we are going to play for the audience the final piece of the drama as it unfolded. In a way, the stage was set earlier when the controversial disrobed Catholic priest and unofficial spiritual leader of the Paiutes of Little Bend where this saga originated, refused to testify. He had been subpoenaed to be a witness but refused to cooperate even under threat of a Congressional contempt. Unfortunately, there is only the audio. We pick up where the real fireworks started. Here we go."

"Leave my family out of this. We are not here to discuss me."

"You are a product of a culture and a race that has benefitted mightily at the expense of the native people. No wonder your views are what they are. But, if you want us to sit idly and be subjected to your poisoned taunts, you are mistaken."

"I am sure you know how your family came to own the ranch you call home. Did your family keep records of how your great grandfather, a regular in the US Army during the Civil War came to own a thirty-thousand-acre parcel of land which belonged to the Howachapi? The Chief gifted the parcel to your great grandfather. That's what you are going to say. You have the signed document to prove it. But, did you ever question why the chief was so generous to your great grandfather? I am not sure if you know. Let me refresh your memory, just in case: to obtain the release of his daughter who was kidnapped and held for ransom by your ancestor."

"That is a lie."

"Well, then. Would you tell us the truth?"

"I don't have to tell you anything. Yes. We have the documents to prove our ownership. You know I am a proponent of integration. Trying to blackmail me won't work. These tactics won't work. They won't

change my views."

"It is important for people of this country to understand the bigotry that exists and there is no better way of exposing it than by having people like you shown in your true colors."

"If you think you can intimidate me, forget it. Your demands are irresponsible. Times have changed, but your attitudes have not. You fought with the US army and the settlers for decades even though you knew it was suicidal. You haven't learned a thing from your failed policies. Your leaders led you to certain death and starvation. You want to blame it on everyone else. You should instead be taking a supplicant and conciliatory approach keeping the welfare of your people in mind."

"You haven't heard it all. You are nothing but a hypocrite, to sit there and tell us to beg for assistance and to preach to us that we must try and integrate into the society. Madam, more than anything, what we want is to preserve and protect our traditions and our way of life. Does that mean something to you? The privileges you enjoy have been built upon the fears and tears of millions of helpless native people."

"Madam, if you believe we came here to beg for welfare, you are quite mistaken. We asked you to tell us the truth. You won't and you can't, for obvious reasons. But, take notice. Truth will prevail and we will prevail. You should be the one talking conciliation because your inheritance is one of the first cases we are going to challenge in court and move for restoration to the rightful owners."

"I object to this vilification of my family and me. Mr. Chairman, I demand that the witnesses be censured and their testimony expunged from the records."

"Order. Order. I appeal to your good senses. Please refrain from personal attacks and inflammatory statements. I shall examine the statements and issue a decision whether they should remain on record. Please continue Congresswoman Orwell."

"I have nothing more to add."

"Congressman Conway."

"Mr. Chairman, I am appalled at the insults that have been hurled at my fellow representative in the house. We are here for a fair and honest hearing and there is no place for personal attacks. We can't bully or shout down the voice of disagreement. I am concerned because what I have to say may not meet with the approval of the native panel and I need assurance that the scenes won't be repeated."

"*Your concern is noted. Again, I appeal to everyone to conduct themselves with dignity and composure befitting the integrity of this institution. Please proceed.*"

"*Thank you Mr. Chairman. Ms. Orwell touched upon some of the opinions I happen to agree with. We must, as a people, native, settler and immigrant, move forward professing our allegiance to the United States of America, as one nation. Integration is vital to the future of this country and the future of the native people. As a nation we are rich in diversity and it is essential we allow the diverse communities of people to thrive and persevere with their customs and traditions. That is what makes us who we are. However, we must be cautious about encouraging practices that have a violent past and whose revival can only serve to promote aggression and bad blood. Cultural traditions such as the Ghost Dance and the Sun Dance, and many more, may have had a relevant past but have been sullied by the abuse of their intended practices. I have a fervent request to the native leaders here to forsake attempts to revive such controversial traditions.*"

"*Sir, these dances and traditions are neither controversial nor provocative. You make them appear to be something they are not. We would welcome you to attend and witness for yourself the enactment of these rituals. Knowledge can dispel superstitions.*"

"*I think I have better use for my time. I do not need to learn more about them to change my views. They are what they are and you would be well advised to distance yourself from them.*"

"*Maybe your time was better spent, plotting with your hooded friends, how to carry out hateful acts against minorities and native villagers.*"

"*This is an insult. I won't put up with it.*"

"*Are you a Klan member?*"

"*How dare you attack me for questioning the relevance of a Ghost Dance?*"

"*Gentlemen. Please.*"

"*I won't sit here and listen to these half-witted savages denounce me and muddy my reputation. You want to preserve your culture. A hideous Ghost Dance is what you call religion. You see visions and that's culture.*"

"*Mr. Conway, the dance you called hideous is sacred to us. The*" *visions you ridiculed are the mainstay of our beliefs. They may not pass muster with your right-wing Christian values. We do not seek your approval."*

"We do not ridicule Joseph of the Old Testament or the Apostle John for their dreams and visions. Yes we respect other religions and cultures but we respect humans more. We expect the same."

"You called us half-witted savages. We shall see whether these savages have enough wit to bite you. We shall unveil your true colors. Let the people be your judge once they learn of your anti-racial sympathies and leanings. Your sanctimonious admonishments arise from deep-rooted arrogance. We have not forgotten your past and we won't let you and the world forget it either. Your past is about to catch up with you."

"Mr. Chairman, I object to this character assassination. Must I put up with this abuse because my views are unacceptable to these people? I refuse to be silenced by such trash talk. I demand an apology."

"Ladies and Gentlemen, I am imploring you to conduct yourself in a dignified manner. Let me warn you that I won't allow accusations of a personal nature to be expressed during these proceedings. Mr. Conway, do you wish for more time?"

"I shall conclude with the following statement. I am vehemently opposed to furthering or prolonging native sovereignty. I support abolishment of special status and privileges to any groups based on racial, ethnic, or cultural priorities. I strongly favor integration. I support the principle of one country and one people, no more."

"This is a message to you, Mr. Conway, and to the many such as you out there. For over five centuries you and your kind tried to wipe us off the face of this land. You nearly succeeded but not quite. We are still here and we are not going anywhere. We are the children of this soil."

"You are not worth the stuff we put in our soil to fertilize it."

"Order. No more. We will take a recess."

"Mr. Chairman, we were invited here to offer testimony. We see nothing but a continuation of centuries of bigotry and abuse. We won't take it. We are leaving. We will have no further part in these proceedings. This has crossed the boundaries of civility. We will determine our own future the best way we can. You just helped advance our cause."

"Gentlemen, could I meet with you in private?"

"Sir, no thank you. We have heard enough. We have seen enough. You can thank your colleagues for this. True reform must start from the heart. As long as we have people in leadership roles that secretly subscribe to principles of racism and racial superiority, we won't get a fair shake. We will find our own solutions. We are wasting our time here."

"Please take your seats. I request you take a seat."

"There is no need for us to remain. We came in good faith. We have no more faith in your good intentions. Goodbye."

"Thank you. Madeline and Lisa, from Albany, NY. Folks, stay tuned. We will let you make your own conclusions. This is democracy in action. There will be lots more information leaking out in the coming days about this. We will have more for you on Nightly News."

"We owe Orwell and Conway a huge debt of gratitude for what they did."

"We must be smart. We must attack the weak links, those with dubious legacies and get under their skin until they wilt or break down. They will melt down once we apply real heat. The media will take care of the rest."

"Father Tosco, you stood up to them and that was a great example. They didn't seem to know how to handle it when you refused to testify."

"I didn't want the focus directed away from you. They must learn to deal with you. They were not after my opinions. They wanted to hold me to the fire so that they can divert attention from the native cause."

"This was nothing more than a delaying tactic. It's not by accident they kept talking about due process."

"Nothing good would have come out of these hearings if not for this."

"We must keep an eye on the media and how they portray us. We'll go after those that paint us in a negative light. We will demonstrate in front of the offices of those that bend the truth to attack us."

"The media behave like sharks. They will injure or devour their own kind if they can get an advantage. If we go after one media outlet, others will dive in to inflict the damage, not out of sympathy for us but to gain advantage for themselves."

"We should plan another nationwide action to protest against the government's humiliating treatment of our leaders at the hearings. This would be a good time to do it."

"We should block all passage through reserved lands, be it a highway, railway, bridge, or waterway that was built without easement rights."

"If there are buildings or businesses built on native property, we should block access to them too. If there are military bases on reservations, we should set up picket lines in front of them."

"We should do it soon while the buzz is fresh and our people are smarting from the slights."

"We should have a very large turnout in all parts of the country to convey the full gravity of our intent."

"We will do it as we did before, in silence, with dignity and no violence."

"It has produced a bigger mess than before."

"Do you think the natives are going to take this lying down?"

"They won't. I am sure they are planning something even as we speak."

"I can't imagine what got into them to act the way they did? It totally undermined the hearings and our plans."

"Maybe it was done by design. Maybe the natives planned this all along much as Conway and Orwell did. Conway has become the poster-boy for the anti-native, anti-immigrant, and anti-all-that-is-not-white lobby. Ms. Orwell has reassured herself of re-election."

"Conway is nobody's fool. He knew precisely what he was doing, especially after what he had seen, the exchange with Orwell. He was playing to his home audience. Does it make sense? No. Does it win points with his constituents? Of course."

"But he may not have been exactly prepared for the response. The natives apparently knew what they were doing. They had done their homework and were well prepared."

"The natives were not prepared to back down. It's we who came up empty."

"Is there any truth to the charges against Orwell and Conway?"

"The natives don't have to prove anything. They achieved what they wanted. Their focus was on those nations straddling the fence."

"The hearings were in trouble the moment Father Tosco refused to testify. There was a change in tone."

"There is always Father Tosco whenever the Native American issue comes up."

"Tosco. Tosco. Forget about Tosco. Why not just leave him alone. He's trouble. Why even bring up his name?"

"I suggest that the president schedule a meeting with the UNNA leadership. It would make them feel satisfied they are being acknowledged at the highest levels."

"Not only will it nail him, this will be the cross that is nailed to him. He won't be able to shake this off. What a breakthrough."

"I was lucky to stumble on this."

"This is good fieldwork agent. It's a lucky break, but luck favors those that are persistent and painstaking in the search for truth."

"Thank you."

"I don't want any loose ends. By the time this becomes public, the whole case must be pieced together, zipped up tight like a body bag."

"There will be no escape from this one. I was extremely careful and checked out all the leads, personally."

"Good. Remember, a successful agent is one who is never seen and never heard from in public. That is the type of work we do. The reward for us is in doing what we do and doing it as best as we can. We protect our country from dangers, seen and unseen with no personal rewards for success."

"I understand, Sir."

"There is a lesson in all of these. If you dig in the right places and dig deep enough, you'll find gold or more dirt as the case maybe. Good work. Keep me posted."

"Thank you, Sir. I will."

"I think we should temporarily halt our plans."

"I disagree. It's important we push ahead."

"We should reciprocate goodwill with goodwill."

"Should we not at least wait to see what's on the table before we throw a monkey wrench at it?"

"We don't have to cancel anything, just postpone it."

"There has been a lot of grass-roots work and we can't let it go to waste. I support the idea of going ahead with our original plans."

"Is the government tossing a few bones our way hoping we take the bait and go home happy? These feelers are nothing but bait. It will weaken our resolve if we get sidetracked."

"Let's postpone the action for the time being. If not, the government can clam up and we could lose the opportunity for dialogue."

"We forced them to stand up and take notice. We must push ahead with our plans. We can't trust their sincerity."

"I don't think we should give up what we planned. We can't expose our strategy too soon. We must watch the opponent's moves and adjust accordingly."

"We should accept the president's invitation. We can meet with the president without conceding anything."

"Let's hear what the president has to say."

"If a photo opportunity is all he wants, we will walk away. We have done it once. We can do it again."

"Francis, I didn't want to be in this position. It happened. But then I realized it was God's plan. He had a mission for me. I had my choices, to put all this behind me and go back to the diocese or stay and help these people. I chose to follow the dictates of my conscience and stayed here."

"Are you still happy with your decision?"

"Yes. But it's not been easy. I go through periods of self-doubt and guilt. I take comfort in prayer to help overcome those dark periods."

"What becomes of your future? Will you start your own church?"

"Never. In my heart and soul, I am a Catholic priest and I will stay committed to my vocation. There's nothing I do now that's different from what I did before."

"How do you know you made the right choice?"

"Because I didn't make the choice for the wrong reasons. I didn't make the choice for comfort, fame, personal gratification, or wealth. I made the choice in favor of my fellow human beings, especially those who are less fortunate. It was the right choice."

"What happens if the Paiutes decide they do not want a Christian church here anymore? Where does that leave you?"

"I am well aware I can run out of my welcome here. Yes. I am expendable. It is their land. No. I have no contingency plans. I trust in the Lord. I won't join some other Christian denomination."

"People criticize you for baptizing without due preparation and pretty much on the spot, on demand."

"There is nothing wrong with that. I only baptize people who ask for it and who are serious about it. We baptize infants. This is a mission and we don't have the system for formal preparation. John the Baptist baptized Jesus when he asked for it."

"There is talk that you are a cult leader and you have plans to use the natives to achieve your goals."

"There is no cult movement here and I am not trying to establish an independent church. I am doing God's will. I live day-to-day. I have no idea what tomorrow may bring and I don't prepare myself for what that may be."

"Peter, I support what you do. Of course, I have been exposed to your ministry a lot more than most other clergy. You have become a catalyst for change whether you want it that way or not. There are priests who, though not openly, do express displeasure at the way you were disgraced. There are priests who privately disapprove of the autocratic behavior of church leaders. They want more openness and transparency. They want to have a say in the church's priorities. They question the wisdom of constructing a new cathedral at such high cost while ignoring many important social programs."

"Francis, I didn't set out to change the diocese or challenge the church. I am here to help a small community of natives. Along the way I had to come to terms with what was more important to my vocation. I have come to accept that serving my fellow humans is more important than obeying the commands of the diocese. What I am doing is not a political movement; this is not a schism; this is not a cult and this is not a new church. I am the voice crying out in the wilderness. Love one another as Jesus loves us."

"That cry unfortunately rings alarm bells in the inner halls of the diocese."

"They demand absolute obedience. The mission of the church gets lost in their desire for control."

"Father Tosco, you are doing all the right things for the right reasons. If I can be of any assistance, it will be my privilege to answer your call. Every time I visit with you, I return with a renewed conviction in the vocation I have chosen. I experience a deeper passion to serve my fellow humans. Fear not. The Lord is with you."

"David, I have a dinner reception coming up at the White House with representatives of UNNA. There will be a press conference afterwards. I need to get a speech ready."

"Sure. What's the tone?"

"Light, friendly, and informal; contrite but not apologetic; accommodating without being condescending."

"Theme."

"Restore trust relationship with native nations. History of unspecified injustices since the time of white settlers; abuses continue; reverse wrongs, and protect the future."

"Anything else."

"Find the speech we did last year in Palm Springs to the Mohave National Alliance. I like that speech. Add some of the same ideas."

"It was not a formal speech. It was more of a town hall meeting."

"That's right. It was effective though. Capture some of the same feeling and create a policy speech around it. Got it?"

"Key ingredients you want?"

"Name change to Native Americans: Agree in principle, subject to approval of Congress."

"Native American Day: Agree; date to be announced."

"Ban on Native Dances: Revoke."

"Recognition of UNNA: Submit to Congress. Will sign bill if passed."

"Pardon for Peltier: Will submit to Attorney General for legal review."

"Bureau of Native American Affairs: Appoint two directors from panel submitted by native nations."

"Protection of native reserved lands: Reaffirm"

"Representation of Native Americans in Congress and Senate: Submit for Congressional consideration"

"Establishment of Appellate Court to adjudicate Native American disputes: Will consult with Justice Department for feasibility."

"Monsignor, I wanted to give you a heads-up in person about my investigation so far."

"Why do I need a heads-up?"

"Because it concerns Father Tosco."

"It's always Father Tosco, of course. That is not my concern any longer. He is not a member of the diocese."

"It will be your concern very soon."

"Why?"

"Remember Shakespeare's Julius Caesar: 'The evil that men do lives after them.' So it is with Father Tosco."

"Has some evil befallen him?"

"Monsignor, you misinterpret. The evil Father Tosco has done has now come back to haunt him. But it will affect you and the diocese."

"I can't imagine what more damage he can do?"

"A lot more than you can imagine. Before I tell you about it, I have a request. This conversation must remain confidential. It must be shared with no one, not until I give the okay."

"I can't agree. Why?"

"All right. I know you can't withhold information from the bishop. That's fine—and your legal department."

"Why all the warnings?"

"We still have ways to go before we complete the investigation. I don't want any part of it compromised."

"Why are you sharing information with me now?"

"You will feel vindicated for the actions you took against Tosco."

"I seek no such comfort. I did what I had to do."

"The diocese could be facing a lawsuit."

"We have attorneys to address such issues."

"But, it's good to be informed and prepared."

"What should we be prepared for?"

"The information must remain confidential."

"All right. How bad is it?"

"As bad as it can get."

"You are being melodramatic."

"Not intentionally. The potential risk to the diocese is high. The measures you take will decide how high it will be."

"Tell me what's going on?"

"How well do you know Father Tosco's background before he became a priest?"

"I review the profiles of all the priests of the diocese."

"Did you come across anything of special interest in Tosco's file?"

"I can't talk about what's in his file."

"You don't have to divulge any sensitive information. I just want to know if you came across something shocking, not what it is."

"I don't remember having seen anything that stands out in my mind."

"If he were involved in a court case, it would end up in his file, correct?"

"Yes, I am sure."

"I take it that there is nothing of a criminal nature in his file."

"That's correct."

"I would presume you are aware that prior to his ordination, Tosco spent a year with the Arch Diocese of Los Angeles."

"Yes. Deacon Tosco was sent to LA to study multi-media communications."

"At USC."

"Yes."

"I guess it's common practice for someone in that situation to be stationed in one of the local parishes. He would provide some services in return for room and board."

"He would be like a Priest in Residence. That's common practice."

"Deacon Tosco resided at the Church of Our Lady of Immaculate Conception."

"I don't remember. But, if that's what you uncovered, that's fine."

"What are some of the things he would have done at the parish?"

"As a Deacon, he would help out wherever he could, with the choir, RCIA, communion, confirmation preparation, and generally assist at church services."

"Would the pastor report back to you on his progress?"

"No, not unless there was something of importance or we asked for one."

"Was there such a report on Deacon Tosco?"

"Not that I can remember. Why did you investigate his past records?"

"Remember some time ago I discussed with you my fears that Tosco may be gearing up to start a cult movement?"

"Yes."

"Cults have the potential for serious trouble. More often than not, the cult and the FBI end up on opposite sides of the fence. We intervene as early as possible to prevent the cult from doing irreparable harm. It starts with a study of the cult leader from the early stages of his formation. I have done a thorough investigation of Tosco and his background. He has no criminal record, not even a traffic citation. What happened at St. Bonaventure is of no interest to us. I have studied his editorials in the Sunday bulletins; nothing really controversial there. I have talked to parishioners about his homilies and his talks to groups. Nothing of relevance came up. Nothing suspicious, until, I backtracked to his Deacon days in Los Angeles."

"Criminal."

"Could have been. Deacon Tosco assisted with the parish youth group. During my interviews with some of his wards and co-workers, there were a few casual remarks, rumors of a friendship with a member of the youth group."

"It's nearly twenty years now."

"My job is never easy."

"Tosco was there, no more than one year at the most. I am surprised people could remember."

"It's amazing what people can recall. There was nothing specific, no scandal. Little-by-little I pieced together the unconfirmed story of a romantic relationship. It was obvious that Tosco was the object of an infatuation and there was nothing to indicate he reciprocated."

"It's not uncommon. Priests do attract attention. Tosco must have been a good-looking young man."

"It remained an innocent rumor until I got to meet the subject."

"It was not one-sided after all; he had an affair"

"Not really."

"He fathered a child."

"No."

"The girl was a minor."

"No. It's a whole lot more complicated."

"Tell me."

"It was a boy, a minor."

"You were able to track him down."

"Didn't take a lot of effort. We already had a dossier on him."

"He has a criminal background."

"He is serving a life sentence."

"What for?"

"Abduction, sexual assault, and mutilation of a minor resulting in death."

"Murder."

"The girl committed suicide."

"You interviewed him?"

"Of course. It's a story we see so often but shocking all the same. History repeats itself."

"He was molested as a minor?"

"Correct."

"By Tosco?"

"Including Tosco. The kid was raised in foster homes and apparently had been physically and sexually abused repeatedly as a minor."

"It would have come up at his trial. He was himself a victim and that would have been relevant for the defense."

"That probably saved him from death row."

"If Tosco were implicated, we would certainly have heard about it."

"He was not. That's the interesting part. There was no mention of Tosco at the trial."

"But he talked to you about it."

"Not spontaneously. Only when questioned specifically about his relationship with Deacon Tosco."

"He could be lying."

"I am pretty certain he is not."

"How can you be sure?"

"He was very protective of Tosco. The infatuation has not worn off. He didn't want to acknowledge it at first."

"Accusing a member of the clergy of sexual misconduct would have been risky at the time. Nobody would have believed him. The victim could easily become the villain."

"I got the feeling there were no such compunctions influencing him. He had a crush on Tosco."

"He had nothing to lose by bringing it up at his trial."

"He talked about his childhood molestations, but not about the affair with Tosco. I found it very odd until I got a better understanding of his reasons. He had a genuine affection for Tosco and wanted to shield him. He was adamant there was no criminal molestation. He was in love with Tosco and he felt he and not Tosco initiated the relationship. If at all, he felt guilty of seducing Tosco. At best, he was certain what happened was consensual."

"Consensual or not, he was a minor. It was a crime."

"Statutory rape."

"Why is he talking about it now?"

"A man serving time in prison without the possibility of parole is a man with no hope. He's destined to live out his life behind bars. When he sees a ray of hope that he can get his sentence commuted or reduced, it's tempting."

"You gave him that ray of hope?"

"I promised him free legal consultation to explore options for a retrial. It would be up to the attorneys to decide if there's enough new evidence to file for a judicial review."

"That was enough to make him talk."

"That's all it took for him to shed his inhibitions about discussing his affair with Tosco. He came to realize he was the victim regardless of who initiated it. He has woken up to the truth that sexual exploitation has many faces. He was a minor and Tosco an adult. Tosco was the abuser. He was a member of the clergy, a person of trust, someone with higher moral responsibility; his guilt is greater; he was the only guilty one."

"No one will believe him now, not after so much time has passed? He is a convicted sex offender, a felon. He could be lying. He may have benefitted if he had brought it up at his trial. He didn't. What good is it talking about it after all these years?"

"He's a monster, in jail, for his crimes. There is yet another young woman in a convalescent home condemned to a vegetative state as a result of his brutal attack on her earlier. He deserves no compassion. But, I am not investigating him; it's Tosco. His testimony is important to expose Tosco."

"What are his odds of getting a reprieve by exposing Tosco now?"

"Anything better than nothing is good. If he can get a retrial; if he can prove that the Tosco molestation occurred; if a sympathetic judge or jury hears the case; if all of these factors work in his favor, he could get maybe a reduced sentence."

"That's a lot of 'ifs'. How can he convince anyone that he's not making this whole thing up for his benefit?"

"Realistically, I don't think there's anything he can do or say that'll make a difference."

"Yet, you got his hopes up."

"I need his testimony to expose Tosco. I want to show the world who the real Tosco is, a predatory wolf in clerical clothes."

"Where does the diocese come in all of this?"

"His testimony will reflect back on the diocese. Tosco was your ward at the time the molestation happened."

"I am not a legal expert, but don't you think the statute of limitations would have expired for this guy?"

"Tosco is not being prosecuted. But his role would become public. Attitudes have changed. People tend to believe in clergy sex abuse."

"The worst that can happen to the diocese is a mention in this guy's testimony, which may or may not be made public. I don't see how it can be damaging to the diocese. If Tosco is sued, the diocese has no longer any obligation to provide legal defense."

"It's the publicity that can be most damaging to the diocese. I am sure some paper would love to get its hands on this story. The diocese will get dragged in whether you like it or not."

"I don't see it doing much damage to the diocese."

"I am no attorney to assess damages. But, I do know that attorneys aren't charitable institutions. They are not after moral victories. They want cash, hard currency. Nailing Tosco or getting a reduced sentence for this guy won't be enough enticement for a good attorney to take up this case."

"I will discuss the matter with our attorneys."

"Please do. Let me add a few words of caution. There is an unknown risk in any exposure to the diocese. The statute may protect you in Tosco's case. But, there will be an assumption that the diocese sheltered a sex offender. Is Tosco's an isolated case? The public may want to know more. The attorneys definitely will want to know. It may prompt others to come forward and some of them may fall within the statute and some may prove genuine. The diocese could come under scrutiny. There may be nothing to hide but only you would know that and maybe some you don't know."

"I want to keep the diocese out of the news. The bishop wants it so."

"Father Tosco, you have been advised of your right to remain silent and to be represented by an attorney."

"Yes."

"You have declined legal representation, is that correct?"

"Yes."

"Do I have your permission to record your statement?"

"Yes."

"The statement you provide and the answers to the questions I am going to ask you are given of your own free will and may be produced as evidence in a court of law."

"Yes."

"If you do not understand a question, feel free to ask me to rephrase it or repeat it. You can also choose to decline to answer."

"I understand."

"While a deacon, you worked as an Assistant Youth Coordinator at the Church of Our Lady of Immaculate Conception within the Arch Diocese of Los Angeles. Is that correct?"

"Yes."

"You were enrolled at USC at that time. You resided at the parish and performed various tasks in return for room and board. Is that correct?"

"Yes."

"Have you maintained contact with members of the parish after you left?"

"No. Maybe for a short while after I left. I don't remember."

"What would you say is a short while?"

"No more than one year after I left, if at all."

"What was the nature of the contact?"

"I don't remember if I had any. If there were, it would have been a card or a phone call. Again, I'm not sure if there was any."

"Do you remember someone by the name of William Dupree of Los Angeles County who was a member of the youth group?"

"No, I don't."

"Did you accompany the youth on field trips and camping trips?"

"I could have. It's more than likely I did go on field trips. I do not recollect if I did or not. I was there less than a year."

"Do you remember having a special relationship with any one youth while staying at this parish?"

"What do you mean by special relationship?"

"Anything more than usual and routine interactions."

"Such as what?"

"Were you romantically involved with anyone in the youth group or in the parish?"

"No."

"Did you have sexual relations with any of the youth of the parish, consensual or otherwise?"

"No. I did not."

"Have you physically, sexually or emotionally abused any minor ever?"

"No, I have not."

"Have you been accused of sexually molesting or behaving inappropriately with a minor?"

"No."

"Mr. Dupree claims he was part of the youth group that went with you on a summer retreat to a campsite in the San Bernardino Mountains."

"It's possible; I have no recollection of Mr. Dupree or a camping trip."

"Mr. Dupree has stated that you took him under your wings to help him with his personal problems."

"It could have happened. It was part of my job to work with the youth. I may have worked with him individually if he was having a problem."

"He says that you made a great impression on him and since he and you both shared a similar childhood, he looked up to you as a role model."

"You like to hear that you connected with some of them."

"In his words, he was infatuated with you."

"I am not aware of anyone being infatuated with me. I don't even remember who he is."

"He says that on that particular trip, someone stole marijuana into the camp and a few of them smoked it. Were you one of them?"

"No."

"Have you smoked marijuana or used illegal substances?"

"I have never smoked marijuana. I have not knowingly used illegal substances."

"Mr. Dupree was one of them that did. He was on a high. He says he then crept into your tent and spent the night with you. You had your own separate tent, correct?"

"I told you I don't remember going on such a trip. If I did go with them, I would have had a separate tent. I can tell you I never shared a tent with any of the young people."

"Mr. Dupree says you had sex with him that night."

"Never. That is not true. I can swear I didn't."

"He believes you were not responsible; he initiated it."

"No such thing ever happened."

"Mr. Dupree is currently serving a life sentence for kidnap and sexual battery on a minor. During his trial, it was revealed he had a long history of being abused as a child. Surprisingly, he never mentioned his relationship with you."

"Because it never happened."

"Because he says it was consensual."

"It never happened."

"He does not consider the sexual episode as anything extraordinary. During the trial and after, he started to make a connection between his past experiences and his adult sexual aggression toward children. I am sure you are aware of the cycle of behavior of sexual predators."

"All that is irrelevant. I had no sexual relations with him or anyone else."

"Are you saying he made this whole thing up?"

"I can only speak for myself."

"In other words, you are calling him a liar."

"You asked me a question and I gave you an answer."

"Mr. Tosco, it's well-known that abused individuals have a tendency to become abusers. Even now, Mr. Dupree sounds apologetic for having seduced you. He earnestly believes you are no sexual predator. Regardless, the fact remains, he was a minor and you were an adult. You committed statutory rape. Needless to say, his sense of sexual propriety is deviant, resulting in horrible crimes. He has been punished for what he did and has been incarcerated for life. But you and other abusers like you who took advantage of his innocent childhood are the real guilty ones. You should be the one spending your life in prison."

"Sir, I told you I had no sexual relations with him or anyone else. Stop making these false accusations."

"Adults contributed to his contorted mental state. They must also be held accountable for his adult perversions. His crimes reflect a desire for revenge for the abuse he endured as a child. He deserves some reprieve, does he not?"

"I do not know this person."

"I visited him in prison and listened to his story. I felt sympathy for him. You can deny all you want and he has no proof. There are no witnesses. You can hide behind statutes that limit your exposure to prosecution. But a young man is condemned to rot in prison the rest of his life. He didn't know the gravity of his actions. He needs counseling. He does not deserve to be locked up for life."

"There is nothing I can do to help him. I didn't have any relationship with him and I am not responsible for his actions."

"I know you are and you know you are. Come clean, Tosco. You can acknowledge your sins. Your confession may give him another chance to live as a free man. You are protected by the statute of limitations. You are safe. It may affect your reputation. But, your reputation is damaged already, beyond repair. Redeem yourself and save your soul. Think of the good you can do."

"Stop! I have heard enough. I have committed no crime. I do not know who this person is and I have had no sexual relations with him or anyone else. You are asking me to do something I can't do. I won't lie."

"You know you are lying? A lie repeated a thousand times does not make it true."

"A truth rejected a thousand times does not make it a lie."

"Think about it, Tosco. Don't let this opportunity go by and don't let a poor guy live and die behind bars. If you change your mind and want to come clean, here's my card and my direct number is on it."

"It won't happen. I don't need your card."

"I'll leave it here, just in case. You may be called to testify if the case is re-tried. It would be wise to consult with an attorney."

"I have no need for an attorney. I have nothing to hide. I speak the truth."

"Truth alone won't help you. I can help you. But you must come clean."

"There is only one truth. Truth is sufficient."

"Over the last several months, my philosophy on life has changed. My views on life, people, religion and relationships have been turned upside down. I thought I had a firm handle on my convictions rolled into a neat little package. It all started to unravel when I met with you and Father Tosco. It's been a positive experience, though. I now have a new sense of purpose. I feel like my life's work has just started."

"Malcolm, it's people like you and Father Tosco who have given us hope and confidence. With your help, we have come a long way."

"We have come to trust ourselves. We no longer feel we are at the mercy of what others are doing to us. We are confident we control our destiny."

"We won't let challenges befuddle us nor allow others to exploit our weaknesses."

"More than anything, we have lost the sense of fear, fear to act, and fear of consequences."

"We are faced with many tough issues but we are ready for action."

"I will do my best to keep the native issue alive in the media."

"We are indebted to you Malcolm. We know you are facing considerable personal and professional risks because of your support for us."

"The risks don't bother me. Changes are happening faster than I anticipated. But, it's still not fast enough. The president addressed issues that no president before him has dared mention. But true change must take place in the hearts and minds of ordinary people. As Frost once wrote, I have 'miles to go before I sleep'."

"We native people are not convinced that statements coming out of Washington, from the president to the congress and other leaders, are genuine."

"There's a misconception that we can be bought off with a little goodwill."

"A show of goodwill won't work anymore. We need to see action."

"There's a lot more that needs to be accomplished before we can say for sure that congress has a genuine interest in improving our welfare."

"If the government feels that we can be appeased easily, they will stop addressing the real issues. We must remain vigilant against complacency."

"New immigrants to this country enjoy greater recognition and benefits than the native people. Sarah Winnemucca once said, 'Maybe it would have been better for native people to have boarded ships, put out to sea, and returned through Ellis Island as new immigrants.' Does that tell you something?"

"Malcolm, what do you make of the allegations against Father Tosco?"

"It's sad, Sarah, what they are doing to him. I don't believe any of it."

"He is being targeted because of his support for us."

"I know what they are doing. They want to silence him. The FBI leaked information that he's been interrogated in connection with a sex abuse case. That's all it takes. It's a clever tactic. He has been cut down at the knees without even being accused of any wrongdoing. All they had to do was quietly leak to selected media that Father Tosco has been accused of sexually abusing a minor boy. Truth is irrelevant. He has been condemned and punished before he knew what happened."

"I can't even think of him as a criminal, let alone a sex offender and a pedophile. Anything is possible in this world, but not with Father Tosco."

"I know he's innocent. I met him and asked him if there's any truth to the rumor. He swore he has committed no such crime. That's enough for me. His word is proof."

"But, the damage has been done. Such is the nature of the allegation. Proof or lack of proof won't matter."

"The FBI will stop at nothing to destroy us. We are the real targets. Father Tosco happened to stand in the way. He's paying a heavy price."

"It is the FBI behind this. I have no doubt about it. The prison has no record of anyone visiting and interviewing Mr. Dupree. Only the FBI has that kind of clout."

"They hold a grudge against native people. They always have. They laid siege to Pine Ridge and riddled the village with machine gun fire killing natives indiscriminately. Yet, their fury is unabated. They are still out for revenge for the death of their two agents. They will stop at nothing to inflict damage on native people and those who support us."

"The FBI agent has been running around here like a tom turkey in heat. I know he met with Father Tosco several times. He's behind all this."

"Father Tosco is in grave danger. The Catholic Church has denounced him. Now, he's being accused as a homosexual pedophile. He could come under attack by right-wing Christian zealots. Attacks on him will be condoned as religious fervor gone out of control. Kill in the name of religion and it'll have the sanction of God in people's eyes."

"It's sad that this is happening to a man who preaches love and peace."

"He has his own enemies. Add your detractors to the list. They all want to silence and neutralize him. I'm sure they feel once he is finished, they can come after you. You are in a tough spot. You will be discredited if you stand up in defense of an accused child molester. If you do not defend him, you are a self-serving callous group of ungrateful cowards."

"We will stand by him, regardless of the consequences."

"He must remain here. He has nowhere else to go. He has sacrificed so much for us. It's our turn to show him how much we appreciate him."

"It won't be easy to convince him to stay. He may feel that he's become a distraction and a liability to you. He won't endanger the native reform movement, even at risk to himself."

"How can anyone take the word of a criminal over his?"

"Malcolm, how can we help him? We must do something."

"That's why I am here. That's what I too want to do."

"He stays inside the rectory and seldom comes out. Only Sarah has met with him a few times. He refuses to meet anyone else."

"Maybe he will meet you."

"There is something fishy about this case. I am going to get to the bottom of it. The FBI went out of their way to dig this up and then they leaked it to the media. AIM has been getting a lot of media attention lately, not because they have done anything new. AIM is referred to as a domestic terrorist organization and their past actions are recalled as if they have current implications. The picture is coming slowly into focus. They want to portray the Native American community as a den of violent terrorists who harbor sexual predators and pedophiles."

"They can come after you too. Be careful Malcolm."

"Let them try. I'm itching for a fight. I'm ready. My reporter's sixth sense is screaming at me this is a trap. They think they are clever. But, they have overlooked what I can do. I am an investigative reporter. I am capable of doing some digging myself. I won't rest until I uncover the truth."

"They won't hesitate to hurt you."

"I am not afraid. In Vietnam, I knew danger and lived with danger as a constant companion, day and night, front and back, above and below. With danger there came an excitement. I can't explain it. Maybe it's the feeling that you are outwitting death with each step you take, with each movement you make. There was no time to be afraid, no time for rational thoughts. There was a feeling that each day you lived was a gift. You saw the guy next to you cut to pieces and wondered if you were the next or why you were spared. That's the kind of excitement I am feeling now. In Vietnam, I was not sure why and for what I was fighting. It's different now. I know clearly why I am in this fight. It's for justice. It's for truth. It's to save Father Tosco from the clutches of these evil men. It's to support you and this native movement. It's for the future of this country. It's to help preserve the American way of life."

"Nothing short of brilliant, Agent."

"Thank you, Sir."

"The bureau needs bright people who are capable of thinking outside the confines of a box. You have upheld my trust in you."

"Thank you, Sir."

"You have proven yourself well. More will be expected of you. The more you prove your ability to succeed, the more complex the cases directed to you. You will reap greater rewards; they will be more than satisfying. There is nothing more exhilarating than having power in your hands; power of knowledge; power to uphold the security of your country; power to eliminate the enemies of the state; power to access the innermost secrets of people in government here and abroad. It's waiting for you."

"I am ready, Sir."

"This is the type of action we desire; clean, covert and complete."

"There will be no retrial. Dupree will remain in prison."

"It does not matter. Shed no tears for him. Dupree is a criminal. He is expendable. It is Tosco we wanted, our target and victim."

"There will be no case filed against Tosco. He won't be indicted, nor tried nor convicted."

"We have accomplished all we wanted. That's the beauty of a sex abuse scandal. He will never be clean again. Tosco will never be the same. He will live in infamy forever. People love filth over truth. Tosco is toast."

"If he had any plans for creating a cult, it's now dead in the water."

"The natives will think twice before they sing his praises. His moral standing has been shattered beyond repair. They can't have a suspected pedophile as their spiritual leader. This will set them back. It will hurt their movement. They won't recover. We will juxtapose Tosco and AIM with the native movement at their every move."

"It didn't cost the Bureau one dime to complete the assignment."

"That was pure genius to get the diocese to settle and literally fund the operation. That was brilliant. I am impressed."

"I can't claim credit for all of the successes. I took your hints and worked with them. I would never have made the connection to his hidden homosexuality had you not expressed doubts about his sympathy for the gay group at his first parish."

"Agent, be proud of your accomplishment. There are always helpful clues lying around in every case. It's the good agent who finds them and when he finds them, pursues them to the end. Take rightful credit. In most cases, that's all we are left with, satisfaction in a job well done. There are no medals, no 'employee of the month' posters and certainly no mention in the media. The bureau's role in this will remain invisible."

"That's fine with me, Sir. You put your trust in me and I came through. I seek no greater satisfaction."

"There are no reports, no memos, no records, and no minutes of meetings. It is a case that never was. But, I shall remember. Thank you, Agent. This country is indebted to you."

"For my on peace of mind, I must ask you this question."

"Go ahead Francis."

"Is there any truth to these allegations?"

"No."

"That' all I needed to hear."

"Why are you here Francis?"

"You need me now."

"Stay away from me. I am damaged goods. I am done, Francis. There is no future for me. You have a future, but you won't if you stay around me."

"Pull yourself together Peter. You are the same person you always were. There're a lot of people that need you, including me."

"I don't want to drag you down with me."

"Stop worrying about me. I can take care of myself."

"I am a sinking ship. If you stay with me, you'll be caught in the wake and sink with me. I can't let you get destroyed for my sake."

"Who says I want to be destroyed?"

"They'll find a way. They won't let you stand in the way. It's over Francis. They are too strong; they will stop at nothing. They did it to me. They will do it to you and anyone else who comes into conflict with them."

"Who are 'they'?"

"I don't know, but there are too many of them. The locals, the police, the politicians, the media, the FBI; the list is endless. I have no defense; no weapons to fight with, anymore. I am at the end of my line."

"You are your own worst enemy now. You fought with 'them' all the time. You must continue. You can't tire. We won't let you. You have the most powerful weapons available; truth and innocence. You will prevail."

"This is different Francis. How can I look people in the eye when I know what they are thinking? How can I stand in front of a congregation and preach about God when I know they suspect me as a sex offender."

"But you are not. Doesn't truth mean something?"

"It means nothing Francis. The world wants to believe that I am another sleazy, debauched hypocritical clergyman. How am I to prove that I did no wrong? The person who can is my accuser. Does anybody want to know the truth? Does anyone want to believe me? I have lost the moral high ground. Without the strength of my integrity, I am nothing."

"You stood up against injustice because you had faith in God and you. It was not something someone gave you. You had it and you built it into a fortress around you. Nobody can break it down, except you. You are the same person. You have done no wrong."

"I thought I was doing something right. I believed in the purity of my purpose. I felt it was strong enough to shield me to withstand any onslaught. But they found the chink in my armor, the one weak link that can destroy me without striking a blow. They destroyed my character."

"Father Tosco. Listen to me. I do not have the ability nor the experience to give you comfort. I respect the Father Tosco who never bent his knees to anyone but God, nor lowered his gaze before another human. I trust you are innocent. The native people believe you are innocent. Malcolm believes you are innocent. Above all, God knows you are innocent. Do not betray our trust in you."

"Why Francis? Why? Why has God let me down? Why has he let this happen to me? Why has he forsaken me?"

"Evil directed toward you is not the result of evil you have committed. I wish there are answers. I wish I could say the words to console you and soothe the anguish in your heart. Jesus too suffered as he approached his crucifixion and death. He suffered and died for doing the right thing. Jesus will support you. Only he can comfort you."

"I can face God knowing that I'm innocent. How can I look at the faces of people who have no way to know that I am innocent?"

"You are looking at yourself now. You are angry and feeling despondent. But it will pass. Lift up your eyes to God. He is just. You have done his will. He won't forsake you. He will show you the way. Then look into my eyes and the eyes of your friends around you. You'll see the answer."

"I have let the people down, people who put their faith and trust in me."

"You haven't let anyone down. An entire community of people saw hope in your vision and experienced strength in your actions. They trust you. I trust you. It can't be we are all wrong. Don't let yourself and us down."

"I don't know what to do. I can't continue the ministry."

"I suspected you would say that. That's why I am here. I will be here until you regain your confidence. I know you will. God won't let you down."

"No. Don't do it Francis. Don't."

"It's too late. I have done it. I have taken a leave of absence. Tomorrow, I will lead the ministry. You can join me if you feel up to it. You and I are instruments in the hand of God. His holy purpose must endure."

"Nations are waking up to the call of unity. Like old bark on a tree, they are shedding centuries of ill will and mistrust and joining hands together across the nation. The call of the eagle has been sounding clear and loud and the message of unity is taking hold."

"The Ghost Dance religion spread from a remote little western farm to the farthest ends of this land, by word of mouth. People were desperate for change. They were energized by hope of a new awakening. We see the same hope in our people now. They shall not be denied."

"It's exciting to see nations reviving their ancient rituals and traditions with confidence. Nothing can stop them now. They do so without fear. They have found trust in themselves."

"We, the Paiutes of Little Bend can proudly say, 'It started here. We started the fire that now consumes the land.'"

"We are like seeds of the 'goat's beard', caught in the wind, spinning out of control and parachuting into unknown lands. The Supreme Spirit has a mission for each of us and for the native people of this land. We will survive. We shall live forever."

"Father Tosco is hurting. His heart bleeds in pain for his support of the native cause. I hope time will heal his wounds. I have no medicine to soothe the hurt in his soul."

"Father Francis is here and he has taken the load on his shoulders. His commitment is no less fervent. But, I do worry about Father Tosco's health."

"Let him be. He'll come out of this darkness of despair enveloping his soul. He'll find comfort in his faith in God and our faith in him."

"The Herald broke the news of the settlement the Diocese of Salt Lake City reached with Mr. Dupree and his attorneys. Five-hundred-thousand dollars to settle a case that never was. Why? We probably will never know. Not uncharacteristically, the bishop and the VG have refused to discuss details of the settlement or to confirm there was a settlement. People are not happy. There will be questions raised in the coming days about this. Did the diocese have skeletons in the closet they wanted to keep hidden? What are they? Why were they in such a hurry to settle out?"

"That's a lot of money. Does Dupree get to keep it?"

"Not one penny, if I'm to trust his word. He didn't know anything about the settlement until I told him. That got him really worked up. The attorneys got a free bonus."

"Maybe the FBI guy got his hands greased too."

"If the FBI thought they could get away with it trampling upon and destroying lives, they're quite mistaken. We reporters have our sources too. I interviewed Dupree in prison."

"That's impressive."

"Why did he cooperate with the FBI then? Why did he accuse Father Tosco?"

"False hope and greed. The FBI agent created the story and used him. He knows he's been duped. He's an angry man now. The attorneys got a lot of money for doing very little work. He went ballistic when I told him how much money had changed hands. Just for good measure, I informed him that there are no prison records to confirm his interview with the FBI agent."

"Did Father Tosco have any connection at all with Dupree?"

"Dupree was a member of the youth group of the parish when Father Tosco was a deacon there. That part is true. But that's where truth ends too. Dupree only remembers him vaguely. There was no summer camp. There was no sexual molestation. It was all a fabrication."

"People are not going to believe him and his change of heart will do no good for Father Tosco."

"It may do no good for Father Tosco now. But, people can be fair minded too. I want to publish as much of my interview with Dupree as possible. I hope people will turn skeptical and start questioning the veracity of the story that was leaked to the press."

"How did you get Dupree to cooperate? You had nothing to offer in return."

"He realized that he had been used, that this was all a set up to get a statement from him to frame and destroy Father Tosco. Once he realized he was nothing more than a pawn in a high-stakes game where he was not a player, he wanted no part in hurting an innocent man. He's not remorseful or reformed by any means. He would have stuck with his story if he had even a remote chance to win reprieve from prison. There was none. There was no attorney to take up his case, no new evidence and certainly, no review by a judge. It was all a big fat lie. He feels betrayed and abused. That's hard to swallow, even for a criminal."

"It may be too little too late, as the saying goes."

"As a reporter, I search for truth and believe in telling it as it is. I am not a romance writer seeking to tickle and titillate the reader. I have no time for frivolity. I suspected there was some sort of a conspiracy here and I was right. The bureau will never admit to anything, and they'll stymie any and all investigations into their role. The diocese and the VG in particular may have had their own axe to grind with Father Tosco. There had to be some collusion between the bureau and the diocese. I can't fathom why else the diocese would cough up this kind of money to assist a condemned criminal. But the Diocesan hierarchy cannot escape the scrutiny like the FBI can. There will be repercussions."

"You are going to make a lot of people uncomfortable."

"If it does, then I've done my job. The FBI will remain untouched by this scandal. This is not an indictment on the bureau. But there are rogue elements within the bureau that think and act as if they are above the law."

"The VG will have to do some explaining for his part in this scheme."

"The diocese and particularly the VG will come in for some harsh questioning as to the role he played. The bishop will be challenged for his elusive existence in the shadows and letting the VG run the show. Yes. The VG will find himself on a very hot seat."

"How will this affect Father Tosco? Will he feel vindicated?"

"Father Tosco is not accused of a crime and won't be. This whole revelation of his innocence won't wipe clean the state. But, right now, he's a prisoner within himself. We can only hope this has not scarred him permanently. I pray he will recover reasonably intact."

"You're challenging very powerful institutions. They're not going to take it kindly. You are taking on a lot of personal risk. Is it worth it?"

"If you don't fight back, these institutions will be emboldened even more. They have no conscience, no ethics, no morals, and no remorse. They may be big and powerful, but they must be forced to play by the rules. Otherwise, our democracy has no meaning. I have no fear of consequences. I am lucky to be alive today. When my comrades fell around me and I was spared, I knew that each new day for me was a gift. I don' take it lightly but I will use it responsibly."

"You inspire us and scare us at the same time Malcolm. The native movement will survive and can't be ambushed by these attacks against Father Tosco. But, I am scared for your safety. We need you Malcolm; but we need you alive."

"What is my life worth? I asked myself that question a long time ago as a young conscript in the jungles of Vietnam. Why was I there? Who was I fighting? What was at stake for my country? Why was I killing people who were defending their own land? I never found the answers. The thought of a tomorrow never crossed my mind. I did what I was told to do without hesitation. Even the slightest indecision would have put my fellow soldiers and me at great risk. Somehow I survived while many didn't. What did I do to deserve being alive? I do not know. Since then I have followed one simple rule: Do my job without fear to the best of my ability and let tomorrow be what it is."

"May the Great Spirit be with you, Malcolm. You have been a true friend. May our struggle for justice be worthy of your sacrifice."

"This country was built on the principles of individual freedom and human dignity. We can't let those principles fall victim to abuse by the mighty and the unscrupulous."

"Tomorrow I will concelebrate with you."

"No. You are in grave danger, Francis. The church won't tolerate your defiance."

"For the last three weeks, I conducted services here. Do you think the diocese does not know? Do you think they're going to be happy about it?"

"There is a difference Francis. You are at a mission and you conducted services as a Catholic priest. They may not be happy with you, but you have not broken any rules. When you concelebrate with me, it is different; I am an excommunicated priest."

"Peter, I understand what I am doing. Do you think I am afraid of punishment? If I were, I wouldn't be here."

"Francis, you're just beginning your career. The stakes are too high."

"I can't explain to you what I have experienced during the last three weeks. In this wilderness, among a group of people who are not Catholics, maybe not even believers, I experienced what it is to be a Christian. I experienced what it is to answer the call of Christ to be a disciple and what my vocation truly means. It has been so uplifting."

"It is foolishness what you're saying. Listen to me Francis. It's too soon to think, say, and act in this manner and invite the wrath of your superiors. Don't risk it all on my behalf."

"Don't fool yourself, Peter. I am not doing this out of a sense of loyalty to you. I have great admiration for what you have done. But, I am doing this out of my own convictions. I am doing this out of a realization that this is what God wants me to do; this is why I became a priest and this is what being a Christian is all about."

"My future is fraught with uncertainty. The future of the mission and my role among the natives is hanging by a thread. It's too risky, Francis."

"I didn't come here looking for security or comforts. You followed your convictions without fear. I follow mine without fear. The disciples had no idea what they were getting into when Jesus called and they followed. But they had faith in Jesus. I have prayed and put my faith in Him. I decided to come here after much consideration. There is no turning back."

"O Lord, Thou art great and merciful. I kneel before thee and glorify thy name. Thy spirit burns brightly within me and thy warm embrace removes the fear in my heart. Thou O Lord hast called me and thy servant answers with a humble heart. I see thy light piercing the darkness. Thou art my light and comfort. Thou hast answered the prayers of thy servant. I shalt not walk in fear."

"Peter. Father Peter Tosco. What are you doing?"

"Mysterious are thy ways O Lord and simple are thy precepts. Thou hast opened the eyes of thy servant and taught me that thy wisdom is infinite and often beyond human understanding. Thy right hand hath touched me and I feel no fear. There is nothing more I shall want. The curtain of doubt has lifted and I see thy will at work upon this land and the native people thou hast placed upon it. Thou hast shown me that they too are thy children, thy chosen people and you shall not forsake them. Thou hast called Francis and he too hath surrendered to thy will. Have mercy on me O Lord for doubting thy purpose. This is thy mission and these are your children. We are instruments of thy divine plan. I surrender to thy will. For thine is the power forever. Amen."

EPILOGUE

"On this hallowed ground, on the same day, three very long years ago, two of our brothers fell, never to rise again. One was my husband, the other a dear brother. They died young, not knowing why their lives were cut short so tragically and so very quickly. They died never to know what became of their sacrifice. But they live in our hearts and in our minds, and their memories shall never fade.

"We have come a long way from that fateful day. We are no longer the tiny fearful band of native Paiutes of the Little Bend Valley. We are the veterans of many a war, still small in size but infused with a sense of purpose and the vision of a secure future ahead. We have overcome many obstacles; many more lie ahead. But we are confident and we will confront them without fear.

"The destiny of the native people shall never again retreat into the dark shadows of time. We are the salt of this land and we shall endure until the end of time. Today, we look toward the glory of the rising sun and we see the children of the soil united as one, within the binding bond of an unshakable brotherhood of nations. We are back, and a new chapter in the history of Native Americans has just begun.

"Brothers and Sisters, I ask you to raise your eyes and your arms toward the Great Mystery, the Almighty Spirit that watches over us and guides our endeavors. Let us recall our ancestors who have traveled to the spirit world and pray for their guidance even as we honor their memories. Join me, Paiutes of Little Bend, children of the soil, in dedicating this sacred ground to the memory of our two brothers, who sanctified it by their blood. . Painful memories of their passing will never ease or pass. Rather than let sorrow lead to despair, their sacrifice will be a shining light guiding us to a better tomorrow.

"We commit this day to two very dear persons who live but whose sacrifices are no less than the two who died. They are non-natives, but their commitment to the native cause was instrumental in establishing national unity and exposing the injustices perpetrated on native people.

The names of Father Peter Tosco and Malcolm Donahue shall forever be enshrined in the annals of native history and lore and in our hearts.

"I salute the great leaders of many nations, the members of the Supreme Council, elected officials and benefactors and my Paiute brothers and sisters, for what they have endured and the determination and resiliency they have shown in the face of tragedy and loss. Together we shall rise again, proud to be Native American and proud to be American."

The End

ABOUT PAUL PG

As a youth growing up in my native land of Kerala in Southern India, I had been fascinated by western movies and stories of cowboys and 'Red Indians'. I had wondered why native people living in a faraway land were called Indians. I carried that interest with me as I immigrated to the United States and over time had some direct and mostly tangential contact with Native Americans and their way of life. It was appalling to me that this land that welcomed me with open arms had little of that warmth for the native children of the soil. The only crime the native people of this land are guilty of is that they were here before us. We coveted what was theirs and they tried to protect what was theirs!

If this story inspires genuine appreciation for this uniquely special community, I shall be gratified.

CPSIA information can be obtained at www.ICGtesting.com
Printed in the USA
LVOW06s1341111015

457805LV00001B/136/P